HOLOCAUST AS FICTION

HOLOCAUST AS FICTION

BERNHARD SCHLINK'S "NAZI" NOVELS AND THEIR FILMS

William Collins Donahue

Vincennes University
Shake Learning Resources Center
Vincennes, In 47591-9986

833.914
D674h
2010

First published in 2010 by PALGRAVE MACMILLAN® in the United States—a division of St. Martin's Press LLC, 175 Fifth Avenue, New York, NY 10010.

Where this book is distributed in the UK, Europe and the rest of the world, this is by Palgrave Macmillan, a division of Macmillan Publishers Limited, registered in England, company number 785998, of Houndmills, Basingstoke, Hampshire RG21 6XS.

Palgrave Macmillan is the global academic imprint of the above companies and has companies and representatives throughout the world.

Palgrave® and Macmillan® are registered trademarks in the United States, the United Kingdom, Europe and other countries.

ISBN: 978-0-230-10807-3

Library of Congress Cataloging-in-Publication Data

Donahue, William Collins.
    Holocaust as fiction : Bernhard Schlink's "Nazi" novels and their films / William Collins Donahue.
        p. cm.
    ISBN 978-0-230-10807-3 (alk. paper)
    1. Schlink, Bernhard—Criticism and interpretation. 2. Schlink, Bernhard—Film adaptations. 3. Holocaust, Jewish (1939-1945), in literature. 4. Holocaust, Jewish (1939-1945), in motion pictures. 5. German fiction—Film and video adaptations. 6. Film adaptations—History and criticism. I. Title.

PT2680.L54Z65 2010
833'.914—dc22   2010018527

A catalogue record of the book is available from the British Library.

Design by Scribe Inc.

First edition: December 2010

D 10 9 8 7 6 5 4 3 2

Printed in the United States of America.

For Marie, forever

Contents

PREFACE

Over the last twenty years, one of the most vital sources for teaching and research in the area of German studies has been Holocaust studies. Indeed, scholarly attention to the Holocaust of the European Jews has been part and parcel of "German studies" since the field's inception. These two areas of inquiry (for lack of a better term) have virtually grown up side by side. Over breakfast one morning during one of the annual meetings of the German Studies Association in the late 1990s, one of my colleagues joked that it seemed to her—given the number of panels and papers then dedicated to the Holocaust—that we had essentially become the "Holocaust Studies Association." That was probably somewhat of an exaggeration even at the time, and it is certainly less true now. But she had a point.

To be sure, this alliance was never uncontroversial; already at that time, a number of U.S.-based colleagues objected that this attention to the Holocaust distorted our view of Germany and German culture, and actually undermined enthusiasm for all things German among American students. To summarize crudely, they asserted that we were shooting ourselves in the foot by attempting to "cash in" on the media attention paid to the Holocaust that had begun in the wake of the television drama *Holocaust* (1978), and perhaps reached a pinnacle with the film *Schindler's List* (1993), coupled with the dedication of the U.S. Holocaust Memorial Museum in Washington, DC, the same year. I would venture that on this issue, a particular asymmetry then dominated, and perhaps still characterizes, the German-American relationship. Though it is perhaps impossible to prove—and I will not attempt to quantify it here—far fewer Germans than Americans appear to enthusiastically welcome the role accorded the Holocaust within German studies.

This was made unmistakably clear to me in 1996, when I participated in a Fulbright scholarly trip to Germany under the rubric "Jewish Studies in Germany Today." Because things have changed so much in the interim, it may be difficult to appreciate the climate at the time. Fourteen years ago, it was a delicate matter for a group of American scholars to travel to Germany in order to investigate the state of Jewish studies, the quality of

Jewish life, and the place of Holocaust remembrance in German public culture. Indeed, the editors of the German weekly *Die Zeit* ran a short piece on that Fulbright seminar, describing our topic as "especially sensitive and important for German-American relationships."[1]

In those days, all Fulbright affairs began in Bonn, which, of course, was then still the capital of the German Federal Republic. As is still the custom, we were briefly, yet ceremoniously, greeted by numerous high-ranking ambassadors, politicians and diplomats, but our first substantive lecture was given by the outspoken Dieter Mahncke, who was then coming to the end of a high-level appointment in the defense ministry and who now serves as a distinguished professor at the College of Europe. Mahncke's essential message about Holocaust education and German youth was politically correct in the main. Of course he endorsed an honest treatment of the Nazi past, particularly with regard to the genocide against the Jews, but he worried out loud about *overdoing* it, especially vis-à-vis third-generation Germans. And he warned us "American Jews" in particular about foisting ever more Holocaust education upon the already overburdened German youth. We ought not bring this agenda to Germany, which had already done so much to commemorate the Holocaust, he argued, for that would amount to pedagogical "overkill."

Many of us were taken aback by this preemptive scolding—as Robert Cohn and I reported in various publications[2]—which is not to say that we did not share some of Mahncke's fundamental concerns about overtaxing young people. Our group was actually divided and, in some cases, simply uncertain about what, if anything, should be done about Holocaust pedagogy, either in the United States or in Germany. We were caught off guard in part because of Mahncke's misconception about our group's mission and its allegedly homogeneous ethnic-religious composition. We were not all Jews, and our main charge was, after all, to take stock of what was then going on in German academia with regard to Jewish studies generally—not to prescribe additional measures or to recommend policy. Mahncke confirmed his misgivings regarding our group in a follow-up letter, which he wrote to Cohn and me in response to our op-ed piece in *Die Zeit*. He was sorry, he noted, but not really surprised, to learn of our criticisms, because "already at our meeting in Bonn it had become clear to me that many in your group come to Germany with prejudice and little good will, also with little openness to what we are now doing and what we have accomplished [with regard to Holocaust education] in the last fifty years."[3]

We had described his words of warning as "blunt" and reported that some in the group perceived them as threatening. Understandably, this touched a nerve. Mahncke responded, "Some acquaintances who also read the article [in *Die Zeit*] asked me whether it might be the case that any German who fails to approach you [Americans] with a bowed head and muttering 'mia culpa' [*sic*] would seem to you 'blunt' or even 'threatening.'"[4] It was also interesting to note the contradictory role accorded American Jews in this exchange: in defending his use of the word "overkill," Mahncke takes cover behind an anonymous *Jewish* student: "That is what the American—Jewish—student from Stanford, whom I quoted, meant when he spoke of 'overkill,' and I admit that it is a bad word, but it makes the point."[5] Ironically, here Mahncke rests upon the authority of the very group (American Jews) whom he had at first attempted to lecture on this matter. He gives voice to an often unspoken tension between Germans and American Jews. If he was right about the pervasiveness of his point of view, then he stood for a much larger group that simply was less willing to speak its mind so candidly. It is hard to tell. But whatever the case may then have been, I do not think this stark we-they mentality holds today, at least not to the same degree.

In 1996, Mahncke prophesied, "We can overburden and exhaust young people for whom this is history—and precisely this is what I want to avoid!"[6] On this point he is certainly correct, and one wonders if we have not long since reached that juncture despite the best intentions of some pedagogues. In my own experience—and this must inevitably remain anecdotal—I can only confirm a general state of "exhaustion" among many Germans of my generation (and younger) when it comes to the Holocaust. Many will politely listen to my concerns but will then confess over a beer (or two) the very exhaustion and "overkill" of which Mahncke had warned some years ago. They have had this topic drummed into them—so they tell me—at school, in various subjects over many years by numerous teachers, and simply cannot muster much enthusiasm for it. These are not deniers or extremists of any kind but instead mainstream, young to middle-aged, and generally extremely well-educated colleagues. Some have even admitted that they offer the Holocaust as a topic in their courses or guest lectures because they believe it plays well to American audiences. This is what Americans expect to hear about Germany, they surmise.

If young Americans are in fact more inclined to show an interest in this topic, they nevertheless share something in common with their German counterparts. I posit a convergence of views—among Americans and Germans but perhaps more globally as well—when it comes to exhaustion with regard to the Holocaust and pedagogical approaches to the genocide. It is perhaps folly to make such broad generalizations about diverse groups; nor do I expect readers to accept this assertion blithely in lieu of more specific arguments made later in this study. Nevertheless, I want to argue that this new commonality of sentiment, if one can call it that, may explain the international appeal of the works of Bernhard Schlink. Surely this author is by no means an exclusively "German" phenomenon, as he himself rightly understands. The present study of Schlink and of the films inspired by his "Nazi novels," as well as of selected other works, diagnoses a broad, cultural desire to shift the Holocaust from its position of trauma-inspiring singularity back to a place of considerable historical distance. This has nothing to do with Holocaust denial for the simple reason that the Holocaust cannot be historicized or "normalized" without first accepting its facticity. As recently as 2005, Ronald Smelser opined that we can safely distinguish the Holocaust "master narrative" (foregrounding Jewish suffering) from various dubious "counternarratives" offered by popular culture.[7] I am not so sanguine. Based on the popular novels and films examined in some depth here, *Holocaust as Fiction* argues that it is the cultural venue itself that enables us to "feel" at once engaged with the Holocaust while enforcing an absolute distance from its essential character of atrocity, fundamental criminality, and human suffering.

It was a popular cultural vehicle—the once controversial, but now widely admired, television drama *Holocaust*—that was given credit, in the United States and particularly in Germany, for raising consciousness about the Shoah (Hebrew for "calamity").[8] Up to this point, the austere and demanding agenda of teaching about the Holocaust had been the preserve of highbrow cultural productions that often either preached to the choir or reached a very limited audience (or both). The television soap-operatic docudrama, however, achieved such a powerful cultural impact for a set of specific and, I would argue, anomalous reasons—ones that do not necessarily apply in the case of subsequent works of popular culture that ostensibly take the Holocaust as their topic. *Holocaust as Fiction* offers an array of specific arguments about Schlink's "Nazi novels" and the films they have inspired, but the larger admonition it proposes is this: we need to attend to the manner in which popular culture—whether in Germany, in the United States, or elsewhere—purveys an unmistakably "light" approach to the Holocaust. In doing so, I hope not to have fallen into the trap of extrapolating simplistic assumptions about the consumers—or producers—of popular culture. For to enjoy the relative "avoidance" embodied in Gerhard Selb (Schlink's very appealing ex-Nazi private eye) says nothing conclusive about one's "Holocaust credentials" or knowledge—except, perhaps, that one is "taking a break" from the serious and more demanding task for which Germans have created an enormous word: *Vergangenheitsbewältigung* (Mastering the Nazi Past). To draw premature or uniform conclusions from escapist, fantasy, or other "allohistorical" popular works about the audience they serve is to cast a very broad net, one that would logically snag a host of other works of popular culture, such as Mel Brooks's *The Producers* (which was recently reprised in Berlin) or Quentin Tarantino's *Inglorious Basterds* (2009), which features an elaborate—but patently imaginary—plot of Jewish-American revenge. There is no reason to assume a monolithic reader or viewership for any of these. We can, and should, imagine consumers moving in and out of various cultural venues. But we should not have any illusions about what these works offer in the first place.

ACKNOWLEDGMENTS

I thank the many colleagues and students who over the last ten years have agreed and disagreed with me about Bernhard Schlink. I am especially grateful to the students in Dr. Hannes Kraus's 2007 seminar on contemporary literature at the University of Duisburg-Essen. They forced me to consider *The Reader* not only as a preeminently German work but also as a particularly American novel. I am equally indebted to my Rutgers and Duke students from the course "Germany Confronts the Holocaust." They wrote many thoughtful responses that changed my thinking on the books and films examined in this study.

For fruitful debate, commentary, and advice (on the book proposal, the manuscript, and/or the lectures I gave in connection with this project), I wish to thank Richard Levy, Paul Reitter, Jeffrey Schandler, Martin Kagel, J. M. Ritchie, Susanne Kord, Bill Niven, Mark Roche, Claudia Koonz, Jochen Vogt, Caroline Schaumann, Leslie Adelson, Sander Gilman, John McGreevy, Susan Rosa, Stanley Corngold, Stuart Taberner, Paul Cooke, Stephan Braese, Dan Magilow, Scott Denham, Hanno Loewy, Karina von Tippelskirch, Clayton Koelb, Brad Prager, Michael Geisler, Alex Sagan, Martha Helfer, Katharina Hall, Monika Betzler, and Peter Böhm. Of course only I am responsible for those times I did not take their sound advice.

I received helpful feedback at the 2008 meeting of the group "Interdisciplinary German Studies of the Southeast" (Emory University) and no less from the 2009 Duke German Jewish Studies Workshop, where I presented the book project. Some of the material in this book is revised from articles that first appeared in *The German Quarterly*, *Seminar*, and *German Life and Letters*.

At Duke's Perkins/Bostock Library—undoubtedly one of the university's greatest treasures—I want to thank especially Heidi Madden for her substantive and incredibly quick responses to anxious, last-minute inquiries. I have not yet succeeded in breaking down her cheerfulness and good humor, though I may at times have come very close. Kevin Smith's speedy assistance with illustration rights was invaluable.

In the last stretch, Eric Downing's encouragement and Sander Gilman's enthusiasm sustained me. A special word of thanks to Michael Halfbrodt, translator at Aisthesis Verlag; his careful work and eagle eye went far beyond creating a German version of this study. Maryska Suda copy edited under great pressure of time and with her characteristic acumen. They both saved me from error on more occasions than I wish to admit. For his intelligent and scrupulous proofing of this study, I offer my heartfelt gratitude to Rory Bradley. Throughout it was Molly Knight's generous and patient research assistance that helped this book see the light of day. She can finally rest assured that those frantic emails are a thing of the past.

I could never have written this book without the support, sacrifice, and love of my family—Olivia, Molly, and of course Marie, to whom I dedicate this book with love.

A NOTE ON TRANSLATIONS

Translations of Peter Schneider's Vati, Schlink's detective fiction (as marked), as well as all German secondary literature are my own. For Schlink's *Der Vorleser*, I have used Carol Brown Janeway's estimable translation, *The Reader* (1997), throughout, though frequently with some revisions. These passages are cited in shorthand as "Janeway, *The Reader*."

Since this book is intended for readers who may have no German—but equally for those who wish to examine the original texts—I have provided both the German and the English translation in every case. In Chapters 2 and 3, where I examine *Der Vorleser* and its critical reception intensively for the first time, I have, in the main, provided both languages in the body of the text. Elsewhere, I have relegated the German to the notes, unless there was a specific reason to do otherwise.

MIGHTY APHRODITE—OR HOW TO HAVE IT BOTH WAYS

HOW DID THE HOLOCAUST EVOLVE FROM SOMETHING allegedly undepictable into the stuff of pulp fiction? How did it evade the strictures of Adorno's famous injunction not to make art of the Holocaust and become a vehicle for popular entertainment? When critics first began asking these questions, the assumption was often conspiratorial: the author or filmmaker was essentially being accused of consciously evading and trivializing the Holocaust. For example, in the wake of the release of Roberto Benigni's *Life Is Beautiful* (1998; *La vita e bella*, 1997), it was alleged that the film purveys ahistorical fantasies that have no relationship to history. Its International Movie Database (IMDb) tag line, for example, announces it as "an unforgettable fable that proves love, family and imagination conquer all"—leaving some to ask if those millions of Holocaust victims simply lacked the requisite love, family, or imagination. But others quickly intervened to explain that the *discourse* is self-reflexively antirealistic and thus proclaims itself a fiction, not factual history.[1] This is the familiar, if not entirely convincing, argument that a work's self-reflexivity insulates it from being misconstrued by less-astute readers or by viewers who fail to grasp this subtlety. At any rate, the best take on the film I know of comes from a German-Jewish émigré to the United States, who wrote a letter to *The New York Times* in the wake of the controversy over the film, explaining that she and her friends—all of whom had family members who were murdered in the Holocaust—would frequently engage in this kind of narrative fantasy. "Rewriting" the actual fates of their deceased loved ones into fantastical tales of heroic escape and survival became, she said, a regular childhood game—one she immediately recognized in Benigni's popular film.

This kind of crude binary division between fact and fantasy fails to capture the more interesting problem presented in what I am calling the

"Nazi novels" (as well as the films based on them) by Bernhard Schlink. This corpus includes the "Selb trilogy" of detective novels, a television film based on the inaugural novel in that series (*Death Came as a Friend*; *Der Tod kam als Freund*, 1991), the runaway international bestseller *The Reader* (*Der Vorleser*), as well as the recent Hollywood film of the same title (2008, dir. Stephen Daldry). In each of these works, it is not a matter of denying history but rather of retiring, rewriting, or simply thumb-indexing the Holocaust. In the novels under consideration—as well as in the two films discussed here—we encounter repeated, and sometimes even "muscular," affirmations of guilt and responsibility. In addition, we find some thoughtful, anguished passages about the complexities of coming to terms with the Holocaust and its aftermath. What is truly interesting, however, is the way in which these explicit (I would say, even ritualized) confessions of guilt and nuanced reflections on coping with the burden of the Nazi past lead not to a more differentiated consideration of the genocide but precisely away from it. It is not quite a case of "remembering to forget" (to borrow a clever phrase from Barbie Zelizer),[2] but rather of recalling, in a highly selective way, particular aspects of Holocaust history (usually those that highlight the observer's "victimization") in order to then move on. Paradoxically, by facing the Holocaust so "squarely," Schlink has significantly contributed to an ongoing, broadly international cultural process of putting the Holocaust behind us. In this sense, I argue that Schlink's novels provide a key literary component to the culture of postunification "normalization" that Stuart Taberner, Paul Cooke, Bill Niven, and others have diagnosed as the new German cultural dispensation.[3]

To some ears, "normalization" sounds a chord of deep suspicion. Indeed, Niven has shown that when Helmut Kohl first conceived his policy of normalization, the German chancellor and self-styled architect of unification was clearly more interested in simply moving forward than in performing the difficult work of national *Vergangenheitsbewältigung* (Mastering the Nazi past).[4] In his discussion of contemporary literature, Gavriel Rosenfeld, too, consistently opposes "normalization" (which he views as almost tantamount to Holocaust evasion or denial) to a more positively valued "memory culture."[5] Yet German public culture since unification has been characterized by a spate of well-regarded architectural Holocaust commemoration, ranging from the Jewish Museum in Berlin to the massive Monument to the Murdered Jews of Europe situated next to the Brandenburg Gate and, perhaps not coincidentally, next to the U.S. embassy.[6] In fact, some observers, including Timothy Garton Ash, hold contemporary Germany as an international model for coming to terms with state-sanctioned atrocities.[7] While the term "normalization" remains fraught with controversy, it can, and often does, designate the way in which the Federal Republic of Germany (FRG), in its official commemoration policies, unambiguously confronts the Holocaust while simultaneously placing it at a historical distance. This is no longer the FRG of the student movement, for example, when serious public intellectuals (including Adorno, Grass, and Böll) thought Vergangenheitsbewältigung so crucial because Nazi structures of thought and behavior were *still* prevalent. For them, confrontation of the Nazi past was virtually tantamount to contending with the present. Nor, obviously, is it the German Democratic Republic (GDR) of the Cold War, where commemoration of the anti-Nazi resistance constituted that state's founding myth, in the process seriously distorting, among other things, Holocaust commemoration itself. Unification made at least two things possible: telling a larger, more consensual truth about the Holocaust *and* integrating it within the annals of European and world history. Treating the Holocaust historically does not necessarily mean, as Saul Friedländer cautions us, that we simply draw a *Schlußstrich*—that is, put it definitively behind us—though that remains one danger.[8] Historicization in this sense is a meaningful and perhaps inevitable form of *appropriation*, and one that historians like Raul Hilburg, Omer Bartov, and Gerhard Weinberg have long advocated. Thus, normalizing the Nazi past clearly means quite different things in different contexts. This book provides a series of case studies demonstrating the often problematic role popular culture plays in this normalization campaign.

It is easy, perhaps particularly for Americans, to think of normalization as something peculiarly German. In the sense discussed—that is, as a *German* response to the conflicted process of coming to terms with the Holocaust and their Nazi past—it is simply axiomatically so. But in the larger sense in which I shall use the term in this study, it means not only transcending the political limits of the Cold War dispensation of a divided Germany but also moving out from under the "shadow" of the Holocaust—and this is something that many people living well beyond the borders of Germany seem to crave. The worldwide popularity and success of Schlink's work cannot be understood, I argue, without viewing this phenomenon from an international perspective. I take on part of that challenge in my final two chapters, "Victims All: *The Reader* as an American Novel" and "Going Global: The Hollywood *Reader*." By expanding normalization specifically to include the United States, I hope to both better account for Schlink's transnational appeal and avoid the cliché of the American intellectual berating Germany for its alleged failure to properly fulfill its obligations vis-à-vis the Holocaust. This condescending posture is clearly obsolete, and, in any case, I surmise that it is deeply unwelcome. To put it succinctly, Schlink is actually more of an American phenomenon than a German one; the traditional approach of studying discrete cultures demarcated by clear national boundaries is simply no longer valid.

About a decade ago, colleagues at Princeton University speculated that *The Reader* constitutes *the* German literary phenomenon of the last quarter century.[9] In the last 15 years, as far as I can judge, Schlink's book has garnered more critical attention from American than from German scholars, unless one considers the dozen or so teaching guides, geared toward the German *Gymnasium* (the rigorous high school college preparatory track), that have appeared in Germany since the novel first achieved such widespread acclaim in the mid-1990s. Oprah Winfrey's selection of *The Reader* for her on-air book club in 1999 exponentially increased the sales of the book in the United States (and beyond), by some accounts making its author a very wealthy man. *The Reader*'s prominent place in public culture seems quite secure and perhaps is even on the rise: it remains an extremely popular choice in U.S. German college programs, it has established itself as a staple of the German Gymnasium curriculum, it is a regular part of the German "A-level" exams in British preparatory schools, and it continues to be prominently displayed in leading German and American bookstores. All of this was true even before the premiere of the Hollywood film (in December of 2008), which is sure to increase the book's sales even more. The cover of the new Vintage paperback edition features a selection of erotically charged images of Kate Winslet and David Krossreplacing the much blander one sporting a faded cluster of flowers. (In some cases, prefilm book editions were provided with stills from the movie's deleted scenes.) The German pedagogue Ekkehart Mittelberg rightly refers to *The Reader* as "a recognized school text" (eine anerkannte Schullektüre) of the higher-level German Gymnasium (Sekundarstufe II),[10] and in his popular teaching guide, Michael Lamberty declares it to be "the internationally most successful German novel of the last decade" (der international erfolgreichste deutsche Roman des letzten Jahrzehnts).[11] This all indicates that in examining the cultural career of *The Reader* (and related works), we are not simply focusing on the choice of a single critic but instead upon a text that has, in a sense, already made cultural history. The Schlink phenomenon cries out for further study.

Much has already been written on *The Reader*, most of it affirmative, if not celebratory. Despite the "second wave" of harsh criticism that some (incorrectly) date to Jeremy Adler's 2002 polemical letter to the editor of the *Times Literary Supplement*, the press surrounding the novel (and Bernhard Schlink in general) has remained, on the whole, astoundingly positive. In this book, I respond to selected aspects of that scholarship in some detail, without, however, seeking to summarize it in its entirety. In other words, this study is not the source to consult if one is looking for what Germans would call a *Forschungsbericht* (comprehensive research report). What is needed, I believe, is a focused critical study, not one more encomiastic reading.

There is some value, I hope, to the close attention paid here to these widely received, taught, and debated novels and films. Yet this study's strength is also its weakness: by focusing primarily on Schlink and the Schlink-inspired films, we can easily overlook the wider and more variegated context of German literature and film that addresses the Nazi past. In this respect, I hope that my *Holocaust as Fiction* can work in concert with more ambitious and broadly conceived recent studies, such as Caroline Schaumann's *Memory Matters* (2008), Chloe Paver's *The Third Reich in German and Austrian Fiction and Film* (2007), and Erin McGlothlin's *Second Generation Holocaust Literature* (2006), as well as Stuart Taberner and Karina Berger's coedited volume *Germans as Victims in the Literary Fiction of the Berlin Republic* (2009). A principle of complementarity may be said to govern these two quite different approaches: I have the luxury of examining a relatively few (albeit very influential) works in depth, whereas the works of Schaumann, Paver, McGlothlin, and Taberner-Berger (among many others) provide a breadth and scope unavailable to me in this study.

Beyond this aspect of mutual benefit, however, I would suggest a dialogical, even interrogatory, relationship as well, and not only with respect to the pointedly divergent views on Schlink one finds in their studies. In a larger sense, I propose that *Holocaust as Fiction*, in its insistent focus not only on the texts themselves but also on the larger social meaning of these works, offers an amicable challenge to the aforementioned scholars. For example, both Schaumann and the team of Taberner and Berger suggest that we have entered a new, more nuanced dispensation in which it is possible to now consider German victimhood alongside that of the Jews. It may well be true, as Taberner and Berger contend, that we are currently witnessing a "more differentiated, less ideological memory discourse" marked by "the integration of the story of German suffering into the larger wartime narrative, with varying degrees of complexity and attention to the causal link between German perpetration and German victimhood."[12] Schaumann, too, makes the case for juxtaposing quite disparate narratives—"the texts of female victims, bystanders, and co-participants, their daughters and granddaughters, German-gentiles and German-Jews, both from the Federal Republic and [the] GDR"—in order to complicate what had been perhaps too simple an opposition between victims and perpetrators.[13]

There is undoubtedly great value in this inclusive approach, and there is an unmistakable optimism and even idealism to their critical assumptions. Yet my own study leads me to issue a word of caution. It asks, by virtue of contrasting methodology, how these scholars constitute this "changed memory discourse."[14] It may not be sufficient to find evidence in diverse works that scholars happen to find interesting, perhaps precisely because these texts conform to a discourse to which they may already be committed. We need to know how these works function socially—how and where they circulate. Who reads, assigns, and discusses these works? What role do they play in the curriculums of schools and universities? What, if any, is their international resonance? Do we find them prominently displayed, year after year, among the offerings of major bookstore chains and in airport bookstores? Too little attention is paid, I would submit, to these fundamental questions that directly bear on the parameters of public culture.

In divining a "new memory discourse," we must not overlook the fact that many preunification texts, such as Schlink's inaugural Selb novel (1987), enjoyed a powerful resurgence in the postunification period. It was adapted as a made-for-television film in 1991, suggesting more continuity than some critics have acknowledged. More recently, of course, the entire Selb trilogy has been reprised and offered in English translation for the global market, just as it had already been reintroduced to the German-language market in the wake of the unparalleled success of *The Reader*. Chronologies that date this putatively new memory discourse to the post-Wende period (or "turnabout," the widely used German euphemism for unification) risk obscuring these important cultural continuities, resurgences, and contradictory developments. The story these critics tell about an altered memory culture, while not wrong, is neither as uniform nor as linear, I believe, as commonly depicted. In short, they tend to overlook Ernst Bloch's concept of "the simultaenity of the nonsimultaneous" in cultural representation. The claim that a more capacious definition of victimhood has replaced a "rigid" model entails oversimplifying layers of culture that remain antagonistic in complex ways. For example, by attending to a stratum of German culture that clearly fell below the radar of official Holocaust commemoration in the FRG during the postwar period—as I do in the next chapter—we can see that an emphasis on *German* victimhood, already "contextualized" within unmistakable indicators of German perpetration, was socially acceptable well before the putative onset of this new dispensation.[15] You just have to know where to look.

Finally, I take issue with the claim that this new, inclusive memory discourse actually welcomes *commensurate* depictions of Germans as victims (of Hitler, of Allied bombings, etc.) alongside those of Jewish victims of the Holocaust. Of course, much depends on what counts as depiction. Does any passing reference or allusion to Jewish victimhood suffice? Or must it be more substantive? How do metonymic evocations of Jewish suffering hold up to palpable, explicit, and "on-screen" portrayals of German suffering? The devil, as we will see, is very much in the details. Truly commensurate juxtaposition of victimhood is, in fact, scrupulously avoided, as I will have occasion to argue here—and not necessarily only on altruistic or ethical grounds but also for reasons of efficacy and pragmatism. German victimhood simply fails to stand out when explicitly and substantively juxtaposed with the suffering of Holocaust victims.[16] Indeed, we may come to appreciate that this more capacious memory discourse has been made possible precisely by all those cultural instruments that powerfully distance the Holocaust from active public consciousness. The "Schlink phenomenon" is surely a prominent part of this hydraulic relationship.

In addition to being a writer of detective fiction, short stories, and novels, Bernhard Schlink is a prominent law professor and a justice of one of Germany's state supreme courts. His biography as an eminent jurist and public intellectual has always played a significant role in the reception of his fiction. How could it be otherwise? While it would be far too simple to say that Schlink's stature as a jurist ensured the success of his fiction, the two are clearly not unrelated—especially insofar as the detective fiction and the novel under consideration are centrally concerned with matters of law, prosecution, crime, discovery, and punishment. To separate the two would be as absurd as if we in the United States were to discuss the widely read fiction of Scott Turow and "forget" that he is an accomplished lawyer, former prosecutor, and the author of the classic law-school initiation book *One L*.[17] Of course, simply merging the two in an unqualified manner is also problematic. I argue that Schlink's relationship to his fiction has, for too long, been a one-way street: the affiliation of author with narrator (usually Michael Berg of *The Reader*) is generally, if loosely, upheld insofar as it flatters either the fictional or the real-world author. But as soon as one sounds a genuinely critical note, one is likely to get a condescending lecture on the discrete status of author and narrator—as if one had skipped out on that lesson of elementary narratology.

Schlink himself has been rather gracious in response to criticism,[18] far more so than many of his supporters who—in their vigorous insistence on the previously mentioned distinction between author and narrator—seem, in the end, suspiciously defensive of the author.[19] Yet Schlink is also, to some extent, responsible for the perceived merging of personas that his defenders decry: he has spoken out publicly on numerous occasions in ways that substantially overlap with key views of his beleaguered narrator(s), a point critics have noticed, emphasized, and advocated.[20] So if readers are to some extent "confused," it is not completely without reason. At any rate, all of this cannot be laid at the feet of "lazy" or uncritical readers. The reception of Schlink's work, as I detail here, is thus characterized by two diametrically opposed trends: on the one hand, a persistent marketing trend that closely aligns author and work, and on the other, a defensive critical position that seeks to redeem the work or the author (or both) by maintaining their distinct character. Schlink, I contend, is implicated in both. As a public intellectual, of course, Schlink has, in interview after interview, forcefully confronted the Holocaust; that much is beyond question. But his fiction, as I argue throughout this study, responds more to the phenomenon of "Holocaust exhaustion" and effectively sequesters the genocide of the European Jews in favor of an emphasis on the plight and burden of Germany's subsequent generations. He does so, as he explicitly argues, precisely in order to give third-generation Germans the relief they need to come out from the shadow of the Holocaust and achieve a healthy sense of national identity.[21] Interestingly, this very point (regarding the national self-esteem of the third generation) is cited in a number of pedagogical guidebooks as something worth rehearsing with students.[22] Möckel goes so far as to meld author and narrator in order to make the point that it is not just Schlink the jurist, but the novel itself, that brings respite to the third generation by removing the question of guilt.[23]

As I try to show how the novels and films promote this posture of moving on and away from the genocide, some critics will no doubt think it sufficient to point to some of the author's nonfictional writings that establish his unimpeachable Vergangenheitsbewältigung credentials.[24] Indeed, Schlink himself has done so. Responding to my previously mentioned contentions about Hanna and Selb (which I expressed in several published articles and provided to Schlink at his request), he writes, "I've read your essays with interest . . . You derive from my fiction certain positions about coming to terms with the Nazi past. Allow me to point out that I have said what I have to say on this issue in a number of articles."[25] This is certainly true; and it is fair to draw our attention to these extrafictional essays as well,[26] for as I have said, the author's stance as a jurist has strongly inflected the Schlink phenomenon that has, in turn, shaped the reception of his novels from the outset. However, the essays he mentions fail to address the concerns that others and I have raised. The very writings to which Schlink refers may actually provide his fiction with a kind of ideological "cover": the fact that the author's own views are widely disseminated—he issued definite hermeneutic guidelines not just in abstruse legal journals, let it be noted, but on radio and television talk shows and in popular magazines—may discourage readers from pursuing certain criticisms and objections they may otherwise have had. At any rate, the fiction also needs to be read as fiction in its own right, so that we may finally ask if it expresses something *more* or *other* than what the author elsewhere argues or consciously intends.

I have confessed to an interest in the wider cultural meaning of the texts and films under consideration. To some, this means abandoning the novels as literature and the films as works of art in their own right. This need not be so. I think one can attend both to the sociological meaning of art and to its aesthetic dimensions. Whether I succeed in every case in serving two masters will be up to the reader. But I must caution from the outset that the commitment to an exclusively "artwork aesthetic" seems to me an odd approach to novels and films that, by their very design, are meant to be widely accessible and that, by virtually all accounts, are aesthetically conventional in nature. Let us be frank: there is an evident bias in the academy against reception criticism, principally because it seems (and perhaps not infrequently *is*) derivative: the image of merely cataloguing the views of others (in place of one's own analysis) is often called to mind. To the contrary, I contend that a judicious use of reception data—particularly for works that circulate in such popular genres as detective fiction and "dominant" cinema—can only enrich our analysis and render it more complex. Though I will not reiterate their contributions here, the pathbreaking work of Hans-Robert Jauss, Stanley Fish, and Jan Radway informs my interest in interpretive communities and reader response.

For this study, I have widened the scope of my original examination of numerous newspaper reviews to include the dozen pedagogical manuals published in Germany to provide guidance in teaching *The Reader*. Rather than grouping my findings in a separate chapter, I have distributed the insights I have gleaned from these handbooks throughout this study, wherever I have found them to be most relevant to a question under consideration. It would be difficult to overestimate the value of these teaching guides, in particular, as they often include rationales for teaching the book in the first place as well as synopses of the pedagogues' (often considerable) experience in having taught Schlink over the past 15 years in German schools. Again and again, one reads how well this novel goes down: it is "easily accessible to everyone" (allen leicht zugänglich)[27] it is deeply relevant to almost any conceivable subject in the Gymnasium curriculum, not to mention to university-level law school students;[28] it offers identification figures in the persons of *both* Michael and Hanna;[29] and finally, it presents a truly gripping story. Möckel, for example, assures her fellow teachers, "In my experience, the novel has proven itself as a text that fascinates pupils of various age groups. It provides a gripping story, contains surprise twists and turns of events, and rivets the reader by way of its narration through to the end."[30] These teaching guides are a real treasure trove; there is enough here of interest—including very telling exercises for student projects, classroom activities, exams, and papers—to justify a chapter or study in its own right. I have not taken that option but hope that others will.

Of course, those who view broader cultural readings as essentially opposed to close, aesthetic ones harbor their own bias. Lurking within some of the approaches that effectively ignore the wider cultural circulation of art can be found the central weakness of the critical paradigm, one that its adherents believe to have overcome long ago, namely that of the New Criticism. By starting with the assumption that Schlink's novels are ipso facto "well wrought urns" containing elaborate structures of irony, ambiguity, balance, and tension, they may be importing answers to an investigation the nature of which was never fully articulated in the first place. This accounts, I think, for the fact that critics can confidently espouse coherent, close readings that are meant to "solve" an alleged misconception, but that they do so without asking themselves just how the respective "misreadings" arose in the first place. I offer this brief example to illustrate the point. McGlothlin diagnoses a "false understanding"[31] with respect to readers' identification of Berg as representative of the second generation. She takes pains to correct this erroneous view by offering her own "careful reading of the text,"[32] which she hopes will demonstrate that the protagonist's experience is, in key respects, "idiosyncratic" and "anomalous"—that is, not in the least representative.[33] McGlothlin's analysis is all to the good, except that it is never explained why "*Der Vorleser* is so readily viewed by readers not only as a paradigmatic second-generation text, but indeed as a better, more accurate version of *Väterliteratur*."[34] How were all those readers duped in the first place? Are they necessarily wrong, if the novel itself, as McGlothlin concedes, "posits Michael's experience with Hanna as representative of an entire generation's encounter with the past"?[35] My own approach, while far more sympathetic to these discarded "popular" interpretations, actually accommodates both readings and, moreover, seeks to theoretically account for the fact that Schlink, by his insistence, actually invites this bifurcated hermeneutic.[36] "Mighty Aphrodite," whom I shall now introduce as a characteristic semiotic strategy, is already present in this apparent discrepancy between popular and academic reception.

This study's point of departure is the observation that Schlink's novels have inspired curiously divergent readings. I will argue throughout this book that the ambiguity inherent in these novels (and to some extent in the films they have inspired) is of a very specific kind, reserving Chapter 2 for a special discussion of *ethical* ambiguity. Critics have, of course, long embraced ambiguity as a prerequisite to hermeneutic sophistication, as William Empson's classic *Seven Types of Ambiguity* attests. This concept has retained its importance even for subsequent movements far more politically committed than Empson's New Criticism. For example, ambiguity (or related terms such as "undecidability" and "liminality") becomes a marker of literary distinction for structuralists and poststructuralists alike. This emphatic valorization of aesthetic ambiguity comports particularly well with literary high modernism as it was understood in the postwar years.[37] In a lecture on the works of Franz Kafka I attended years ago, Harvard professor Judith Ryan masterfully delineated at least a dozen critical approaches, ranging from biblical, to historicist, to biographical, to Marxist, to structuralist, to Freudian, to deconstructionist, and so on. She presented each paradigm as tantalizingly responsive to a certain aspect of Kafka, yet it is somehow never fully satisfying. Each approach answered at least one burning question yet left us frustrated in other respects. To me, this remains a model of high modernist hermeneutic ambiguity—a puzzle not for its own sake but a profound challenge precisely to our established systems of meaning-making that otherwise characterize hermeneutical practice in the extraliterary "real" world. One can come at Kafka from almost any position and be, as Ryan masterfully shows, partially "right" yet always, at the same time, profoundly "wrong."

While Schlink's texts possess a kind of multivalence, the model of ambiguity that best applies to his novels is quite different in nature than the one adumbrated here; indeed, it is essentially binary. On numerous key hermeneutic questions, the "Nazi novels" of Bernhard Schlink give rise not to a rich Kafka-like penumbra of semiotic meanings (and rich deferral of signification) but instead a bimodal interpretive structure that I am, for the fun of it, calling the "Aphrodite strategy." I take this term from the many well-known depictions of Aphrodite (or Venus) in painting and sculpture that show her both as a voluptuous nude and as an

undeniably modest woman. Typically, she is depicted in the act of cover-
ing her breasts with one hand and her pubic area or pudenda (i.e., *Scham-
stelle*) with the other. But this is, of course, a losing proposition because
the one hand is (thankfully) never sufficient to cover both breasts, and
even when the artist allows her to make use of her long and flowing hair
(as in the famous fifteenth-century Botticelli painting), she never quite
manages to conceal her nudity, which, of course, is the whole point. It is
perhaps worth remembering that this gesture of modesty constitutes the
core aesthetic conception of these many Aphrodites—it is not imposed ex
post facto, as were the veils and scraps of flowing cloth that were painted
over the genitalia and (female) breasts of Michelangelo's Sistine Chapel
nudes. On the contrary, Aphrodite (as I am schematically deploying this
figure here) is meant to simultaneously exhibit and conceal bare female
flesh.[38] Thus we can enjoy her delicious nakedness precisely because we
can partake of the illusion that we are not voyeurs. She is not placing her
"wares" on display, as in some storefront on the Reeperbahn (Hamburg's
notorious red-light district). Her unmistakable gesture of modesty allows
us to see her (and ourselves) as "pure." She lets us have it both ways.

What does all this have to do with Schlink? I employ this "Aphrodite
strategy" heuristically to help us identify a whole series of similarly struc-
tured hermeneutic options in Schlink's novels. This semiotic technique of
"both-and" (*sowohl-als-auch*) not only allows readers to see a thing from
two distinct points of view, but it usually requires us to do so from two
diametrically opposed perspectives that not only enhance but also, in a
sense, require each other. One of these perspectives, I argue, is hermeneu-
tically "dominant" (e.g., Aphrodite's nudity), whereas the other is "reces-
sive" but palpably present (e.g., the gestures of modesty) in a manner that
provides "plausible deniability" to the first option. So even as we feast our
eyes on the fleshly charms of curvaceous Aphrodite, we can, with logical
consistency and good conscience, claim that we are glimpsing a chaste
virgin.

Such is the hermeneutic structure that allows us, for example, to see
Gerhard Selb (of the eponymous detective trilogy) both as a fantasy resis-
tor figure and as a figure of harmless fun. Aphrodite, so to speak, is at
the heart of what, in Chapter 1, I call the "popular culture alibi"—the
notion that popular culture can at once be socially critical (and therefore
worthy of the hallowed imprimatur Vergangenheitsbewältigung) and also
dismissed at will as mindless entertainment. Aphrodite is also present in
two diametrically opposed notions of ambiguity discussed in Chapter 2:
the first notion, the dominant one in the reception data, views ambiguity as a "gray zone" of high moral sophistication, whereas the other

deploys ambiguity as a means of avoiding the nuances of ethical inquiry. She is there again in Chapter 3, where I discuss the intriguingly dualistic nature of guilt—as both a bold confession of (juridical) responsibility and its opposite; she is present, if you will, in the curious manner in which guilt metamorphoses from shame into a badge of virtue and honor. The ambiguous Aphrodite makes her presence felt in other chapters as well—as, for example, when we see that the narrator of *The Reader* is set up as both a deeply flawed and scarred human being (analogous to the modesty gesture), only to be offered ultimately as a winsome identification figure fully capable of representing the aspirations (or fantasies) of second-generation observers of the Holocaust. Her presence is so ubiquitous, so to speak, that I have shamelessly appropriated and adapted the title of Woody Allen's film, *Mighty Aphrodite*, to describe the omnipresence of this structure. She provides a handy visual metaphor for my analytic approach and helps set the stage for questions that should bedevil any reader of Schlink.

For example, how can Hanna Schmitz seem like a consummate Holo-caust perpetrator to some and a mere guilty bystander to others? It is not enough to simply wish away one of these options or to "prove" that one is invalid or misconceived. Any credible approach must take account of the *dual and mutually exclusive* messages being sent at various levels through-out the novels. On all the key questions regarding story and discourse, critics are not merely of different minds—certainly not evenly or hap-hazardly distributed over the hermeneutic horizon—but curiously polar-ized (though admittedly not in even quantities). Many, for example, view Hanna as the mother figure she is presented as being on several occasions. But for those who resist this identification, there is the requisite passage where Berg denies what he has elsewhere affirmed. The text always con-tains some irrefutable evidence—just as those depictions of Aphrodite do—for *both* positions. So how do we adjudicate the contradictions? By suggesting the presence of "Mighty Aphrodite," I hope, above all, to fore-ground the key interpretive challenge, even if readers accede variously (or not at all) to the specific conclusions proffered in this study.

The evidence I offer is of course also textual—based on close read-ings of differential semiotic structures—but my argument depends on a political and poststructural hypothesis as well: in the end it is the dom-inant second-generation mind-set (a term that will admittedly require some clarification) that ensures that the "dimension of voluptuousness" will prevail. Because we—and not just Germans, or even Germans of the second generation—share Berg's sense of being burdened and exhausted by the rigors of Vergangenheitsbewältigung, we need him to be right.

For American readers, too, he is a hero drawn in our own image, and therefore his flaws serve only to further ennoble him. If and when this readership itself changes—when mass consumption reading practices are no longer determined by the hermeneutics of Holocaust exhaustion—the social meaning of Schlink's work may change as well—but not until then.

Throughout this study I make use of generational terminology. "First generation" refers to those Germans who were adults during the Nazi period, and "second generation" refers to those who were children at that time or else born shortly after the war. There is admittedly a high degree of inexactitude in this usage. What constitutes a generation, after all? Precisely where do we draw the line between the two? The liminal—and highly contested—case of Günter Grass illustrates the difficulty. To what generation do we ascribe the 17-year-old SS recruit? (Grass, by the way, was the same age as Hanna Schmitz when she joined the SS.) To what extent can we assume the existence of a common factor that allows such generational groupings to be meaningful in the first place? As the sociologist Karl Mannheim observed in his magisterial essay of 1928, "Das Problem der Generationen," these are all valid objections, and indeed there are other good reasons for remaining skeptical of this imprecise usage.[39] Yet none of these arguments outweighs the utility of these generational groupings, as long as we remain aware of their tentative and largely heuristic value.[40] A wholesale rejection of generational terminology would demand too high a price, requiring us, for example, to do without Christian Rogowski's poignant reflections on teaching—as a German in the United States—American students about Germany, Nazism, and the Holocaust.[41]

Beyond Schlink and the immediate questions raised by his texts (and related films), I pursue three larger issues in this book. The first of these has to do with that impossible genre, Holocaust literature (or film). How can one criticize this or that work without offering at least an operational definition of one's own? I do not adhere to a static view of "Holocaust literature": the "didactic" era, during which Holocaust literature or film recapitulated key historical events of the genocide in a documentary or autobiographical fashion, has more or less ended. Schools, museums, and memorials have largely taken over this pedagogical function, releasing art to do what it does best—that is, probe, interrogate, and unsettle conventional wisdom on what the Holocaust legacy should mean in contemporary life. Of course, those earlier—generally more direct and didactic—works also persist into the present, providing continuity, complementarity, and a baseline for those that follow. More recent approaches that treat the Holocaust "epiphenomenally" may well prove compelling, insofar as they embed a jarring, or unexpected, confrontation with the genocide within the life of subsequent generations in a manner commensurate with the way we might encounter the Holocaust today—namely, as a history characterized by profound "disbelief" (Friedlaender). To admit that evasion is a risk that accompanies such indirect epiphenomenal approaches is simply to concede the freedom inherent in aesthetic experience. Yet this "secondary" treatment of the Holocaust need not ipso facto disappoint. As I have elsewhere demonstrated with reference to selected works by Uwe Timm, Thomas Bernhard, Martin Walser, Thomas Brussig, and Walter Kempowski,[42] there is in fact much to be gained precisely via this method of indirect reference. The sudden eruption, or even slow recognition, of Holocaust themes may, in the context of a work predominantly concerned with other matters, provide readers a powerful, memorable, and productive opportunity to consider the role the Holocaust *should* play in contemporary culture. These works inquire about the conflicted meaning of historicization and memory rather than presume it to be settled. And the surrounding narrative can function as an elaborate frame that quite effectively sets off the subtle Holocaust "detail."[43] Alas, Schlink's relegation of the Holocaust to epiphenomenal status provides all the distance but few of the rewards associated with this method of indirection.

Expanding the category of German Holocaust literature to include the contemporary authors mentioned here (even with the crucial modifier "epiphenomenal"), and furthermore to place Schlink in this context at all (albeit critically), widens the rubric in ways that will seem impermissible to some. Indeed, we would do well to recall the austere admonitions of Theodor Adorno, Lawrence Langer, and Alvin Rosenfeld—rigorous gatekeepers all, the latter two ceaselessly warning against the implicit "mental comfort" offered to readers and viewers of Holocaust fiction that compromises truth for the sake of entertainment value.[44] They are particularly alert to (as they would see it) the illicit aesthetic pleasures that are smuggled into works classified under this rubric. Their reservations issue a solemn cautionary note. After citing a particularly disturbing passage from *Night*, in which Elie Wiesel reports the incineration of live babies, Rosenfeld asks, "Has there ever before been a literature more dispiriting and forlorn, more scandalous than this?" In the same, influential essay, "The Problem of Holocaust Literature," he defines the genre as "a literature of decomposition" (in multiple senses of the word) and asserts apodictically that we must simply admit that "at Auschwitz humanity incinerated its heart."[45] Frankly, it is hard to imagine applying these same criteria to the works of Schlink or to the films they have inspired—certainly Rosenfeld would not permit us to do so—despite their overt thematization of Nazism and the Holocaust.[46] Whether we may wish to expand the borders of Holocaust literature or not, readers and film audiences surely do already—and in no small part due to marketing. In widening the circle—acknowledging that popular culture has long since done so—we need not give up our critical sense. Our task, rather, is to differentiate works that function critically from those primarily in the service of evasion. By reminding ourselves of the stark, prescriptive strictures of earlier theorists, we come to recognize Holocaust literature not as a normative, protected field but as a richly heterogeneous and contested one.

The second overarching matter, previously mentioned in passing, is the question of ambiguity and its assumed relationship to higher-level moral inquiry. This is the focus of Chapter 2. The conventional wisdom is that as we move beyond the black-and-white ethical certainties of the past, we proceed into a land of richer ethical ambiguity. There are several problems with this assumption, with which the critical literature is rife. First is the frankly incorrect assertion that Holocaust literature has, until recently, trafficked almost exclusively in monochromatic figures and simplistic attributions of guilt and innocence. Second, there is a flip side to this undertheorized affiliation, namely one that deploys ambiguity (perhaps unconsciously or inadvertently) precisely to halt the process of painful ethical deliberation. Related to both of these issues is the way in which a "gripping" fictional account is asked to substitute for the tedious work of historical investigation, encouraging readers to bypass the travail of dealing with ethical nuance. These are matters that, I hope, may enrich other discussions beyond Schlink.

The third major question of this study is an old one: it concerns the ability of popular culture to provoke serious social criticism. This is not a question that I would presume to try to settle in the abstract. While my own penchant for assessing the vagaries of reception data keeps me from articulating any dogmatic position, I must confess that a good deal of skepticism runs through each of the subsequent chapters. Ever since Andreas Huyssen (who, I believe, took his cue from Heinrich Böll) affirmed the efficacy of the television series *Holocaust* within German public culture[47]—to the chagrin of modernist authors who had tried their hand at Holocaust literature but to far lesser effect—critics have been increasingly willing to embrace popular culture as an effective vehicle for confronting the Shoah (Hebrew for "calamity") and other atrocities. The most extreme disciple of this school of thought may be Hanno Loewy, who suggests that Holocaust allusions in certain episodes of *Star Trek* may prove a more effective tool of Vergangenheitsbewältigung than the self-consciously thematic works of Holocaust enlightenment by the "founding fathers" of this genre, for example, Peter Weiss, Rolf Hochhuth, Elie Wiesel, and others.[48]

The fundamental theoretical reconceptualization of literary realism that we have encountered in the last decade and a half may have played a role in paving the way for this trend. Though not the first, Robert Holub is probably the most lucid propagator of the "ideological reading" of realism. In his *Reflections of Realism*, he espoused the thesis that realist texts typically—even programmatically—obscure their own artifice and, in the process, serve to "normalize" certain regressive social conventions, such as quietism, anti-Semitism, and misogyny. Several years thereafter, Dorrit Cohn forcefully argued against the affiliation of a consistent political or ideological position with any particular literary genre, and with realism in particular.[49] Realism, she argued, is neither essentially reactionary nor politically conservative, as it had often been deemed to be. At about the same time, Eric Downing published a series of articles in the esteemed *Deutsche Vierteljahrsschrift*, culminating in the pathbreaking book *Double Exposures*,[50] in which he argued for the critical potential of realist literature (though not of all kinds), essentially overturning the modernist caricature of realism as naïve and un-self-reflexive.[51] This theoretical paradigm shift, valuable in its own right and long overdue, may paradoxically have opened the floodgates to a less critical and less nuanced view of all realism—extending, I suspect, to the kind of popular realism that was not really the concern of Holub, Cohn, or Downing.[52]

What remains curious, I think, is the way in which the cultural studies approach has effectively "disappeared" the once-dominant ideological reading of realism that assumed that the genre itself was authoritarian (or worse) as well as unreflective and affirming of the status quo. Deeply problematic in itself—for it was always overly broad—this older view of realism seems to have been replaced, in our time, with one that simply installs the opposite presupposition. At any rate, in this study I find myself confronting, again and again, the uncritical assumption that *popular* realism—that is, utterly conventional realism—can eo ipso fulfill this important "enlightenment" function, often without any interest on the part of critics who make this claim to try to determine (beyond their own assertions) whether the work in question actually succeeds in doing so, and without articulating criteria that would even address the question. I discuss this matter in some depth in Chapter 4. Picking up on this leveling, antimodernist backlash, one pedagogue unreservedly recommends Schlink for the classroom precisely because he (Schlink) lets us have it both ways: his novels, she asserts, are at once eminently consumable *and* intellectually and aesthetically challenging. Drawing on the language of cultural studies, she effortlessly places Schlink in the "postmodern" tradition that self-consciously rejects the division between high and low culture, between "serious" and entertaining literature.[53] *Holocaust as Fiction* advocates not a return to the high-handed Frankfurt School dismissal of popular culture, but rather a more considered, pragmatic, and skeptical approach—one that negotiates between the Scylla of the Frankfurt School and the Charybdis of cultural studies based on the articulated merits and demonstrated social meaning of individual works.

I begin this study in Chapter 1 with a discussion of a genre generally acknowledged to be "lightweight" in aesthetic terms, namely detective fiction. I think it helps set the stage for narrative tropes and strategies that recur in the later, putatively "weightier" novel. At the same time, it reminds us of the pleasure and playfulness that is part of all art—the very ingredient that makes "Holocaust art" such an impossible genre in the first place. I have chosen not to recapitulate all the scholarly debates, nor have I fully recreated the scholarly apparatus from the three articles I previously published on Schlink. Though I draw freely on my prior work, reproducing and modifying some of it here, I have self-consciously aspired to a lighter approach in my own writing. In this spirit, I have attempted to write a book that will be accessible not only to my academic colleagues but also to the many college and high school students (as well as their teachers) who may compose the bulk of Schlink's readers today.

I have assumed that readers may wish to consult the various chapters selectively. Indeed, *Holocaust as Fiction* may rightly be considered a series of interconnected essays. Chapters 2 and 3 especially presume a sustained interest in textual detail and critical reception; the others are more essayistic in manner. To those who opt to navigate the book from cover to cover, I confess at the outset to a degree of redundancy. It is not possible to discuss the detective fiction without mentioning the later novel that would emerge from the same fiction laboratory. And the fundamental question of the narrator's position cannot be entirely sequestered (or so I decided) to a single chapter. Whenever possible, however, I have tried to reduce the overlap by pointing readers to the more substantive discussions, wherever these might be found. Nevertheless, intrepid readers will notice that Hanna Schmitz, that central and very fraught figure from *The Reader*, makes an appearance in almost every chapter of this study. Given her importance to each of the questions I treat here, I simply saw no way of restricting her to a single chapter. Those confronted with an all-too-familiar argument are hereby advised—as the Germans say—"to read diagonally" whenever necessary.

After the release of Daldry's Oscar-winning film, Schlink proclaimed that *The Reader*—hailed by some survivors, refugees, and others as the latest and highest expression of Holocaust literature—is not really about the Holocaust at all. So is Schlink just moving the goalposts? Is he responding to the needs of the global film market? Whatever the case, there is undoubtedly something intrinsic to this body of work that lends itself to diametrically divergent, *and* interdependent, readings. "Mighty Aphrodite" reminds us not to fall into the either-or trap of surface contractions and instead to consider the ways in which these binaries may actually function in tandem. I invite readers to explore this enigma with me in the following pages.

CHAPTER 1

RESISTER AFTER THE FACT

SCHLINK'S *SELB* TRILOGY AND THE POPULAR CULTURE ALIBI

It [the detective novel] is seldom praised and often read, even by those who despise it—what do we have here? There must be something to this case after all.
—Ernst Bloch, "A Philosophical View of the Detective Novel"

In a mystery novel everyone is suspect, simply by virtue of being there. It's a kind of moral realism, which is the main attraction of these books. (Only the detective is exempt, since he—or she—is the fairy responsible for restitution and retribution.)
—Ruth Klüger, *Still Alive: A Holocaust Girlhood Remembered*

IMAGINE A POPULAR, BESTSELLING PIECE OF CONVENTIONAL German fiction that features a loveable ex-Nazi who makes overtures to an attractive young member of the opposite sex. This figure with a "burdened past" eventually acknowledges having been involved in some nasty business but pointedly never specifies her responsibility for crimes during the Hitler period. Imagine further that this character, who is definitely, although nebulously, connected to Nazi crimes, is portrayed as a "moved mover," that is, as a lower-echelon actor with accomplices and superiors at least as guilty as she—and probably, we are led to believe, much more so. Hypothesize further that this novel places the ex-Nazi principally in the context of German (rather than Jewish) suffering, and that she is portrayed as having paid the price (or at least a very high price), while the truly guilty go unpunished. Imagine this ex-Nazi as a victim, unfairly manipulated by others both during and after the war. Finally, consider that this figure is given substantial extenuating circumstances—perhaps even an alibi for never revealing what she did during those infamous "dark years." Would such a novel necessarily be cause for controversy? Is it *intrinsically* problematic?

One may well suspect—not least because of my use of the feminine pronoun—that in this hypothetical situation, I have been referring to Bernhard Schlink's bestseller *The Reader* (1995), which of course does present a sympathetically drawn ex-SS member in the person of the illiterate Hanna Schmitz. But I refer, rather, to another novel by Schlink—one that appeared contemporaneously with the *Historikerstreit* (historians' debate) of the late 1980s and managed to evade the critical scrutiny that subsequently plunged *The Reader* into controversy.[1] How did Schlink's *Selbs Justiz* (1987; coauthored with Walter Popp; published in English as *Self's Punishment*, 2005), whose endearing hero, the ex-Nazi Gerhard Selb, meets all the criteria enumerated in the hypothetical scenario, elude the moral-historical categories that allegedly dominate postwar German culture? The answer is not hard to divine: it did so simply by being what it is, namely, pulp fiction. As a detective novel, it sits squarely within that undemanding cultural stratum designated as being unmistakably "U-Literatur" (*Unterhaltungsliteratur*), that is, pure entertainment with no obligation to instruct, ennoble, edify, disrupt, subvert, or—least of all—defy commodification, as Adorno would have stipulated. This stuff is truly Teflon-covered, and criticism that seeks to saddle it with any sense of social responsibility simply slips off without gaining purchase. Yet at the same time—and this is the truly interesting paradox—we seem willing to credit mass entertainment precisely with such social-critical potential when it pleases us to do so, as is clear from the case of the 1978 German broadcast of the American television series *Holocaust*. After widespread initial doubts about the capacity of popular entertainment to do justice to the subject matter, critics came to value the tremendous role this soap-operatic drama played in raising consciousness about the Holocaust in both Germany and the United States.[2]

Despite general reservations (or perhaps even deep-seated prejudice) about detective novels, I wish to examine the Selb trilogy first, because it so closely parallels certain thematic and structural patterns that recur somewhat less obviously in *The Reader*. Indeed, the trilogy serves as a kind of x-ray for diagnosing that better-known novel. Because these detective novels fly below the radar of high culture, they illustrate an instance of Blochian nonsimultaneity,[3] that is, a notable incongruity that complicates a widespread conception of German culture as being uniform with respect to this question or as being perpetually, insistently—and, some would say, obsessively—on the lookout for politically incorrect literature about Nazism and the Holocaust. In point of fact, *Vergangenheitsbewältigung*

(Mastering the Nazi past)—as Lisa Heineman's remarks on the career of Beate Uhse demonstrate—has, from the beginning, been a rather uneven and class-inflected matter in German public culture.[4] It may ultimately be folly to take Gerhard Selb, the eponymous hero of Schlink's detective trilogy, too seriously. Yet it is here that Schlink rehearses what I will call his "perpetrator formula," a recipe that calls for a likeable Nazi who feels guilty, though never of anything concrete; repentant, though without any substantive exploration of the conversion; and, above all, compromised—even betrayed—by a hierarchy where the real evildoers are always elsewhere. It is interesting to enter Schlink's narrative laboratory for another reason as well: the detective novels, while avatars par excellence of belletristic literature, are by no means aimed at a social class lower (or other) than that envisioned as the target group for Schlink's later novel, which supposedly has grander aspirations. It is clear from the advertising that the publisher is courting the very same readership for both. If the Selb trilogy and *The Reader* indeed reach the same (or similar) readership, then there is all the more reason to inquire into the ideological use being made of these apparent confections.

Edmund Wilson began his celebrated three-part salvo against detective novels by reminding his *New Yorker* readers of the genre's popularity among those who (he thinks) should know better: "For years I have been hearing about detective stories. Almost everybody I know seems to read them, and they have long conversations about them in which I am unable to take part. I am always being reminded that the most serious public figures of our time, from Edmund Wilson to W. B. Yeats, have been addicts of this form of fiction."[5] To these, he might well have added the names Brecht, Benjamin, and Bloch, all of whom had an intimate appreciation of this mass cultural genre.[6] Though Wilson writes as a cultured despiser of detective fiction—he famously dubbed it "a field which is mostly on a sub-literary level"[7]—his observation about its readership remains pertinent for our discussion. We cannot simply dismiss it as pabulum for the masses,[8] as he would have liked to do. And even if we could, this would only make it more interesting for critics who continue to view detective fiction as an important source of social commentary.[9] If Hanno Loewy is right to suggest that German popular culture provides a potentially more meaningful forum for coming to terms with the Nazi past than many a high cultural effort,[10] we would certainly want to take this genre into account. As one critic notes, "a peculiar quality of almost all Schlink's texts is that they treat explosive issues of recent German history in a brilliant manner and manage expertly to combine suspenseful entertainment with profundity. In the detective novels as well, topics such as the Nazi past, the relationship of East and West, as well as the relationship of Germans and Jews are raised in a manner that does justice to their complexity."[11]

While we may ultimately want to challenge the latter part of this claim, what is of interest for the time being is the assertion that Schlink's work, including his detective fiction, represents a kind of *littérature engagée*. Schlink himself has never been shy about advocating for these *Krimis* (detective novels); on the contrary, he has repeatedly stressed the continuity in his writing, even going so far as to state that he could not have written *The Reader* without the experience he had gained in writing the detective novels.[12] At any rate, it is impossible to conceive of the pleasure (and therefore the meaning) that these books provide without attending to the person of Gerhard Selb, the private investigator whose Nazi past permeates the series as a whole. I will first treat the inaugural volume of the trilogy, *Selbs Justiz* (1987), and then consider how *Selbs Betrug* (1992; *Self's Deception*, 2007) and *Selbs Mord* (2001, *Self's Slaughter*, 2007) qualify the portrait I have drawn.[13]

This is the mystery our private investigator is initially asked to solve: someone has broken into the computer system of a major German chemical concern, and it becomes the job of the aging detective Selb, an old friend and the brother-in-law of CEO Korten, to find the culprit. As is the case in so many detective novels, the narrative accoutrements can be as important as the "analytic drama" itself. Selb's mild hedonism, relaxed air, self-deprecating attitude, and his role as an aging underdog—throughout, he appears charmingly old-fashioned—make him a distinctly likeable figure from the outset. He is "a man with a ruptured past," as one critic observes, "but one who has learned from it."[14] He loves good (usually Italian) food and beautiful (always younger) women. He pursues an attractive, young secretary, Frau Buchendorff, throughout most of the first book, and similar love interests in the latter two, but is favorably contrasted with his more flamboyant skirt-chasing friend Philipp. Within the first third of the novel, Selb deftly tracks down the hacker, who turns out to be both a rival for the affections of the beautiful Buchendorff and an ecological activist who attempts, in his own misguided way, to curb illegal pollution that is being emitted intentionally and systematically by the Rheinland Chemical Works, a thinly veiled reference to the Sandoz chemical spill scandal of 1986.[15]

At this point, the plot takes a fateful turn. The hacker Mischkey is unexpectedly killed in a suspicious car crash, and Selb begins to have pangs of conscience for exposing him despite the fact that he had done so without the intention of having him murdered. And so our protagonist turns inward. But since this is a detective novel, "inwardness" is a distinctly relative term. The search for Mischkey's murderer (now funded by love interest Buchendorff) becomes, as Selb says, a quest for "a clarity about myself."[16] What this investigation ultimately produces, however, is less a searching exploration of one man's Nazi past than a fairly concerted effort to "normalize" his biography. The title *Selbs Justiz* refers most immediately to the vigilante-style justice meted out at the novel's end. Yet it might just as well denote the novel's dogged attempt to justify the protagonist's career. The last two-thirds of this entertainingly written work essentially tell how a bright, educated, and socially privileged young man could plausibly have been duped by his Nazi superiors, not to mention by a deceitful Jew, into prosecuting innocent men for capital crimes during those "dark" Nazi years. The loveable, avuncular Selb is an ex-Nazi with a heart of gold.

He first broaches his "burdened" past with Frau Buchendorff, who, as a member of the second generation, needs to be filled in on his backstory. Selb confronts his past with what appears to be disarming honesty: "I'd been a convinced National Socialist, an active party member, and a tough prosecutor who'd also argued for, and won, the death penalty . . . I had faith in the cause and saw myself as a soldier on the legal front. I could no longer be utilized on the other front following my wound at the start of the war."[17]

No cowardly evasion here: Selb appears to put it all on the table, manfully taking responsibility for his youthful convictions. And he favorably contrasts this unvarnished account with "the sanitized version" he is apparently accustomed to telling.[18] But this admission actually conceals, precisely in its stalwart assertiveness: broad statements stand in for the enumeration of specific crimes and individual responsibility. It is the classic case of shutting down further conversation by means of an aggressive "confession." Frau Buchendorff only wants to know why Selb has left the legal profession and why the once powerful state's attorney (*Staatsanwalt*) is now a has-been private detective. Without showing any interest in Selb's fearlessly acknowledged "Nazi convictions" or in the associated harsh death sentences, she focuses exclusively on the lucrative career he has given up. In the film version, which I discuss later, she smiles admiringly and warmly when the detective expresses his disgust at the insincere "rehabilitation" of his Nazi jurist colleagues: "[To them] this reinstatement was a kind of reparation. That disgusted me."[19] His aura of principle and conviction works its magic on her, furthering the erotic tension that has been developing between them.

Selb's response to her inquiry about his career choice announces the fundamental strategies the novel will deploy to come to terms with the

Nazi past. After 1945, he says, "I'd lost my faith. You probably can't imagine how anyone could believe at all in National Socialism. But you've grown up with knowledge that we, after nineteen forty-five, only got piece by piece. Around the time of the Monetary Reform they started to draft incriminated colleagues back in. I could have returned to the judiciary then, too. But I saw what the efforts to get reinstated, and the reinstatement itself, did to my colleagues. Instead of feeling guilty they only had a sense that they'd been done an injustice when they were expelled."[20]

Even for a genre not particularly distinguished for luxuriating in excessive inward reflection, this conversion account seems astonishingly perfunctory. Selb sheds his attachment to Nazism like a youth who, as he attains the age of reason, parts ways with his childhood notion of religion: "I'd lost my faith." He furthermore espouses the dubious proposition that highly placed, well educated, and powerful actors like himself knew less about the evils of Nazism than the allegedly historically privileged second generation. While this may be quite true in some cases, with respect to specific historical discoveries and their postwar dissemination, a statement of this generality—"you've grown up with the knowledge that we . . . only got piece by piece"—seems designed for blanket exculpation. Lastly, and this theme runs throughout the Selb trilogy, our protagonist comes off as morally superior to all of his former Nazi comrades—as a cut above those former colleagues who returned unrepentant (or worse) to their positions in the justice department and would later show up in the infamous *Braunbuch* exposé published by the German Democratic Republic (GDR) for distribution in the Federal Republic of Germany (FRG).[21] Selb alone has learned from his experience and, not unimportantly in creating sympathy for him, has paid a self-imposed price of reduced salary and prestige. Further, we are given to believe that Selb's divorce had to do with the fact that his wife never shed her Nazi "faith" in the same thorough way as Selb did: "It was bad with my wife, who was a beautiful blonde Nazi and remained that way till she became a nice, plump Economic Miracle German."[22] These other figures—so cleanly distanced from Selb—clearly stand for the failed denazification effort in postwar West Germany.

The inaugural novel as a whole, as well as the trilogy that it introduces, seeks not so much to explore the criminality of Selb's suspects but to explain away his own, and it does so by propagating the all-too-familiar notion of the unwitting cog in a much bigger enterprise—the duped accomplice. When Judith (as Frau Buchendorff is now more intimately known) angrily accuses Selb of being a "nobody" who simply carries out the work of others ("Du bist auch so ein Irgendwer, der für die Mächtigen die Drecksarbeit erledigt"),[23] she clearly does not intend to evoke sympathy on his behalf or pay him a compliment. Yet with these words she gives expression to the novel's carefully executed strategy all the same. All we need now is one additional ingredient—already adumbrated here—namely, Selb's *unknowing* complicity. This is supplied by the evil Korten, who, we discover (and this is the novel's real discovery), has used Selb as a pawn throughout the Nazi and the postwar years. Though undoubtedly trite, the chess metaphors reveal the detective's self-image as he moves toward solving the book's real crime: "Of course I'd let myself be manipulated as a prosecutor, I'd learned that much after 1945 . . . Nevertheless, I didn't think it was the same thing to be guilty of having served a putative great but ultimately bad cause, or to be used by someone as a pawn on the chessboard of a small, shabby intrigue I didn't yet understand."[24]

Clearly, Selb seems to prefer to have become inculpated via Nazism—presumably because his involvement could then be explained away as youthful delusion set aside in more mature years and with the benefit of hindsight. In any event, his awareness of being "abused" or "taken advantage of" (*mißbraucht*) dates to the postwar period.[25] Thus, the apparent mutual exclusivity of these two options is only rhetorical. The novel has it both ways. Selb's experience of Nazism is both the freely embraced "reputedly great thing" that sours only in hindsight *and*, as we discover in the course of this story, a grand deception that trapped him into doing evil. Emphatically, it is the latter scenario that structures the remainder of the novel. And it is of generic (and not only ideological) consequence that he observes, once again, that this shabby intrigue was something he does not yet fully understand. This is the meat of the "mystery."

During the war, the Rheinland Chemical Company made use of Jewish slave laborers, including one Karl Weinstein, once a prestigious professor of organic chemistry in Breslau, who is now pressed into the service of this company's war effort. In 1943, Weinstein denounces two of his (non-Jewish) German colleagues, Tyberg and Dohmke, telling the Gestapo that the two were involved in a conspiracy to sabotage production. At the forceful urging of the federal prosecutor Gerhard Selb, both are quickly convicted of treason and the latter is hanged. It turns out, as Selb discovers only many years later, that Weinstein, prompted by the power-hungry Korten, had knowingly provided false testimony in the hopes of preserving his own life. As Sarah Hirsch, Weinstein's *Lebensgefährtin* and the novel's authoritative Jewish survivor of the Holocaust, puts it, "They didn't even promise him his life, only that he might survive a bit longer."[26] Though he was clearly acting under duress, the novel's main Jewish character is portrayed as deceitful and somewhat cowardly, a point his wife corroborates: "My husband didn't cope well with life, nor was he very brave."[27] Also noteworthy is the way Schlink moves Selb into a position analogous to that of Weinstein vis-à-vis the villainous Korten: both are manipulated pawns in Korten's dastardly scheme to take over the reins of corporate power. "She didn't realize," the detective tells us, "she was not only telling his story but also touching upon my own past."[28] All of the various plot strands, at first so inchoate and apparently unrelated, lead back to Korten and his conspiracy: "The conspiracy—with me as the dupe. Set up and executed by my friend and brother-in-law. And I'd been happy not to have to drag him into the trial. He'd used me with contemptuous calculation."[29]

By the time Selb asks himself what to make of his own guilt,[30] the question seems almost moot. This has the effect of unburdening others as well, such as the dim-witted Schmalz, who is portrayed as yet another helpless pawn of Korten despite the fact that it was he who physically threatened Weinstein and actually murdered Mischkey. A bit like Hanna in *The Reader*, Schmalz is the proximate, but clearly subordinate, perpetrator. Of course, this model of guilt, one in which only a few superiors—or perhaps ultimately only one—are blameworthy, while all the rest appear as cogs or subordinate functionaries, is both well-known and shopworn. Indeed, the implicit Hitler-Korten analogy is already clearly suggested with the murder of the computer hacker, Mischkey. Crucial in this analogy is Schmalz's role as hit man, one that significantly requires no written command from the *Generaldirektor* (read, führer). Instead, we learn of a general ethos of violence and of a hierarchical chain of command in which well-understood signals, rather than explicit orders, are given to overzealous subordinates.[31] This is a page right out of Holocaust historian Raul Hilberg's *The Destruction of the European Jews*—one that, however, interprets the absence of a written order from Hitler as the prelude to a functionalist explanation of the genocide rather than as an exculpation of lower-level perpetrators.[32] As one of Selb's longtime friends suggests, it might well have been "the case that the chain was so well-oiled that everyone knew what was meant without it being spoken out loud. But if it was oiled like that, it certainly can't be proved."[33]

Accordingly, it is supremely satisfying—if not quite legal—to kill off Korten. After considering his several options, Selb realizes that Korten could easily twist, or entirely evade, any actual attempt to bring him to justice. For this reason, he decides to take matters into his own hands—literally—by pushing his nemesis off the rocky cliffs of Brittany. He realizes that this is not quite right, and he suffers the requisite pangs of conscience in the immediate aftermath. Yet he is confirmed in his vigilantism by one of the novel's principal surviving victims, the German Tyberg, the other member of the duo who had been falsely accused by Weinstein and condemned by the Nazi court in 1944 but who had somehow escaped capital punishment. From a structural and generic point of view, we might say that Tyberg was spared precisely so that he could play this crucial postwar role for Selb. In the final episode, he calls Selb to signal (again, in rather transparent "code") his approval of this ultimate installment of "Self's justice" (the more literal translation of the novel's German title, *Selbs Justiz*). We learn that "Tyberg had understood. It felt good to have a secret confidant who wouldn't call me to account."[34] This moment of absolution refers, of course, backward as well, for it was none other than Selb who, as the ferocious young Nazi *Staatsanwalt*, tried to have Tyberg executed. The German word I have translated as "confidant" here (*Mitwisser*) also means "accessory," which offers a juridical connotation that puts Tyberg squarely in Selb's camp. This, in turn, gives Tyberg's approval a far richer dimension—Selb is not only exonerated for Korten's murder in the present but, implicitly, also for his role in state-sponsored murder during the Nazi period. But this goes far beyond mere forgiveness; it constitutes a genuine role reversal, for in this manner, Selb is transformed into Tyberg's ex post facto avenger. Moreover, by murdering Korten, Selb has achieved what he believes West German courts could not, or would not, have done. In taking on this role, albeit belatedly, Selb does not only rehabilitate himself. Perhaps even more importantly, he lifts this unwanted burden off the shoulders of the second generation—who, as we shall see in subsequent chapters, are sometimes depicted as "victimized" precisely by this unwelcome task, one they did not choose, of having to prosecute various kinds of Nazi-era crimes.

If we are to conclude that the Selb trilogy is not merely a collection of unrelated investigations unified by the coincidence that they feature the same detective but instead is a concerted, consistent exploration of the ex-Nazi Gerhard Selb, then we will need to pay some attention to the other two novels, where we find a reiteration and elaboration of the formula already established. These subsequent volumes contain frequent reminders of Selb's Nazi past. But what, at first blush, seems a bold confession regarding, for example, "the havoc I wreaked at the time I was a state prosecutor," turns out, upon closer inspection, to be just as vague and summary a gesture as the one we encountered in the inaugural novel.[35] For example, at one point in *Selbs Betrug* (Self's Deception) we learn that our protagonist played a role in sending Russians and Poles to concentration camps: "I remembered the senior public prosecutor's memo that had crossed my desk in 1943 or 1944 at the Heidelberg Public Prosecutor's Office, which had decreed that any

Russian or Polish workers taking their tasks too lightly were to be sent to forced labor in a concentration camp. How many had I sent? I stared into the rain."[36] Three aspects of this passage are already familiar: first, the initial reminder that superiors ordered the action, in this case, the *Generalstaatsanwalt* (chief public prosecutor); second, the suggestion that Selb was lied to and manipulated, which is conveyed by the claim that only lazy workers were to be transported to camps for the exclusive fate of *Zwangsarbeit* (forced labor); and third, the paucity of any specific information on Selb's Nazi-era crimes. It is no coincidence that the detective's reflections break off just as he asks himself the tough question regarding his own role.[37] Selb's passivity in this scheme is underscored—both in the English and German editions—by means of the technique of deferred agency. In this case, the policy memo seems to have come to him of its own accord.

While this can be understood as psychologically well-founded from Selb's point of view (after all, who would wish to recall such things?), none of the other fictional figures, in particular those who actually engage him on the topic, appear at all interested in pursuing it. Lacking in all three novels is a representative of the second or third generation who displays any kind of sustained interest in Selb's or Germany's Nazi past, despite the fact that, according to Selb at least, this is precisely the generation best poised to comprehend Nazi crimes. Instead, these conversations about the war merely afford him the opportunity to remind us how much better he is than those former Nazi colleagues who reentered government service without ever really having shed their fascist convictions.[38] In language strikingly familiar from the first volume in the trilogy, Selb reflects, "In 1945, they turned their back on me for having been a Nazi public prosecutor, and when they wanted the old Nazis again, I turned my back on them. Because I was no longer an old Nazi? Because the let's-look-the-other-way attitude of my old and new colleagues at the bar rubbed me the wrong way? Because I had definitely had enough of others laying out for me what is just and unjust? . . . I can't say, Leo. Back in 1945, being a public prosecutor was simply over for me."[39] The importance of these sentiments for our understanding of Selb can be gleaned from their almost literal reiteration yet again in volume three, though this time not as tentative questions but instead as firm statements of conviction.[40] Once again, we meet Selb the lone moralist, who refuses to be corrupted by postwar laxity in coming to terms with the Nazi past. Ironically, in these passages, Selb confirms one of the main complaints of the so-called '68ers, namely that the postwar German judiciary and justice department (not to mention other governmental agencies) were packed with unrepentant and unreconstructed ex-Nazis.[41]

The detective who repeatedly insists on the importance of facing the past is, ironically, a bit hazy with regard to his own—except when it comes to his wartime sufferings. Both *Selbs Betrug* and *Selbs Mord* go further in establishing the protagonist as victim than had *Selbs Justiz*. In both sequels, we get an elaboration of the fact, already stated in the first volume, that Selb was seriously wounded on the Eastern Front and rendered incapable of further duty as a soldier. Now we read that these injuries resulted from a particularly horrific attack on his tank brigade in Poland, and it was for this reason (and not because he meant to) that he ended up as a Nazi *Staatsanwalt* (Public Prosecutor).[42] Unlike his explications about his role as Nazi prosecutor, which are preemptive and summary, Selb pauses here to tell us what it felt like to be trapped in a tank, unable to see the enemy, and then to suddenly hear the explosion that would take the lives of his comrades and end his career as a soldier. This episode is amplified to include the victimhood of Germans in general when, for the first time since 1942, Selb returns to Berlin, where he is reminded of the widespread destruction wrought by Allied bombing that left the city in ruins and took the lives of his parents.[43] In contrast to the semantically rather thin affirmations of "guilt" for a career as a Nazi prosecutor, the passages regarding the protagonist's own suffering are, understandably, emotionally more intense and richer in descriptive detail.[44]

This carries over into the narrative present when, in *Selbs Mord*, the protagonist is attacked, first by a group of skinhead neo-Nazis who compel him to scream "Heil Hitler" at the top of his lungs before tossing him into the Berlin *Landwehr* Canal,[45] and later by a group of self-appointed "antifascist" thugs who just happened to have witnessed this scene of humiliation and decide to punish Selb (by once again thrusting him into the same canal) for this public display of alleged Nazi sympathies.[46] Selb does nothing to deserve such violence and thus gains our unalloyed sympathy. Yet he cannot help viewing these attacks in relationship to his own Nazi past, about which these hooligans could of course have known absolutely nothing: "I wasn't seriously injured . . . But something [other than my body] did hurt. I had had the opportunity to rectify what in those days I did wrong. When do you get that kind of opportunity? But I did it wrong again."[47] There are two ways of reading this remark: either it is an obvious trivialization of his own Nazi past—one Schlink has perhaps included in order for us to gain a critical perspective on his detective narrator—or it is a serious proposition. In light of the generic bias in favor of reading *with* the private investigator (and on this more later), I would suggest that we are meant to see these two events (his service as a Nazi prosecutor and this attack by neo-Nazis) as indeed analogous—comparable at least insofar as the compulsion Selb experienced in the latter situation provided a commensurate opportunity to make amends for the earlier one. Selb failed to resist the skinhead gang, just as he once failed to stand up to his Nazi superiors. Again, he did what he was told; and again, it is suggested, he did so under threat of physical violence. We are thus invited to project his unmistakable status as victim in the recent attack back onto his Nazi past. Where, in all this, is the convinced young Nazi eager to serve on the Eastern Front at a time, as we now know, when some members of the *Wehrmacht* (German army) actively assisted the SS in the prosecution of the Holocaust?

Selb does make amends, however. In fact, all three adventures in each of the novels can be seen as reparation. In murdering Korten, he has, as we have observed, carried out a form of retributive justice largely unavailable in postwar Germany. Despite occasional self-doubts, which only serve to render him more likable, Selb defends his murder of Korten as an act of justifiable homicide, honoring the ancient call for revenge.[48] More importantly, this act reverses the passivity and subservience he practiced as a young Nazi *Staatsanwalt*, when he unknowingly did Korten's bidding. We witness Selb redressing his Nazi past in the subsequent novels as well. In helping the young activist Leo Salgar avoid capture, he in no way endorses her misguided efforts at "postmodern terrorism."[49] On the contrary, Schlink does not allow his narrator to miss the opportunity to denigrate the political radicalism and violence associated with the 1968 student movement,[50] which Selb clearly thinks is the inspiration for Leo's unsavory methods.[51] But Selb is sympathetic to Leo's goals of preserving an ecologically safe environment, just as he was of Mischkey's in volume one. And he vigorously defends his extralegal efforts to protect her, on the grounds that these represent a corrective for the overly submissive attitude toward authority inculcated in him (and his generational cohort) during the Nazi period: "I've been a man who minds his own business, a cobbler who has stuck to his last too often in life. As a soldier, a public prosecutor, as a private investigator, I did what I was told, it was my job, and I didn't go messing about in matters that were other people's domain. What we are is a nation of cobblers who mind their own business, and look where it's gotten us."[52] To clarify the already transparent allusion, Tyberg responds, "You're talking about the Third Reich?"[53] So it is not merely in doing good deeds today, but also in reversing the authoritarian character traits he imbibed during the Nazi era, that Selb rehabilitates himself. This is most clearly evident in the final installment of the trilogy, in which Selb inadvertently becomes the advocate of a Jewish family that had lost its stake in a bank when it was "Aryanized" in the 1930s. Though only occasionally in clear view within a novel that comprises a number of convoluted plot lines, the story of "Labans Kinder," the Jewish family persecuted during the Nazi period, finally gives Selb the chance to champion their cause, and, more specifically, to reverse the experience of his younger years when he stood idly by while his prosecutor cronies joked about dispossessed Jews seeking justice from their office.[54]

Lacking any clear idea of Selb's actual guilt, we respond more to this palpable series of moral reversals, gradually gaining the impression that he has atoned for whatever deficiencies he once had. In conjunction with the other elements we have seen on display throughout the trilogy—blustery but vacuous confessions of guilt, constant passing of the buck to superiors, self-presentation as the manipulated victim of others' intrigues—this trajectory of moral betterment only serves to further camouflage the particular crimes of his past. Selb himself encourages this process of obfuscation by casting his adversaries as the embodiment of fundamental moral vices rather than as perpetrators of specific historical crimes. This is already apparent with respect to Korten in volume one—observe how Selb performs the same trick on Weller and Welker, the antagonists from volume three. Their vices are in fact so generic that they—who, of course, were never Nazis—begin to merge with the Nazi arch villain Korten: "Yes, so they were. Third Reich, war, defeat, reconstruction, and economic miracle—for them these were only different circumstances in which they played the same game: they multiplied what they had or what they controlled . . . What did governments, systems, ideas, human suffering or joy—what did any of these matter, if the economy didn't flourish? . . . Korten was also like this . . . Just like the others [Weller and Welker], his own power and success had become one with that of the firm."[55] If these murky characters can metamorphose so easily into Korten by virtue of their greed and pursuit of power, there must be nothing unique about Nazi-era crimes. What we have witnessed throughout the trilogy, then, is a two-pronged strategy in the representation of perpetrators. On the one hand, evil is concentrated in the person of one or a very few highly placed superiors and thus safely isolated from midlevel bureaucrats like *Staatsanwalt* Selb. On the other hand, even these highly placed perpetrators are drained of virtually all historical specificity—despite initial references to the contrary—such that, in the end, we have just plain old "bad guys." This is how popular fiction contributes to "normalization" without ever seeming to overtly engage the debate.

GERHARD SELB ON THE SILVER SCREEN:
WHAT QUESTION DOES HE ANSWER?

As we have seen, there is a contradiction at the very core of this fictional detective. On the one hand, he needs to be proximate enough to evil so as to be a credible convert in the postwar period. One cannot be said to have "turned away from Nazism" in any meaningful way if one was never deeply involved in it in the first place. Thus, Schlink (as well as Popp) places the protagonist within the upper reaches of the SS: he is a *Staatsanwalt*—a state prosecutor—who has, as he manfully confesses, successfully argued for the death penalty in Nazi courts. On the other hand, Selb somehow needs to be distanced from this activity, which Schlink attempts to do by stressing his protagonist's tender age and attendant naivety. Even the quick pace of detective fiction cannot mask this contradiction, for at no time in German history could one attain the position of state prosecutor without having attained the age of majority—and then some. It is now, as it was then, a position of considerable prestige and power, and one that demands a very high level of education. Selb is, after all, "Herr Dr. Selb," a doctor of jurisprudence.[56]

By the time the third installment appeared in 2001, critics were complaining that Selb's advanced age simply strains credulity. In chapter three of *Selbs Mord*, the detective admits to being "über siebzig," (over seventy)[57] and he marks the time rather clearly as January of 1997: "We followed the television news of Bill Clinton's reelection and inauguration."[58] The interior mention of Selb's age seems calculated to win our sympathy; this was always a central part of his characterization.[59] The critical mention of his advanced years is focused only upon the question of his believability as a detective in the present: how could such an elderly man credibly play this role—especially such a physically demanding one? Though it may seem churlish to raise historical questions about figures in the fun genre of detective fiction, the novel's own attention to chronology would seem to justify our query. So rather than ask how the geriatric Selb can get around to do his sleuthing, let us ask how old that "young" Nazi Staatsanwalt could possibly have been.

This does not require much detective work or "new historical" mining of arcane data. If we look at the infamous *Braunbuch*, which lists the ex-Nazis in positions of authority in West Germany in the mid-1960s, we gain a useful picture of Selb's jurist cohort. Let us stipulate from the outset that the *Braunbuch* is a problematic source: it was collated and published for polemical reasons by the GDR and was clearly intended to add fuel to the fire of '68er outrage against the Nazi "fathers." Further, it is not complete (infamously eliding ex-Nazis in the Eastern Bloc), nor is it free from error. But if we ask only about the *ages* of ex-Nazi state prosecutors, judges, and those holding positions of similar rank in West Germany, we are not likely to encounter a great deal of distortion. Recall that this is precisely the professional cohort with whom Selb repeatedly affiliates himself. This group is prominently referenced in *each* novel, sometimes on multiple occasions. It turns out that their average age in 1942—the earliest that our wounded Selb could have returned from the Eastern Front to take up his role as state prosecutor—was just over 34 years (34.32, to be precise).[60] The average age of the entire group listed in the *Braunbuch* (1,002 entries) is somewhat higher (36 years).[61] The vast majority of Nazi state prosecutors were born within the first decade of the twentieth century, many within the first five years of the century. Even if Selb were exceptionally young for his cohort, he would have been 10 or 15 years older than Günter Grass, who was recruited into the SS at the truly tender age of 17. Moreover, the members of the group with whom Selb compares himself would themselves have been pushing *eighty* years of age when the first installment was published in 1987.

These data may appear out of place to connoisseurs of this consummate genre of entertainment. Yet detective fiction is known not only for extravagant plot devices but also for its love of empirical data, close attention to detail and temporal sequence, as well as a valorization of deduction from carefully placed cues and plot segments—as anyone who has read Sherlock Holmes surely knows. The point, at any rate, is to show how the detective's age is prominently thematized, but in one direction only, and that an essential element of refashioning Selb into an ex post facto resister requires us to take the bait and not pursue the question of chronology and age in a direction that is clearly less favorable to the detective. Obviously, a thirty-something, highly placed lawyer would be held to a much higher standard of behavior than the naïve youth we are led to believe young Selb was at that time.

The question of the detective's allegedly tender age becomes a real stumbling block for the visual medium of film, because here the young detective needs to be depicted directly—and played by an actor—rather than merely referenced within the older protagonist's reminiscence. Nico Hofmann, director of the television film *Der Tod kam als Freund* (which is very closely based on *Selbs Justiz*), appears to grasp and address the problem of the "two Selbs" rather directly, as we will notice when we examine a key scene that he has added to the plot. But before doing so, let us cast a glance at the larger popular cultural context in which Selb and company circulate.

Film scholar Anton Kaes proposes that we consider film as a kind of "answer" or "response" to a set of larger social questions posed within the wider realm of public culture.[62] In order to understand a particular film's "intervention" or place within this popular cultural dialogue, or multilateral web of communication, it may be useful to attend to prior treatments of the same, or similar, set of themes or problems. In the case of *Der Tod kam als Freund*, and of Selb in particular, it is probably Stanley Kramer's *Judgment at Nuremberg* that most memorably and perhaps controversially set out the terms of debate regarding "second-tier" perpetrators like Selb.[63] It premiered in Berlin in 1961 to a stunned German audience; apparently, Willy Brandt was himself at a loss for words.[64] In attending to the film's many controversies (e.g., over how much these midlevel perpetrators actually knew of the death camps, and the matter of collective guilt more generally), it may be easy to forget that this work actually establishes a consensus regarding this group of defendants. To the very end, former Minister of Justice Ernst Janning (powerfully portrayed by Bert Lancaster), who represents the most honest and morally upright of all the accused, maintains that he was not fully informed about the extermination camps. Having called chief judge Dan Haywood (played by Spencer Tracy) to his prison cell after his conviction, Janning insists, "Those millions of people—I never knew it would come to that." What is perhaps too easily neglected in the wake of Haywood's condescending response—"Herr Janning, it came to that the first time you sentenced to death a man you knew to be innocent"—is the extent to which Janning and Haywood, both moral authorities, actually agree. While, in some sense, they are clearly adversaries, they ultimately concur on what the crux of the matter is for this film, namely that certain members of the legal and military elite constitute a privileged social class that *should* have known better, even if they did not have specific knowledge of the Holocaust per se. Before he lectures Janning on the value of a single human life, Haywood first thanks him for his testimony, not only because "it needed to be said" but also because only he—that is, Janning—was in a position to do so. "Maybe we didn't know the details," Janning concludes, "But if we didn't know, it was because we didn't want to know."[65]

This is bad news for Selb, so to speak, because as a Nazi *Staatsanwalt*, he would presumably belong precisely to the circle of second-tier actors scrutinized here. Abby Mann, who wrote both the play and the film script for *Judgment*, has repeatedly stressed his interest in this group of lesser-known defendants. He chose to focus not on the notorious ringleaders who were prosecuted first but instead on the well-educated and privileged "doctors, businessmen, and judges" who proved, both in the actual verdicts of the latter Nuremberg trials as well as within the drama of this mass market film, to be accessories to murder. We should remember that the term "judges" is, for Mann, a capacious rubric that includes a state prosecutor like the eponymous detective Selb. Further, Mann specifically includes a member of the detective's own cohort, so to speak: Emil Hahn (who is played by the actor better known to American audiences for his role as Colonel Klink in the popular television series *Hogan's Heroes*) is a *Staatsanwalt* just like Selb and is one of the trial's four main defendants. In conducting his research for this project, Mann consulted the august Telford Taylor, one of the judges from the first Nuremberg trial, who assured Mann of this group's singular importance: "He said the most significant of trials was that of the judges of Germany. Why? Because these judges' minds had not been warped at an early age. Having reached maturity long before Hitler's rise to power, they embraced the ideologies of the Third Reich as educated adults. 'They, most of all,' Taylor said, 'should have valued justice.'"[66] This is an "argument" the film also makes, almost verbatim.[67]

Though it strains credulity to the breaking point, Selb's putative "youth" lifts him out of this category, which probably explains why he is a fictitious rather than historical figure. We are asked to believe that he was simply too young to come under this kind of indictment. This discrepancy might be overlooked within a fast-paced novel, but it is complicated in the film, particularly when the villainous Korten and Schmalz appear to belong to precisely the same age cohort as Selb. The visual contradiction must be dealt with; how can Selb otherwise be set off as naïve and essentially good?

Director Nico Hofmann must have sensed the dilemma of placing these men side by side. Nothing in Selb's physical appearance—neither as the handsome young *Staatsanwalt* nor as the older detective—will support the claim of innocence due to tender age. Furthermore, Hofmann must have been aware that portraying the vehement young state prosecutor in his black robes before a Nazi court as he aggressively cross-examines the Jew Karl Weinstein presents a peculiar challenge as well—and not only because the young Selb may remind us of the youthful defense lawyer in Kramer's film, played by Maximilian Schell. Somehow, Hofmann, too, must answer the "charge" of the Nuremberg judgments—as well as that of Kramer's and Mann's *Judgment at Nuremberg*—namely, that such a highly placed figure working within the SS is justly regarded as an accessory to Nazi crimes. I do not, of course, contend that either Hofmann or Schlink are specifically responding to Kramer's film; that matters very little, in fact. Nor does it matter that many Germans viewed the Nuremberg trials themselves as an illegitimate form of "victors' justice" (*Siegerjustiz*)—a point the film thematizes, by the way; for the very denunciation of the Nuremberg trials may, on the contrary, show how firmly it remains lodged in the cultural memory, if primarily in a negative way.[68] While Kramer's iconic film, as well as Mann's play (which has recently been staged in Germany),[69] represents an instance of popular culture commensurate with Schlink's detective trilogy, the juxtaposition remains, for my purposes, heuristic. The cultural "question" about the culpability of highly educated and privileged members of the SS—the prior cultural query, if you will, to which Kaes advises we seek the "response"—might just as well have arisen in the contentious debates surrounding Bitburg, Hochhuth's play *Juristen*, or any number of other events and works.

Hofmann resolves the problem by essentially abandoning the "youthful naiveté" defense and instead builds upon two other tropes from the novel, namely, that of Selb as the unwitting executor of another's diabolical plan and Selb as a person of goodwill and innate compassion. To accomplish this, however, he requires plot material not available in the novel. So he makes up a past for Selb as an amateur boxer. He places the handsome, half-naked young man in the ring with an opponent who seems nearly defeated after being pummeled by the muscular and adept young prosecutor. The prominent scar on Selb's face ("Schmiß") is a sign of his young male's courage—it is the physical evidence of his membership in a student dueling fraternity. Clearly, he is unafraid to endure pain. Profuse amounts of sweat bespeak not only his great exertion and stamina but also accentuate his powerful upper body. Though locked in primal physical conflict, Selb remains the picture of manly composure. He now has his opponent on the ropes and could easily inflict real damage, for he is the undisputed alpha male in this duo. But he graciously keeps himself in check, pointedly resisting Korten's vociferous exhortations: "Keep punching, Selb! Finish him off! Knock him out!" (Schlag zu, Selb! Mach ihn fertig! Schlag zu!) Instead, Hofmann's Selb backs off and gives the other guy a chance to recover his balance. The message is clear: Selb fights fair or not at all. But when he turns his back, his opponent takes full advantage of his momentary inattention and brutally beats him. Korten crudely berates him for letting this victory slip through his fingers, calling him "feige, inkonsequent" (cowardly and lacking in perseverance). The image of a verbally abused, betrayed, and bleeding Selb speaks volumes.

Clearly, Korten is not on hand merely to support a friend in an amicable, off-hours boxing match. He has something riding on this contest—presumably a bet—and he is using Selb to attain it. Even here—preeminently here—Korten is pulling the strings in a scheme Selb does not seem to comprehend. This interpolated scene with Selb as the good-hearted, duped boxer and Korten as the "crooked manager" partakes of a larger literary and filmic genealogy that, among other things,

Figure 1.1   Selb as victim of his own kindness: he is too principled to take advantage of his boxing opponent. (Still from *Death Came as a Friend*.)

communicates hierarchy, exploitation, abuse, and victimhood. Hofmann may in fact be quoting the legendary scene with Marlon Brando in *On the Waterfront* in which the young boxer sees his future sacrificed to the greed of his unscrupulous managers. He "could have been a contender," he famously says, if not for the nefarious interference of his greedy and corrupt handlers. The actor who plays the macho, young Selb even looks a bit like the young Brando.

The second device Hofmann devises to communicate a sense of what we might call Selb's "plausible naivety" clearly derives from the novel but appears in the film in a revised, streamlined fashion. As useful as the German Tyberg was in providing absolution to Selb at a key point in the novel, this figure drops out entirely of *Der Tod kam als Freund*. Instead, Hofmann reserves the survivor role exclusively for the Jewish "Frau Weinstein," as the woman who was Herr Weinstein's lifelong companion is known. (In the novel she is Sarah Hirsch, but she is still Weinstein's common-law wife.) This means that the friendly Vera Mueller of the novel, who, as an American Jew, also confers forgiveness upon Selb, is cut from the film as well.[70] All the attention is thus focused on the Auschwitz survivor. We can divine strategic as well as ideological reasons for this decision.

Hofmann cleans up a perhaps too cluttered plot by eliminating Tyberg and Mueller, but he may also be acceding to the new dimensions of public culture that emerged in the early 1990s, in which the authority of the Jewish survivor of the Holocaust became particularly prominent. At any rate, it is Frau Weinstein, as I shall call her, who provides the ultimate alibi for Selb's ignorance as state prosecutor.

As he goes back in his mind to those key war years, Selb becomes vaguely suspicious of Korten, but he still genuinely does not know—even these many years later—what precisely led to the trial and convictions in which he played a leading role. He needs to visit this Jewish survivor to discover the truth. She tells him, in the slow and careful speech one associates with painful testimony, that Korten extorted Weinstein's denunciation by threatening to have him deported to the camps. Selb, visibly shaken, is so surprised that he has her repeat this. Indeed, he finds it so difficult to integrate this fact into his life story that he must replay the scene back at his hotel room over a number of strong drinks. Despite all the various modes of Vergangenheitsbewältigung that permeated German public culture up until this point—notorious trials, informational films, controversial plays, the popular television series *Holocaust*, news reports, and so on—Selb seems to never have considered until now that he could have been an accomplice to murder.

Frau Weinstein's primary function as a character is simply to play this role of informant. She does not scoff at Selb's ignorance or gullibility and does not lecture him on the need to carefully consider how such "evidence" is obtained in the first place, especially in an authoritarian regime; nor does she suggest that he should have been skeptical of Weinstein's statements, given his vulnerable situation as a Jew performing forced labor during the Third Reich. To the contrary, she takes Selb seriously, accepts his inquiry as legitimate, and confirms his naivety as fully plausible. In this respect, her indictment of Korten is truly secondary. In genre or structural terms, this plot segment lends respectability to Selb's musings about his Nazi past as a query worthy of "discovery" within a detective novel—indeed, as *the* principal unknown datum awaiting the detective's careful investigation. Perhaps inadvertently, Frau Weinstein simultaneously reinforces Selb's status as structurally parallel to that of her husband, for though not equally at risk by any means, both played the same role as pawns in Korten's dastardly scheme. Weinstein was indeed a knowing accomplice, though under considerable duress. But poor Selb was an unwitting one—unaware of his crime even until Frau Weinstein provides this crucial piece of testimony. His lack of awareness of his role as Korten's accomplice is so thoroughly established in this scene that we

Figure 1.2   Frau Weinstein, improbably bald after fifty years. As a Jewish survivor, she is the film's principal authority. (Still from *Death Came as a Friend*.)

are left to wonder if one can speak of Selb's "guilt" at all. As a Jewish survivor—improbably still bald after all these years[71]—Frau Weinstein thus verifies his abuse and victimhood in a way that is ideologically far more valuable than Tyberg's exonerating phone call ever could be.[72]

Of course the entire investigation into Selb's Nazi past is, from the visual point of view, somewhat of a foregone conclusion, since viewers will very likely already know who the villain is almost from the very beginning of the film. Actor Werner Kreindl's masterful rendering of the malignant Korten, with his eerily glassy eyes and balding head, seems an intentional citation of Gustav Grundgren's Mephistopheles; but even if viewers do not quite make that connection, one cannot miss the fact that Korten is, from the outset, played as "demonic." We just do not yet know the backstory. In this sense, the entire film serves to "explain" its initial disturbing image of Korten.

Figure 1.3   Korten as "demonic," evocative of filmic depictions of Mephistopheles. (Still from *Death Came as a Friend*.)

THE EXCULPATORY GENRE OF DETECTIVE FICTION

There is another, more subtle technique of normalization that has less to do with character and plot than with the genre itself. In his illuminating discussion of detective fiction, Ernst Bloch establishes the "most decisive criterion" of the genre—indeed, this "principal earmark of the detective story"—as "the darkness at the beginning."[73] By this he means the following: "In the detective novel the crime has already occurred, outside the narrative; the story arrives on the scene with the corpse. It does not develop its cause during the narrative or alongside it, but its sole theme is the discovery of something that happened *ante rem* . . . The main point is always the same: the alpha, which none of the characters appearing one after another admits to have witnessed, least of all the reader, happens outside the story like the fall from grace or even the fall of the angels (this in order not to shun all-too-mythical coloration)."[74]

If Bloch is right, the very emplotment of Nazism within the detective genre provides all manner of ideological relief. Nazi crimes are, according to strict generic regulations, *ante rem*—"unknown"—even to the detective, who in this case was a highly placed official. Casting Nazism as "the alpha," as a fall from grace, of course remythologizes these years and resuscitates the postwar demonic thesis. The absolute separation of readers and characters from "the darkness at the beginning" is the sine qua non to which Bloch returns throughout his study.[75] Finally, this darkness is always something radically "other" that can only be explored authoritatively in and through the detective story itself. Thus, prior to any of the exculpatory strategies encoded within the protagonist and his story, the very genre of detective fiction mystifies Nazism by making it the great, unknown, foundational crime. For similar reasons, W. H. Auden dismisses the claim that detective fiction indulges fantasies of violence.[76] On the contrary, and in agreement with Bloch, he argues that "the magical satisfaction" of detective fiction derives principally from the pleasing "illusion of being dissociated from the murderer."[77]

This morally questionable upward transferring of criminal responsibility that this kind of fiction makes plausible represents a trite rehashing of the *Machtergreifung* (seizure of power) thesis, according to which those hundreds of thousands of Germans who facilitated the Holocaust are to be seen not as accomplices and accessories but as victims of the dictator Hitler. The trick, of course, is to espouse this doctrine while denying that one is doing any such thing. In a humorous allusion to Eric Segal's *Love Story*, Selb tells us that he neither envies nor forgives Korten for his posthumous prestige, because "[*committing murder*] means never having to say you're sorry."[78] And with this single remark, we are instantly thrown back into the undiscriminating stew of "U-Literatur," a fun genre where weighty issues are merely exploited for their entertainment value. Anyone who does not understand this, as we are sure to be reminded, simply does not know how to have fun—or, I am tempted to say, must be an academic (!). Apparently, popular culture's prerogative is to deny any responsibility for supplying culturally affirmative ideology (in the sense Horkheimer and Adorno used the term),[79] while taking credit for isolated moments of "progressive" enlightenment. Such moments—in which, for example, Selb is himself placed in question—can of course be found, just as critics eager to recover *The Reader* as a progressive Holocaust novel have recently discovered the protagonist of that novel to be "ironic." Before exploring that point further, however, let us step back to take stock of the broader relationship between the Selb detective trilogy and *The Reader*.

FROM DETECTIVE FICTION TO HOLOCAUST LITERATURE

I began this chapter with the assertion that Schlink's detective novels are interesting not only in their own right but also insofar as they lay bare the perpetrator formula that is also featured in that better-known novel.

First and foremost, we see in Hanna Schmitz an elaboration of Gerhard Selb. Like Selb, if guilty at all, she is, then, at most "guiltlessly guilty" ("schuldlos schuldig"). As in the case of our likeable detective, Hanna is unquestionably placed at the scene of crimes but is never specifically and individually responsible for any particular deed. There are always others on hand, a number of who (such as the male guards at the horrible church fire) were her superiors. As an illiterate ethnic German (*Volksdeutsche*), she is given an even more compelling explanation than Selb for her ignorance of the larger Nazi enterprise. True, there is no single villain such as Korten, around whom the narrative crystallizes guilt and draws off the last vestiges of her responsibility; as a result, she does retain a modicum of (always nebulous) guilt. But with regard to the worst of the crimes of which she may be guilty—transporting women from work details to their death in Auschwitz or standing by while women burned to death in a locked church—there were always other, more highly placed actors who willingly exploited her ignorance and handicap. During her trial following the war, the other defendants openly deride her; it becomes clear in the course of that trial that these codefendants have manipulated Hanna into accepting the lion's share of guilt by affixing her signature to a document she could not have read, let alone have written. Rather than speak the truth about her illiteracy, she accepts the judge's verdict for a crime she certainly did not commit. She is prosecuted aggressively by ex-Nazi lawyers (perhaps one of Selb's unrepentant colleagues) and defended by an inept rookie. Not unlike our Selb, she is much abused during *and* after the war.

But to argue that Schlink's Selb trilogy represents a kind of dry run for the later novel—and that an ideological consistency with regard to Vergangenheitsbewältigung pervades all these novels—is of course not to say that Schlink has simply resuscitated Selb in the person of Hanna. Despite further parallels at the level of plot (e.g., Selb, too, loses his virginity to a woman who is old enough to be his mother), there are significant differences, particularly with regard to the respective narrators.[80] It would not have been possible to maintain the shroud of secrecy around Hanna *and* make her the first person narrator, as this would also have deprived her of her illiteracy alibi. For even if the book had been written in hindsight, that is, from the vantage of her newly acquired literacy, the ability to narrate and reflect intelligently (or even coherently) on her preliterate days would have cast considerable doubt upon her illiteracy excuse. It is clear that Michael Berg has inherited, so to speak, some of Selb's duties. Whereas Selb himself bemoans that he is much "mißbraucht," Michael will have to do this both for Hanna and himself. Selb's robust overstatement of guilt serves as the model for the characterization of Berg in *The Reader*, where a structurally similar overstatement of guilt (as I explore in Chapter 3) serves to create sympathy for this narrator. Ironically, when Korten advanced a suspiciously vague notion of complicity—"We are guilty all"—Selb rejected it in favor of determining specific and individual responsibility.[81] In *The Reader*, however, the claim of feeling trapped in a hopelessly complex web of guilt functions quite differently—namely, to foreground the plight of the second generation—and is therefore allowed to stand.

Like her literary precursor, Hanna undergoes a self-imposed punishment (actually two, if one includes the suicide) and is ultimately rehabilitated: she learns to read, imbibing the classics of Holocaust literature in one fell swoop, and leaves her life savings to the sole Jewish survivor of the church fire. Yet her rejection of Nazism is no more reflected upon than Selb's simple and sudden "loss of faith." Here, as there, Schlink fails to give us any substantive or nuanced insight into perpetration of or into the actual, and presumably painful, process of denazification.[82] Though Schlink undoubtedly moves closer to the Holocaust with *The Reader*, both that novel and the Selb trilogy refer to the genocide only elliptically, and both are primarily concerned with German, not Jewish, victims. Hanna and Selb are both redeemed, albeit in strikingly different ways: Hanna's suicide amounts to a self-imposed death sentence, whereas Selb is portrayed as a resister after the fact. At this point, we may note that by emphasizing his "Langsamkeit" (slowness to react) so extensively, particularly in volume three of the trilogy, Selb implies that he in fact never needed to rehabilitate himself because he was always good—just too slow in responding. In castigating himself for too tardily reacting to current challenges of neo-Nazism, Selb explains that this is a problem that has haunted him since his youth: "I've always been a bit too slow, not just since I've gotten older."[83] Hanna's trajectory can be seen as tracing this same pattern of delayed reaction. Only the ideological value of casting himself in this light can explain the relentless repetition of this motif, which soon becomes tedious.[84] This mantra, along with the claim that only the second generation could fully grasp Nazism, helps make plausible, at least at first blush, the notion that Germans were unable to mount an effective resistance at the time because they simply lacked the necessary perspective on events available in subsequent years.

IRONY, SELF-REFLEXIVITY, AND THE
AUTHORITY OF THE DETECTIVE

It remains to be asked whether these novels—the Selb trilogy, on the one hand, and *The Reader*, on the other—also share an unreliable narrator. Do Selb and Berg invite the kind of fundamental criticism that would undermine the very mode of Vergangenheitsbewältigung that I have argued is typical of both? Can we salvage Schlink by means of irony—that is, by arguing that we are actually *meant* to read against the grain? This is precisely the argument that some advocates of *The Reader* propose. Though they adduce a variety of reasons for doing so, each argues that we are intended to see past Michael Berg rather than to uncritically share his point of view. For Joseph Metz, the novel's thematization of reading and misreading self-consciously evokes the postmodern ethos and thus frees us from the exclusive viewpoint of Berg;[85] for Martin Swales and Bill Niven, the issue of shame opens the novel to divergent perspectives.[86] In contrast, and for reasons I delineate at greater length in Chapter 4, I take the view that Berg's narration is effectively "einsinnig" (unimental perspective), to borrow a term coined by Friedrich Beissner to characterize Kafka's prose.[87] This means that though one can always justify a variant view, Berg generally invites a consonant reading. With his hyper-self-criticism, he is always one step ahead of the critics; his circumspection and self-deprecating remarks serve only make to him more trustworthy, not less.[88] Of course, no such argument—on either side—can be made in absolute terms. If pain is what the patient says it is, irony must be what the reader claims it is. I would only want to share the burden of proof fairly with those who wish to place Berg fundamentally in doubt. In arguing for the efficacy of the television drama *Holocaust*, Huyssen based himself on documented responses of the target audience.[89] Critics who wish to qualify *The Reader* as serious Holocaust literature, specifically by placing Berg in question, do so over the objections of most readers.[90] While it is surely the business of critics to take issue with popular readings—and this present study is no exception—proponents of the "ironic reading" of Berg need to tell us precisely *why* a piece of popular realist fiction so consistently misses its mark.[91]

If narratorial irony is a debatable matter in *The Reader*, it is all the more difficult to claim for the detective novels. Yet we should be aware that this same procedure could conceivably be carried out on Selb as well. A perceptive critic will notice that the villainous Korten actually speaks some truth, especially when he refers to the mass reinclusion of ex-Nazis in the West German establishment,[92] and also when he indicts Selb for indulging in a cowardly act of self-exculpation by focusing exclusively on his (Korten's) role: "The perpetrator now wants to play judge, isn't that so? So, you see yourself as innocently abused?"[93] Korten's challenge inadvertently identifies *in nuce* the strategy for coming to terms with the Nazi past that the novel, in large part, advocates and that was widespread in the postwar period, as historian Konrad Jarausch shows.[94] Are we now to believe that this eleventh-hour "insight"—this "self-reflective" moment—actually undermines all that has gone before? Have we discovered a "disruptive" moment, one that perhaps salvages an otherwise retrograde mode of Vergangenheitsbewältigung? Or is Schlink playing to two audiences simultaneously? The irony thesis may be very flattering to readers, yet it is crucial to notice that Selb, like Berg, reliably anticipates the very criticism we may wish to credit ourselves with having discovered. In this respect, we are always outflanked. He and Berg concede their errors in such a disarming manner that we are all the more willing to accept the novels' overriding message that ex-Nazi perpetrators are often enough just another kind of victim, caught within a hierarchy and ruthlessly manipulated by their superiors.

It may be that we know what we are getting into when we take a detective novel in hand. Perhaps we can see through the questionable use of the Nazi past and still enjoy *Selbs Justiz* as the fairly good story it is (it is the best of all Schlink's detective novels). Perhaps consciousness of the genre's naivety no more detracts from our enjoyment than it would in the case of fairy tales, folk ballads, or children's literature. But while the genre may come equipped with certain self-inoculating devices, we should not be too quick to consider the matter settled. Though some readers will claim to distance themselves from Selb—and perhaps they really do— the tendency in detective fiction generally, as John M. Reilly observes, is just the opposite.[95] W. H. Auden goes further in suggesting "readers' enjoyment of detective novels relates to their sense of guilt, and a fantasy of being restored to an Edenic Great Good Place."[96] If this is true in a general sense, detective fiction that thematizes Nazism and the Holocaust may have some role to play in the psychic management of guilt and the construction of a positive German national identity.

Finally, the generic shibboleth of poetic justice would seem to provide a fictional escape from West Germany's real-life failure to pursue Nazi criminals in any thoroughgoing manner during the postwar period.[97] The appeal of this kind of fiction may be the sense of completion and retributive justice missing from modernist treatments and, to some extent, even from historical depictions of the crimes of the Holocaust. Nadya Aisenberg explains, "In real life, many crimes go unsolved even when investigation takes place, many are covered up and not even investigated, or a court case is dismissed on a technicality even when the identity of the criminal is known. But in the world of fictional homicide, justice prevails, the criminal is punished, order is restored. Poetic, not civic, justice rules. Because of this, readers experience the pleasure of narrative closure."[98] From this perspective, Korten functions as a symbol for unsolved Nazi-era crime, while his murder provides a pleasurable resolution that can be seen as vicarious compensation for the real-world dearth of criminal prosecution and punishment of Nazi perpetrators. Ralph Giordano has named this failure Germany's "second guilt" ("die zweite Schuld"), and it is precisely this issue (rather than any real complicity in the crimes of his parents' generation) that gives Berg such pause.[99] Readers may therefore have more than sufficient cause to look for fictional heroes to fill the gap left by reality.

This fantasy resolution, however, comprises only the final phase of the fictional reconstruction of Nazism. As we have already noted, the concentration of responsibility in the hands of just one actor (or a very few) was an important prerequisite, and one that echoes official West German pronouncements regarding German war guilt from Konrad Adenauer to Helmut Kohl.[100] The other crucial ingredient in this fictional management of Vergangenheitsbewältigung is the conception of the crime itself. To be sure, Korten threatens and manipulates the Jew Weinstein. But this abuse is no different in kind than that meted out to gentiles (indeed, this is how Selb becomes a victim on par with Weinstein). Korten's ruthless pursuit of power is in fact no different from any other story. The fact that he maintains his power in the postwar period by the same unscrupulous means (viz his use of Schmalz to murder Mischkey) suggests, as we have seen, that there is nothing unique or historically specific about his wartime transgressions: he simply took advantage of larger political developments to satisfy his pitiless ambition. Thus by naming, while marginalizing, the Holocaust—Weinstein's widow served that function in book one, and the Laban family does so in the final installment—as well as by normalizing Korten's Nazi past as the coincidental setting for a universal narrative of corruption and domination, the novel has already supplied a gratifying resolution, well before Selb takes justice into his own hands and murders Korten.

The real genius of the Selb trilogy, implicitly at least, is to deny that there is any such message. It is just entertainment. But we are then constrained to ask how the topics of Nazism and the Holocaust lend themselves to such great fun. *The Reader*, with all its overt ambition, could not make use of the popular culture alibi and thus has not evaded the critical scrutiny spared Schlink's earlier novels. Furthermore, to view Schlink's detective trilogy as a fantasy form of Vergangenheitsbewältigung does not preclude sympathy and understanding for the real need it fills. As in so much American popular cinema, Schlink has not striven for historical accuracy or even analytical insight. Instead, he has provided his readers with something much more basic, namely, a consolation prize. Whereas the German high cultural tradition—as documented in Judith Ryan's *The Uncompleted Past*—agonizingly reflected on the *missing* resister to Nazism, popular culture simply brings this figure into existence by fiat.[101] Gerhard Selb is not the ex-Nazi that many Germans may actually have known, but he is the one they *wish* they had known. He is macho, confident, and witty, yet also vulnerable and self-deprecatory. He is honest (in his own terse way), was never very guilty to begin with, and is eager to make things right in the present. He is an ex-Nazi who, by finally killing the holdover Nazi villain, refashions himself into a kind of resister after the fact. For what more could one possibly ask?

CHAPTER 2

SOOTHING FICTIONS

AMBIGUITY AS DEFENSE

The Reader is a small, quiet, intellectual book that asks the big moral questions. It has a distinctly Mitteleuropean feel, an air of allegory and moral meditation. Hardly a prescription for a bestseller.

—Dinitia Smith, *The New York Times*

IN THE BROADWAY VERSION OF *CABARET*, THERE is an unforgettable song in which an older Berlin widow recounts personal and economic hardships she experienced throughout the first decades of the twentieth century, particularly during the early tumultuous, inflation-ridden years of the Weimar Republic. This time around she will marry for money, not love. The white spotlight starkly illuminates this solitary figure on the dark stage, and with a haunting refrain that does not lack a touch of defiance, she implores the audience to put themselves in her place: "What would you do?" Any impulse we might feel to judge this beleaguered rooming-house proprietress is thereby muted. Hanna Schmitz, in Bernhard Schlink's best-selling novel *The Reader* (1995), virtually poses the same question. But here the stakes are much higher: as a guard in an SS unit assigned first to Auschwitz, then to a women's camp near Krakow, Hanna's last assignment is to oversee inmates as they are being evacuated westward near the end of the war. One night, while the prisoners are confined in a local church, an Allied bomb ignites the steeple, gradually setting the entire building ablaze. As the prosecutors in Hanna's war crimes trial argue, "Die schweren Türen hielten stand. Die Angeklagten hätten sie aufschließen können. Sie taten es nicht, und die in der Kirche eingeschlossenen Frauen verbrannten."[1] (The heavy doors held fast. The accused could have unlocked them. They did not do so, and the women burned to death.)

During the trial, Hanna twice turns the investigation back on the judge: "Was hätten Sie denn gemacht?"[2] "Die Antwort des Richters," we read, "wirkte hilflos, kläglich. Alle empfanden es. Sie . . . schauten auf Hanna, die den Wortwechsel gewissermaßen gewonnen hatte."[3] "'What would you have done?' The judge's answer came across as hapless and pathetic. Everyone felt it. They . . . stared in amazement at Hanna, who had more or less won the exchange."[4] This is an astonishing feat since the judge has really only asserted a fairly rudimentary moral precept, namely that there are some things that, in the absence of an immediate threat to life and limb, one simply must not do. "Was hätten Sie denn gemacht?" (And what would you have done?) With this question, Hanna is of course asking us as well. And, as in *Cabaret*, we are called to understand, if not quite condone, her behavior. Or, more precisely, we are invited to sympathize, in part because we never learn exactly what her behavior and actions were that night.

The novel's tremendous international popularity and critical acclaim surely have to do with its ambitious and laudable agenda. *The Reader* sets out to explore the very real plight of second-generation Germans, who, in their unenviable effort to confront a catastrophe they did nothing to bring about, share a great deal in common with the novel's larger, international readership. More daring, perhaps, is the novel's depiction of Hanna as a woman responsible for her actions (whatever they may have been), while, at the same time, her choices and behavior are, to a fateful degree, determined by her underprivileged upbringing, by the larger sociopolitical environment, and by her specific disability. This more nuanced depiction of a perpetrator has been hailed as an advance over the simplistic, moralizing approaches of the past, which, we are told, tended to place perpetrators and victims at monochromatic extremes.

For several years after the initial German publication, no one seemed seriously disturbed—apart from the occasional, sparsely worded reservation embedded in a larger encomium for the book—by the rather strong suggestion that Hanna's illiteracy provides an alibi of sorts for joining the SS and carrying out her "duties." Indeed, none of the German language reviews of the original publication found anything substantially wrong with the characterization of Hanna. The author himself confesses some reservations about this strategy: "I was even afraid to publish it in Germany because I thought maybe people might misunderstand it as [an] apologetic, sort of whitewashing book."[5] Schlink is, as we will have occasion to notice again later, a perceptive critic of his own work; and in this case, at any rate, his fear was fully justified.

In the wake of the 1997 publication of the English translation, and, more precisely, of the book's subsequent U.S. popularity and critical acclaim, three Americans, all of them actively engaged with the

Holocaust as academics or authors, and all of them Jews, registered unmistakable discomfort with the depiction and implicit ideological function of Hanna's character. The first to sally forth was Cynthia Ozick, who, in the March 1999 issue of *Commentary*, faults the novel for indulging in a kind of ahistorical fantasy: "The plot of Schlink's narrative turns not on the literacy that was overwhelmingly typical of Germany," Ozick notes, "but rather on an anomalous case of illiteracy, which the novel itself recognizes as freakish."[6] Though Eva Hoffman finds a bit more to like in the novel, the title of her review in *The New Republic* that same month, "The Uses of Illiteracy," points to her chief reservation. "In linking illiteracy and brutality," Hoffman argues, "Schlink is introducing explanatory ideas about the Holocaust that have been deeply discredited precisely by that event."[7] Holocaust historian Omer Bartov, in his 2000 article "Germany as Victim," locates the novel's distortion both in the absence of depiction—Jewish victims, though obliquely referred to, have no real presence in this book—and in the spurious conjunction of Hanna's victim status with that of Michael Berg. As a result, the agitated, ceaselessly ruminating narrator becomes, for Bartov, "a victim's victim."[8]

Under pressure to "explain" an entire generation's vexed relationship to its parents, it is not difficult to see how Hanna must perforce appear both likeable and, in a sense, reproducible. If we are to understand, rather than condemn, the second generation's attachment—and recall that Berg insists that we cannot have it both ways—then we, as readers, must have some sympathetic experience of this intergenerational bond. Schlink achieves this through a sleight of hand that has been lauded by numerous critics: he introduces a weighty "issues book" with an unlikely erotic preamble that readers simply love. But it is more than mere sugarcoating. By appealing to the erotic, Schlink evokes universal categories of human attraction and bonding that appear to require no explanation whatsoever, insofar as they are biologically grounded, "automatic," and thus decision-free. Yet even before Michael "has the good fortune to be seduced by an older woman," as the anonymous reviewer for *The Economist* saw it,[9] Hanna is presented as a person who responds to human need with spontaneous generosity. Her introduction to Michael, and to us, comes when she rescues the unknown boy, who is apparently ill and filthy with his own vomit, cleaning him up and escorting him safely home. Her basic impulses, when not encumbered by other factors (such as those that will lead to her career as a camp guard), are thus established as startlingly humane.

It is through his experience with Hanna, let us recall, that Berg feels qualified to represent "a German fate." We should not conceive of

Hanna's cultural deprivations too narrowly, as Ozick and perhaps even Hoffman appear to have done, for what Schlink is saying is not merely that an inability to read and write per se accounts for brutality. Nor does he mean that this alone provides a fully adequate explanation of evil. On a more charitable reading, Hanna's handicap may function as a metaphor for deprivation more generally, meant to explain why some people turn to evil. Certainly this is the way Stephen Daldry chooses to portray her in his compelling 2008 film of the novel (see Chapter 6). It is precisely because this explanatory model enjoys popular credence that Hanna, too, for all her apparent particularity, comes to stand for the many. What we see in her is not the great enigma of evil, from which we shrink in horror and incomprehension, but a virtual textbook example of the sociological conception of criminality, which we tend to embrace. Hanna in fact embodies the liberal credo on criminality, which may explain some of the book's appeal in countries far from Germany—such as in the United States (on *The Reader* as an American novel, see Chapter 5). While she evokes the horrors of the Holocaust—though relatively indirectly, as both Bartov and Hoffman rightly point out—she simultaneously makes the Holocaust appear more amenable to explanation in terms of familiar ideas about human behavior.

In the last pages of the book, we learn (via the prison warden) that Hanna has accepted her incarceration like a nun embracing solitude: "Über viele Jahre hat sie hier gelebt wie in einem Kloster. Als hätte sie sich der hiesigen Ordnung freiwillig unterworfen, als sei die einigermaßen eintönige Arbeit eine Art Meditation."[10] (For many years she had lived here as if in a cloister. As if she had submitted willingly to the prevailing order, as if the somewhat monotonous work were a kind of meditation.) As in Schiller's *Maria Stuart*, we encounter a woman who freely submits to a patently unjust punishment for a crime that we know she has not committed, in order to pay for a lesser offense, but one that has been left curiously unspecified here. She struggles to gain literacy and then promptly (and, in my opinion, incredibly) reads all the classics of Holocaust literature, but not before becoming an activist for better prison conditions. Before she can enjoy the clemency that has been granted her after 18 years of prison, she hangs herself in her cell on the very morning of her release, rendering what some deem a final, moral act of self-condemnation. To top it all off, Hanna leaves her life's savings to the sole remaining survivor of the church fire.

Given multiple incentives, both textual and extratextual, to see Hanna as a kind of prototypical perpetrator, this character seems destined to expand or multiply to fill the historical void. We know a great deal about the Nazi elite, but what about those many, many others—those "hundreds of thousands," according to Raul Hilberg's best estimate—whose actions made the genocide possible? Bearing the "Allerweltsnamen (common name) Hanna Schmitz,"[11] she has become the "Jane Doe" of the second-tier perpetrators. The novel cannot, however, answer the historically specific question, to what extent are we actually entitled to think of Hanna as having multiple historical "siblings"? Nor, if we are honest, is this a question with which the text is seriously concerned. We cannot, of course, blame Schlink for our own desire to substitute fiction for history. It may be more correct to speak of a hermeneutic "distortion" that has its roots in readers' psychospiritual needs rather than in the conspiratorial intent of any particular literary work. But if so, it is nevertheless a hunger that *The Reader* fully satisfies.

Though it has been hailed as a significant advance in the literature of *Vergangenheitsbewältigung* (Mastering the Nazi past),[12] this book is in fact remarkably lacking in description of the Nazi past or the Holocaust in particular. For a courtroom drama centering on Holocaust crimes—one cannot help but think of Peter Weiss's classic *Die Ermittlung* (*The Investigation*, 1965) as the gold standard—we encounter astounding lacunae.[13] Schlink has made this possible—and apparently plausible—by a number of ruses: an inept judge, an inexperienced defense attorney, Hanna's illiteracy, and a kind of reverse deus ex machina in the form of the handwritten report of the church fire that incriminates Hanna by pure chance, and in a manner her codefendants could not have fully expected or planned. In this way, the court and, above all, the novel's readers are spared the painful recounting of the details of camp routine, as well as of the horrific events of the death marches. Even when he goes off to Struthof later, to learn about the camps firsthand, Berg "spares his readers the sickening details," as Suzanne Ruta notes with apparent gratitude.[14]

The chief excuse Berg offers for himself (and therefore for us) for not reiterating the details of the trial, particularly those pertaining to the testimony of the Jewish witnesses, is the state of "numbness" that overcame him whenever the topic arose.[15] "Wie der KZ-Häftling," Berg imagines,

der Monat um Monat überlebt und sich gewöhnt hat und das Entsetzen der Neuankommenden gleichmütig registriert. Mit derselben Betäubung registriert, mit der er das Morden und Sterben selbst wahrnimmt. Alle Literatur der Überlebenden berichtet von dieser Betäubung, unter der die Funktionen des Lebens reduziert, das Verhalten teilnahms- und rücksichtslos und Vergasung und Verbrennung alltäglich wurden. Auch in den spärlichen Äußerungen der Täter begegnen die Gaskammern und Verbrennungsöfen als alltägliche Umwelt, die Täter selbst auf wenige Funktionen reduziert, in ihrer Rücksichts- und Teilnahmslosigkeit, ihrer Stumpfheit wie betäubt oder betrunken. Die Angeklagten kamen mir vor, als seien sie noch immer und für immer in dieser Betäubung befangen, in ihr gewissermaßen versteinert . . . diese Gemeinsamkeit des Betäubtseins beschäftigte [mich] und auch, daß die Betäubung sich nicht nur auf Täter und Opfer gelegt hatte, sondern auch auf uns legte, die wir als Richter oder Schöfen, Staatsanwälte oder Protokollanten später damit zu tun hatten.[16]

[It was like being a prisoner in the death camps who survives month after month, and becomes accustomed to the life, while he registers with a dispassionate eye the horror of the new arrivals: registers it with the same numbness that he brings to the murders and deaths themselves. All survivor literature talks about this numbness, in which life's functions are reduced to a minimum, behavior becomes completely selfish and indifferent to others, and gassings and burnings are everyday occurrences. In the rare accounts by perpetrators, too, the gas chambers and ovens become everyday scenery the perpetrators reduced to their few functions and exhibiting a mental paralysis and indifference, a dullness that makes them seem drugged or drunk . . . The defendants seemed to me to be trapped still, and forever, in this drugged state, in a sense petrified in it.][17]

There is, of course, considerable truth to the narrator's claims: witnessing barbarity can indeed damage the psyche, perhaps irreparably. Such, at any rate, was Himmler's conviction and the principal reason he felt it necessary to rotate his executioners through the extermination camps and the *Einsatzgruppen* (mobile killing units) on a three- to six-month tour of duty.[18] Perpetrators no doubt availed themselves of a number of methods for the requisite "production of distance," as Zygmunt Bauman has suggested.[19] Their "psychic hardening," as Eva Hoffman calls it, may indeed account not only for their willingness to murder but also for the postwar denial of guilt.[20]

But at what point does this blanket assertion of "numbness," applied here to perpetrators, victims, and postwar observers alike, become an imprecise and perhaps counterproductive hypothesis? To whom, and in what degree, does this apply? The literature on trauma and posttraumatic stress disorder is vast and growing; though the matter of "secondhand trauma" is still hotly debated, the phenomenon itself—the psychic and somatic retreat from overwhelmingly threatening stimuli—is now widely understood, and is deeply entrenched in popular culture.[21] This helps explain the broadly sympathetic reading Berg has received with respect to this undeniable burden of witnessing the genocide—even via secondhand accounts and museal representation. In attributing this kind of mental shutting down, or *Betäubung* (numbing), to so many—and notably to postwar innocents such as himself—Berg's concerns are clearly broader;

here Schlink is obviously counting on the reader's own sense of saturation with Holocaust horrors, a point made overtly later in the narrative.[22] For Berg, we are all victims of the Holocaust, a point to which I will return in Chapter 5. Because there is a grain of truth in this observation as well, one that resonates with the reader's own natural defenses against depictions of atrocities, critics have, until fairly recently,[23] overlooked the patent absurdities contained in this extended lamentation.

We know, for example, that some of the perpetrators returned home and bragged about their murderous "work." Others sent pictures from the front documenting the mass executions—against orders, by the way—along with greetings to their families. Diaries, such as those on display in Buchenwald, reveal doctors who were more interested in camp cuisine than in the "selections" they conducted between meals and naps. Certainly, Viktor Frankl's famous memoir of Nazi internment, *Man's Search for Meaning* (1962), fails to corroborate Berg's summary claim that inmates' behavior was typically "teilnahms- und rücksichtslos." Neither does Ruth Klüger's acclaimed autobiography, *weiter leben: Eine Jugend* (1994), which recounts the author's internment in Theresienstadt and Auschwitz, confirm these sweeping assertions, any more than does Anna Pawełczyńska's 1973 study, *Values and Violence in Auschwitz*.[24] Furthermore, the perpetrators convicted at the Frankfurt trial (1965) hardly appeared to be reduced to a state of *Stumpfheit* (stupor, obtuseness), as if "betäubt oder betrunken" (anesthetized or drunk). On the contrary, they were often quite spirited, self-righteous, argumentative, and arrogant; they occasionally smiled, and even laughed, in the face of their accusers.[25] But neither is Berg entirely wrong: one does find—even in Klüger, for example—precisely this sense of being mentally and physically overwhelmed. His error lies in having generalized this phenomenon so indiscriminately. Given the critics' silence, one almost feels that Berg has hit upon a widespread consensus. Perhaps we want to believe that the Holocaust makes moral zombies out of all of us.

In a characteristic move, Berg "retracts" his questionable equation of victims, perpetrators, and ex post facto observers with an apologetic disclaimer: "als ich dabei Täter, Opfer, Tote, Lebende, Überlebende und Nachlebende miteinander verglich, war mir nicht wohl, und wohl ist mir auch jetzt nicht"[26] (as I compared perpetrators, victims, the dead, the survivors with one another, I felt uneasy, and I still feel unwell)—which may explain why no one has thought to scrutinize his concatenation of questionable associations. Unfortunately, this is rather like asking the jury to ignore a sensational outburst that would otherwise directly affect the verdict: the request may simply ensure that the case is not overturned on appeal.[27] The effect of this strategy is directly observable in Thomas Klin-genmaier's explication of Hanna's career as essentially passive—a woman who "lands" in the SS (as if by the ineluctable pull of gravity) and "there, in this moral stupor, about which Berg later broods, conducts her ghastly service."[28] In a similar vein, a popular teachers' guide misses an opportunity to problematize this notion of "numbness" by posing this question to students: "Why is this numbness a necessary reaction?"—a leading question, to say the least.[29]

Related to this is Berg's suggestion that he need not evoke sympathetic Jewish victims because, after all, even the book authored by the two survivors of the terrible fire fails to do so: "Es lädt nicht zur Identifikation ein und macht niemanden sympathisch, weder Mutter noch Tochter, noch die, mit denen beide in verschiedenen Lagern und schließlich in Auschwitz und bei Krakow das Schicksal geteilt haben . . . Es atmet die Betäubung, die ich schon zu beschreiben versucht habe."[30] (It does not invite one to identify with it and makes no one sympathetic, neither the mother nor the daughter, nor those who shared their fate in various camps and finally in Auschwitz and the satellite camp near Cracow . . . It exudes the very numbness I have tried to describe before.)[31] Even the Jews' memoir exudes this "numbness"; they, too, went around as if in a stupor. The tactic is pretty clear: Berg is seeking justification for the very claim he has already admitted is discredited. We should note that this particular reiteration of the Betäubung phenomenon, something Berg here pointedly reappropriates, actually follows his repentant renunciation of this self-same gesture noted earlier.[32] Berg's use of (imaginary) survivor literature to sanction his evasion of Holocaust atrocities is perhaps the most questionable move in this sustained effort to justify the summary and indirect fashion in which the events of that night are finally reported—in a passage that takes up just two-thirds of one page.[33] This is a fraction of the space accorded the dubious "numbness doctrine" that is reprised in various guises throughout the novel.

Now it is surely a perilous undertaking to equate readers' responses with the text itself. The question we must ask, rather, is the extent to which they are responding in a reasonable manner to a work of conventional literary realism. Are they distorting and simplifying a far more complex work? Or are they responding sensibly to cues that have been deftly planted by an author who has had considerable prior experience in the mass entertainment genre of detective fiction? Are they responding plausibly to an author whose expertise consists in the efficacious presentation of evidence and testimony? We may not be too surprised to discover that Oprah Winfrey, who did not demur from using her on-air book club discussion of *The Reader* to introduce a heart-wrenching segment on adult illiteracy, repeatedly misstates the case by suggesting that Hanna's own life was at risk when she decided not to help the trapped women.[34] But we would not necessarily lay this misconstrual at the feet of Schlink himself, even though he was present for the discussion and did not object to this particular reading. (However, he did intervene at other points to offer corrections.) It probably does say something about the novel itself when a reviewer as perceptive as Scott Malcomson of *The New Yorker* holds the book to be about "the minor trial, circa 1965, of a guard who failed to be heroic."[35] Similarly, Richard Bernstein of *The New York Times* is following carefully executed textual cues when he deems Hanna to be a double "scapegoat," manipulated both by her codefendants and by the nation as whole.[36] Perhaps, then, Oprah can be forgiven for her insistent application of Elie Wiesel's famous admonition to Hanna. Taking up Hanna's question to the judge ("What would you have done?"), Winfrey asks her audience to put themselves in Hanna's place. But notice what has now become of that place: "it's not the actual acts," she says, citing the misconstrued authority of Wiesel, "it's the indifference of the other people who did nothing."[37] Hanna, who failed to "act heroically" in not opening the church doors, has metamorphosed into a bystander or, at worst, a fellow traveler.[38] Dripping with condescension toward American popular culture, the German press, including the august *Frankfurter Allgemeine*, suggested that the fault for such a simplistic reading lies with Oprah (and all she represents) rather than with the novel itself.[39]

Ambiguity and Moral Sophistication

In negotiating the treacherous moral maze of evaluating how people behave under dictatorships, there are two characteristic mistakes. One is the simplistic, black-and-white, Manichaean division into good guys and bad guys . . . The other, equal but opposite mistake is a moral relativism that ends up blurring the distinction between perpetrator and victim. This kind of moral relativism is frequently to be encountered among liberal-minded Westerners.

—Timothy Garton Ash, "The Stasi on Our Minds"

Berg's rejection of moral righteousness, and his insistence on viewing Hanna from a number of perspectives—that is, both as a manipulated underling and as a relatively free moral agent—have inspired not a few reviewers to associate this novel with such lofty things as "moral poise" and "moral fastidiousness."[40] But what do the critics really mean with their recourse to the language of morality? We cannot proceed with our discussion without considering, at least briefly, the critical climate that to some degree explains the success of *The Reader*. On this point, we would do well to begin with eminent Holocaust refugee, learned modernism expert, and Cambridge don George Steiner, for it was doubtless his glowing review in the *London Observer* that inaugurated the proliferation of the language of morality so rife in the subsequent criticism.[41] In claiming that "*The Reader* . . . is rapidly becoming a touchstone of moral literacy," it is clear that Steiner is fundamentally interested in the power of literature to humanize, for he goes on to assert that "the whole concept of the 'literate' is the crux [of the novel]."[42] This is an interesting position, and one that lives on in the numerous pedagogical guidebooks that feature illiteracy (and its overcoming) in prominent ways,[43] which perhaps should not surprise us since these pedagogues tend to view themselves as influential forces in the moral and civic education of their charges. Crucial in Steiner's assessment is the causal link he posits between Hanna's newfound literacy and her subsequent suicide: "Literacy has made remembrance unendurable," he opines. Silent on the question of Hanna's illiteracy and the nature of her crime, Steiner only asserts that "the evidence against her is damning." Dearer to his heart is the other side of the coin, namely, her eleventh-hour attainment of literacy, a development that, in Steiner's view, very nearly takes on the role of an avenging nemesis. It is as if the moral law that Kant thought lies in every human heart blossoms under the radiant power of literacy.

In order to justly find Hanna guilty of a capital crime—and therefore deserving of the death penalty she subsequently imposes on herself—Steiner must bridge a yawning textual gap (Iser's famous "Leerstelle"), which he does, apparently, based on his own personal experience of Nazi persecution. The fact that the novel might be taken in opposite directions—"damning" Hanna outright, on the one hand, or simply deeming her an unheroic bystander, on the other—constitutes what is perhaps the book's crowning postmodern achievement. Given the narrator's fundamental evasiveness, survivors of the Nazi genocide may simply, of their own accord, assign some specific, "damning" responsibility to Hanna. After all, they know better than the emotionally anaesthetized narrator, for they, or their immediate family members, were there. Other readers with no firsthand experience of the camps—who of course constitute the bulk of the novel's current and future readership—remain entitled, perhaps even invited, to see Hanna not principally as an agent of evil but as a victim of circumstance. This latter tendency, extensively represented in the criticism, is evident in a telling remark of Carl Macdougall, who celebrates "this extraordinary little novel" for "risking the notion that a perpetrator of evil is as much a victim as those who are murdered in the name of racial purity."[44] *As much a victim*? There is surely more of a "risk" to this notion than Macdougall cares to acknowledge. The novel's structural elasticity—which allows readers to insert other readily available Holocaust narratives virtually at will, while at the same time excusing its own evasiveness precisely by referring to an amorphous plethora of Holocaust narratives already circulating in the wider culture[45]—surely accounts, in part, for its widespread appeal.

Though Steiner explicitly connects "moral literacy" with an act of retributive justice and thus a sense of closure, those who follow in his wake suggest something quite different, namely that the moral importance of this book lies in its refusal, as Robert Hanks puts it, "to allow clear-cut answers" about Hanna.[46] Indeed, it is the persistent nebulousness of Hanna's criminal responsibility that figures most prominently in this kind of praise, as Bernstein's remark makes clear: "This is not a dilemma that can easily be resolved, if at all, and it is a mark of Mr. Schlink's depth and honesty that he makes no effort to resolve it."[47] Similarly, Peter Mosler registers his gratitude for Schlink's "discovery of the gray zones" ("Entdeckung der Grauzonen").[48] There is, in all of this, a general sense of liberation from the putatively outmoded and simplistic moralizing strictures that have thus far governed thinking about the Holocaust. Natasha Walter represents a common sentiment when she observes, "Most of us can only deal with the Holocaust by relying on blanket condemnation, and Schlink wants to shake us from that position."[49]

On the one hand, in these pronouncements, one senses a postmodern valorization of ambiguity per se, that if taken to its logical extreme would, of course, undermine ethics entirely. But the much more plausible reason cited for celebrating a story that "throws up in the air all our notions of guilt and atonement" is that such an approach promises to engage the reader in a way that traditional Holocaust literature, with its cast of inhuman perpetrators-as-monsters supposedly cannot.[50] The novel thematizes its putative departure from this strategy by noting the proliferation in the postwar period of impoverished, monochromatic Holocaust iconography; and interestingly, here, as in the bombing that ignites the horrible church fire, the Allies are pointedly made responsible. Moreover, Schlink himself emphasizes nothing so much as his effort to "humanize" Hanna, showing that she is not some evil alien creature but a fellow human being.[51] This, in turn, is said to make the Holocaust "real" to a whole new generation of readers.

The prospect of seeing oneself—and, thus, "the human"—in a despicable criminal of course boasts a venerable literary pedigree (one that is at odds, we might note, with the genre of detective fiction discussed in Chapter 1). "Shakespeare, Schiller, the Schlegel brothers, and E. T. A. Hoffmann all had a weird interest in the extreme villain," Peter Schneider reminds us. He also notes, "Schiller considered the fictional representation of evil as an educational duty of literature. He wanted to break down the easy contempt of the lawful citizen toward the criminal by exploring the psychology of the criminal."[52] Can Schlink be said to stand in this worthy tradition of Schillerian "aesthetic education"?[53] Does he not seek precisely to "break down the easy contempt" that he associates, above all, with his own generation's summary disavowal of its parents? If so, then we would indeed want to approve the critics' admiration for the novel's daring suspension of moral certainties in a way that possibly forces readers to identify with perpetrators.

Yet this is hardly the case. Dostoevsky, let us recall, challenges us to enter into the twisted mind of his protagonist Raskolnikov, but only after he has given us the gruesome murder scene, complete with split skull and bloody hatchet. To be sure, Schlink does not entirely suppress the depiction of atrocity, but he does obfuscate the connection between perpetrators and crime, so that we are left with the feeling—if we can believe the critics—that there is some deeper truth to this mystification of criminal responsibility. Yet this enterprise seems doubtful, at best. While there is surely an enduring mystery regarding the degree to which Hanna was nudged into her role by her underprivileged upbringing (i.e., the irresolvable mix of social determination and free will), there is no essential or higher moral truth in failing to connect crime with criminal. We can only acknowledge with humility the "overdetermined" status of Hanna's crime once we know what that crime is. This obfuscation allows critics to cease thinking about the vagaries of criminal responsibility, rather than impelling them to pursue its complexities. In characterizing the depiction of Hanna in terms of a profound moral stalemate, these critics cooperate in the novel's normalization of a matter that should instead receive further scrutiny.[54] Rather than acknowledging the failure of the justice system to uncover specific and individual responsibility, or pointing to the unfinished task of Holocaust historians—to explore the culpability of the vast lower tier of collaborators—the critics remain in thrall to the novel's implicit injunction to go no further. By wrapping themselves in the mantle of an alleged "moral complexity," they undermine the very thing they claim to value, namely, moral discourse itself.

CO-OPTING THE GRAY ZONE

> Levi understood that human cravings for simple understanding include the need "to separate evil from good, to be able to take sides, to emulate Christ's gesture on Judgment Day: here the righteous, over there the reprobates." The gray zone, however, defied such neat separations. Indeed, Levi argued, it ought to "confuse our need to judge." Nevertheless, moral judgments resound in Levi's writing . . . [His] moral agenda is demanding.
> —Jonathan Petropoulos and John Roth, *Gray Zones*

We should perhaps recall the provenance of the term "the gray zone," for what is now being used approvingly with reference to Holocaust perpetrators was coined by Primo Levi to refer to the specific dilemma of the *Sonderkommandos*. As Jonathan Petropoulos and John K. Roth explain, Levi "used that phrase specifically to refer to the 'incredibly complicated internal structure' of Auschwitz, which created moral ambiguity and compromise in ways large and small. He was struck particularly, but not only, by the ways in which the German organization of the camp led Jews, however reluctantly, to become complicit in the destruction of their own people. Focusing attention especially on the Sonderkommando, the Jews who were conscripted to work in the gas chambers and crematoria at Auschwitz-Birkenau, the camp's killing center, Levi said that 'Conceiving and organizing [those] death squads was National Socialism's most demonic crime.'"[55] The gray zone, as Levi defined it, was never meant as a brief for moral ambiguity per se; nor was it intended to undermine moral judgment. Rather, his purpose is clearly to complicate moral inquiry rather than to quash it.

Levi's statement on the Jewish prisoners who, under incredible duress, served as members of the Sonderkommando—charged with dragging corpses from the gas chambers, removing from them whatever remained of value to the Nazis, and conveying the bodies to the ovens—should not be misconstrued. He famously said, "No one is authorized to judge them, not those who lived through the experience of the Lager and even less those who did not."[56] Levi's insistence that these prisoners not be condemned as willing collaborators is itself a moral intervention, and it is meant precisely to block the appropriation of the gray zone by those perpetrators who possessed relatively more agency and freedom. In any case, it is mistaken to view Levi as the father of moral relativism concerning the Holocaust. On the contrary, his work is characterized by a profound moral ambivalence, qualification, and subtlety. This was grounded above all in his self image: "Although Häftling 174517 [Levi's prisoner number] knew that he was the Holocaust's innocent victim, Levi also felt shame, a key component in what he called the survivors' disease."[57] Precisely because he doubted "the moral instinct of humanity"[58] and worried that the Holocaust, or something akin to it, might indeed recur, Levi felt the need to keep ethically alert. "What could humankind do, he wondered, to keep such threats [e.g., the recurrence of genocide] at bay? One of Levi's responses was to study the gray zone and to grasp why there must be caution as well as boldness in making moral judgments."[59] "*Especially* when the gray zone was under consideration," Petropoulos and Roth remind us, "moral evaluation had to be made."[60]

As previously noted in some detail, the principal means by which *The Reader* avoids moral accountability is by postulating what I have called "the numbness doctrine." Interestingly, it seems not to apply even to that core group of prisoners with whom Levi was most concerned, namely, the members of the so-called Sonderkommandos. Confronted with the proximate reality of mass death and its consequences like no other group, these inmates responded only partially with the "numbness" repeatedly invoked by Berg. In the place of blanket mental and spiritual deadness, historians Gideon Greif and Michael Berenbaum diagnose a far more mixed palette of emotional responses to the horrors of camp life. In his essay "Between Sanity and Insanity: Spheres of Everyday Life in the Auschwitz-Birkenau Sounderkommando," Greif elucidates "other gray zones that existed in the lives of Sonderkommandos: for example, in the tension between an unfeeling, numb, and even robotic mind-set on the one hand, and a compassion for other victims," on the other. "Among the Sonderkommandos," he shows, "the impulse towards suicide and the desire to survive and bear witness also existed simultaneously amidst a rush of conflicting emotions."[61] Berenbaum also documents a spectrum of emotional and moral responses, such as "the contemplation of suicide, the sense of abject powerlessness, the refuge in numbed feelings, robotic behavior, and the outrage they felt at the fate of children."[62]

Betäubung was never just a way of making plausible Berg's failure to narrate the gruesome details of the trial testimony, however. Instead, it is part and parcel of the novel's larger "gray zone campaign," for implicit in this numbness is a regression to the essential, preconscious, and routinized bodily functions and dissociation from precisely those higher critical faculties that make moral judgment possible. It is thus no coincidence that both historians mentioned here describe it as "robotic"—that is, not fully human. But if we cannot even generalize this numbness for those who should be the most likely candidates (the Sonderkommandos), then how much less are we entitled to apply it to all those other groups that Berg indiscriminately places under the Betäubung umbrella—perpetrators, postwar judges, juries, lawyers, and student observers like himself? In this inventory of potentially numbed observers, we should not, of course, forget to include ourselves—as readers placed alongside the sympathetically drawn Berg (more on this later), we, too, are being invited to view ourselves as anesthetized into a state of moral suspension.

"Die Angeklagten kamen mir vor, als seien sie noch immer und für immer in dieser Betäubung befangen, in ihr gewissermaßen versteinert." (The defendants seemed to me to be still, and forever, caught up in this numbness, turned to stone, as it were.) Such are Berg's thoughts as he watches the trial. But can Hanna Schmitz and her colleagues legitimately be placed within Levi's gray zone? Is this the moral sophistication hinted at by the critics and promulgated by pedagogues?[63] Does this constitute Schlink's daring move—to apply categories of moral insight originally developed for brutalized prisoners to the perpetrators? It will not do to argue prescriptively by reminding readers, as Petropoulos and Roth do so well, that Levi was acutely aware of this danger and strenuously countered it.[64] Instead, one must look at the novel itself and specifically at the characterization of Hanna as an illiterate ethnic German (*Volksdeutche*) of the lower economic class. As I elaborate at some length in Chapter 6, she cries out for inclusion within this zone of moral indeterminacy. Portrayed as having childlike mental capacities when it comes to moral reasoning (a point perhaps best captured in Daldry's recent filmic depiction), Hanna is presented to us as an actor reduced to what Lawrence Langer famously dubbed "choiceless choices"[65]—a term that was first developed specifically for prisoners forced to work for the SS. Late in the novel, after her attainment of literacy, she invokes Levi almost verbatim in solemnly telling Berg (and us) that no living person has the right to judge her. In short order, she carries out this judgment on herself via suicide, making her form of *Selbs[t]justiz* (self-administered justice) sympathetic to many readers. And we might note in passing that she "confirms" Gerhard Selb's contention that only the second generation possesses the necessary perspective on the Holocaust, for though she kills herself, she does so only in the aftermath of a second-generation consciousness-raising. In this respect, she provides an object lesson for Selb's thesis and another instance of the *Langsamkeit* (slowness to react) that he endearingly exemplifies.

If the novel and the 2008 film it inspired contain any intriguing premise at all, it is this: that lower-tier collaborators suffering from economic disadvantage and a concomitant lack of education do in fact require closer consideration and perhaps more nuanced discussion and research. To suggest that the underprivileged and socially vulnerable represent a fertile recruiting ground for coconspirators and collaborators of violent, lawless political movements is not in itself an implausible idea—one thinks, for example, of the conscripting of child soldiers for military campaigns in the Sudan and elsewhere.[66] Indeed, this line of thinking easily overflows the temporal confines of the Holocaust and causes us to ask much more far-reaching, potentially uncomfortable questions. If we were to take this idea seriously, then we could not safely isolate evil within Nazi Germany but would have to ask how such widespread moral collapse might potentially apply to other countries and other times as well, as I discuss further in the final chapter of this study, "The Hollywood *Reader*." But this supposed affiliation of the underprivileged with criminality might also function in a manner that is irresponsibly over-broad. We know, for example, that many other members of Hanna's social class did not collaborate. Why, for example, did the illiterate farmer who saved the life of Ava Schieber[67] choose to risk his and his family's life to do the right thing, while Hanna joined the SS? We simply need to know more about what she did and why she did it. But at this crucial point, the novel's plot dissolves into an exculpatory fog. Here we might speak of a literary strategy of innuendo fully at odds with historical inquiry—a strategy that vaguely suggests "causality" while at the same time discourages the only kind of investigation that could actually establish it or something close to it. It remains a mystery (to me, at least) how one of the most agreed upon and established notions of criminality—the sociological explanation—can be applied to the Holocaust in such a casual manner and then emerge to be celebrated as an "innovation" in Holocaust literature.

If the novel places Hanna within Levi's gray zone, it does so obliquely, as if the author sensed that even perpetrators as socially disadvantaged as Hanna cannot, in the end, be compared with the brutalized, captive members of the Sonderkommando. (Here we may recall Schlink's fear of having written a "whitewashing" book.) Rather than explore the vagaries of class as one, perhaps very important, determinant within a complex mix of historical factors, *The Reader* envelops both Hanna and us in a mental fog that impedes moral reflection rather than furthering it—all the while allowing us to feel good about ourselves. It gestures toward all those revered icons of postmodern sophistication: open-endedness, indeterminacy, fragmentation, and lack of resolution. But in fact, and paradoxically, the novel's deployment of the gray zone promises consolation and closure by encouraging us to give up the pursuit of tedious and complex ethical questions. As we briefly saw, Levi's postulation of a "gray zone" for the Sonderkommandos prompted careful investigations that resulted in the discovery of contradictory and complexly layered sentiments and behaviors on the part of these prisoners. Schlink's recourse to the gray zone, in contrast, seems decidedly antihistorical, since it implies that there is no need to seek further because we already know that we cannot know. It retroactively justifies the failure of many families to pursue information about the wartime activities of their first-generation members by making this seem the natural state of affairs. Here, once again, is a consummate "Aphrodite" moment, as we are being invited to view this ignorance as profundity itself. In this way, the notion of a gray zone, like the numbness that constitutes it, functions as a defense against confronting Holocaust atrocities.

In the end, one cannot avoid the conclusion that the effort to implicate the reader, no matter how laudable, is simply a ruse. The great discovery at the heart of this novel—what "explains" so much else in the text—is Hanna's illiteracy, not her actual complicity in crimes against humanity. In what might strike us as a bizarre reversal of definitions of the human, readers now identify with the humanized Hanna exclusively as one determined by forces beyond her control. As one of Oprah's discussants crudely put it, "So but for the grace of God go I,"[68] a sentiment replicated, somewhat more guardedly, in the elite reviews.[69] If *The Reader* actually prods readers to consider themselves as potential perpetrators, we would then need to pose the next question—of what kind? If readers' identification extends only to the conception of the perpetrator as a victim of circumstance ("there but for the grace of God"), then what manner of moral accomplishment is this?

More fundamentally, we might ask what else may be at stake in tapping into this long cultural tradition of attempting to link the bourgeois reader with extreme criminality. Is this not itself a kind of evasion or a reprieve from the tedium of history? This convention is so much a part of the aesthetic tradition that one can easily take it for granted. It seems "natural" that art pose transcendent historical questions precisely in order to engage the reader on an intimate level; otherwise, literature could easily become merely historicist or antiquarian in nature. On this point, it is again Primo Levi who provides a fresh perspective: "I do not know, and it does not much interest me to know, whether in my depths there lurks a murderer, but I do know that I was a guiltless victim and I was not a murderer."[70] With his refusal to speculate about what might have been, Levi reminds us of the potential for moral evasion that lies within this aesthetic tradition. It is not my point to discredit the Schillerian philosophy of aesthetic education that asks readers to place themselves in the position of the radically marginalized and socially deviant. There may indeed be much to admire in this gambit—perhaps. As an educator myself, and specifically as a teacher of literature, I myself am inclined to this humanist view. But Levi reminds us that within this very vehicle of potential moral edification inheres its very opposite. In engaging the subjunctive and hypothetical, however laudably, we may also, at the same time, be fleeing the unbearably actual and historical. And by privileging an imaginary identification of ourselves with Holocaust perpetrators, we also may be inadvertently endorsing the notion of the moral "undecidability" of their actions. The simultaneity of these two "moments"—that is, of moral illumination via self-projection, on the one hand, and avoidance of intolerable knowledge via flight into the subjunctive, on the other—is what makes the "Aphrodite" function relevant here as well—for this enables a simultaneous embrace of, and flight from, moral thinking. Could this be what lies behind the critical elevation of these "interesting ambiguities"?[71]

From this perspective, we would need to revisit Hanna's famous interrogatory—"What would you have done?"—as I shall do in greater depth in the next chapter, for it is perhaps the example par excellence of the retrospective hypothetical that at once represents a deeply relevant intervention and a diversionary tactic. At this point, however, I would rather emphasize the way in which Levi's remark spotlights an aporia of Holocaust literature, for the "mental comfort" that Lawrence Langer and Alvin Rosenfeld have identified as a hallmark of so many accessible works does not simply derive from a thematic distortion or substantive evasion of the genocide. It rather goes to the nature of art itself, which provides comfort not only through beauty of form—whatever that may be—but also in this fundamental subjunctive move through which "historical" literature is made relevant to the present reader.

To celebrate the novel's treatment of "moral complexities and ambiguities inherent" in the narrative situation is, of course, an understandable reflex.[72] We do not, with good reason, celebrate didactic fiction that merely rehearses well-established ethical positions. My point here, however, has been to suggest that an unreflective embrace of moral ambiguity may, in the very name of complexity, effectively deny it. In the case of *The Reader*, the critical valorization of ambiguity serves to enforce a simplistic binary division of perpetrators into, on the one hand, the notorious evildoers (with whom the novel is frankly not concerned) and, on the other, a vast, undifferentiated category of what historian Richard Levy refers to as the "middle management," a group that is represented, problematically in this case, by Hanna and her siblings. Schlink has advocated the novel—over the more explicitly propositional essay, for example—as a particularly apt venue for issues that remain essentially problematic, open-ended, and irresolvable.[73] This may be true; but notice what becomes of the ethical "gray zone" in the judgment of one of Schlink's greatest promoters, the critic and publicist Tilman Krause. "If there is a moral" to the story,

Krause concludes, then it is this: "One will never understand everything, therefore one ought, in order to be fair, to withhold condemnation."[74] In this, he seems to concur with Hanna. In her last meeting with Berg, as we noted, she insists that only the dead have a right to judge her, for they alone understand her adequately—"Auch das Gericht konnte nicht Rechenschaft von mir fordern" (Even the court had no right to call me to account).[75]

In the end, we may also need to ask if the critics' embrace of ambiguity does not bespeak more exhaustion with ethical thinking than engagement with it, a point I pursue in the penultimate chapter of this study. Schlink is no doubt right to discard the monster thesis—a project Peter Schneider had, by the way, already undertaken with his 1987 novella *Vati*. But the result should be greater complexity, not another cliché. If the new trend in Holocaust literature is to explore the perpetrators' tangle of motivations, we will need more, not less, analytical rigor. The widespread and fundamental critique of rationality that has characterized modern intellectual life—variously associated with critical theory, poststructuralism, and postmodernism—may have produced a rather lopsided climate that does not bode well for this task. As philosopher Vittorio Hösle observes, while we continue to observe the rules of technical and instrumental reason in our daily lives, we tend to forfeit those of value-rationality as ipso facto unattainable.[76] Yet if we are to proceed beyond self-congratulatory images that ratify our own alleged "numbness" and sense of victimhood, foregone conclusions regarding an assumed state of moral ambiguity will have to give way to a scrupulous investigation that seeks to understand specific responsibility for crimes in light of real historical constraints. This task may well lie beyond the scope of good fiction—and may thus represent the real limit to literary approaches to the Holocaust.

CHAPTER 3

"WHAT WOULD YOU HAVE DONE?"

GUILT AS VIRTUE

Im gesamten Text zeigt sich die ausgeprägte Neigung Michaels, sich schuldig zu fühlen.

—Magret Möckel, *Bernhard Schlink, Der Vorleser*

Qui s'accuse s'excuse.

—Anonymous

"IS CHEATING WRONG?" I ASK MY STUDENTS. Without hesitation, most affirm that it is, unequivocally. And they give good reasons: it undermines the educational enterprise, destroys trust, and renders efforts at assessment questionable. "But have you ever done it?" This is clearly the more uncomfortable question. Statistics suggest that two-thirds to three-quarters of my class will indeed have cheated on an exam or homework assignment by the time of graduation. Their personal implication in a general moral query does not keep them from upholding the basic principle—in this case, of academic honesty. But not so when it comes to the Holocaust.

Again and again, students tell me that because they cannot know for certain how they would have conducted themselves, they cannot now condemn Holocaust perpetrators—"After all, what would I have done?" They do not doubt for a minute that the genocide was wrong. But their uncertainty—or, perhaps, humility—regarding their own hypothetical behavior tells them to break off this line of inquiry. There is indeed much to admire in this attitude, for they have evidently learned to eschew simple moralism and to avoid self-righteous posturing. The sentiments of my students, it turns out, echo the findings of a 2001 *Spiegel* survey in which 53 percent of those asked responded that forgiveness was required for Holocaust perpetrators: "You also have to be able to forgive. You just don't know what you would have done in that situation."[1] But do we know what we are "forgiving"? Or is this perhaps a code word for not wanting to know?

HANNA'S CONFESSIONS

It may come as little surprise, then, to learn that my students—like many other readers of *The Reader*—react with fundamental sympathy to the question Hanna Schmitz puts to the chief judge during the early phase of her trial for crimes committed during the Holocaust.[2] "What would you have done?" she asks the judge. The question is breathtaking because it contains so much more than it actually says. She does not contest the fundamental charges made against her; she is in fact admitting guilt. "Yes, of course I did it," she seems to be saying—"Did I have a choice?" All she wants to know, some twenty years after the war has ended, is this: what would someone else have done in her place? And not just anyone—for this judge, whatever quirks he may otherwise display, is an extremely well educated, highly placed member of society, someone with unmistakable privilege and power. In comparison, Hanna, whom we will soon discover to be illiterate but already know to be vastly less fortunate educationally and socially, is a real nobody. If even the presiding judge cannot successfully explain something that he claims is *obvious*—something that, by his own account, constitutes a fundamental moral precept—then he must cede the exchange to Hanna. This he fails to do, and those in attendance, the narrator tells us, unanimously conclude that Hanna has won the day: "Die Antwort des Richters wirkte hilflos, kläglich. Alle empfanden es. Sie reagierten mit enttäuschtem Aufatmen und schauten verwundert auf Hanna, die den Wortwechsel gewissermaßen gewonnen hatte."[3] (The judge's answer came across as hapless and pathetic. Everyone felt it. They reacted with sighs of disappointment and stared in amazement at Hanna, who had more or less won the exchange.)[4]

With this pivotal scene, Schlink achieves—I would argue—an astounding degree of consonance between the *intradiegetic* auditors present in the fictional courtroom and the *extradiegetic* readers of his novel. Both groups are intently "reading" Hanna in order to figure her out; and both, I contend, conclude that she is fundamentally sympathetic, at least for now. Yes, grave crimes have been alleged and will, in due course, be explored. But for now, within this power play between judge and underprivileged defendant—one that we, as readers, have directly witnessed (as opposed to distant war crimes we will only hear about)—the underdog has prevailed. And we cannot fail to cheer her on, at least provisionally. Schlegel and Hölderlin have articulated the ways in which the "sensuality" of art possesses the potential to speak more compellingly, and possibly even more complexly, than abstract philosophical argumentation.[5] But like Plato, they were also keenly aware of the ways in which aesthetic devices, precisely because of their very "sensuousness," can distort rather than enlighten. Which of these options (that are present in all art) predominates here? In what follows, I will explore the manifold ways in which "guilt" is deployed in *The Reader*. To some extent, the novel purveys a suppler notion of guilt than what would be admissible in a court of law. On the other hand, we will see how guilt simultaneously becomes a signifier for suffering and, indeed, for virtue itself. It will be helpful in this discussion to keep in mind that Hanna, despite those powerful instances of quoted speech, remains a figure *within* Michael Berg's fictional memoir and serves, I will argue, primarily to characterize him. We have no direct access to Hanna—or anybody or anything else, for that matter—except through Berg. She is, in this sense, his "construct." In talking about her, he is always, in a sense, talking about himself.

Hanna's admission of guilt—implicit in her showstopping questioning of the chief judge—comes before we know to *what* she is admitting. More precisely, it occurs at the outset of a trial in which we learn *nothing* more about her actual culpability, but a great deal more about the myriad ways in which she was compromised, victimized, betrayed, and simply used by those more powerful than she. I have elsewhere argued that this intentionally amorphous portrayal of Hanna's criminality greatly diminishes the novel's moral thrust. Schlink repeatedly asserts that he sought to portray the dilemma of loving a perpetrator, but then skews the issue by blurring her criminal responsibility through a technique I have called "enforced mystification."[6] Here I want to explore something different, though clearly related—namely, the ways in which the very confession of guilt becomes not a tool of discovery, analysis, or epiphany, but rather their opposite. In both Hanna and Berg, we observe how confessing guilt can be deployed to retard further analysis, derail the process of discovery, and ultimately establish the confessed perpetrator as the narrative's "real" victim.[7]

The first of these functions is evident when the judge pauses to answer what appears to be such a simple question. Here Schlink effectively slows the narration in order to build drama. A long paragraph (long for this novel, at least) separates Hanna's fateful question from the judge's feckless response, giving us a chance to wonder how this will all play out and perhaps to ask ourselves how we might respond in his place. Hanna's dramatic question directly follows an acceptance of responsibility that is, at first glance, no less comprehensive and "muscular" than Gerhard Selb's: "To the judge's questions, Hanna testified that yes, she had served in Auschwitz until early 1944 and then in a small camp near Cracow until the winter of 1944–45, that yes, when the prisoners were moved to the west she went with them all the way."[8] (Der Vorsitzende ließ sich von Hanna bestätigen, daß sie bis Frühjahr 1944 in Auschwitz und bis Winter 1944/1945 in einem kleinen Lager bei Krakau eingesetzt war, daß sie mit den Gefangenen nach Westen aufgebrochen und dort auch angekommen war.)[9] Then her guileless challenge to the judge literally stops the action, at least for the time being. By agreeing so early to the basic charges, she frustrates not only the defense strategy of her codefendants, who are clearly settling in for a protracted trial, but also, from a narratological viewpoint, the very master plot of a courtroom drama.[10] Unwittingly, she halts the arrow of the classic Aristotelian "analytic drama" in midflight. In part, this is attributable to her ignorance of sophisticated societal and judicial conventions: "Sie hatte kein Gefühl für den Kontext, für die Regeln, nach denen gespielt wurde, für die Formeln, nach denen sich ihre Äußerungen und die der anderen zu Schuld und Unschuld, Verurteilung und Freispruch verrechneten. Ihr Anwalt hätte, um ihr fehlendes Gefühl für die Situation zu kompensieren, mehr Erfahrung und Sicherheit haben oder auch einfach besser sein müssen."[11] (She had no sense of context, of the rules of the game, of the formulas by which her statements and those of the others were toted up into guilt and innocence, conviction and acquittal. To compensate for her defective grasp of the situation, her lawyer would have had to have more experience and self-confidence, or simply to have been better.)[12] Though this passage begins with a capacious admission of "guilt" on Hanna's part, no further elaboration of her specific criminal responsibility is offered; instead, we are told how very "innocent" she is of prevailing conventions that would require her to act in an adversarial manner.

And because we are readers of an entertaining novel, rather than prosecuting attorneys, I submit that we are primed to accept a candid general admission of guilt in lieu of protracted, and necessarily tedious, demonstrations of specific crimes. Having come clean early, she gains our trust and spares us the gory details. By acknowledging responsibility, she sets herself apart from her scheming codefendants and, in this respect, recapitulates a successful exculpatory strategy, one that was made famous by Albert Speer at the Nuremberg trials and reprised widely in the German press during the mid-1960s on the occasion of Speer's release from Spandau prison.[13] Hanna's "astonishing" honesty (to use the language of the novel) functions, in other words, as a preemptive strike against our prosecutorial scrutiny, quashing our curiosity before it has even been properly piqued by the courtroom proceedings.

Hanna's memorable "confession" becomes, in this sense, a credential—one that enables her to credibly contest more specific allegations. For example, "Sie wollte auch nicht akzeptieren, daß sie bei einer früheren richterlichen Vernehmung zugegeben hatte, den Schlüssel zur Kirche gehabt zu haben. Sie habe den Schlüssel nicht gehabt, niemand habe den Schlüssel gehabt, es habe den einen Schlüssel zur Kirche gar nicht gegeben, sondern mehrere Schlüssel zu mehreren Türen, und die hätten von außen in den Schlössern gesteckt."[14] (She also did not want to acknowledge that she had admitted, in an earlier deposition, to having had the key to the church. She had not had the key, no one had had the key, there had not been any one key to the church, but several keys to several different doors, and they had all been left outside in the locks.)[15] This statement, viewed initially as a specific and perhaps minor qualification to a more general acceptance of guilt, has tremendous implications. It cannot be an effort to evade guilt—for that she has already admitted. Rather, she—and she alone—simply wants to set the record straight. And we, of course, are all ears, for she is one of the very few defendants to do so.

It has become a canard of commemorating the Nazi past in Germany that defendants invariably deny their guilt. This was true at the Nuremberg trials and again at the Frankfurt Auschwitz trials.[16] These repeated denials, evasions, and "clever" refutations of responsibility were made unforgettable for Americans via *Judgment at Nuremburg*; and for Germans, Peter Weiss's *Die Ermittlung* (The Investigation, 1965) memorably drove this point home. It was a message that, at any rate, was almost inescapable. Margarethe von Trotta's *Die bleierne Zeit* (1981) shows us, in what is perhaps that film's most important scene, impressionable and vulnerable schoolchildren being compelled to watch Alain Resnais's painfully graphic documentary, *Night and Fog (Nuit et brouillard*, 1955).[17] The two most deeply affected viewers are, of course, the adolescents Marianne and Juliane, the title characters of the film's English-language release. We are of course constrained to watch the Resnais film *with* them, and are no less affected. Together with them, we hear the grandiloquent voiceover of the *Night and Fog* narrator, who sonorously reminds us not only that most of the Nazi perpetrators went unprosecuted but also that those who were charged and tried almost unanimously denied their guilt at every turn. "'I'm not guilty,' says the *Kapo*; 'I'm not guilty,' says the officer. 'I'm not guilty.' Then who is guilty?" asks *Night and Fog*'s narrator in overwrought, slightly histrionic tones.[18] The suggestion—both Resnais's and von Trotta's—appears to be that the next generation will have to make good where the first has so obviously failed.

Figure 3.1   "Who is guilty?" The admonitory voiceover from Alain Resnais's *Night and Fog* as depicted within von Trotta's *Marianne and Juliane* as an interrogation of the second generation.

It is against this cultural backdrop that Hanna's stunning admission of guilt needs to be read. The adamant and mean-spirited denials of her codefendants within Schlink's story constitute only the local and specific iterations of this much broader refusal of guilt, which, as I have suggested, has already been enshrined and rehearsed by a number of popular-culture vehicles. From this perspective, Hanna's admission serves not only to frustrate juridical and narrative expectations, but—perhaps more fundamentally—it also functions as a source of great relief. For in accepting so much guilt so readily, she thwarts another process: the transfer of "guilt" or "responsibility" to the second generation, performing (or at least attempting) an end-run around the trauma of the second generation. From this point of view, we can see the deployment of Hanna's robust confession as an effort to erase the cultural mourning of the second and third generation that Eric Santner writes about in his influential study, *Stranded Objects*—a mode of confronting the past that, as Santner rightly points out, was in fact always limited to a rather small demographic group.[19]

This depiction of Hanna as the exceptionally honest perpetrator, I propose, helps to explain the drama in the courtroom as the auditors await the judge's response. The "hush"—a response that readers of the novel are of course invited, in some sense, to recapitulate—has less to do with what might be said than with what has already been said, for Hanna has already punctured the narrative balloon. To echo Hans-Robert Jauß, Hanna has already engaged, and radically altered, the audience's "horizon of expectations" with regard to defendants accused of such crimes—and all this quite apart from the judge's response.[20] We are left to wonder, is the trial essentially over? Can we pack up and leave? Is it now just a matter of wrapping things up? Hanna brings this tension to a premature culmination.

It may be this general sense of relief that prompts us to let down our guard and relax our analytical inquiry. Her qualification of some of the "details," as we saw in Chapter 2 with regard to the locked church doors, can, in this sense, be read as further proof of her candor. What we may too easily overlook is the way in which these "minor revisions" to the general charges, when tallied up, effectively reduce Hanna to the status of guilty bystander—or perhaps even less, given the general chaos that apparently prevailed on that fateful night. Indeed, if we carefully examine the language of the novel, we will see that her "negligible" qualifications of the accusations effectively exculpate her of all the major charges in the end. This is not a matter of a simple reversal, however. My argument is precisely *not* that the novel appears to do one thing but actually accomplishes another. Rather, what is much more intriguing is the way in which it does both *simultaneously*. It makes us feel that we are experiencing a capacious admission of guilt, all the while significantly diminishing and qualifying that guilt.

Of the three main charges made against her, the church fire remains the most egregious. Tellingly, Berg cannot even recall the first charge, as that allegation is so minor. With regard to the forced evacuation of the camps—what we now generally know as "death marches"—she admits, as we saw previously, that 'when the prisoners were moved to the west she went with them all the way."[21] The testimony itself only really places her at the scene of a crime—and, in the case of the death march, one that is hardly referenced, let alone evoked in any kind of emotional detail. And though it may seem pedantic, we perhaps ought to notice the convenient intrusion of the passive voice: "the prisoners were moved to the west"— certainly, were this an actual trial, the lawyers would have pounced on this. This fictional trial is being held in the wake of significant public discussion of the Holocaust in Germany, as Rebecca Wittmann has recently shown.[22] The historian Konrad Jarausch describes the public culture of West Germany in the early 1960s thus: "Despite all denials of individual responsibility, the enormous extent and the new quality of the crimes committed during the war of annihilation and genocide could hardly be disputed—especially since thousands of witnesses, be they surviving Jews, former slave laborers, or liberated prisoners of war, still found themselves in Germany."[23] The novel asks us to believe that Hanna, while capable of a sudden and dramatic spurt of intellectual growth later on (in prison), has remained—throughout the postwar period and up to her trial and subsequent imprisonment—as ignorant and incurious about the Nazi period and her role as an SS officer as she was at the time of her wartime "service." Readers will variously judge the plausibility of this belated conversion scene. To me, its very narrative convenience strains credulity. Even that master of self-exculpation, Gerhard Selb (Schlink's fictional private detective whom we encountered in Chapter 1), allowed that much more about the dimensions of the Holocaust became known in the postwar period. Why is there no trace of this ex post facto "knowledge" to be found in the context of Hanna's great admission of guilt? Its absence is one key factor in positioning her confession as a courageous act attesting to personal integrity. If readers consistently fail to notice this lacuna, they do so, I would argue, because, generally speaking, we are not accustomed to contest an admission of guilt, especially one that comes as such a surprise.

This same analysis could be applied to her "work" in the camps. She confesses, as previously noted, to having "served in Auschwitz until early 1944 and then in a small camp near Cracow." What kind of "service" did she provide? Did she participate in the infamous selections? Here, too, she distinguishes herself from the other defendants (as well as all those famous deniers we may have in our cultural memory) by stepping forward and admitting guilt. She alone concedes the charge, adding that they all acquiesced in the selections, implicating, in one fell swoop, each of the codefendants: "Aber wir alle wußten."[24] (But we all knew.)[25] It is this expansive confessional moment that unleashes the ire of the other women, one of whom erupts in a vituperative outburst: "'You dirty liar!'" she screams, while "another of the accused, a coarse woman, not unlike a fat broody hen but with a spiteful tongue, was visibly worked up."[26]

Significantly, it is at this retaliatory moment that we first hear of the charge that Hanna subjected certain girls to her own "persönliche Selektion,"[27] that is, to special work conditions in her private quarters. For a moment, we are invited to see Hanna as a sadist who perhaps took advantage of these girls for some kind of sexual gratification. But within the space of a few pages, two "expert" witnesses step forward and essentially dismiss the worst of these allegations.

First and foremost is the testimony of the surviving daughter—who of course speaks with the unimpeachable authority of the Holocaust survivor (a topos Schlink reprises from the first Selb novel, in which the Jewish survivor "Frau Weinstein" performs this function). To be sure, this "authority" is a bit of an anachronism because the status of survivors' testimony was not, at the time of the fictional trial, nearly what it would become by the 1990s, when the novel was first published.[28] She spontaneously rises to her feet when she hears the angry codefendants accuse Hanna of targeting young girls for some kind of special treatment, exclaiming: "Oh God! . . .

How could I have forgotten?"[29] The ejaculatory and staccato formulation underscores our encounter of her outburst *in media res*: these vicious accusations have clearly unearthed a painful and important memory that she has not yet had a chance to adequately process, and one apparently not contained in the published memoir that plays such a crucial role in the trial. The retrospective narrative suddenly moves to her present state of mind, and the drama escalates as we make an important discovery—along with the courtroom audience—all of which represents another technique of binding readers to the perspective of the courtroom spectators.

Despite the fact that this scene has the unmistakable feel of a revelatory moment, it may simultaneously strike readers as deeply familiar. Schlink is here making use of a stock trope of courtroom drama, namely, the unexpected informant (usually speaking from the spectators' seats) whose sudden and authoritative eruption proves fateful for the defendant. True to literary, and especially filmic, convention, "She did not wait to be called to the front. She stood up and spoke from her seat among the spectators."[30] Yet no sooner has the daughter-survivor corroborated the basic facts of the allegation (yes, Hanna did indeed sequester certain girls for some kind of special service) than she *reverses* the malign interpretation placed upon them: "*But it wasn't like that at all*, and one day one of them [one of the sequestered girls] finally talked, and we learned that the girls read aloud to her, evening after evening after evening. That was better than if they . . . and better than working themselves to death on the building site. I must have thought it was better, or I couldn't have forgotten it."[31] Thus, Hanna can perhaps be credited with giving them a kind of reprieve, within the very limited options available to her then as a low-level guard. Granted, in her courtroom testimony, the survivor now wonders whether it was indeed better for the girls, but she states, for the record, that she certainly believed it was so at the time, inviting us to think that Hanna might very well have come to the same conclusion. (In Stephen Daldry's film, this scene is handled quite differently; see Chapter 6, "The Hollywood *Reader*").

When the survivor completes her impromptu testimony—its very spontaneity offering yet another degree of authenticity—we witness a truly filmic moment. Hanna, who, up until this point, has not acknowledged Berg's presence, dramatically trains her gaze upon him—the one person in the courtroom who could corroborate her longstanding practice of having literature read aloud to her by subordinates. A word from him might establish her as the good camp guard who did her best in a bad situation—one who offered defenseless girls a respite before their inevitable return to Auschwitz. But it could equally expose her as illiterate. We can almost see the novel's "camerawork"—first, a close up of Hanna as she seeks out Berg; then, a point-of-view shot featuring the bewildered young law student.

Was she asking him to speak or to remain silent? Berg insists—invoking the formulaic language of melodrama—that there was no request at all: "Her eyes found me at once, and I realized she had known the whole time I was there. She just looked at me. Her face didn't ask for anything, beg for anything, assure me of anything or promise me anything. It simply presented itself."[32] Perhaps so—or perhaps he was simply unable to acknowledge her importuning, thus repressing another painful "betrayal" on his part. Why does she turn to him precisely at this—and only this—juncture? Frankly, it does not matter whether she was asking for silence or for testimony, nor does it matter that Berg adamantly maintains that he detected no appeal in her countenance. The very fact of this dramatic gesture—the only time she ever looks Berg directly during the entire trial—tells us, unmistakably, that she sees him as deeply relevant to the Jewish survivor's testimony as well as the claims of her malignant codefendants.

If this is a cue for him to rise to his feet, as the survivor did, and to speak what he knows about Hanna's predilection for being read to, he clearly fails to take it. Yet this omission is richly overdetermined, for Berg's neglect to address the court fulfills simultaneously at least two important functions. First, it serves to enshrine Hanna as an even more beleaguered and abandoned defendant, one whose former lover chooses silence over the opportunity to put in a good word for her. In the sentences that directly follow, we get a clear sense not only of Berg's shame and discomfort but also, first and foremost, of Hanna's downtrodden state: "I saw how tense and exhausted she was. She had circles under her eyes, and on each cheek a line that ran from top to bottom that I'd never seen before, that weren't yet deep, but already marked her like scars."[33]

At the level of plot, Berg must of course fail to speak both in open court when Hanna seeks him out and later when he makes a fumbling attempt to have a word with the presiding judge about Hanna's illiteracy. It is crucial to the story line that Hanna's conviction appear *both* deserved (for she has clearly been involved in some wrongdoing) *and* somehow fundamentally unjust. If Berg were to "prematurely" defend her, he would clearly compromise the aura of injustice that so crucially surrounds her throughout much of the novel. On a more banal level, Berg's failure to speak publicly, and even privately, with the judge motivates his almost compulsive musings regarding Hanna's innocence. In other words, precisely because he never did address the court, he must address himself, again and again, on this topic. The absence of one kind of testimony results in the overabundance of another.

He formulates a *plaidoyer* for Hanna on three occasions, but none is more masterful than when he first makes the case *against* Hanna, only to then expertly take it apart, piece by piece. No handbook on trial rhetoric could trump Berg's method of dispatching opposing arguments in advance only then to refute each one by one—leaving us (the jury) to embrace his own, more benevolent view of Hanna. After "discovering" her illiteracy—and recall that there is no specific evidence for this; it simply comes to him one day while he is walking in the woods—he formulates the novel's toughest interrogation of Hanna, if only in his own mind: "But could Hanna's shame at being illiterate be sufficient reason for her behavior at the trial or in the camp? . . . Why opt for the horrible exposure as a criminal over the harmless exposure as an illiterate? Or did she believe she could escape exposure altogether? Was she simply stupid? And was she vain enough, and evil enough, to become a criminal simply to avoid exposure?"[34]

It matters a great deal that exoneration, when it comes, issues from the same person who articulates these unsparing charges. And it further matters that the following exculpation comes from a former intimate who knew that reading aloud to her was an eminently plausible accounting for the girls' "special treatment":

> Both then and since, I have always rejected this. No, Hanna had not decided in favor of crime. She had decided against a promotion at Siemens, and fell into a job as a guard. And no, she had not dispatched the delicate and the weak on transports to Auschwitz because they had read to her; she had chosen them to read to her because she had wanted to make their last months bearable before their inevitable dispatch to Auschwitz. And no, at the trial Hanna did not weigh exposure as an illiterate against exposure as a criminal. She did not calculate and she did not maneuver. She accepted that she would be called to account, and simply did not wish to endure further exposure. She was not pursuing her own interests, but fighting for her own truth, her own justice. Because she had always had to dissimulate somewhat, and could never be completely candid, it was a pitiful truth and a pitiful justice, but it was hers, and the struggle for it was her struggle.[35]

Critics who choose to view this defense as simply part of the novel's ongoing ambiguity regarding its principal perpetrator—a back-and-forth about the "real" Nazi-era Hanna—are, I believe, overlooking the lawyerly manner in which Berg prosecutes this acquittal. This is by no means the rhetoric of ambivalence or indeterminacy. On the contrary, Berg carefully lays out the case against Hanna, lets our anger build, and then deftly defuses and neutralizes each of the charges.[36] Furthermore, it constitutes only one leg of an effectively deployed tripartite exculpatory "testimony."[37] This powerful vindication of Hanna reflects not just the rhetorical expertise of our young fictional lawyer but, as I will argue in another chapter, that of the jurist-author himself.

It may seem curious to have elaborated on a charge that Hanna vehemently contests—the alleged abuse of the girls—within a larger discussion focusing on confession and admission of guilt. However, this detour was necessary in order to see how the novel rehabilitates Hanna's confessional sincerity. By way of the Holocaust survivor ("It wasn't that way at all") and Berg ("She accepted that she would be called to account, and simply did not wish to endure further exposure"), we learn both that when she admits and contests guilt, she is telling the truth.

Yet I wish to argue that a meaningful confession—even if primarily gestural and implicit—lurks within this passage after all. Well before we get to Berg's powerful verbal defense of Hanna, the novel has already raised doubts about a key presupposition of the principal allegation, namely the putatively *premeditated* and wholly calculated quality of her decision to privilege the protection of her shameful secret (illiteracy) over speaking the truth about her role as member of the SS during the war. The richly ambivalent glance that suddenly focuses on Berg in the spectators' gallery of the courtroom—possibly unreadable even to Hanna herself—suggests that she was seeking *something* significant from him. Perhaps she was prepared to reveal her handicap then—that is certainly one valid reading— but she needed his support and encouragement to follow through. Failing that, one could conclude, she falls back into her old patterns of behavior, thus inculpating herself further. I dwell on this point because it may well constitute a moment of confession—to herself, if not to the court.

In appealing to Berg at the very moment that her wartime practice of having young inmates read to her comes to light, is Hanna not, in effect, exposing herself—revealing what she will later be accused of so assiduously concealing? Is she not, as it were, saying, "Yes, of course I did this, but *you* should know what this means." Like Berg, we are being asked to connect the dots—to link these two stages of her life and notice what they have in common. No, she has not quite verbalized the fact of her illiteracy, but she seems to be asking him (and therefore us) to do so on her behalf, or at least to understand the underlying circumstance that will make that conclusion so compelling. At the very least, we witness an opening, a moment of extreme vulnerability, in which Hanna appears to let down her guard. It passes quickly, to be sure, but is marked in the novel as a pivotal moment of recognition. The "absolution" she receives with regard to this charge, then, is not exclusively—or perhaps even principally—due to Berg's extraordinary skills as a virtual defense attorney but to her own anguished "confessional" gaze.

We will never know if she was "actually" prepared to publicly admit her illiteracy, and thus to explain what must otherwise have appeared to the court and its spectators as very odd behavior, or whether she sought only to explain herself, privately, to Berg—to say, with this indecipherable look, that he, at least, should know that her practice of having others read aloud to her represented an opportunity for beauty and edification rather than an instance of brutality and exploitation. This, at any rate, is a hermeneutic option that we, as readers (and perhaps particularly as viewers of the film), are well poised to choose, as we witness directly only the positive, loving side of this reading practice. The counterpart scenario, dating to the now distant war years, has the status—at best—of dubious conjecture. We have, as it turns out, been prepared—almost from the very beginning of this fictional memoir—for this exculpatory moment, for there, where we are first introduced to Hanna, we are told that that her fundamental benevolence could be misconstrued as violence. The retrospective Berg, writing at age fifty, long after the trial and Hanna's demise, and reminiscing about his first encounter with her, says, "When rescue came, it was almost an assault."[38]

Hanna's third confession, which centers on the church fire in which all but two of the prisoners are killed, is patently false. Even at the time of this admission (still a few pages before Berg's realization of her illiteracy), we doubt her full culpability. The other defendants seek to heap the blame for the report entirely on her; and though we do not yet know of the specific handicap that would render this impossible, it seems very unlikely. Once again, repeating the well-worn pattern, all the other defendants deny any and all responsibility, refusing to admit that helping the prisoners was feasible, or an option they were even aware of, given the general confusion at the time. Hanna alone struggles through the judge's questioning, refusing one pat excuse after another: no, she wasn't afraid the prisoners would overpower her were she to open the doors, and, no, she did not fear being "arrested, convicted, shot," should they escape while she had responsibility for them.[39]

All of Hanna's "answers" are, of course, egregiously insufficient. Yet she comes off as significantly more sympathetic than her cohort because she is *trying* to tell the truth. Her fumbling attempts to explain herself frequently take the form of incomplete sentences that trail off into ellipses, leaving us to wonder how they could possibly end. Yet her repeated efforts give the impression of a woman who is valiantly attempting, however unsuccessfully, to confront her past, and this alone makes her look a good deal better than her codefendants.

The report in question, written for the Nazi authorities at the time of the incident, places responsibility on (or, to speak from the Nazi perspective of the time, gives credit to) the female guards: "The guards who remained behind, the report indicated, had allowed the fire to rage in the church and had kept the church doors locked. Among the guards who remained behind, the report indicated, were the defendants."[40] While the other defendants, eager to scapegoat Hanna, dismiss the report as patently wrong, Hanna concedes that it had been carefully redacted in order to put events in a more positive light. The criterion she adduces for the cover-up are twofold, that is, a desire to divert attention from the male guards who fled as well as to deflect any scrutiny of the women who remained.[41] Though these corrections may first appear lost in the rancorous dispute over authorship, they nevertheless serve an important purpose.

Hanna's concession about faking the report is not just one more way of upgrading herself vis-à-vis her codefendants. Actually, it reinstates much of what the others had previously said in order to exonerate *themselves*. Her testimony on this point in fact reprises one of the key mitigating factors of that night: the armed SS guards, the men who had been responsible for the command of the death march in the first place, had fled the scene, leaving unarmed women guards to cope with the crisis: "Some of us were dead, and the others had left. They said they were taking the wounded to the field hospital and would come back, but they knew they weren't coming back, and so did we. Perhaps they didn't even go to the field hospital, the wounded were not that badly hurt . . . We didn't know what to do. It all happened so fast, with the priest's house burning and the church spire, and the men and the cart were there one minute and gone the next, and suddenly we were alone with the women in the church."[42]

In other words, the inexperienced female guards, who had never before had to face this degree of responsibility, were effectively abandoned. While Hanna's responses to the judge never justify their failure to aid the burning women, they do succeed in depicting a crisis atmosphere in which perhaps no clear *decision* seemed possible, especially when all the (male) decision makers had fled the scene. Hanna does not overtly evade responsibility—this is her chief virtue vis-à-vis the others—yet the dispute over the authorship of the report and the polarization of the defendants more generally (all of them against Hanna) tends to obscure their broad agreement on the events of this night. More than anyone else—except for Berg, who adds in other crucial factors—Hanna helps to diffuse responsibility, while seeming to be the one defendant willing to accept it "manfully." Rejecting the accusation of having penned the report, she flatly states, "No, I didn't write it. Does it matter who did?" In a manner that none of the characters could possibly appreciate, she is dead right, for they all have much more in common than any of them, or most readers, seem to realize.

Yet she does "confess" to having written the document in the end. Even before we learn of her illiteracy per se, this move enhances her victimhood more than it enlarges her juridical guilt. We have witnessed the painful badgering and manipulation of a woman who is trying to confront her Nazi past, one who, albeit with little success, is attempting to sift out what is true and false in the notorious report. In this immediate context, her confession reads as a cry of surrender as she is outmaneuvered in court. When we later learn that she alone has been given a life sentence, while all the others received limited sentences,[43] our sense of the injustice done to her only increases. The subsequent revelation of her illiteracy advances the process of her victimization, for it reminds us of how she was at a disadvantage from the very beginning. Unable to read the court order to appear in the first place, she is charged with the additional crime of attempting to evade arrest. Incapable of reading the deposition and other materials, she could not prepare a proper defense. And finally, since she is unable to read and comprehend the survivors' memoir, which was distributed in advance of the trial and served as crucial testimony to which all parties attested, she finds that she has agreed to things she never meant to. These cumulative injustices semiotically congeal around the false confession she gives at this key point in the trial, the moment that seals her fate: "Once Hanna admitted having written the report, the other defendants had an easy game to play. When Hanna had not been acting alone, they claimed, she had pressured, threatened, and forced the others. She had seized command. She did the talking and the writing. She made the decisions."[44] Within the space of a few pages, Hanna metamorphoses from admitted perpetrator into chief victim, for the illiterate Hanna is portrayed as lacking precisely the autonomy and self-sovereignty that would be required to execute so many key decisions.

By the time the judgment against her is handed down, she has no further desire to communicate anything to Berg: "When the trial was over and the defendants were being led away, I waited to see whether Hanna would look at me. I was sitting in the same place I always sat. but she looked straight ahead and through everything."[45] Here, Berg is, of course, reminding us of that dramatic visual appeal she made earlier in the trial. He has carefully positioned himself to receive another such look, to be identified once again as someone who could help her case, if only he would choose to do so. And because readers of memoir literature tend to identify with the narrator, it can be said that we, too, are being offered this position of potential rescuer. It is a reminder for us to engage what we "know" of Hanna from that sensuous first third of the novel in order now to come to her aid, if only in our minds. While her string of confessions—some true, some false, some implicit—has clearly not served her well at the court of justice, it seems to have paradoxically enhanced her position significantly in the minds of readers. As she is being led away, Berg leaves us with his impression of a stoic scapegoat—a woman whose look is described as "proud, wounded, lost, and infinitely tired."[46]

What remains truly interesting is not just this insistent process of exoneration but the simultaneous assertion—and acceptance—of her guilt. Again and again, readers conclude, as Ekkehart Mittelberg does in his Cornelsen teachers' guide, "Quite apart from the questionable accusations made by her codefendants, Hanna's guilt remains pronounced."[47] But if one examines the handy chart he has constructed, listing all the incidents relating to Hanna's guilt, we notice a curious reversal. The woman who so bravely stepped forward to confess her guilt—thus distinguishing herself from the vast majority of defendants—turns out to be a garden variety perpetrator at best: she is guilty, first, of "unterlassene Hilfe" (failure to assist) during the church fire (though with all kinds of extenuating circumstances, as we have seen),[48] and second, of following orders by participating in the "selections" (though here, too, her "special treatment" of the vulnerable young girls may seen by some as a kind of "resistance"). Guilty of following illegal orders and of not helping when she could have—this is all that remains if one subtracts the incidents that are clearly either false charges or false confessions. Perhaps it is because, in the end, she sounds so much like others of her generation that readers fail to see the way in which she is systematically absolved of even these last two charges. Mittelberg's chart makes another point, though again inadvertently. The heavy charges come relatively early in the novel; thereafter, the guilt discourse steadily softens to the point of atonement.[49] But the real determinant of this strategy, in the end, may depend not upon phrasing, narrative placement, or guided student exercises but upon an external factor. German readers, in particular, may have a difficult time consciously acknowledging the way in which a Holocaust perpetrator—*any* perpetrator—has been effectively exonerated, for this would be tantamount to breaking a powerful postwar taboo. No matter how disadvantaged, a perpetrator of the Holocaust is ipso facto guilty. Paradoxically, the "fact" of Hanna's guilt may qualify her as an ideal candidate for exculpation—her unquestioned perpetrator status is the very thing that makes it "safe" or permissible to view her with sympathy. In this sense, Schlink has achieved what his narrator could not: the possibility of *simultaneously* condemning and understanding Hanna Schmitz. But if true, it is certainly not entirely his doing but rather a function of the contemporary public culture, and it may not be immutable over time.

The pattern of establishing one's status as victim by confessing exaggerated, amorphous, or wholly misplaced guilt is introduced long before we ever discover that Hanna was once an SS guard. Berg inaugurates this semiotic chain as a boy during his conflicts with Hanna. It continues into adulthood and remains, as we shall see, a staple of his depiction of their relationship, whence it flows generously (if uncritically) into his discussion of German "collective guilt" and, specifically, second-generation guilt, as he establishes himself and his relationship with Hanna as paradigmatic for this generational experience.

Hanna and Berg have two major quarrels, one of which becomes physical. These occur close together, during Berg's spring break from high school. The two of them have already decided to take a four-day bicycle tour of some idyllic countryside, stopping in four small towns, where they will register in hotels as mother and son. But before they set off on that trip, on the very first day of his Easter vacation, Berg rises early, determined to surprise Hanna by showing up unannounced in the streetcar she conducts. He does so, but initially enters the second car because he notices she is busy talking with a colleague in the first. Eagerly, he waits for her to notice and join him, but she never does come into his car, and he becomes convinced that she has simply chosen to ignore him. He abruptly exits the streetcar without ever having made contact, walks the long way home, and confronts her later about this slight.

The second conflict also arises from Berg's desire to surprise his lover. He steals quietly from their bed in the hotel early one morning in order to fetch breakfast and flowers, leaving a note just in case she were to awake in his absence. He returns to find an enraged Hanna, who has no knowledge of any note and who clearly feels abandoned. Before he can explain himself, she strikes him across the face with the thin leather belt from her dress. Poised to do it again, she strikes the air instead before collapsing into a sobbing, remorseful heap. Did she find a note and, lacking the skill to read it, simply assume it was a breakup note, a "Dear John" letter, as it were? Or did Berg's missive go missing for some plausible reason—perhaps a gust of wind? This point is never resolved.

What links both episodes—perhaps too conveniently—is Hanna's profound fear of being abandoned, rejected, and denied. Though each is, of course, narrated by Berg (like everything else in the book), the first seems particularly sympathetic to him. He goes to great lengths to meet her on her turf and feels utterly rejected when she does not enter his car, though she clearly had the opportunity to do so. His status as underdog is enhanced by her harshness in their subsequent verbal exchange: she mocks his class privilege, denies that he possesses the power to hurt her, and demands that he leave. He learns to deal with this kind of conflict by falsely confessing guilt: "But half an hour later I was back at her door. She let me in, and I said the whole thing was my fault. I had behaved thoughtlessly, inconsiderately, unlovingly. I understood that I had upset her. I understood that she wasn't upset because I couldn't upset her. I understood that I couldn't upset her, but that she simply couldn't allow me to behave that way to her."[50] Moreover, this mode of submissive confession becomes the modus operandi that characterizes their manner of conflict resolution and, therefore, their relationship in general: "I had not only lost this fight. I had caved in after a short struggle when she threatened to send me away and withhold herself. In the weeks that followed I didn't fight at all . . . Whenever she became cold and hard, I begged her to be good to me again, to forgive me and love me."[51]

Hanna, of her own accord, abruptly ends her violent outburst over Berg's disappearance on that morning during their Easter bike trip as soon as she notices that his lip is bleeding. Instantly, her wrath subsides, and she tends him like a gentle nurse, showing that she is not an intrinsically violent person. (Her behavior would otherwise have lent credence to her codefendants' accusations against her at the trial). On the contrary, she may in fact be a decent person, though perhaps typical of her class and time in her readiness to use physical punishment—after all, she figures as the "mother" in this unequal relationship. In any event, she is shocked by the sight of blood and is immediately moved to mercy. But even in this case, where Berg would not need to take the blame, given her sudden about-face, he does so implicitly: Hanna says that she never saw the note that Berg claims to have left. He holds his tongue, tacitly conceding the point, even though he is certain he left one.

Hanna appears imperious in one scene and cruel in another; Berg is clearly the injured party in both. But this one-sidedness crumbles in retrospect when we realize that her illiteracy directly accounts for the first outburst and certainly played a substantial role in the second, insofar as she was unable to read the additional letters in which Berg expressed what he could never say to her face-to-face.[52] What emerges from these observations is this: Berg employs confession not as a way of expressing sincerely felt guilt and responsibility but rather in order to preserve an important relationship—one in which he is clearly the junior, less powerful partner. Simultaneously, these false confessions serve to characterize Berg as a victim, even when he does not overtly seek this status, for these acts of submission add implicit insult to injury: not only must he put up with unreasonable behavior, he must also take responsibility for it.

Even before he explicitly argues that his relationship with Hanna constitutes a preeminent paradigm for the dilemma of the second generation as it seeks to come to terms with the Holocaust, we can already see the essential outlines. Schlink has long maintained that the central question of *The Reader* is, how could one have loved a perpetrator? I have argued in various ways that Hanna's perpetrator aspect is so studiously played down that this dilemma cannot really arise. But surely Schlink is not entirely mistaken: his novel does indeed present a paradigm for the second generation's painful relationship to its parents. However, its function and meaning are not to be sought in loving the perpetrators but instead in confessing undue, and even false, guilt. Indeed, this fictional relationship is put forward, in part, as a way of imagining how and why an entire generation could use the often-ritualized language of confession and guilt as a way of cozying up to a more powerful partner.

In this unacknowledged semiotic economy, Hanna might stand in for the United States as the dominant—but still desired—senior partner who requires "unreasonable" acts of contrition in order to maintain the relationship. If, as Santner and others have postulated, the mandate to confront the past appears, in the minds of many second-generation Germans, to emanate from the United States, then it is not unreasonable to hypothesize a second-generation imaginary in which an unequal love relationship, such as that between Berg and Hanna, takes on this additional symbolic function. In this way, this otherwise perhaps trivial and dysfunctional relationship rises to the level of a compelling, if inevitably controversial, *political* metaphor. This may in part explain the book's popularity: it gives postwar Germans a (necessarily indirect) means of expressing a sense of injustice at being required to enact public rituals of guilt for crimes for which they cannot really be held personally responsible. This claim for broader significance can only fully be appreciated, however, once we better understand Berg's strategy of systematic "over-confession."

Berg's Guilty Virtue

As we have seen, Berg begins by distinguishing his actual innocence with regard to their disputes from the nominal guilt he confesses in order to make things right between him and Hanna. But he soon begins to deploy confessional language in a manner that no longer acknowledges this distinction.

While he ostensibly embraces a deep-seated guilt for the collapse of the relationship, and even for its very existence, the story insistently sends another message. Around the time of his sixteenth birthday, he begins to feel attraction to younger girls of his own age group and starts a flirtation with one of them, Sophie. Though he shares other important aspects of his life with his school friends, he never lets on that he is conducting an affair with a 36-year-old street-car conductor—a woman whom he acknowledges could easily be his mother—in a cold-water flat on the other side of the railroad tracks, as it were (in German, literally in the *Bahnhofstrasse*, the train-station street), far away from the upper-middle-class milieu of his upbringing. Hanna is fully aware of his desire to be with his school friends. As a kind of a farewell gift, she arouses him to unprecedented heights of erotic fulfillment—"Als wir uns liebten, hatte ich das Gefühl, sie wolle mich zu Empfindungen jenseits alles bisher Empfundenen treiben, dahin, wo ich's nicht mehr aushalten konnte. Auch ihre Hingabe war einzig." (When we made love, I sensed she wanted to push me to the point of feeling things I had never felt before, to the point where I could no longer stand it. She also gave herself in a way she had never done before)[53] Thereafter she dismisses him unceremoniously with the laconic directive: "Jetzt ab zu deinen Freunden" (now off to your friends).[54]

Despite some very good reasons for his silence about Hanna—in West Germany in 1958, this would have offended the regnant Adenauer-era canons of public morality—and despite Hanna's own reservations (she agrees to the Easter vacation bicycle excursion only under the pretense of appearing in public as mother and son), Berg repeatedly castigates himself for his failure to "acknowledge" her publicly. Reiterating *her* contentions from earlier quarrels, Berg confesses to having "disavowed" and "disowned" Hanna.[55] His self-accusations reach their zenith in response to the scene at the community pool, where Hanna puts in a brief and final appearance. Here, one must set aside the image of the svelte Kate Winslet from the film. The novel describes Hanna as a "powerful" and muscular 35-year-old (see Chapter 6). This stark difference in bodily appearance—between her and a pool full of lean teen-agers—can only intensify Berg's hesitation, thus mitigating his alleged offense against her.

He notices her from a distance, but in his shock at her unannounced presence in this unexpected setting, he simply cannot decide how to respond: "In dem kurzen Moment, in dem ich dabei meinen Blick von ihr ließ, ist sie gegangen."[56] (And in that briefest of moments in which I took my eyes off her, she was gone.)[57] His subsequent response reveals how he has internalized the blame that he had earlier recognized as being false, perhaps even coerced: "My body yearned for Hanna. But even worse than

my physical desire was my sense of guilt. Why hadn't I jumped up immediately when she stood there and run to her! This one moment summed
up all my halfheartedness of the past months, which had produced my
denial of her, and my betrayal. Leaving was her punishment."[58]

I think we are meant to see that, here, Berg is needlessly beating
himself up. Granted, he may indeed have felt a growing distance as he
began to explore—and desire—the company of friends his own age. Yet
must the fading of a first love strike us as particularly blameworthy, let
alone surprising? Why should it have produced such pronounced guilt
or, indeed, the strongly worded "betrayal" he confesses almost ritually?
Critics will rush in to explain that this is Berg's "subjective truth" of his
adolescence, and it must be respected as such. That is certainly true. But
what concerns me here is more the manner in which these self-flagellating
confessions are meant to be read *simultaneously* as both justified (precisely
as a statement of his subjective experience) and unjustified, namely as an
overassignment of guilt that therefore draws our attention to his deformation and suffering as a result of this problematic relationship. Schlink is
surely banking on this dual perspective.

Berg's (and possibly Schlink's) desire to restrict his account to the
protagonist's contemporaneous, teenage mind-set, and thus to highlight
his deep internalization of the guilt discourse, emerges clearly when we
reflect that the larger fictional memoir is a product of the 50-year-old
Berg reflecting back on his youth and young adulthood. He already
knows, as he relates this story of his agonizing "betrayal," that Hanna
had actually left town for fundamentally different reasons: she had been
offered a chance for a promotion at her job, but this would have required
some kind of written exam, and she was simply not prepared to allow her
illiteracy to come to light. Much later, in the context of his memories of
the trial, Berg writes, "Seltsam berührte mich die Diskrepanz zwischen
dem, was Hanna beim Verlassen meiner Heimatstadt beschäftigt haben
mußte, und dem, was ich mir damals vorgestellt und ausgemalt hatte. Ich
war sicher gewesen, sie vertrieben, weil verraten und verleugnet zu haben,
und tatsächlich hatte sie sich einfach einer Bloßstellung bei der Straßen-
bahn entzogen."[59] (I was oddly moved by the discrepancy between what
must have been Hanna's actual concerns when she left my hometown and
what I had imagined and theorized at the time. I had been sure that I had
driven her away because I had betrayed her and denied her, when in fact
she had simply been running away from being found out at the streetcar
company.)[60]

So, despite the fact that the entire fictional memoir is written in the
firm knowledge of Hanna's illiteracy, and notwithstanding the fact that

the temporal distance (some 35 years) is clearly, and even dramatically, marked in numerous places throughout the novel (and in particularly poignant ways at both the beginning and the end), our narrator-protagonist chooses to keep the real reasons for Hanna's departure secret from the reader for an extended period of time.[61] First-time readers, caught up in the suspense of the novel, tend not to notice the memoirist's perspectival and temporal shifts back and forth from—to borrow the language of film narratology—close-ups to long shots, as it were. Once recognized, this ploy can seem a bit manipulative or self-indulgent, even if we concede that it may be necessary to maintain a sense of narrative suspense up to the point of the disclosure of Hanna's illiteracy. But apart from these merely functional, narratological considerations, it is important to notice that this elastic memory perspective serves another function as well. It encourages, perhaps even requires, us to savor Berg's guilty feelings without having them prematurely undermined by an alternative explanation for the breakup. By delaying the revelation, Berg can have it both ways: we learn, long after the agonizing events themselves, that he was hardly to blame at all. Yet we also learn that he still *feels* guilty: "Allerdings änderte der Umstand, daß ich sie nicht vertrieben hatte, nichts daran, daß ich sie verraten hatte. Also blieb ich schuldig. Und wenn ich nicht schuldig war, weil der Verrat einer Verbrecherin nicht schuldig machen kann, war ich schuldig, weil ich eine Verbrecherin geliebt hatte."[62] (However, the fact that I had not driven her away did not change the fact that I had betrayed her. So I was still guilty. And if I was not guilty because one cannot be guilty of betraying a criminal, then I was guilty of having a loved a criminal).[63] If he cannot be guilty of Hanna's sudden departure from his hometown, then he will be guilty of something else. No revelation about her can alter this ironclad fact about him. In this sense, we might say that his "guilt" is indistinguishable from a religious conviction: it simply cannot be falsified. Clearly, Berg must have his guilt.

There is much that is of interest in this curiously durable assertion of ongoing guilt, in particular as it connects with broader statements about collective and second-generation guilt. Logical consistency is clearly not a priority, as his shift in self-accusation (first for having failed to acknowledge an older lover, later on, for having loved a criminal) is fully evident. We are simply not inclined to be too hard on him because, to the young Berg, she wasn't a criminal at all; and to the older law student and future lawyer—not to mention to the reader—she can only seem to be a "criminal" in a relatively limited sense.

More significant, though, is the manner in which Berg (and perhaps Schlink himself) offers this bimodal conception of guilt as a valid metaphor for grasping the larger situation of the so-called German "second generation." Semantically, his final avowal of "having loved a criminal" not only builds the bridge to the discourse on the plight of the second generation but also constitutes its core "argument." Recall that Berg seeks to establish himself as iconic of the second generation precisely through his relationship to Hanna. The principal difference, he claims, is that he could not distance himself from her so cavalierly, definitively, and self-righteously as many of his fellow students did from their parents. They made it too easy for themselves, he argues, by attempting to cover over their "Schuld und Scham"—"guilt and shame"—with "auftrumpfende Selbstgerechtigkeit"—"swaggering self-righteousness."[64] "War die Absetzung von den Eltern," he wonders (not without a modicum of self-righteousness), "nur Rhetorik, Geräusch, Lärm, die übertönen sollten, daß mit der Liebe zu den Eltern die Verstrickung in deren Schuld unwiderruflich eingetreten war?"[65] (Was their dissociation of themselves from their parents mere rhetoric: sounds and noise that were supposed to drown out the fact that their love for their parents made them irrevocably complicit in their crimes?).[66]

His fraught relationship with Hanna becomes an avatar of second-generational woes precisely because it exhibits the guilt and entrapment (*Verstrickung*) that some overzealous students sought to elide with their denunciatory fervor: "Wie sollte es ein Trost sein, daß mein Leiden an meiner Liebe zu Hanna in gewisser Weise das Schicksal meiner Generation, das deutsche Schicksal war, dem ich mich nur schlechter entziehen, das ich nur schlechter überspielen konnte als die anderen."[67] (How could it be a comfort that the pain I went through because of my love for Hanna was, in a way, the fate of my generation, a German fate, and that it was only more difficult for me to manage than for others).[68] In order to make this claim stick, Berg feels the need to make Hanna more of a criminal than almost any of the fathers whom his generation so eagerly and indiscriminately pilloried. Let us set aside, for the moment, the fact that this claim represents an internal contradiction in the novel (and not just for the reasons stated here). Instead, let us read *with* Berg in order to grasp how the guilt discourse that he has carefully developed over the course of the memoir is made to culminate in his epiphanic statement on the second generation's predicament:

Though he qualifies that last sentence with the word "but," Berg also encourages us to see this statement as a logical consequence of the foregoing. He has, of course, thought of Hanna as a mother figure, as we have seen, at various points. Indeed, he remembers two bath scenes in which Hanna and his mother are specifically juxtaposed. Moreover, the entire analogy he proposes here depends explicitly on us recognizing Hanna as not just any, but as a preeminent, representative of that "first" Nazi-era generation of adults. Given her status as parent figure, then, he ought not, by his own argument, feel very guilty: for "love of our parents is the only love for which we are not responsible." With this claim about second-generation guilt—one widely and approvingly commented upon in the criticism—Berg brings to culmination a process he began long ago: the practice of strongly asserting, while simultaneously undermining, his "guilt."

COLLECTIVE GUILT AND THE SECOND GENERATION

The ideological value of reiterating this trope of "guiltless guilt" can best be appreciated by placing it, as Berg explicitly does, within the context of the controversial notion of collective guilt: "Whatever validity the concept of collective guilt may or may not have, morally and legally," he declares, "for my generation of students it was a lived reality."[69] Berg is rightly dubious about the concept as a legitimate legal doctrine but insistent on its *punitive* effect upon the second generation. This unchosen but nevertheless "lived reality" thus takes on a life of its own—affecting his entire generational cohort, regardless of their actual moral or legal responsibility. Accordingly, this phenomenon begins to look a lot like Hanna's confessed guilt—that is, grossly out of proportion to any demonstrable wrongdoing and thus a sign, rather, of *injustice*: a classic Aphrodite moment.

Schlink the jurist is in fact known to take the notion of collective guilt quite seriously. In an essay entitled "Die Bewältigung von Vergangenheit durch Recht" (The Mastery of History through Law), he meditates on the "rational core" of this otherwise widely discredited notion of supra-individual guilt: "Solidarity with perpetrators entraps you in their crime and guilt—this is the rational core of the concept of collective guilt. Guilt is not passed along like an infection from the sick and guilty parts of society to the healthy ones, nor is it handed down from one generation to the next genetically. The concept of collective guilt can only sensibly mean that whenever a society practices solidarity with the perpetrators of crime, it thereby acquires a share in the criminals' guilt, and [accordingly] assumes responsibility with respect to the victims."[70]

While juridical guilt must be both specific and individual,[71] collective guilt results from the failure of a *community* to expel members guilty of an egregious crime: "Insofar as the perpetrators of the Third Reich were not banished, prosecuted, and condemned, but rather tolerated, respected, and allowed to retain their professional positions, thus advancing their careers, and were accepted as parents and teachers—[for all these reasons,] the generation of perpetrators and that of their children have become entrapped [together] in the crime and guilt of the Third Reich."[72]

This formulation of collective guilt, which Schlink elsewhere derives from ancient Germanic clan law,[73] is remarkably similar to the one we find in the novel (which is perhaps one more reason why readers, justly or not, tend to conflate author with narrator). Note the almost identical diction in Berg's rendition when he indicts his parents' generation for tolerating unrepentant, unprosecuted ex-Nazis in positions of leadership. Later he reprises and expands upon the guilt not of the actual Nazi perpetrators but of those who tolerated and promoted them in postwar Germany.

Up until this point, we encounter a fairly consistent presentation of the concept of collective guilt across juridical and novelistic discourses—or to put it otherwise, both the jurist Schlink and his fictional narrator are in agreement about what constitutes this kind of German guilt—the kind Ralph Giordano famously dubbed "die zweite Schuld" (the second guilt). But this is simultaneously the point where the two significantly diverge, for just as Berg indicts his parents' generation, he begins to turn these very accusations back upon himself. (This constitutes a large part of Berg's recantation of the student movement's "interrogation of the fathers," a topic I treat at some length in the next chapter.) We should note the self-lacerating, not quite convincing, effort to take upon himself a degree of guilt that he does not deserve. We are, of course, meant to see that Berg is being far too hard on himself. In what sense can he—then a hormonally driven adolescent of just 15—be said to have "chosen" Hanna? And even if he did so, what does this really have to do with tolerating ex-Nazis in positions of social and governmental power? Just as illiteracy is meant to establish Hanna as essentially "unmündig" (disenfranchised, not fully responsible), Berg is clearly introduced as a minor who cannot, in any meaningful sense, be held responsible for failing to expel ex-Nazis from civil society. Berg is not guilty of trying to talk himself into a position of innocence (as he accuses himself); on the contrary, he is, if anything, guilty of taking on a surfeit of guilt. Schlink the jurist surely understands this, as in one of the key legal writings we have already examined, he candidly asserts, "Children are not free to expel their parents, nor is the second generation in a position to isolate the first."[74] Berg becomes the poster boy for the nefarious effects of collective guilt as "erlebte Realität" (lived experience).

The Reader is ultimately designed to stage the tragic impossibility of collective guilt as an actionable charge with any substantial relevance to the second generation. Schlink concedes, "There could never have been a sufficient and consistent expulsion [of perpetrators], so that the guilt (or entrapment) contains an aspect of the unavoidable or, if you will, the tragic."[75] Guilt that is tragic and unavoidable—and this perhaps explains the Oedipal motif with Hanna as mother figure—is always already the attribute of a victim.[76] Berg emerges as the casualty of *fate*, in a plaintive formulation he has already employed to great effect.

Like many of his generational cohort, Berg's "guilt" therefore functions more as a code word for the deep mental and spiritual discomfort that derives from his close association with first-generation perpetrators and those who tolerated them after the war. It signifies the sense of being entangled (*verstrickt*) in a web of culpability that is not really of his own making. Simultaneously, however, it expresses the *unjust* imputation of collective guilt that accrues to him and his generation simply because of an accident of birth. In this sense, it expresses what historian Konrad Jarausch diagnoses as the postwar "misery of being German."[77] As he explains, "Though German identity had been badly damaged by the crimes of the Nazis, it did not disappear entirely but, rather, transformed its character into a 'community of fate' [Schicksalsgemeinschaft]. As a result of the Second World War, being German became an international stigma that had to be borne stoically and, at best, could be attenuated through good behavior."[78] A large part of this collective bond derived from a sense of shared victimhood.[79] Berg's ritually confessed, but fundamentally undeserved, guilt may serve as a powerful symbol for this sense of victimhood and thus explain the readiness with which second-generation German critics embraced him as their representative. Lurking just beneath the surface of this self-flagellating rhetoric of the repentant "perpetrator" is that of the misunderstood and much abused victim. In this sense, perhaps, Berg can be said to represent "das Schicksal meiner Generation, das deutsche Schicksal" (the fate of my generation, the German fate).[80]

"Confession," as Peter Brooks reminds us in his illuminating study *Troubling Confessions: Speaking Guilt in Law and Literature*, "has for centuries been regarded as the 'queen of proofs' in the law: it is a statement from the lips of the person who should know best."[81] Yet it is the false confession that brings most clearly to the fore the distinction between the constative and performative aspects of confession. It is the latter, at any rate, that seeks to alter the status quo. Brooks explains, "When one says 'Bless me Father, for I have sinned,' the constative meaning is: I have committed sins, while the performative meaning is: absolve me of my sin. The confessional performance of guilt always has this double aspect."[82] By drawing our attention to this second function of confession—the performative—Brooks helps us understand the overdetermined status of Berg's false confession. In accusing himself so relentlessly, he not only portrays himself as the victim of an indiscriminate and unjust notion of collective guilt, he simultaneously begins the process of reintegrating himself—and his generational cohort—within the international community. Secular modes of confession, no less than their religious antecedents, remain the royal road to reinstating membership within the community: "Confession alone will bring release from the situation of accusation and allow reintegration with normal social existence and community."[83]

Berg's rhetoric was never meant to be taken very seriously as "constative confession," but rather was meant to function in its performative dimension by helping to bring about a kind of reconciliation of the pariah status of second-generation Germans. Thus, Berg's anguish is meant not only to give voice to the "misery of being German" and its related "international stigma" but also to help overcome and heal them. In "Die Gegenwart der Vergangenheit" (The Presence of the Past) and elsewhere, Schlink notes the dilemma of second-generation Germans travelling abroad who have a Holocaust identity imposed upon them regardless of their personal efforts to confront the Nazi past.[84] This is clearly a broader phenomenon, as Christian Rogowski and others have commented upon with respect to their experience with Americans.[85] Berg's ritual confession of guilt can, from this perspective, be seen as the offering that is (or was) expected of Germans of that generation. It may contain an aspect of repressed resentment and obsequiousness, as he offers here the discursive tribute still expected by the Western Allies in the 1990s, and perhaps by the United States above all. In any case, by avoiding the indiscriminate accusatory gesture that brought his '68er cohorts into such disrepute, Berg deftly positions himself and his generational cohort for a far more sympathetic cultural reception, both at home and abroad. In this respect, *The Reader* represents the literary analogue par excellence to the wave of Holocaust commemoration that marked German public culture in the wake of unification, as Niven has persuasively documented.[86]

The final image we have of Berg is similar to the one he drew of Hanna as she exited the courtroom after her conviction—distraught, beleaguered, and burdened. Which raises the question, does Hanna somehow benefit, retrospectively, from the narrative campaign that insists on the subjective nature of guilt that may have no juridical objective correlative? Would it be implausible to theorize that conceptual patterns that were developed essentially to exonerate and reintegrate nominal perpetrators such as Berg might—somewhere in our undisciplined minds—come to include the first generation?

CHAPTER 4

FATHERS AND SONS

TWO KINDS OF SECOND-GENERATION VICTIMS

> Wir sind eine sehr selbstgerechte Generation gewesen—und geblieben . . .
> Mir ist es unheimlich, diese selbstgerechte moralische Eifer. (We were a
> very self-righteous generation—and still are. I find this holier-than-thou
> fervor bizarre.)
> —Bernhard Schlink, *Der Spiegel*, January 24, 2000.

OSTENSIBLY A NOVEL ABOUT THE HOLOCAUST, *THE Reader* is also a prominent and widely hailed narrative about the proper reception of '68. And it is an unmistakably revisionist message: there is no sense here of pride or accomplishment in having confronted the Nazi "fathers." Berg beats a hasty retreat, arguing first that the '68ers' accusations were largely overblown rhetoric that masked an unacknowledged, self-serving agenda. Even if some parents did deserve to be confronted, the second generation cannot really be credited with having done so: The iconic Michael Berg argues, in essence, that the children cannot be said to have failed to condemn the crimes of their parents, for this was an impossible task from the beginning. Yet Schlink never allows his narrator to accuse himself, or the generation he is said to represent, of anything but minor transgressions. For to be guilty of love, as we have seen, is to not be guilty at all. Indeed, this may be the whole point of revamping the image of the '68ers: as long as they are principally identified with shrill, indiscriminate, and moralizing accusations, they cannot qualify as victims worthy of sympathy. In moving them ever further away from the painful details of history and politics, and in portraying them instead as being enmeshed in timeless matters of love or psychological struggle, Schlink can be seen as hewing quite closely—though perhaps inadvertently—to the sometimes astonishingly ahistorical strategy of the student movement. In the remarkable

novella *Vati*, Peter Schneider also gives us a member of the second generation painfully bound by love (or the hunger for love) to a parental
perpetrator. But in this case, the details of Holocaust history cling so
tenaciously to the narrative—perhaps most especially when the son tries
to distance himself from them—that he cannot be remade into some
timeless victim of love or generational conflict. Instead of being ennobled
by the experience, or depicted as having mastered it (even partially), Schneider's second-generation son is truly tainted by his association with that
infamous first generation.[1]

An art-historical digression might illuminate the underlying point
I am making in this chapter regarding the depiction of victims. To
do so, I turn briefly to the well-known sixteenth-century painting by
Lucas Cranach the Elder known as "The Lamentation at the Foot of
the Cross."[2] Though undoubtedly *geschunden* (abused), as art historian
Rüdiger an der Heiden observes in his commentary,[3] Cranach's body
of Christ on the cross is simultaneously idealized. Despite the realistic
rivulets of blood, an ashen face, and punctured side, this Christ exhibits
an athletically buff body that somehow defies gravity. His upper torso
is muscular and well sculpted, his left arm extends powerfully into the
foreground, and the cloth that is typically meant merely to cover his
groin becomes, in Cranach's painting, an extravagant material flourish—
the fabric counterpart to the blast of a trumpet—that announces the
special status of this victim.[4] The thieves, in contrast, are truly ugly.
The "good thief" (i.e., the one who, according to the New Testament,
acknowledges that he deserves his punishment) hangs from the cross
in a manner that stretches and distorts his already unpleasant body. To
be sure, blood streams down his body no less than Christ's, but he is
pudgy, soft, and weak; he bears an unpleasant grimace on his pale face;
and his genitals are knotted in a tightly wrapped cloth that accentuates
his protruding potbelly.

In this contrasting depiction of the three figures of the crucifixion, Cranach is not particularly distinctive. But his remarkable painting provides a
strong visual reminder that some victims invite identification more than
others—usually as a result of carefully executed artistic cues. Of course
I have taken an extreme and temporally remote case to make this point:
Berg is no Christ figure, nor is he in any sense "crucified." Nevertheless,
"Die Klage unter dem Kreuz" should remind us of two ends of the spectrum that may be helpful in considering Schlink and Schneider. Some
victims are indeed drawn in a manner that brings out their *undeserved*
punishment, their implicit nobility, and even heroism, while others—like

the thief—are depicted as repulsive and grotesque in their very suffering, perhaps even because of it.

As hackneyed as the symbolism of the hand held out in an accusatory gesture undeniably may be (i.e., one finger extended in the direction of the accused; three necessarily pointing back at the accuser), it succinctly captures the novel's agenda—namely, to refocus the reader's attention on Berg. It contains *in nuce* the novel's essentially antipolitical strategy or, rather, its use of politics as a vehicle for characterizing the beleaguered protagonist. As noted in Chapter 3, the "guilt" of which Berg speaks is not in any sense juridical; it is not a matter of actual responsibility for criminal behavior but rather a vague and painful sense of entrapment in the previous generation's sins. Whereas Berg speaks eloquently of the debilitating effect of this relationship, his successful career ultimately belies—or at least handily overcomes—most of these wounds. In the current culture of competing victimhood, Berg is the kind of victim one would most like to be, if a victim one must be.[5]

On the other hand, Peter Schneider's fictional Rolf Mengele is an unqualified loser who is truly warped and damaged by his unfortunate parentage. "For Schneider's critics," Birgit Jensen rightly observes, "the protagonist's profound lack of heroism generates only moral indignation."[6] Indeed, the initial journalistic reception of each work reflects, in the main, the critics' reaction to the respective narrators. The critical failure of Schneider's story may have begun, as Peter Morgan observes, with spectacular charges of plagiarism against the author, but it was sustained by a deep dislike of the narrator, who in turn was persistently and uncritically identified with the author and the work itself.[7] Conversely, the overwhelming critical success of *The Reader* must at least in part be attributed to Michael Berg's noted congeniality, his "usefulness" as a generational spokesman, and the maturing '68ers' need for a more respectable past. While the fate of each work appears to be strongly inflected by "extraliterary concerns,"[8] the texts themselves are clearly implicated as well. Schneider achieves a more meaningful treatment of the second generation's ambivalence toward its perpetrator parents because, paradoxically, his fiction rests so firmly on the facts of history, whereas Schlink's novel not only evades specific Holocaust crimes but also provides a series of rather effective alibis for doing so. Both works offer strong criticism of the '68ers' wholesale indictment of their parents' generation. But in the case of Schlink, as we shall see in this discussion, this apparent revisionism proves somewhat of a red herring.

Jeremy Adler's polemical letter in the March 22, 2002, edition of *The Times Literary Supplement* was the first substantial attack on *The Reader* in a European mass-circulation venue. It created only a brief stir in England, but in the German press, it inaugurated a reconsideration of the merits of the novel, with Adler's piece being published in expanded format and offered as an encouragement to further reassessments, which quickly followed (e.g., Norfolk). Literary critics and specialists, however, will know that the real debate dates to the 1997 U.S. publication of the novel, when Cynthia Ozick, Eva Hoffmann, and, somewhat later, Omer Bartov voiced strongly dissenting views. Though all three may have agreed with Adler's charge of *Kulturpornographie*, their central objection focused on the way in which Hanna's illiteracy functions as a spurious alibi, with Bartov also pointing to the novel's studied avoidance of Jewish suffering[9] Assessing the recent *contretemps*, Ulrich Baron strikes a curiously defensive, if not cynical, pose, suggesting that Adler and company simply envy Schlink his "global success" (*Welterfolg*); that the episode merely proves the effeteness of literary criticism in the face of an overwhelming media success; and finally, that the real motive behind the efforts of the *Süddeutsche Zeitung* (where Adler's piece appeared in German) and *Der Spiegel* was essentially commercial. They are alleged to have created—or worse, "imported"—a controversy merely for the purpose of increasing their sales. The novel's contribution to *Vergangenheitsbewältigung* (Mastering the Nazi past), Baron argues, will survive all recent attacks. "Essentially," he maintains, "Schlink's novel is about the simple fact that you can't just disavow somebody you once loved in your youth after it becomes clear that that somebody is a criminal. In such a situation, a shift in perspective comes about that is indeed in favor of the perpetrator."[10]

This may well be true, yet it only raises the question of how this "shift in perspective" actually comes about, especially since such a move "in favor of the perpetrators" will ultimately be deployed to remake the second generation in the oddly idealized image of Berg himself. Baron is surely right to emphasize the close relationship between the two; although, as I will argue, it is not only the love of the children that results in a more positive view of the perpetrators, it is also the reverse: the more positive depiction of the perpetrators allows the children themselves to appear in a substantially more positive light. This point emerges from a comparison between two fictional members of the German "second generation": Schlink's Michael Berg and Schneider's "son" from the novella *Vati*.

The love that children have for their perpetrator parents presents a fascinating narrative premise, and one that both Schlink and Schneider have pursued for its potential to speak to larger generational issues. Yet it is only intriguing insofar as both terms are fully valid. Children who have thoroughly repudiated their parents (and thus cannot be said to love them anymore) make for a less interesting story, while those who remain emotionally connected to parents (or parental figures) who are not in any clear sense perpetrators prove dissatisfying as well, at least as a topic for literature. Schlink's novel, as I have argued, falls into this latter category: Hanna is undoubtedly placed at the scene of several crimes, but in each case, her disadvantaged status as a lower-class, illiterate person tends to relieve her of any specific responsibility.[11]

Berg learns of her handicap in time to make a difference in the trial's outcome, but he does not tell anyone. To understand how this sequence of events effectively vacates the novel's premise, we must see how Berg's reticence becomes coded as a badge of noble anguish—a hallmark of his impossible predicament—rather than as a failing that substantively contributes to the breakdown of justice. As a result of Berg's vacillation, the fraudulent SS report on the night of the church fire retains its legitimacy in the eyes of the court, the other defendants remain secure in their counterfeit alibi, and no discovery is made about who actually had the "last clear chance" to liberate the church's inmates. In other words, the discovery of criminal responsibility, which is the court's only real task, remains utterly thwarted.

This is made possible—and respectable—in part by the novel's selective reading of Kantian moral philosophy on the inviolability of the individual. If Berg is to do anything with his discovery, he should, of course, speak to Hanna herself. But this he simply cannot bring himself to do. The second best option would be to reveal this crucial fact to the presiding judge, but this would violate *her* right to privacy and, more importantly, her autonomy. He learns all this by consulting with his philosopher father, who reminds his son that he—Berg—would not have liked others intervening on his behalf just because they were convinced of the truth of their position. Berg gets as far as an actual meeting with the judge. But the conversation never goes beyond pleasantries and what the judge, in his vanity, assumes is an occasion to offer the young law student some career advice. Berg's failure thus becomes secondary to that of the representatives of the first generation—the father and the judge—who almost intentionally seem to misconceive the issue. The father senses that he has not answered his son's real question, but he does not pursue the matter. He is quite content to leave the matter as an abstract moral dilemma. In fact, he dismisses his son without ever having learned what prompted the visit. And the judge is no better.

But even though he clearly is a flawed human being (and he is unmistakably depicted as being distant and feckless), Berg's father inadvertently offers a rationale for halting what should be the trial's unrelenting search for truth. "We are not talking about happiness," Berg's philosopher father advises, "we're talking about dignity and freedom."[12] So although Berg failed to raise the issue with anyone (until years later when he speaks to the surviving Jewish witness about Hanna's illiteracy), we are still invited, with the blessing of no less a personage than Kant himself, to focus on Hanna as the proper object of our philosophical and ethical concern. It is clearly her "worth and freedom" that are at issue here. As Schlink himself has explained on numerous occasions, when asked about his hero's "moral dilemma," Kant is being invoked to ostensibly protect Hanna from the intrusion of would-be do-gooders, such as Berg and his cogenerational-ists. This argument does not, of course, absolve Hanna but instead enjoins others from intervening on her behalf. If she chooses not to reveal her illiteracy, then she will have brought the unjust sentence—life in prison for her, versus four-and-a-half-year terms for the other guards—upon herself. From the Kantian standpoint (as it is here presented and, as we shall see, later reprised), it is more important to preserve her autonomy than to enforce the truth. Berg's failure to intervene can thus be seen as a sign of respect, despite its fateful consequences for Hanna. Indeed, Hanna's stubborn refusal to reveal her illiteracy becomes, in this manner, associated with freely chosen self-punishment—with expiation, dispro-portionate punishment, even self-sacrifice. Hanna clearly knows that she is inculpating herself and that she could get a better deal if she were to admit her illiteracy. Hanna becomes a scapegoat and Berg, a bit of hero.

The citation of Kant, even by such a weak figure as Berg's father, thus triggers a chain of hermeneutic moves that ultimately upgrades both Berg and Hanna via a process that is mutually beneficial. By respecting Hanna as an autonomous agent, and specifically by not treating her as a means to an end, Berg simultaneously fulfills a Kantian imperative (the injunction against instrumentalizing autonomous subjects) *and* inhibits prosecutors from probing beneath the defendants' web of excuses and lies. Yet what if Berg, in his quest for moral guidance, had instead turned to a philosopher other than Kant, say, to John Stuart Mill and his famous "harm principle"?[13] Would he not then have been required to cast his net beyond the autono-mous subject and consider the *social* good? Mill's calculus—to take just one alternate ethical model—would have demanded that Berg conduct himself in a manner that takes into account the welfare of other concerned par-ties, such as the survivors of that horrible fire as well as all others dedicated to uncovering the truth. But this is a road not taken. On the contrary, in this regard, the novel focuses exclusively on the perpetrators, making them principally responsible for accusing themselves. In this way, it declares the second generation not only not responsible but also morally enjoined *not* to intervene. Elsewhere, Berg will confront the "'68er" agenda to confront the "sins of the fathers" rather directly. Here, the message is already implicit but no less clear: the effort itself is unwarranted.

Lest we see Hanna in too culpable a light, Berg reminds us in a key passage proximate to the second repudiation of the '68ers: "Illiteracy is dependence" (Analphabetismus ist Unmündigkeit)[14]; and, as we well know, "Unmündigkeit" (better translated as being under age or a minor) is the juridical condition *par excellence* for vacating responsibility and punishment. Not until she attains literacy does Hanna become "mündig," as the heavy-handed reference to Kant's *Antwort auf die Frage, Was ist Aufklärung* (answer to the question, What is Enlightenment?)[15] makes clear: "By finding the courage to learn to read and write, Hanna took a step from childhood into adulthood, a step towards enlightenment."[16] The Kantian reference at this juncture analeptically reinforces the earlier one, whose principal message was to remove the task of confronting the Nazi past from the shoulders of the second generation.

In order to burnish Berg's credentials as a victim worthy of our pity, and perhaps even our admiration, it is necessary both to dissociate him from the extremes of '68er rhetoric (those harsh and all-encompassing denunciations of the Nazi "fathers") *and* to dilute our apprehension of the Nazis' crimes. Before turning our attention to the novel's explicit thematization of '68, let us examine another strategy the novel employs to distance its chief perpetrator from concrete acts of criminality. This time it has nothing to do with Berg's action or inaction but rather with the novel's very selective deployment of a crucial historical "intertext": the real-life trial of the notorious female guard Hermine Ryan née Braunsteiner.

A brief consideration of a teaching manual that has been developed for the German *Gymnasium* can demonstrate this point. Greese and Peren-Eckert open their book with the observation, "*The Reader* appears to be one of the few novels of contemporary letters to have established itself within the canon of college preparatory schools."[17] They go on to justify their interest in this work specifically on the basis of its treatment of history: "The relevance of this novel from the point of view of history lies in its treatment of central second-generational questions about the Nazi period. Students become concretely aware of questions of guilt, responsibility, coming to terms with the Nazi past—as well as the matter of becoming entrapped in criminal circumstances, albeit in an 'innocently guilty' [schuldlos schuldig] manner."[18] Following an extensive section on illiteracy, which acquaints students with the seriousness and scope of this disability, the authors turn their attention to the question of Hanna as a "historical" figure, and here they are immediately faced with a dilemma.

On the one hand, their endorsement of the novel as a work that helps young Germans confront the Nazi past clearly depends on Hanna's "historicity." They are, to put it bluntly, concerned that students view her as "definitely real" (durchaus real)[19] and, to this end, provide extensive historical documentation in their appendix, including a fairly thorough report on the so-called Mare of Maidanek (Stute von Majdanek). In comparing the real-life Nazi career of Hermine Ryan—who, after the longest trial ever held in Germany, was condemned to life in prison—with that of fictional Hanna Schmitz, students will discover unmistakable parallels: "In this manner it becomes clear," the authors aver, "that the perpetrator type exhibited in Hanna possesses analogies to the real world. Indeed, it is representative of many actual careers, even if there is no direct inspiration for Hanna."[20] If Germans know anything about real-life women camp guards, their source would most likely be the protracted Majdanek War Crimes Trial of 1975 through 1981, the first and only time female camp personnel were tried in a German court. The most notorious among all defendants was, beyond doubt, Hermine Braunsteiner, as she was known prior to her marriage to the American Russel Ryan. She was convicted of murder in a verdict that left no doubt about her personal responsibility. Judge Günter Bogen specified that she had "contributed, eagerly and for egotistical reasons, to the command of murder. Her contribution renders her responsible for murder."[21] While Schlink does not speak of specific historical models, he has affirmed in an interview that in preparing the novel "he researched and read what little there was to read about women as guards in concentration camps."[22] Our jurist-author, who has written insightfully on collective guilt and the concept of crimes against humanity,[23] was surely intimately familiar with the Majdanek War Crimes Trial.

Pedagogues are right to suggest that some German readers will immediately note stunning parallels between historical fact and Schlink's fiction. Not unlike Hanna, Braunsteiner-Ryan famously challenged the court's right to judge her. As the *Süddeutsche Zeitung* put it, "In the end, she turns the spear [Spiess] around and accuses the court: 'What do you know, gentlemen, what do the others in this courtroom, know about us?'"[24] This echoes—and perhaps directly inspired—Hanna's famous query of the presiding judge ("What would you have done?"), an exchange the novel asserts that she wins. While Hanna can implicitly claim ignorance due to her illiteracy and underprivileged background, Ryan does so explicitly, citing her tender age of 19 and her subordinate position within the camp hierarchy.[25] As noted on several occasions, reminders of Hanna's lower position in the camp-guard hierarchy also serve to inhibit any definite attribution of guilt with regard to key charges. Very much like the fictional

Hanna, Ryan ultimately admits that she is guilty in some kind of general way—just not *that* guilty: "I bear some guilt, but I am no murderer."[26] Compare this to Berg's formulation of Hanna's amorphously lesser degree of responsibility: "I could go to the chief judge and tell him that Hanna was . . . guilty, but not as guilty as it appeared."[27] (Hanna actually serves a few years longer than her historical counterpart, since Braunsteiner-Ryan was released from prison after having served the 15-year sentence imposed on her by the court.) Bundespräsident Johannes Rau's grant of clemency in April of 1996—almost simultaneously with the release of the novel—could not but promote the association of these two "figures," though this is, of course, something that Schlink could not have known, however much it will have colored the novel's reception in Germany. The novel's internal cue regarding their "equivalence" is, of course, Berg's perception of Hanna as "Pferd," a transparent evocation of Ryan's notorious nickname "die Stute."[28] So to see Hanna and be reminded of Hermine is eminently plausible but equally problematic.

The historical intertext may register to the casual reader, but the pedagogues who recommend that their students deliberately reacquaint themselves with the Majdanek trial realize, to their credit, that the comparison quickly breaks down. Ryan was, after all, notorious for ripping children from their mothers' arms, beating them and other prisoners bloody with a riding whip or kicking them with steel-capped boots for the slightest infraction, and murdering them, in addition to other specific crimes. In providing guidance to fellow teachers, Greese and Peren-Eckert offer one of the most perceptive statements regarding the novel's characterization of Hanna that I know of: "In this way [i.e., by comparing the historical person to the fictional one], it should become clear that the trial report contains concrete descriptions of the crimes committed by Hermine Braunsteiner (for example, she is said to have bludgeoned children to death with a heavy soup ladle), whereas the novel provides none of this kind of damning detail. The novel aims to keep the majority of Hanna's concentration camp past in the dark. Hanna is accused of taking part in selections. What this actually means is never specified."[29] Indeed, it is not.

The language employed in discussing Braunsteiner-Ryan's criminal actions is perhaps worthy of note: the subjunctive tense is used ("Sie *habe* Kinder mit Schöpfkellen *totgeschlagen*"), which represents indirect speech, and is conventionally used in the German-language media to render news reports that may not yet be substantiated. In literary terms, of course, this is a distancing mechanism, equivalent in English to "she is said to have *beaten* children *to death* with soup ladels," and is surely a curious way in which to speak about the actions of a convicted felon.

While justifiable on formal grounds (it is, after all, "reported speech," insofar as the authors did not themselves render the verdict), this use of the subjunctive represents a divergence from American and British usage, where phrases of caution (such as "allegedly" or "putatively") fall away once a formal verdict has been rendered in a court of law. We thus sense in this word choice an insecurity about the analogy even before the authors overtly retreat from the equation of Hanna and Hermine. The authors' uncertainty extends, tellingly, to Hanna. First they say that a large part of her concentration camp past ("ein Großteil der Lagervergangenheit Hannas") remains shrouded in darkness. Does this mean that she indeed committed similar crimes and is, in this sense, comparable to Braunsteiner-Ryan? Is the only difference that Ryan's guilt has been demonstrated in court, while Hanna's remains unspecified, in part because her ex-lover withheld a crucial secret? That is one clear implication. They hedge their bets, averring simultaneously that Hanna's actual role in the "selections" is only alleged ("Hanna wird vorgeworfen . . ." [Hanna is accused . . .]) and yet pointedly unspecified. In shifting back and forth between these options, they follow the novel's strategy, in which the *court* convicts her (even "over-convicts" her), while the larger *novel* does not. In other words, they embrace the novel's great "sowohl-als-auch" hermeneutical strategy—wanting to have it both ways.

What they cannot get around is the fact that Hanna appears much more benign than Hermine. The teachers resolve this problem in a time-honored manner, namely by ending the lesson abruptly, citing an "expert," apparently with the intention of wrapping things up definitively. We learn that parallels are lacking in other respects as well: Hermine Ryan never experienced a "Konversion" (as Hanna does in prison), nor did she designate any survivors as her legal heirs. Now clearly backpedaling, they conclude, "Thus her [final] insight as well as her bequest [to the surviving Jew] are to be understood in light of literature's utopian potential."[30] This is a very fine privilege to invoke on behalf of literature, but what is the value of the historical allusion in the first place if it is to be broken off at will and replaced with utopian fantasy? The discussion is halted just where it needs to begin in earnest. What is the role of this "utopian potential" when it comes to Holocaust literature? Is the very novel that was lauded for its historical realism now to be seen as wish fulfillment? Can one convincingly appeal to utopian motives just at this highly problematic juncture, or should we not consider the novel as a whole—indeed, the entire characterization of Hanna—as a product of this rosy perspective?

At any rate, we now better understand how Schlink has humanized his "monster." But it is difficult to take seriously, since the teachers' own lesson draws our attention to the manner in which he carefully obscures the kind of specific and personal responsibility that led to the Majdanek convictions. Interestingly, the state's attorney who prosecuted Hermine Ryan, Dieter Ambach, notes the challenge of seeing the nine defendants as fellow human beings. To him, they were in fact "monsters. I had the greatest difficulty seeing them as normal human beings."[31] One does not solve this compelling problem, however, by concealing the crimes. The challenge of seeing both aspects synoptically—the horrific crimes as well as the vulnerable and somehow loveable human being—is daunting, to be sure, but not impossible, as can be gleaned from Tim Robbins' unsettling film *Dead Man Walking* (1995), in which a searching and sympathetic portrayal of the protagonist (played by Sean Penn) succeeds despite the onscreen depiction of his brutal murder of a young couple.[32] One could also point to certain episodes in the acclaimed HBO television series *The Sopranos* (in which brutal mafia thugs are simultaneously portrayed as loving family men) and of course to Schneider's *Vati*.[33]

One might wish to see Greese and Peren-Eckert's teaching guide as peripheral in its emphasis, perhaps as a mere aberration. But that is not possible for two reasons. First, the general view that *The Reader* provides an appropriate vehicle for discussing recent history ("Zeitgeschichte") is widely held (and not just by teachers), as reflected in the following assertion by an interviewer for *Der Spiegel*: "Perhaps your book has become such a staple in German schools because it can serve as a suitable introduction to an entire nexus of topics, [i.e.] the Holocaust."[34] Second, of the circa one dozen teachers' manuals on the market, all prominently feature the "Holocaust theme"[35] and view Hanna as an exemplary perpetrator. At least five of these explicitly reference Hanna in connection with Hermine Braunsteiner.[36] Köster, furthermore, candidly identifies "justice for the perpetrators" (Gerechtigkeit für die Täter) as one of the novel's chief selling points,[37] and recommends the book in part because its principal concern with the second generation will, he thinks, alleviate the students' need to defend their grandparents.[38] In a larger sense, all of these teaching guides, with their often extensive historical apparatus, share the same fundamental problem: they claim to be providing background information to a novel that gestures toward, but actually shuns, concrete historical detail.[39]

The German student movement that would later become known by the loosely fitting epithet "the '68ers" understood well that soothing fictional constructs could not replace the work of honestly facing the past.

And yet, while denouncing "the crimes of the fathers" was one of the three main pillars of the movement's agenda (the other two being the reform of the authoritarian university system and protest against the American prosecution of the Vietnam War), the '68ers were themselves not averse to playing fast and loose with history.[40] Indeed, one of the most regrettable legacies of the student movement's rhetoric has been its rather free-floating use of the term "fascist" (or, more commonly, "faschistoid") to designate not only the Nazi period but also the United States in its purported "genocide" in Vietnam, as well as almost any aspect of the German establishment to which they happened to object at the moment.

As early as 1961, Ulrike Meinhof sought to characterize the politics of Christian Social Union leader Franz Josef Strauß by comparing him with Adolf Hitler;[41] and with that, the die was cast. For the student leftists, *Gegenwartsbewältigung* (coming to terms with the *present*) would become tantamount to Vergangenheitsbewältigung and vice versa. Following the shooting of protester Benno Ohnesorg in 1967, "students identified themselves," writes historian Belinda Davis, "as a persecuted minority—like Jewish Germans in the Third Reich."[42] The comparison attained a measure of intellectual respectability when Oskar Negt, then a prominent student of Jürgen Habermas, "wrote in the New Left paper *Neue Kritik* a lengthy description of the treatment of Jews under the Third Reich with pointed reference to the contemporary treatment of student protesters."[43] The Berlin underground newspaper *Linkeck* repeatedly published photos of emaciated concentration camp inmates in a context (the Emergency Laws of 1968) that openly sought to equate victims of the Nazis with the student protesters of the day (see Figure 4.1).[44] Rolf Tiedemann (who would go on to edit the works of Walter Benjamin) characterized the government's tactics against students as a "pogrom," while Gudrun Ensslin, future leader of the *Rote Armee Fraktion*, explained the police shooting of Ohnesorg in this manner: "This is the Auschwitz generation and there is no arguing with them."[45]

To what extent Germany's Nazi past served as a legitimate lens through which to view the Federal Republic of the 1960s and 1970s, as opposed to simply offering a ready-made reservoir for incendiary rhetoric, is probably an irresolvable question, certainly one on which historians have yet to achieve a consensus. We can be certain, however, that forces on the Right were at least as willing to indulge in this practice. Segments of the press branded Rudi Dutschke, leader of the SDS (Sozialistischer Deutscher Studentenbund, or the Socialist Student Party), a "little Hitler" and "Führer" of the movement; and when more than a thousand students marched on the Springer Verlag to decry the shooting of Rudi Dutschke

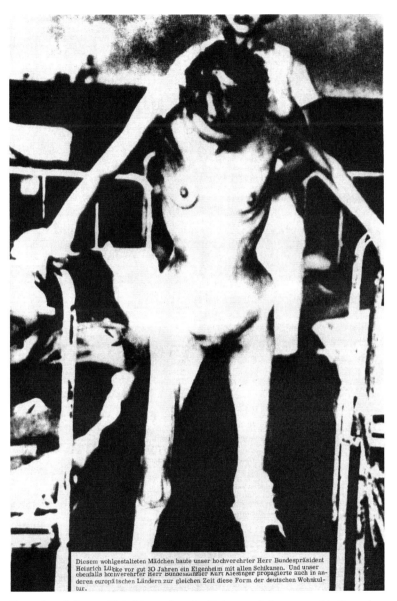

Figure 4.1   Infamous *Linkeck* image featuring Holocaust victim as a stand-in for student victims of police brutality in 1968.

The German caption reads: A good thirty years ago, our highly esteemed President Heinrich Lübke, with all manner of chicanery, built this shapely girl a home of her own. And at the same time our no less highly esteemed federal chancellor, Mr. Kurt Kiesinger, spread this kind of German home decor throughout other European countries as well.

by a reader of *Bild-Zeitung*, the newspaper *Welt am Sonntag* compared the protest, in which students overturned cars in order to block the departure of delivery trucks, to the infamous Nazi book burning of May 10, 1933.[46] Later on, members of the Red Army Faction would explain the 1972 bombing of the U.S. Army base in Heidelberg with the assertion that current German security forces reminded them of "American imperialism, Auschwitz, Dresden, and Hamburg."[47] Across the spectrum we note a hyperbolically ahistorical approach to Nazism and the Holocaust as well as a specious identification with Jewish victims. Schlink's retrospective memoirist has harsh words for the student movement, in which he played a minor role. Is it this questionable appropriation of Jewish suffering that Michael Berg repudiates in *The Reader*? Does he object to the distortion of history? Hardly—in fact, Berg, whose repudiation of '68er activism has been widely lauded in the German press, dehistoricizes the student movement even further by reducing the students' vehement denunciation of their perpetrator-parents to a timeless psychological struggle between generations, one in which National Socialism is merely the incidental catalyst to perennial youthful rebellion.[48]

This radical detachment from German *Zeitgeschichte* ("contemporary history"should be seen as a way of insulating the second generation, retrospectively, from those uglier aspects of *Vergangenheitsbewältigung*, the ones that reflect poorly on the overeager, indiscriminate accuser. Those three fingers that inevitably point back to the accuser—to return to one of Berg's favorite images—become, in this manner, "unbent." One critic is so eager to join Berg in reducing the '68ers to a mere psychological dependency on group identification that he equates the postwar student radicals to youthful members of the Nazi SA; the same youthful rebellion, he claims, explains both movements.[49] While unconvincing, Moers's reading does reflect the novel's ahistorical cues.[50] One of the most obvious of these comes from Berg directly, as he muses, "Sometimes I think that dealing with the Nazi past was not the reason for the generational conflict that drove the student movement, but merely for the form it took. Parental expectations, from which every generation must free itself, were nullified by the fact that these parents had failed to measure up during the Third Reich, or after it ended."[51] Berg acknowledges that for some children of the second generation, the National Socialist past was indeed a real problem. But even then, it is treated, above all, as a *psychological* problem. Accusing the fathers, no matter how good it might feel in the short term, does not really solve the problem. "Pointing at the guilty parties did not free us from shame," he observes, while "coming to grips with our parents' guilt took a great deal of energy."[52] This is indeed how he would most like to portray the conflict—as an intergenerational emotional struggle: "Was their dissociation of themselves from their parents mere rhetoric: sounds and noise that were supposed to drown out the fact that their love for their parents made them irrevocably complicit in their crimes?"[53]

As long as the '68ers were characterized as fanatical, self-righteous, and arrogant,[54] it was impossible to accept them as proper victims worthy of our concern, pity, and admiration. The image of the angry accuser must therefore yield to a pervasive sense of *Verstrickung*, which of course does not quite translate as "complicity" (though Carol Brown Janeway has rendered it just that way for the English edition) but as "entrapment" or "entanglement." Feeling trapped by their parent's guilt is not, of course, the same thing as self-incurred guilt, as second-generation Germans must surely sense. This much-commented-upon anti-'68er invective, thus, surely has less to do with '68 itself than with establishing the "victim" credentials of the novel's real focus group. It constitutes the novel's main contribution to burnishing the image of the second generation.

Berg closes the circle of his revisionist take on the student movement by mobilizing Hanna in defense of "first generation" parents whose guilt remains unclear. Of course the point is not to intervene at any "real" historical or juridical level. I do not argue that Berg (or, for that matter, Schlink) attempts to distort any actual Holocaust criminality. Yet the deployment of Hanna as a stand-in for an unstated number of first-generation fathers does further the agenda of polishing the image of the second generation. Indeed, by emphasizing the relative innocence of all those fathers he just happens to know, Berg effectively reduces the need for accusing them in the first place. The argument that demonstrates this contention may seem somewhat convoluted, but there is a payoff.

Schlink's novel can even be said to take the form of a kind of proof in which the "thesis" (the initial indictment of the '68ers) occurs at the outset of the trial,[55] while the "conclusion" (the "dehistoricizing" passage discussed earlier)[56] emerges after Hanna's "guilt" has been elaborately qualified and obfuscated. Having drawn her to resemble the notorious "Stute von Majdanek" in virtually every respect *except* for the latter's spectacular guilt, Schlink can now deploy Hanna to buffer a whole class of parents whose crimes, whatever they might have been, must pale in comparison: "But what other people in my social environment had done, and their guilt, were in any case a lot less bad than what Hanna had done."[57] The logic of this passage, if one can speak in this manner, is once again to annul, or at least set aside, the juridical meaning of guilt. The "unburdened" Hanna makes others look good by comparison. How does this work?

One of these "others," indeed the only first-generation representative from Berg's "social environment" whom we get to know besides Hanna, is of course his own father. The elder Berg comes across as detached in the interaction described here (i.e., when his son seeks "philosophical" advice regarding his duty to disclose the secret of Hanna's illiteracy). Yet let us not forget that he was somewhat of a resister during the Nazi period: he persisted in lecturing on Spinoza, despite a clear proscription by Nazi authorities, thereby putting himself and his family at some risk. And he paid the price of his disobedience: he was forced out of the university and reduced to eking out a meager living at a small press specializing in tourist books and maps. The novel avoids making him a hero precisely by casting him as a less than exemplary father and family man, and as an aloof professor, distant from real-world concerns. Yet true to its "sowohl-als-auch" strategy, the novel simultaneously establishes him as a fundamentally good man, one who, in a small but not insignificant way, stood his ground. Now, in the postwar period, he may well belong to the group that, through their inaction and indifference, tolerated the rehabilitated ex-Nazis in their midst. But this is a different order of responsibility entirely; it constitutes a "sin of omission," so to speak, rather than one of commission. And as we noted in Chapter 3, it is, at any rate (according to Schlink), both somewhat unavoidable and tragic.

By highlighting a particular kind of postwar *parental* guilt for tolerating ex-Nazi perpetrators in their midst, the novel thus completes its refiguration of the *second* generation. It is no longer just a matter of requiring the first generation to face up to its own responsibility (as the Kantian intertext suggested earlier), nor is it exclusively a matter of retracting ill-considered and overbroad indictments (as Berg persuasively argues). Rather, by spotlighting this first-generation failure, incurred in the aftermath of the war, the novel effectively alters the terms of *Vergangenheitsbewältigung*: it has itself taken on the role of identifying the "real" failing and has, in this respect, become the chief complainant in lieu of the student plaintiffs. Schlink localizes the duty of accusation neither within literature in general nor within a particular genre (e.g., the infamous *Väterliteratur*), but rather within this single novel. In this sense, it retroactively renders obsolete those activist '68ers who felt it was incumbent upon them to accuse their Nazi fathers. Having the object of their ire refashioned into relatively benign fellow travelers—guilty of crimes that at worst were "allemal weniger schlimm" than whatever Hanna did—the second generation is now free, so to speak, to be remolded into a more sympathetic image. They have been released *ex post facto* from their unflattering role as blanket denunciators—"the swaggering self-righteousness I so often encountered among these students."[58]

In drawing attention to this ideological strand of the novel, I have admittedly flushed out into the open aspects that might otherwise blend into the narrative background. Indeed, in using such rationalist metaphors as the novel's "argument," I refer to rhetorical devices that may seem quite foreign—and perhaps objectionable—to readers of prose fiction. Of course one could protest that the novel never really "says" that Berg's father is to be taken as "exhibit A" with respect to first-generation culpability; it is indisputably true that novels rarely operate in this way. Not only does the novel not "argue" in this explicit manner, it certainly does not do so in absolutes. There are, after all, other first-generation "father" figures to be found in the novel, including at least one who appears to have been a hands-on Holocaust perpetrator: I refer to the sinister driver who conveys Berg part of the way to the Strutthof-Natzweiler concentration camp.

But neither does *The Reader* purport to tell an idiosyncratic story of random experience. Berg (and, in his way, Schlink) wants to speak for his generation; and to the extent that he succeeds in doing so, we cannot take lightly his conclusions about either the fathers or the sons. He bases his claim to represent the second generation on the proposition that the intensity of his relationship with Hanna reveals a problem common to others of his nation and generation, but one not as obvious: it is "in a way the fate of my generation, the German fate."[59] Echoing the epiphany that Hanna will experience in prison, Berg's pain and suffering yield a blinding insight into the structural dilemma of his generation. He is not ultimately crippled, but instead is illuminated, by his experience. In this way, Hanna ends by becoming a credential, the basis for his distinctive, yet simultaneously *representative*, status. Hanna, who stands for the first generation, has deeply wounded him, leaving him scarred well into adulthood. But she provides the prerequisite to his quiet heroism—she supplies the necessary *agon* to his *Bildungsroman*.

Peter Schneider is perhaps Germany's best known surviving '68er, at least in the United States. Almost from the time of his own youthful activism, he has taken an increasingly critical view of the student movement. Thus, it is perhaps not surprising to discover that in his novella *Vati*, the protagonist son similarly confesses to an improbable kind of guilt by association and that he, too, takes his cogenerational comrades to task for an all-too-glib indictment of their fathers. But unlike Berg, the young Mengele never garners our respect, admiration, or confidence; instead, he appears to evoke outrage, bafflement, and only intermittent moments of sympathy. First of all, unlike Berg, this narrator cannot even produce a coherent narrative that will easily please the reader. Instead, this maddeningly meandering story takes the form of a kind of letter addressed to an unspecified boyhood friend who, after a long hiatus, registers renewed interest in Rolf (Mengele's son) once the sensational news of the elder Mengele's death has broken. In *Vati*, the son attempts to explain why he went to visit his infamous father and what he did while there. Like the narrator of Thomas Mann's *Mario und der Zauberer*, who seeks to justify why he remained in Torre di Venere long after the abusive nature of Cipolla's performance had become abundantly clear to him, he succeeds only in further implicating himself. Though obviously writing this with the benefit of hindsight (at several key points we are reminded of the temporal distance between the time of narration and the narrated events), Rolf Mengele appears to benefit little from this gift of time. His conclusions seem doubtful, and his intentions are nothing if not contradictory. It is not clear that his "friend"—the recipient of this missive—really likes him or whether his recent interest is simply prurient and voyeuristic. In this sense, the "friend" may provide an image of the implied reader—encouraging us to see not only the son but also ourselves as problematic in our response to Holocaust atrocities.[60]

Whereas Greese and Peren-Eckert can outline a clear 17-point path documenting Berg's process of Vergangenheitsbewältigung, culminating in the writing of the novel itself,[61] no such trajectory could possibly be devised for Rolf, whose stories about his pursuit of the mysterious girl and the theft of cash from his hotel room will strike some readers as extraneous and tedious, perhaps even pathetic, at least at first glance. Like Schlink, Schneider sets out to give perpetrators a human face for the purpose of rendering impossible a fraudulent form of Vergangenheitsbewältigung that simply exiles them from humanity. This is a means of evading, not confronting, the past: "By means of the same defense mechanism, the viewer distances himself from the perpetrators of the Holocaust: there were just a few deviant monsters who did that. We have nothing to do with them!"[62] Closely linked to the untenable "demonic thesis," popular in the early postwar period and in part espoused by Carl Zuckmayer's *Des Teufels General* (1945), and even Thomas Mann's *Doktor Faustus* (1947), the "monster thesis," as both Schlink and Schneider would agree, avoids the real challenge. In one of his intermittent moments of insight, Rolf observes, "The monster they made him out to be made him almost invisible."[63] Schneider announces this provocative undertaking of reclaiming perpetrators of horrific crimes with the very title "Vati": the Auschwitz "Todesengel" (Angel of Death) was someone's "Daddy"—in this case, a highly cultivated man who took a profound interest in his son's education, sent the young boy postage stamps from all over the world, and regularly watched *The Wonderful World of Disney* with a little neighbor-hood boy whom he had taken under his wing.[64] How could this be?

Of course Rolf cannot really answer this persistent question, but his dilemma rings true because he cannot—try, as he may—recast his father as "schuldig unschuldig" (guilty but essentially innocent), handicapped, ignorant, or as some kind of *un*willing executioner. He is no lower-level functionary like Hanna. The immoveable historical reference to Mengele, which is the bedrock referent of Schneider's text, thus provides a rich perspective on the *second* generation as well—one that is notably lacking in Schlink. As Colin Riordan observes, "The original *Bunte* article [which reported the actual meeting of Rolf and Josef Mengele] was so widely read, and the Mengele case so well known, that even the moderately informed reader could hardly have missed the indications that *Vati* was a literary re-working of the Mengele story, even though neither *Bunte* nor Mengele were explicitly referred to in the original volume."[65] Though identifiable as a particular historical case, this reunion of the Mengeles also casts lon-ger shadows: Rolf's failure to confront his father adequately—indeed, his efforts to deny, obfuscate, and relativize his father's guilt—renders him a questionable, though hardly unrecognizable, guide to the task of coming to terms with the Nazi past.

Whereas Berg's evasion controls the very exposition of Hanna, deter-mining our limited view of her from the outset, Rolf is much more like one of us. Though he is the literal author of his story—a fictional memoirist no less than Berg—he cannot change history by fictionalizing it, much as he might wish to, and he is angry about that. He does not even pretend to do justice to the principal victims of the Holocaust, though he well knows what is expected of him in terms of politically correct behavior.[66] In him, we encounter a familiar set of transparent arguments intended to "unbur-den" Daddy: no matter what his father's actual role in the genocide, "Vati" could not have acted alone—he must have had millions behind him. Such thoughts predictably result in viewing this arch perpetrator as the victim of a witch hunt: "The whole world was after my father. Millions of lower level perpetrators hunted the single, all-powerful one, in order to become inno-cent themselves."[67] There is just enough truth in this remark to give pause. And if the father were a fictional figure whose reality depended entirely on the son's ruminations, we might be tempted to soften our view. Yet because he is talking about the real Josef Mengele, who, within the story, confesses to an unshaken belief in Nazi racialist doctrine,[68] Rolf has no chance of persuading to persuade us (or himself) of his father's innocence.

What is more, in this image of a "witch hunt" against Mengele, there lurks the silhouette of Hanna's predicament. As Daldry's film makes quite explicit, we are invited to see her as having been scapegoated not only by the other female guards but also, more fundamentally, by those "million other Germans" who go unpunished (Hare, 42). This is a tactic that one of the teaching manuals employs in order to contextualize Hanna's prosecution.[69] At the very same time, she is a "victim" of the spectacularly unpunished Mengele—one of the many "small perpetrators" offered up in place of the real prize. The specter of Mengele and other first-tier perpetrators (those who were punished as well as those who were not) thus provides a kind of "backstop" for lower-level functionaries, effectively siphoning off their guilt (as Korten does for Selb in the first volume of the detective trilogy) as long as their own culpability remains either unspecified, offstage, or indeterminate. But this same trick does not work in reverse: Mengele's crimes, like those of Hermine Braunsteiner, are a matter of public record, even of Nazi lore. No matter how many accomplices or helpers' helpers they may have had, and no matter how these homunculi may seek to unburden themselves by passing guilt up the chain of command, their crimes are not diminished.

I have made strong historical claims for a novella that does not even use the name Mengele, though it does come extremely close at times, as when the son recalls, "At first I was irritated by the tone the teachers used to call on me in class—the hesitation, the sinking of their voices prior to these three syllables. As if my good Swabian family name were not quite pronounceable."[70] Schneider says he chose the more generic "father-and-son" nomenclature, eschewing even the name Rolf, not to avoid the Mengele connection, which he explains would have been inevitable at the time of first publication (1987). Rather, he sought to encourage resonances that go beyond this specific family (1988).[71] He wanted to bring out the "representative" aspect of this individual family story. It appears, though, that his coyness was attributable, in part, to a fear of litigation.[72] Schneider's use of unattributed quotations from Rolf Mengele in the novella became the basis for a prepublication scandal instigated by Gerda-Marie Schönfeld of *Der Spiegel*.[73] In partial response to charges of plagiarisim, subsequent editions of *Vati* contain the following explanatory note from the author: "The story *Vati* is based on actual events, namely the first and only meeting between the concentration camp doctor, Josef Mengele, and his son, Rolf."[74] Early readers who may have missed the controversy and overlooked the historical allusions built into the text will nevertheless have found substantial guidance in the words of Jürgen Manthey, whose review in the prominent *Süddeutsche Zeitung* (April 11, 1987) was excerpted as follows on the flyleaf of an early edition of *Vati*: "Does it make the story more compelling or even more enlightening that

Mengele is the basis for this narrative? But what meaning would such a story have without the authentic atrocity behind it? An invented Holocaust murderer would only allow the real one to slip away."[75] While it would be naïve to ignore the specific historical reference I have thus far privileged, it would be equally mistaken to overlook the extent to which our protagonist is also a son in a more general sense. Though I continue to refer to Schneider's characters as Rolf and Josef Mengele as a matter of convenience, I take seriously the author's effort to point both toward, and beyond, the Mengeles. It is particularly in the role of son—a role that no one can, after all, freely choose—that the narrator most deserves the sympathy denied him by early reviewers.[76]

Schneider's son is angry at his "Daddy" in the first instance because he is such a horrible parent—a father who has made his son's life undeservedly miserable: "I wanted to get him, bring him down with the injustice of my life of guiltless guilt."[77] The intensity of this brief statement bears some reflection. Rolf pointedly does not spout expressions of exaggerated guilt, unlike his literary counterpart, Michael Berg. On the contrary, he flatly asserts that he has *innocently* come into this "guilt-ridden" life—and, in this respect, Schneider is quite right to claim that *Vati* goes far beyond the particularity of one infamous family. A guilt-ridden life is precisely what Rolf, along with all members of the second generation, inherited through no fault of their own, regardless of their parents' particular involvement, or not, in Nazi war crimes. This is the "erlebte Realität" (lived reality) of collective guilt about which both the fictional Berg and real-life Schlink have spoken so eloquently: it is the rock-bottom "truth" of second-generation experience, untouched by any normative argument about the theoretical or juridical validity of the concept of collective guilt.

The reason why Rolf's honest complaint about an undeservedly guilt-ridden life does not garner more sympathy soon becomes clear, however, as we observe the way in which his anger extends to—and perhaps finds its real focus in—the Jews because of their "role" in his family drama: "Indeed, instead of hating my father, at this moment I hated the victims, who allowed themselves by the thousands to be led to the gas chambers—though they were only guarded by a dozen SS thugs. And they made me—me, of all people—into their avenger."[78] Though he speaks here with unmistakable self-centeredness (ausgerechnet mich), he is simultaneously expressing—albeit with some degree of hyperbole—his rejection of a role with which many members of the second generation may feel they have been unfairly burdened. He resents being forced into the position of serving as the Jews' "avenger" by an accident of birth—an accident that by no means is limited to his particular position as the son of a notorious war criminal. This resentment might seem more legitimate the further away one is from acknowledged leading perpetrators like Mengele, and it would resonate with greater force within the orbit of Berg's less indictable milieu of ineffective, but not felonious, fathers.[79] Do these sons—the ones Berg represents—not have even less motivation to avenge, confront, or accuse, given that they find themselves at a relative remove from the center of perpetration?

In this sense, Schneider's "son" is truly Janus-faced. One the one hand, he triggers generic second-generation concerns with which one might concur—however hesitantly or privately. On the other hand, he represents an extreme case one understandably would want to shun. The second "face" of course predominates, in no small part because he completely succumbs to the temptation of blaming the victims. He simply cannot forgive the Jews for the Holocaust, as Henryk Broder would later famously put it. This is an ugly, though stunningly honest, admission. It is of course only possible because Schneider has not made it easy for readers to identify with Rolf. Unlike his literary counterpart Berg, and without the responsibility of guiding our thoughts and behavior, Rolf can give voice to the pain of the wounded child whose moral compass has clearly been deformed by this accident of birth. He is, in other words, freed from the burden of serving as the exemplary *Vergangenheitsbewältiger*.

In Schneider's story, the son's misplaced anger is, we might say, well placed because it communicates this emotional, rather than historical, truth. And, in this sense, *Vati* can be said to demonstrate the distinctive contribution of literature (as opposed to history and other kinds of public discourse). Pathetically, Rolf seeks approval, love, and validation from a man he hates—from someone who can never meet his emotional needs. His personal development appears to be stunted in other ways, including in terms of a maladjusted sexuality, as we notice in the scene where he pursues an attractive young woman, not seeming to grasp that his advances are unwanted until she ultimately eludes him. When we "overhear" his politically incorrect views on the Holocaust, as if we were party to an intimate therapy session, the account is confessional, subjective, and private, as it is a passage in a letter to a friend. Its impact is all the more powerful, therefore, when we see him as a potential predator who may not even have noticed the young woman's flight. His judgment is clearly impaired, as becomes evident when he assumes, entirely without justification, that the desk clerk is guilty of having stolen possessions from his hotel room. There is little danger of what Dorrit Cohn would call a "consonant" relationship between reader and literary figure, although when Schneider first read from this text to audiences consisting largely of American Jews, he was attacked for inhabiting the persona of the son (simply by speaking in his voice) and, in this way, allegedly underplaying the dissonance and revulsion that readers have otherwise noted. This is one reason, Schneider has said, that he was initially hesitant to have the novella translated into English.[80] Rolf is, plainly, "damaged goods." His wounds cannot be pressed into the service of a larger *Bildungsroman*—deployed, that is to say, as a series of agonistic moments that, in the end, serve to edify. Unlike Berg, whose foibles and setbacks lead him dialectically onward, Rolf remains someone whom we may pity, but not someone we would ever like to be.

Rolf's psychological retreat from Holocaust atrocities leads us into dangerous, and possibly familiar, territory. Responding to pictures of Holocaust victims, he initially reacts in the manner expected of him: "I can not and will not ever deny the crime to which they testify."[81] This is the kind of rhetoric we could expect of Berg; in fact, it sounds very much like a portion of his speech about the burdens and aporias of *Vergangenheitsbewältigung*, discussed in Chapter 5. Rolf qualifies this respectable, Holocaust-affirming statement in a manner that, furthermore, is reminiscent of Berg's "numbness" plea: "I must admit that I am until today unable to grasp these atrocities in all their detail, because whenever I attempt to confront them a blinding vertigo takes possession of me. Perhaps it is a weakness of my constitution, a defense mechanism, a flight impulse—all that may be, but I cannot change it."[82] Berg's disquisition on *Betäubung* (numbing or torpor in the face of inhumanity) is not substantially different. But whereas Berg uses, then quickly retracts, this particular explanation for our need to look away from spectacles of violence—to explain why, in general, we cannot withstand sustained exposure to atrocity—Rolf's response is typically crasser and more self-centered. These pictures make *him* sick; he focuses—with an equal measure of poor judgment and revealing honesty—on himself. Whereas Berg quickly covers his tracks after having wandered dangerously far into the swamp of "equationism"[83] by offering psychological truisms, Rolf flatly states that the vertigo that overcomes him is a protective mechanism rooted in the desire to escape. Berg's very analytical posture—his ability to render retrospective judgment about this phenomenon that once overtook his senses—bespeaks a degree of agency and power that Rolf utterly lacks. In other words, in the very act of articulating his powerlessness, Berg displays the self-assurance that negates that helplessness. His literary counterpart does not rise above this "constitutional weakness" but, rather, is fully subject to it—as he says, "it is beyond my control" (ich kann das nicht ändern).

Schneider deftly reprises Rolf's expression of visceral overload in the context of father Mengele's diatribe in the rain forest. Listening to Daddy's pseudo-Darwinian justification for genocide, Rolf is physically affected: "An overwhelming, disabling indifference came over me, destroying each and every impulse."[84] He attributes this state of physical weakness to the oppressive tropical heat, but we become suspicious about its sudden onset at this juncture. When it appears for the third time, in the context of the stifling police station, there can be no mistaking the mind-numbing, distinction-dissolving function of this infirmity. Rolf has come to punish the hotel clerk, but not to pursue the grander kind of disinterested justice he claimed to seek on behalf of others when he first set out to find his war-criminal father.

At some level, he seems to register the fact that his pursuit of the hotel thief has displaced his principal quest. Looking at the anonymous group of desperate cases assembled on the benches before him, he capitulates in a manner that recalls his (physical) withdrawal from the investigation of his father's past: "You couldn't tell whether they came as accused or as accusers. This distinction seemed completely irrelevant in this heat."[85] Given the story's prominent, tripartite reprise of this experience of somatic retreat from reason and judgment (Rolf actually says "I went around as if numbed" ["Ich ging wie betäubt"]),[86] one cannot avoid the discomfort of a response that seems both eminently understandable and deeply problematic—understandable, because we can imagine the physical pain that renders the pursuit of such thought so challenging, and problematic, because we see this "numbness" ("blindness," "indifference," "vertigo," etc.) deployed in a way that dissolves the distinction between perpetrator and victim—and perhaps even appears to justify this dissolution in the face of the second generation's "disability."

Provocatively, Schneider presents us with a protagonist who only nominally confronts the Holocaust while actually refocusing our attention on *his* personal malady. Indeed, this is Rolf's signature move—to act as if he is "avenging" crimes of the Holocaust (something that is socially acceptable), while he is in fact pursuing his own personal "justice." Despite his meandering, sometimes maddeningly indirect, and self-indicting prose, he admits this outright: "I've already told you what I was looking for in Belem. I wanted to take him to task, to compel him to stand before a German court and take responsibility. Today I realize that this rationale was designed more to disguise my real plan. I wanted to get him, bring him down, confront him with the injustice of my life . . . No, I will say it with words that are simpler but also misleading: I wanted to be redeemed through him."[87] Is this specific proclivity—namely, to focus, however inadvertently, on the damage done to the children rather than on the genocidal crime itself—a strain of behavior that might be relevant to broader swaths of the second generation? Is Holocaust commemoration sometimes more about the second generation's need for "redemption" than about remembering the genocide itself? It is not far-fetched to think that it may be so. In any event, Schneider's damaged, flawed, and often unlikable narrator is a spokesman for this, and it thus remains unlikely that readers who may, at some level, sense in Rolf a kindred spirit will ever overtly acknowledge him as their generational "representative."[88]

How very different is the case of Schlink's Berg? Recall his "numbness doctrine," which is initially invoked as a universal phenomenon equally affecting perpetrators, victims, judges, bystanders, and postwar observers. For Berg, this experience of Betäubung, as I have argued here, figures not as an ignoble impulse to escape but as a serious alibi for shutting down in the face of atrocity and gross inhumanity. Understandably, it has proven persuasive to many because it appears intuitively true: all of us will have experienced this feeling to some degree, if only in response to the daily television news. Berg exploits this in troubling ways, however, in particular by suggesting that Jewish victims' experience of moral numbness in the face of overwhelming evil somehow validates the Betäubung of perpetrators as well as of postwar observers such as himself.[89] In the end, Berg's notion of "universal numbness"[90] or "moral autism,"[91] which initially had not bothered reviewers at all, has simply proven to be historically incorrect: there is in fact plenty of survivors' and perpetrators' testimony that contradicts this overbroad assertion.

Though Rolf set out to distinguish himself from the bulk of those '68ers who so decisively denounce their fathers, in the end, his narrative supports the opposite conclusion. Inadvertently—like so much else in the novella—his behavior suggests that he is in fact an extreme case of a rather widespread phenomenon. Rolf's emotional dependency and life history link him inexorably to the war generation, and it is this inescapable dependency and proximity—not the crimes of the Holocaust per se—that is, for him, the principal insupportable burden. He whines that while the other kids' fathers have some, less obvious guilt, he alone is truly "born guilty" (schuldig geboren). But in a brief moment of honesty, Rolf Mengele states that he knows this to be untrue. He knows he did nothing to deserve his notorious father. He says what so many others of this generation must be thinking. Though, in this sense, a perhaps truer mouthpiece for the anger and frustration of the second generation, Rolf must remain unacknowledged and disavowed. What self-respecting, graying ex-'68er—now perhaps well ensconced in the German ruling establishment—would possibly want to confess an affinity with Rolf? The critical preference has remained—and very likely will remain—with Berg.

BERG AS SCHLINK'S ALTER EGO

> It's a book about my generation, so it's also a book about me.
> —Bernhard Schlink, as a guest on *The Oprah Winfrey Show*

One of the reasons that Berg makes such a positive impression may have to do with his perceived likeness to his creator. Both are successful second-generation lawyers who have criticized '68er "excesses," have affirmed the Kantian inviolability of the autonomous subject, and have articulated the plight of second-generation Germans in remarkably similar ways. Teachers' guides—equipped in some cases with tables juxtaposing similar positions held both by the fictional Berg and the jurist Schlink—frequently play up the parallel between the two.[92] And in interview after interview, when Schlink is asked about his relationship to Berg, he teasingly allows that some of this is indeed autobiographical. When, for example, Oprah Winfrey wondered if he, too, had had a youthful affair like Berg, Schlink smiled wistfully, hesitated, and then coyly declined to confirm this suspicion.

The identification of author with literary figure is as much a staple of amateur literary criticism as it is an offense against serious literary analysis, as Feuchert and Hofmann pedantically intone: "Whoever frivolously equates Michael Berg's arguments with Bernhard Schlink's views thereby violates elementary principles of literary analysis of fiction."[93] Yet the invocation of this canard of narratology has, in its own way, become a cudgel used to quell legitimate debate about the sociological meaning of a first-person fictional memoir that has so insistently been marketed in conjunction with the author's credentials and life story. Nor has it been applied evenly: I recall giving a paper on *The Reader* at the German Studies Association when a respondent argued that my criticisms of the novel (I had not even mentioned the author's biography) could not possibly hold water because the author is, after all, a distinguished jurist and respected public intellectual.

I do not wish to invalidate the fundamental narratological distinction between author and literary figure. It remains a very handy structuralist tool, even in our messy poststructuralist environment. It remains so relevant, however, only because of the ongoing and deeply entrenched *opposing* tendency to meld the two. And this is something that pedagogues, media figures, promotion people, and perhaps Schlink himself have sometimes blatantly encouraged. "Here one has the impression," Cerstin Urban tells us in her teaching guide, "that author and jurist Bernhard Schlink is expressing himself through the novel's protagonist [seine Romanfigur]"[94]—just one example of the critical identification of author and literary figure that can be easily multiplied.[95] Nothing encourages this trend so directly, perhaps, as a chart that Mittelberg includes in his teaching guide, in which Berg's and Schlink's common characteristics are carefully catalogued, for example: "B. Schlink is the son of a theology professor; the father of the protagonist is also a professor . . . B. Schlink grew up with three siblings, as did Michael."[96] And the list goes on. For a whole array of reasons, then, the actual reception of *The Reader*—its "erlebte Realität" (lived reality), to borrow a phrase from the novel's discussion of collective guilt—is such that Berg has, to a significant degree, become Schlink's alter ego, whether we like it or not. This is something no literary-critical maxim can expunge or wish away. The result of this quasi equivalence is clearly beneficial to the literary figure: the author's articulate media presence and his thoughtful interventions in public culture tend to enhance Berg's stature to the extent that we follow the cues of teachers and others and allow the two to become linked in our minds.

Those who want to segregate author from narrator cannot be blind to the semiotic contamination that obtains in the real world, where meaning is negotiated in messy ways and readers of popular novels, unschooled in the niceties of formal criticism, simply make the connections that are so generously offered them. Those critics who seek to uphold these "elementary rules of literary analysis" do so, I believe, because they think they are thereby liberating the novel from a hermeneutic vice that keeps it from achieving its full potential. Free Berg from Schlink, they say, and readers are set free to criticize the narrator; this in turn releases the author from the faults and errors that we may then wish to attribute to Berg. This "liberation" cuts both ways, unlocking the allegedly self-critical potential of the novel, on the one hand, and preventing the author from being identified with politically incorrect views, on the other. Yet unlike the *alliance* of author and narrator noted above, this emphatic *dissection* inevitably makes Berg look worse. I will suggest that this entire argument is beside the point. Berg is not likeable principally because of his similarity to Schlink—he is simply *more* likable for that reason. He is a classic "consonant" literary figure in his own right; he is drawn in such a way that we read with, rather than against, him.[97] Because this is an issue that goes to the very heart of the most fundamental disagreements about this novel,[98] it will require some explanation. I will take one particularly well-argued case as exemplary for this position as a whole.

Feuchert and Hofmann introduce their commentary with the admonition, "When analyzing *The Reader* it is crucial to draw a clear distinction between the level of the novel whose author is Bernhard Schlink and that of the fictional story, whose first-person narrator is Michael Berg.

The controversies over the novel . . . are not infrequently rooted in a naïve equation of these two planes."[99] The debate to which they refer is the radical reassessment of the novel that began to appear in mass circulation venues in 2002, led by critics like Jeremy Adler, Lawrence Norfolk, and Willi Winkler. This view culminated in the damning sobriquet "Holo-kitsch." This group found fault, above all, with the exonerative depiction of Hanna, and laid the fault squarely at the author's feet, blaming him for trivializing the Holocaust. Rather than contest the depiction of Hanna and the message she sends, Feuchert and Hofmann seek only to transfer the responsibility to Berg—and it is in this that they typify a whole group of scholars and critics.[100]

Yet in doing so, they seriously revise our view of Berg. He becomes not just prone to error in a "human-all-too-human" kind of way but pro-foundly guilty of consciously evading the Holocaust. Notice how the logic of their analysis leads them to a wholesale indictment of the narrator that is much stronger than anything we have encountered thus far. Having noted Berg's insufficient response to the sinister Mercedes driver (the one who gave him a lift to the Strutthof concentration camp), Feuchert and Hofmann conclude, "The flashback must be understood precisely in this manner: once again a memory serves to exonerate perpetrators in general, and Hanna specifically. Numbness, indifference, [the indefinable] 'it'— all these code words in the end result in the exculpation of Hanna. Berg thereby accepts approvingly that his arguments could apply to all perpe-trators, and thus ultimately hardly any one would remain responsible for the Holocaust."[101]

Where, in this harsh condemnation, is the loveable, wounded, self-aware, and self-critical narrator we have come to know? In order to ren-der their argument logically consistent, Feuchert and Hofmann give us a figure whom few would recognize from the novel. They overlook the manner in which Schlink specifically mobilizes error and self-critique as a vehicle not for dissonant critique but rather for sympathy—they miss, in other words, the way in which "guilt" can come to be seen as a badge of honor (see Chapter 3). They can of course cite any number of grave errors—above all the "numbness doctrine"—which I myself have roundly criticized as an evasion.[102] But what they fail to notice, I think, is the persistent manner in which Berg beats us to the punch. He is always there first, beating his own breast, and thereby preempting any very serious criticism from us. Are we really inclined to kick this guy when he is down? The reception data suggest that we are not.[103]

There are two additional problems with this reading. First, Feuchert and Hofmann assert that the narrator only lets us know what he himself could have known at the time.[104] But this is clearly mistaken and gives us a rather misleading view of the fundamental narrative perspective—Berg does not in fact keep the reader to the level of knowledge he would have had at the time.[105] Unlike, for example, J. M. Coetzee—whose memoir of South African childhood, *Boyhood* (1997), does in fact hew rather closely to the mentality of the boy—Berg signals from the outset that he is writing from the perspective of the more astute middle-aged man. While it is true that he withholds certain crucial details (such as Hanna's illiteracy) in order to tell a more suspenseful story, what we cannot forget is that from the beginning, he is carefully establishing his credentials as a sagacious sifter of past events. Two brief examples may suffice. First is the eloquent dream sequence (from chapter 2), which poignantly and self-consciously wishes Hanna's house away—first into the country, then into another country altogether. This is a powerful and self-conscious fantasy of removing oneself from the very trap of accidental birth that Rolf so crudely decries in *Vati*, from the involuntary snares of history, and from the unwelcome burdens that come with membership in the second generation. This is an indisputably retrospective view that frames the entire memoir, and Berg renders it (in contrast to Rolf) with a high degree of self-reflexivity, irony, and sovereignty: he knows he is dreaming, knows he cannot "export" Hanna or the Holocaust to other lands or times, and is aware that this is only an option in dreams—or, perhaps, in literature.

Throughout the novel, we find numerous retrospective interventions that testify to a more mature and well-adjusted (if long-suffering) Berg as being the memoir's "true" narrator. When, for example, he speaks about the almost impossible dilemma of dealing with the Holocaust and the problematic legacy of '68, he is clearly speaking from this later, "wiser" perspective that just happens to coincide (sometimes in the very same verbal formulations) with the author's own views.[106] Moreover, in particular with respect to these two key points, he has garnered such a high degree of critical concord that his self-proclaimed status as generational spokesman has been widely embraced. As a spokesman for these foundational second-generation issues, Berg has proven anything but an embarrassment or the fundamentally "inadequate narrator" that Feuchert and Hofmann deem him to be.[107] This does not mean that readers view him without nuance, only that he preempts (and thereby neutralizes) our critique with his own (often hyperbolic) self-accusation, and that his "errors of judgment," such as they are, tend not to be counted against him but rather enhance his status as victim.

Paradoxically, it is not the warm embrace of Berg—which predominates in the first phase of overwhelmingly positive press reception—that demands a flat, or one-sided, view of him. Indeed, these critics found enough to lament about him and his unenviable predicament. It is, on the contrary, Feuchert and Hofmann's argument that would now make Berg (and the generation he is said to represent) into an overwhelmingly negative figure, for they read him as both a consummately *representative* figure[108] and one who consciously excuses perpetrators en masse: "There is simply no way to soften Michael's analysis: in the end it serves unmistakably to legitimate the perpetrators and their deeds."[109] Are readers of Schlink's novel really being asked to identify with this Holocaust evader? This strikes me as tantamount to confusing Berg with the character of Rolf of Schneider's novella.

In pressing their case against Berg's alleged "legitimatization of perpetrators and their actions," Feuchert and Hofmann solemnly conclude, "Therefore an alert reader must of course repudiate [these views]."[110] Yet the less they can show how Schlink actually requires our watchful attention, the more they need to exhort and scold from without. Now invoking the authority of Wolfgang Iser, they claim that readers who fail to remain vigilant overlook the text's subtle "Appellstruktur" (structure of indeterminacy).[111] Like other critics of this bent, they seek to upgrade Schlink's rather undemanding text, which they elsewhere admit to be "extensively conventional" (weitgehend konventionell)[112] by framing it within sophisticated theoretical models. These readings are not invalid and are sometimes quite insightful. Yet, in general, their approach reminds me very much of the old fable of stone soup: all the really flavorful ingredients (such as salt, butter, parsley, cream, and potatoes) are ostensibly superfluous additives to a broth that, until their inclusion, consisted only of water and a stone. When critics like Metz use Lacan, or when Swales draws upon theories of shame to "unlock" the complexities of Schlink's text, they seem to me very much like those generous contributors to the stone soup—which is not to say that they do not end up with a savory concoction.[113] As prescriptive readings that are meant to enrich the hermeneutic process, they succeed. But they stand in splendid isolation from the vast reading practices of others, showing little interest in *why* such divergent readings would emerge and *whether* the novel can be said to support them as well. Like numerous other prescriptive critics, Feuchert and Hofmann never seriously consider the proposition that this specimen of conventional literary realism instigates the very "inattentive" (or "slothful") reading they identify and reject.

Is it not in fact possible that Schlink has constructed Berg precisely to be the flawed, but noble, hero of the second generation? This is probably why Adler, Lawrence, Winkler, and company—by the way, hardly amateur critics who are unlikely to know the difference between an author and narrator—do not demur from attributing weaknesses directly to the book and author. They see that this narrator, despite (nay, because of) his ritual self-flagellation, is not really set up for the kind of serious, thoroughgoing critique elicited by Schneider's "son."[114] Quite the contrary, Berg is still widely viewed as a respectable generational representative—not unlike his creator, whom *The New York Times* christened "the bard of his generation" in 2002.[115]

THE JEWISH IMPRIMATUR ON BERG'S VICTIMHOOD

Berg's oft-quoted dismissal of '68er *Vergangenheitsbewältigung* may distract us from the manner in which he is in fact deployed as the novel's "new Jew" within the perpetrator-victim framework. Far from nullifying this binary in the name of some allegedly higher order of moral ambiguity, the novel, in fact, depends on it. The dyad has admittedly been refashioned, but the basic structure is there, offering Berg an ultimate place of honor. Shortly before the novel concludes, Berg visits the lone, nameless Jewish survivor of that terrible fire. Toward the end of their meeting, she comments on Hanna's "brutality." What she means, we soon discover, is not Hanna's treatment of the inmates trapped in the burning church, or her behavior as camp guard, or even what she did (or failed to do) on the death march, as one might well expect; rather, the survivor is referring to the sexual and emotional abuse that the young Berg endured during the mismatched love affair. "That woman was truly brutal . . . did you ever get over the fact that you were only fifteen when she . . . Did you ever feel, when you had contact with her in those last years, that she knew what she had done to you?"[116] This validation of Berg as victim, bestowed at this privileged moment in the novel by the sole Jewish survivor, may finally explain why Hanna's war crimes have never been clearly delineated: they would have distracted from her victimization of Berg—that avatar of the second generation and the novel's real interest.[117]

The conferral of victim status represents the culmination of a narrative process in which Berg and the camp inmates have been deliberately and rather extensively juxtaposed. This occurred, as we have observed, during that dramatic moment in the trial when the surviving daughter remembered that Hanna had indeed "selected" girls for "special service." Hanna's visual singling out of Berg at this particular moment signals his special relevance; indeed, the very drama of the scene depends on a juxtaposition that functions in two directions—inculpating Hanna insofar as she "victimized" an underaged boy (as the survivor has just affirmed) but also exculpating her insofar as these acts of reading turn out to be benign, even beautiful.[118] This is not simply a crude equation of the two, but an indirect analogy that both defers to the Jewish victims' primacy *and* welcomes Berg into their circle—another instance of the novel's persistent "sowohl als auch" strategy. Berg does not presumptuously claim to be the "new Jew," nor does he seek to displace the Jews, in the hyperbolic, shrill manner of some of his '68er cogenerationalists. He demurs from having Hanna explicitly employ the worn-out defense of "Befehlsnotstand" (just following orders) and instead deftly communicates some of that very same defense indirectly, via her lower-class provenance and illiteracy. Schlink here refines the practice of the unjustified appropriation of victim status notoriously associated with the student movement by both respecting a hierarchy of suffering and redirecting it through the Jews toward himself.

Is this a true refinement or, rather, an offensive ruse? In earlier publications, I frankly argued the latter position. Defenders of Schlink point out, however, that he makes all the politically correct points on the Holocaust agenda. What more could he have his protagonist do? Moreover, can we not make room for second-generation Germans within a more nuanced spectrum of victimhood? Must we persist in simplistic binaries that divide groups exclusively into German perpetrators and Jewish victims? I think we can concede all these points, but without necessarily endorsing the questionable analogy between Berg and the female concentration camp inmates—however qualified it may be—for two reasons. First, the legitimate sense in which the second generation is "victimized" by the Holocaust has little to do with the Jews or with the historical experience of inmates in concentration and extermination camps. The difference is an order of magnitude. To state what should be obvious: being targeted for genocide is simply incommensurate with the stigma of being related to first-generation perpetrators and to those who failed to prosecute them properly.

The more convincing conception of second-generation "victimhood" comes, I would argue, not from Berg but rather from Rolf, who, we recall, powerfully articulated the sense of historical unfairness of being made into a Holocaust "avenger" by an accident of birth. To modify Helmut Kohl's notorious remark, this would be the *Ungnade der späten Geburt* (the *mis*fortune of being born later)—a feeling that, as I argue in the final two chapters of this study, is likely to be shared by many non-Germans as well. Having Berg say—as Daldry does in the film version—that his own suffering was much less than that which Hanna inflicted on others (i.e., the Jewish female inmates) does not remove the fundamental clumsiness of the analogy. Perhaps in the mid-1990s, a point in time at which the Holocaust had already become a pliable metaphor for so many kinds of injustice and suffering,[119] this seemed a respectable gambit. Maybe the Holocaust was (or still is) *the* cultural shorthand for "victimhood" appropriate to popular, mass-market realism, as Eva Hoffman has argued.[120] But the problem here is not (or not only) that an inviolable status reserved to the Jews is being misappropriated but that it so overreaches that it includes its opposite—to say that Berg is like the camp inmates (in however qualified a fashion) is to simultaneously acknowledge that he is nothing like them. This unfortunate analogy helps to explain why the Holocaust had to be strenuously kept offstage in this novel—to do otherwise would have pushed the preposterousness of this juxtaposition to the surface. And it furthermore helps to explain Berg's ultimate "mastery," for, in one sense, he overcomes a victimhood that never really quite existed.

Further, such a conception of victimhood may also seriously sell short the second generation, for if there is any truth to its *ongoing* suffering, how can a successful Berg—who, like his creator, masters his problem by writing about it—serve as its worthy representative? How can he stand for the unfinished anguish, ambivalence, and bitterness of those who feel unjustly thrust into their involuntary historical role? Is he perhaps a less valid representative for the plight of the second generation than an idealized self-image—a fictional character who, no less than Gerhard Selb, is meant to compensate for, rather than engage, historical reality?

Despite its unimpeachable commitment to an enlightened form of Vergangenheitsbewältigung, *The Reader* invites a certain kind of dismissal. Like the work of indictment that it retroactively takes over from the '68ers, the novel claims it is carrying out, through the person of Berg, Vergangenheitsbewältigung itself. Though we can imagine further incremental steps in Berg's ascent toward ever-greater mastery, his work is essentially done within the action of the novel. In the once widely read (but now commonly disregarded) essay "Commitment," Adorno argued that well-meaning, "politically progressive" literature—as long as it remains formally conventional—really only serves to reinforce the political status quo. Schlink's hero is so utterly "consumable" (in this Adornian sense) that it is hard to imagine him sticking in the craw of readers. Because he incarnates such an idealized self-image of the second-generation readers, Berg can only serve as a fascinating, rather than provocative, repellent, or unnerving, character.

In stark contrast, Schneider's Rolf Mengele reminds us that being a victim does not necessarily make one attractive, nor is it a badge of honor or a status symbol. Instead, victimhood is often associated with shame, and not infrequently—as Art Spiegelmann's *Maus* suggests so powerfully—it results in a deformation of character. As the unlovable, "ugly" representative of the second generation, Rolf can give honest expression to irrational anger and hurt. In his injustice toward the principal victims of the Holocaust, we glimpse some of the profound moral harm done to the children of the perpetrators.

CHAPTER 5

VICTIMS ALL

THE READER AS AN AMERICAN NOVEL

All of us, even those who were born later, are to a certain extent survivors of the Holocaust.

—Ruth Klüger, *Von hoher und niedriger Literatur*

It is easy to mistake keening for ourselves for keening for the Shoah.

—Eva Hoffman, *After Such Knowledge*

The Reader was the first German book to garner first place in the *New York Times* Bestseller List.

—Michael Lamberty, *Literatur-Kartei "Der Vorleser"*

GIVEN BERG'S CLAIM TO REPRESENT "A GERMAN fate," as well as the affirmation this claim enjoyed in the German press, one might easily conclude that Schlink's novel is, in some sense, an exclusively *German* work, one that might not translate well to other cultural settings. My suggestion in Chapter 3—that the unequal love relationship between Berg and Hanna may offer a covert model for "managing" the pressures of Germany's key transatlantic relationship—would seem to confirm this view. Yet exactly the opposite is the case. Translated into over 37 languages (and perhaps more by the time this study appears), *The Reader* has long enjoyed the status of international bestseller; and nowhere has it sold more, and presumably had more readers, than in the Unites States. Translated into English in 1997, it was well reviewed in almost all the quality papers and in many minor ones. Despite some noted reservations in a few elite publications (Ozick, Hofmann, Bartov),[1] it continued to gain readers; sales skyrocketed once Oprah Winfrey chose to include it for discussion in her on-air book club in April of 1999.[2] The show, watched by millions, featured Schlink, who, with winsome charm, answered (and dodged) questions about the novel and its allegedly "autobiographical" content.[3] From the standpoint of readership alone, it is safe to say that *The Reader* is indeed an American novel—more so even than the widely read "American" author Günter Grass (whose *The Tin Drum* has reached more American readers than its German original, *Die Blechtrommel*, will ever garner) or the recent bestselling author of *Measuring the World* (*Die Vermessung der Welt*, 2005), Daniel Kehlmann. Schlink's audience exceeds the "American" film sensation *Das Boot*, which has been viewed by a U.S. audiences many times the size of German ones.

But what makes *The Reader* so amenable to the so-called American mind?[4] How is it that a fictional memoir by a second-generation German about his affair with an older woman, whom he would discover only later to have been an SS guard at Auschwitz, could appeal to such a broad swath of U.S. readers? If this novel really represents the latest in German *Vergangenheitsbewältigung* (Mastering the Nazi past), as many critics claim, then how did it conquer the American market where, presumably, this agenda would seem foreign indeed?[5]

What Timothy Garton Ash recently wrote about Florian Henckel von Donnersmarck's *The Lives of Others* applies, *mutatis mutandis*, equally well to Schlink: "It mixes historical fact . . . with the ingredients of a fast-paced thriller and love story . . . You might think that the film is aimed solely at modern Germans, [Anthony] Lane writes, but it's not: *Es ist für uns*—it's for us. He may be more right than he knows . . . Like so much else made in Germany, it is designed to be exportable. Among its ideal foreign consumers are, precisely, Lane's 'us'—the readers of *The New Yorker*. Or, indeed, those of *The New York Review*."[6] Like von Donnersmarck, Schlink has spent a good deal of time in the United States and is intimately familiar with the cultural scene. He was a guest professor at Princeton University and regularly teaches at the Cardozo School of Law (Yeshiva University) in New York City. He knows how to write a book that ostensibly thematizes a particular history, while having broad appeal, in the manner of a Hollywood film. That appeal presumably has much to do with the fact that the book is accessibly written and is divided, like all his detective fiction, into brief chapters that lend themselves well to bedside as well as other *ad hoc* kinds of reading. The fact that the first third features a steamy love affair entirely free of any cerebral content may explain how the novel hooks its readers, at least initially. The erotic prelude—narrated straightforwardly but without lurid detail—surely appeals to many without offending conventional canons of "good taste."

But what is it that keeps American readers going once the novel reveals itself to also be about concentration camps, about a death march—in short, the Holocaust—as well as about the fraught manner in which second-generation Germans have come to grips with all this? Oprah Winfrey thought she could make it speak to larger audiences by emphasizing the theme of illiteracy. She introduced the discussion of Schlink's novel with a detailed report on the phenomenon of illiteracy and its ongoing, widespread, and insufficiently acknowledged deleterious effects on Americans. She may have been on to something after all—despite the condescending remarks with which German newspapers dismissed her efforts—particularly with regard to the sympathy and understanding she sought to generate for "victims" (her word) of this heartbreaking handicap, a sympathy that, of course, rather directly accrues to Hanna.

Yet I think the fundamental appeal of *The Reader* lies elsewhere. While Hanna's illiteracy surely makes her a more palatable character, despite her perpetrator status, this fact does not sufficiently explain the novel's success in the United States—even if the many German teachers' guides that highlight this handicap in some detail also seem to show up in U.S. university settings, where the novel is frequently taught in its original German-language edition. To understand this American appeal better, I think we have to consider the manner in which *The Reader* evokes history very generally (or perhaps only nominally), while omitting "tedious" historical particulars. Relatedly, I will argue that the novel—particularly in its central, iconic courtroom scenes—gestures at traditional Vergangenheitsbewältigung, but, in reality, systematically encourages us to divert our eyes from the genocide's principal victims in order to lament a much broader circle of "victims," namely ourselves—including Americans. Finally, I will examine the novel's presentation of Berg as a prototypical second-generation German, yet simultaneously as an international, even universal, identification figure.

This thesis is bound to evoke numerous objections and must, to be honest, remain, to some degree, speculative. Often it is assumed that the American cultural "use" of the Holocaust is restricted to simple binaries in which Germans unfailingly appear as evil Nazis, and Americans, insofar as they are on the scene, play the roles of heroes and rescuers. While the U.S. cultural reception of postwar Germans is in fact much more complex,[7] the American pop-cultural use of Nazism, as Maria Tatar and others have shown, offers a great deal of support to this simplistic dichotomy in which Americans reserve themselves—perhaps all too glibly given the historical record—for the role of the "good guys."[8] Even when we look beyond popular culture to venues that ask to be taken more seriously, we see that this laudatory view of Americans is enshrined, for example, in the very conception of the U.S. Holocaust Memorial Museum (USHMM) and its permanent exhibit. Yet while it is true that the Holocaust becomes an event in U.S. history, so to speak, simultaneously with the glorification of American troops' liberation of the camps and defeating Nazi Germany, this dominant conception does not do justice to the manifold relationships and associations Americans have with the Holocaust. This point rings true particularly in the wake of the USHMM's widely publicized dedication in 1994 and the extensive media exposure given to other genocidal atrocities (Rawanda, Bosnia, the Iraqi Kurds, etc.) that are often evoked in the context of the Holocaust. In short, I contend that in the course of several decades of Holocaust education and increased public awareness, beginning roughly in 1978 with the broadcast of the television series *Holocaust* and reaching its apogee perhaps in the U.S.-dubbed "Year of the Holocaust," 1993,[9] we have not only witnessed an appetite for positive views about the United States. Rather, what we have seen (as numerous commentators have publicly worried) is a certain "Holocaust exhaustion" or "Holocaust saturation" in the sense of a growing fatigue under the psychic and emotional burden of these awful truths.

"Is the Holocaust being overdone?" Ronald Smelser answers this question by drawing our attention to a vast array of the forms of American popular culture—films, books, video games, and Internet sites—that thematizes the Nazi period with nary a reference to the Holocaust *per se*. Here, he shows, we are served up a strong dose of German soldiers as victims: often, common *Wehrmacht* soldiers are casualties of cruel, frequently anonymous Soviet hordes—but of course never as collaborators in the genocide that began on the Eastern Front. "What these memoirs convey," Smelser elucidates, "is the filth and fear and death of war on the ground against an implacable, often invisible foe. The style is simple; the prose is colorful and turgid. The stories resemble closely those related for decades in Germany in the popular *Landser* series but never translated into English."[10] Popular culture—as I argued in Chapter 1 with reference to Schlink's detective novels—thus appears to offer its own defense against the Holocaust simply by bracketing it out. While voicing some concern about the appetite for this "counternarrative," Smelser does not assume that their avid consumption is tantamount to Holocaust denial: "It just does not mention it," he observes," "or, if it does, confines the villains to Hitler and the SS-police."[11] This enclave of popular culture provides a reprieve from the rigors of official memory culture, which are often perceived as burdensome.

Gavriel D. Rosenfeld takes a darker view. In his "Alternate Holocausts and the Mistrust of Memory," he argues that recent "allohistorical" fiction, that is, fiction that imagines a counterfactual history, testifies to the presence of a worrisome desire to put the Holocaust behind us once and for all. Such fictional "alternate histories of the Holocaust," Rosenfeld proposes, "seem to dovetail with this burgeoning backlash against Holocaust memory . . . Indeed, by depicting memory as a burden that leads to frustration, if not outright disaster, these accounts have challenged the long-held belief in the necessity of remembrance. The significance of this trend is difficult to interpret. On the one hand, these alternate histories may be seen as *descriptive* accounts of the difficulty in coping with the Nazi past. On the other hand, the impatience with memory that suffuses them may well reflect a *prescriptive* desire to be done with the Holocaust once and for all."[12] There are less nefarious ways of reading this literature, as Rosenfeld himself cursorily acknowledges when he suggests that Ransmayr and Ziegler may in fact be critiquing "the virtues of remembrance in contemporary German culture" rather than the memory of the Holocaust itself. In any case, I think we must take seriously the diagnosis of an "exhaustion with memory" that pervades his study.[13]

Nevertheless, we should note that this disposition—while difficult to quantify or even adequately describe—need not be equated with the ignorance or malevolence of deniers and neo-Nazis. Good-faith recipients of Holocaust history may also feel burdened precisely because they believe these things to be true. Contemporary "readers" of the Holocaust—as Inga Clendinnen calls us all—may reject atrocity, recoil from brutality, and perhaps repress genocidal accounts we know to be accurate—not because we contest their veracity, but because we do not want to rehearse them and be spiritually crushed by them. Indeed, the very fact of having been deeply touched—perhaps even somehow wounded—by exposure to Holocaust images can itself lead to a kind of self-sequestration from further contact. This, at any rate, is Ruth Klüger's argument in her acclaimed autobiography *weiter leben*. She pleads with readers not to retreat from the frank discussion of the Holocaust just because they have, in a sense, already "done their time" in confronting horrific images of suffering: "Let yourselves at least be provoked, don't hide behind a barricade, don't say from the very outset that it doesn't concern you or that it only concerns you within a framework that you have delineated neatly in advance with a compass and a ruler. Don't say that you had, after all, already put up with the photographs of the piles of bodies and had contributed your quota of shared guilt and compassion. Get angry . . . look for a fight!"[14] But her very vehemence belies the experience of Holocaust "saturation." As Eva Hoffman puts it, we "struggle to find forms through which to confront the hydra heads of atrocity, to give artistic expression to images and stories from which one wants to, needs to, avert one's mind and eyes."[15] If any of this rings true, is it any wonder that people of goodwill can, in some amorphous sense, consider themselves "victims" of the Holocaust—not victims of the actual genocide, of course, but "victims" of these awful truths that intrude on our lives and perhaps even deform our spirit?

For some time, commentators have wondered—and frankly worried—about what needs Americans might be fulfilling by engaging in acts of Holocaust commemoration. A typical focus for this concern is the afore-mentioned United States Holocaust Memorial Museum. At the entrance facing the Washington Mall (a privileged piece of real estate reserved for time-honored, quintessentially "American" monuments, memorials, and museums), one finds a prominently engraved quotation from General (and later President) Dwight D. Eisenhower expressing his moral outrage at his discoveries in Ohrdruf, a small satellite camp near Dachau.[16] Visitors to the museum follow a carefully choreographed route, which begins with a required introduction by a museum staff member and continues in a crowded elevator car that brings guests to the top floor. On the way up, visitors hear the voice of an American GI who helped liberate one of the camps, while they view footage of the liberation on a small screen.

Edward Linenthal, whose *Preserving Memory: The Struggle to Create America's Holocaust Museum* provides a balanced and illuminating account of the museum's founding, describes visitors' experience:

> From the moment they are herded into the intentionally ugly, dark-gray metal elevators in the Hall of Witnesses which transport them to the begin-ning of the exhibition on the fourth floor, they are bunched together. In the elevator, they watch an overhead monitor with black-and-white film of Americans' first encounter with Buchenwald, Mauthausen, and Ohrdruf, while the voice of a GI recalls the horror of what he saw: "The patrol leader called in by radio and said that we have come across something that we are not sure what it is. It's a big prison of some kind, and there are people running all over. Sick, dying, starved people. And you take to an American [sic], uh, such a sight as that, you . . . you can't imagine it. You, you just . . . things like that don't happen."[17]

Visitors encounter the Holocaust through the eyes of an American lib-erator, who is so overwhelmed that his syntax begins to break down. This carefully executed perspective is reinforced by the first photo visitors see as they exit the elevators—"a black-and-white photo of American troops looking numbly at charred human remains on a pyre."[18] There can be little doubt that the museum invites spectators, at least initially, to assume the role of American "heroes and rescuers," though it would be unfair to the permanent exhibit as a whole to claim that it leaves this simple triumphal narrative in tact. Nevertheless, the case could be made—and indeed has been, as we shall see shortly—that the chief public commemoration of the Holocaust by the United States makes questionable concessions to Americans' vanity, patriotism, and preference for upbeat, flattering historical narratives.

After confessing that he does not know what most visitors make of their USHMM experience (this is, after all, hard to get at), Alvin Rosenfeld goes on to quote, at some length, the account of Estelle Gilson, because he suspects that hers "may be representative of the responses of many of those who come to the museum."[19] Gilson concludes her chronicle: "To have walked through this exhibition alongside fellow Americans—Caucasian Americans, African Americans, Hispanic Americans, Asian Americans, and yes, Jewish Americans—all in their bright summer tourist garb, left me feeling strangely comforted and surprisingly proud."[20] Without missing a beat, Rosenfeld quips, "Comfort and pride are no part of what one typically feels upon leaving the remains of Nazi camps in Poland or Germany or upon concluding a visit to Yad Vashem in Israel."[21] While one could argue that the analogy to concentration camps and even to Yad Vashem is not quite fair,[22] there remains the valid point that Gilson finds the USHMM to have provided some kind of uplifting American social bonding function—having galvanized Americans of the most diverse heritages into one group by way of the Holocaust.

Similarly, Peter Novik prefaces his concerns about American commemoration of the Holocaust with the perhaps-by-now requisite caveat that we cannot know for certain what visitors take from this experience. Though he begins with reflections on the USHMM, he quickly broadens his purview, looking back to the key year 1978 when the television series *Holocaust* was first broadcast in the United States—a watershed year in the American public's Holocaust education,[23] just as it proved to be for German audiences.[24] Throughout this ethically disconcerting time period in U.S. politics and society, particularly in the wake of Vietnam and Watergate, an engagement with the Holocaust may, he suggests, have offered Americans a sense of clear moral order: "So, in one sense, viewing *Holocaust* was a ritual of solidarity expressing abhorrence of 'evil incarnate'— an affirmation of shared values, albeit expressed negatively."[25] In all three of the foregoing examples, it is suggested that Americans derive from the

Holocaust some positive source of cultural identity, be it the image of the innocent American GIs, the morally outraged General Eisenhower, the sense of unity among otherwise radically diverse demographic groups, or the "reassurance that good and evil" remain "clearly distinguishable."[26] If these are in fact fundamentally "American" approaches to the Holocaust, then we are no farther along in our quest to understand the appeal of *The Reader* to American readers, for it would seem to fulfill none of these needs. There are no Americans in the novel, and the only U.S. presence is indirect and negative: Berg tells us that it was an Allied bomb that ignited the church steeple in the first place, setting in motion the most devastating event in the novel—the burning of the church together with all its *ad hoc* inmates. We may note in passing that this mention of an "Allied bomb" probably goes unnoticed by the bulk of U.S. readers, who are regularly characterized, fairly or not, as notoriously uninformed in matters of history.

Nor can Schlink's "American" Jewish survivor (who is referred to as "Ilana" in the film but goes unnamed in the novel) fulfill the role of a character with whom readers potentially identify. Rosenfeld has argued in "*The Americanization of the Holocaust*" that a fairly recent interest in survivors and rescuers belies a peculiarly American inability or unwillingness to face the true horrors of the Holocaust; in short, and paradoxically, Americans seek consolation in the very focus of their "Holocaust" narratives.[27] While the Hollywood film depicts the (now fully American) Jewish survivor in a notably conciliatory fashion (see Chapter 6), this is not the case in the novel. Though the Jewish woman Berg visits near the end of the narrative—the only living survivor of the church fire—has notably found refuge in the United States, she plays an overall far too meager role—her character is too cool, and too sparsely drawn, to elicit this kind of emotional investment on the part of U.S. readers.

Finally, it can hardly be said that *The Reader* presents a touchstone of moral certitude. Just the opposite appears to be the case. Numerous critics, as we saw in Chapter 2, hail the novel as achieving moral sophistication precisely because it denies the easy reassurance that good and evil are indeed clearly distinguishable. On the contrary, Hanna is said to confront us with a moral "gray zone." The extent of her moral freedom has been significantly circumscribed by her handicap, and we, like Berg, are left with the dilemma of either understanding or condemning. Doing both simultaneously seems impossible.

If these were the only "American" ways of confronting the Holocaust, we might find ourselves at a dead end. But, in fact, as both Novik and Alvin Rosenfeld argue, the Holocaust has, perhaps from the very beginning of its public commemoration, offered Americans a way of expressing, dramatiz-ing, and perhaps even "treating" their sense of victimhood. The appropria-tion of victim status that we witness in the following is both disarming in its unabashed bluntness and surprising for its apparent ubiquity in American culture. Novik writes,

> Both inside and outside the political arena, it became common to invoke the Holocaust to dramatize one's victimhood—and survival. As "persecuted evangelical Christians," said Ronald Reagan's interior secretary, James G. Watt, he and his wife could see "the seeds of the Holocaust-type mentality here in America," and for that reason they were strong supporters of the Washington Holocaust Museum. Returning to television after a sex and money scandal led to his and his wife's departure from their PTL [Praise The Lord] Ministry, Jim Bakker told viewers that "if Jim and Tammy can survive their holocaust of the last two years, then you can make it."[28]

If these were merely isolated instances, such shocking misappropriations of Holocaust symbolism might be less worrisome. Yet Rosenfeld deems them not exceptional, but emblematic, of a "culture that seems to encour-age and reward victimhood status . . . And so we have proliferating images of the Holocaust serving as ready-at-hand emblems of accusation in con-temporary debates about AIDS, abortion, child abuse, gay rights, the rights of immigrant aliens, etc . . . In this imaginary world, Holocausts threaten from every corner, and all are victims or potential victims."[29]

He gives the example of the immensely popular Pat Robertson, whose words, regularly heard by millions via the Christian Broadcasting Net-work, cannot easily be dismissed: "Just what Nazi Germany did to the Jews, so liberal America is now doing to evangelical Christians . . . It's no different; it's the same thing. It is happening all over again. It is the Democratic Congress, the liberal-biased media, and the homosexuals who want to destroy all Christians. It's more terrible than anything suf-fered by any minority in our history."[30] To underscore the already obvious analogy, "footage of Nazi atrocities against the Jews appeared on screen" while Robertson spoke.[31] Given the quotations from Jim Bakker and Pat Robertson, we may be tempted to conclude that this phenomenon is restricted primarily to right-wing religious fundamentalists. Yet this is not the case either. In his analysis, Rosenfeld targets the leftist secular Jewish artist Judy Chicago—and specifically her controversial "Holocaust Proj-ect"—for scathing critique, and Novik reminds us that none other than Woody Allen, in the wake of scandals about his personal life, resorted to Holocaust analogies (comparing himself to survivors) in order to find the strength to get through the ordeal.[32]

If there is something to this trend of co-opting Jewish suffering, then how is this need met by *The Reader*, a novel, as I have already argued, that hardly provides us with a palpable Jewish survivor or victim who might serve as the identificatory vehicle for readers' self-pity? True, we do have the testimony of that Jewish daughter; and while her description of the death march and the fire in the church adds information and intensifies the drama, it constitutes a very small part of the novel as a whole and is not, as far as Holocaust literature is concerned, particularly graphic. Moreover, neither she nor her mother figure as "flesh and blood" characters in this novel.[33] How can victim roles be wrested from figures who never really embodied them in the first place?

American readers clearly gravitate not toward the Jews but toward the Germans, Hanna and Berg. They do so, as it were, at the behest, and with the permission, of the Jewish Holocaust victims. In a dramatic passage toward the novel's end, Berg receives the victim mantel, as Ernestine Schlant first pointed out in her study *The Language of Silence: West German Literature and the Holocaust* (1999), from none other than the surviving daughter. While she refuses to grant Hanna explicit absolution, she does anoint Berg as Hanna's preeminent victim. And if we are honest, she implicitly rehabilitates Hanna simply by accepting the tea tin—Hanna's personal legacy to her—as a replacement for the one she lost in the camps. It does not take a semiotician to see this as being restitution, and thus reconciliation, at some level. In both cases, and in fairly direct fashion, the Jew is made to endorse the German's status as a victim (a move, as we have noted elsewhere in this study, that Schlink already rehearsed in *Selbs Justiz*). Daldry's film exploits and expands upon this key exchange, as we will see in the next chapter.

Perhaps it was a sign of the times that Schlink felt compelled in the mid-1990s to fictionally enact this Jewish acknowledgment of Germans' victim status. Today we are freer, I think, to consider the vulnerability and undeniable suffering and death of millions of Germans without necessarily equating them with Jewish victims of the Holocaust in this strained and unconvincing manner. Upon reflection, it seems artificial, to say the least, to have Berg "recapitulate" the fate of the young Jewish girls who were sequestered for special reading detail at the Auschwitz satellite camp, because in this way, he essentially "occupies" their victimhood, as it is their victimhood—as Berg well understands—that in part transfers to him. He does not demur from imagining abuse scenarios that equate him with these Jewish girls (e.g., "Would she have sent me to the gas chamber if she hadn't been able to leave me, but wanted to get rid of me"),[34] even while arguing eloquently that Hanna would never have done such a thing. He has it both ways: mighty Aphrodite again.

It may be that American readers needed the blessing, so to speak, of Jewish victims in order to take seriously the suffering of the Germans. But if this is so, it seems necessary to distinguish among German victims and specifically to extricate Hanna from her symbiotic relationship with Berg, for these really are of two distinct kinds, after all. She remains an image of the abjected other, whereas Berg rises to the level of a heroic protagonist—a traumatized postwar reader of the Holocaust whose mastery of the events is above all evidenced by his advancement to the position of author of this account. American readers might sympathize with Hanna as someone less fortunate—someone, I dare say, they are grateful not to be. In Berg, on the other hand, they see an image of themselves.[35]

In the case of Hanna, readers' "sympathy" is not really an opportunity for identification so much as an opportunity for what Julia Kristeva has called "abjection": the expulsion of qualities that cannot be admitted to consciousness but whose very exclusion is constitutive of our subjectivity.[36] In terms of popular realism, Hanna's illiteracy functions perfectly. By definition, it represents something that readers—through the very fact of reading the novel—are not. More important, and more psychically rewarding, one might say, is the fact that readers can reject all that is uncomfortably associated with Hanna—such as her preethical thinking that leaves her entangled in crimes against humanity. It has often been said, as noted in Chapter 2, that this novel represents a breakthrough in moral sophistication precisely because it dares to represent ethical ambiguity. But what readers really enjoy is the abjection of this unpleasant ambiguity. Hanna Schmitz is not really a "Jane Doe" perpetrator after all—"mit dem Allerweltsnamen Schmitz" (with the extremely common name of Schmitz). She is, rather, a pitiable illiterate person whom readers are quite happy to see expunged from the narrative. Her death proves as "satisfying" as did Korten's in the detective series. Or, to put it perhaps more accurately, her character provides both the *frisson* of high-level moral ambiguity and the ultimate relief of eliminating this irritant from the narrative. Like so much else in this novel, this turn of events also adheres to the law not of simple binary oppositions (either-or) but rather to illusorily concomitant propositions.

Ironically, the characterization of Hanna as morally illiterate—incapable even years after the fact of recognizing ethical options—may render her even more "alien" than if Schlink had depicted her criminal complicity more directly. Readers shy away from—and abject—the lack of agency embodied in Hanna on trial—the Hanna who speaks the novel's most famous lines. Ultimately, it is not the act of murder that renders an individual inadmissible—including innumerable literary figures, by the way—but rather the lack of agency that characterizes Hanna for most of the novel—up until her miraculous reversal in prison. Confessed murderers can be reconciled and (to use Peter Brooks's formulation) readmitted to the circle of civilized humanity.[37] And perpetrators can become objects of unmistakable personal identification, as the Episcopal bishop of New York made clear in "the first major public event in which Christians *as* Christians were involved in Holocaust commemoration." In his opening remarks to a plenary session of a 1974 conference at the Cathedral of St. John the Divine in New York City—the first of many such U.S. conferences—he said,

> If we look into our souls, we know that we too were there at Auschwitz; that any one of us could, under certain circumstances, have committed those atrocities . . . I entered the Marine Corps as a rather decent, Christian American boy; I was trained to kill; and I did kill . . . I found my soul somehow so warped and immunized by the propaganda to which I was exposed that I could do these things without feeling . . . I have had my Mylai in my own life, so that our Mylai did not surprise me when it came; and I think that perhaps any one of us could also have had his or her own Mylai, his or her own Auschwitz.[38]

Some may take offense at the bishop's comparisons of My Lai, Auschwitz, and his own career as a U.S. Marine, but the shortcomings of equationism are not my point here. Rather, in closing our discussion of Hanna as an abjected object of apparent pity, I want to draw our attention to the missed opportunity her characterization brings with it. By not giving Hanna a specific role in the genocide, Schlink's novel deprives readers of the opportunity to compassionately imagine the acute mental suffering of an actor who has confronted her own participation in mass murder. Failing this, readers are denied the chance to identify with Hanna as a complex moral agent. The gifts Hanna offers the lone Jewish survivor suggest repentance, remorse, and the need for reconciliation—but for what? It is not enough—simply from a narrative point of view—to say that all this is well known and need not be repeated here. The failure to *dramatize* it within the novel—indeed, the conscious decision to relegate Hanna's belated conversion, as it were, to brief secondhand summary reports—means that she essentially remains as the creaturely, inarticulate, overgrown child, incapable of thinking and acting like an adult for the greater part of her life. The result is a caricature of a perpetrator—a scapegoat whose suicide enacts the very abjection readers secretly desire.[39]

To emphasize "roads not taken" can be a risky enterprise in literary criticism. In response to the argument I have offered here regarding Hanna's potential depiction, I can well imagine the reaction of a cherished mentor, the great Harvard Germanist Karl S. Guthke, who delighted in hurling the following admonition at seminar students when he thought they might be going dangerously off track: "That is precisely the novel that *wasn't* written; stick to the text we have before us!" This is still pertinent advice that I have, from time to time, handed on to my own students. Yet it bears perhaps too great an imprint of *textimmanent*—or, in the United States, "New Critical"—assumptions, which most of my teachers absorbed as they came of age professionally, but that, in terms of a critical framework, cannot adequately address Holocaust literature. So to grasp how, in this case, Hanna evokes sympathy but also, at a deeper level, a kind of revulsion, it is indeed helpful to understand precisely what she is not, or alternatively, what she might otherwise have been. At the same time, it is helpful to take that sage advice and stick to the narrative, because there is also a clear narratological rationale for limiting the discussion of Hanna's "conversion." To write this development into the novel, instead of leaving it essentially as an epilogue to her suicide, would have meant a major shift in focus. Hanna's story would have become the lightning rod for readers' emotional investment; the novel's dearth of concern for Jewish victims would have become even more evident; and, above all, Berg's own *via dolorosa* would have been relegated to secondary status.

Despite all of Oprah's promptings, American readers are not really invested in either Jewish victims or in Hanna as a "perpetrator-victim." They are, to put it perhaps a bit too polemically (and yet to echo the analyses of Novik, A. Rosenfeld, Langer, and others), primarily interested in *themselves* (ourselves) as victims, and no one fills this need better than Berg. There is something acutely distasteful about using actual Holocaust victims as props for self-pity, as the examples of Woody Allen, Judy Chicago, Jim Bakker, and Pat Robertson make abundantly clear. Simply quoting their crudely self-serving misappropriations of Jewish suffering and death makes the point. But what about affiliating oneself with the sufferings of second-generation Germans? That is an option that, I would argue, might seem perfectly respectable to Americans but in fact is something that remains highly problematic in Germany.

Henryk Broder's charge that "the Germans will never forgive the Jews for Auschwitz" still haunts German public culture.[40] Overt sympathy for the dilemma of second-generation Germans—succinctly formulated by Schlink as the psychic suffering that results from having loved perpetrators—was, and perhaps still is, taboo. To many, and perhaps for good reason, it frankly seems indecent to focus on this kind of pain—no matter how legitimate and worthy of cultural expression—as long as the official Holocaust-commemorating agenda appears to require public rituals that are concerned exclusively with the genocide itself—as well as with its principal victims, the Jewish population of Europe. In 1996, a year after *The Reader* first appeared, the Hamburg sociologist Sybille Tönnies identified what she regarded as an unseemly trend of Germans trespassing on the turf of Jewish victimhood.[41] Given this climate, one can understand why Schlink chose to place a novel that is essentially about the woes of second-generation Germans under the rubric of more traditional Holocaust literature, to which early critics readily assented, as we have noted, by filing *The Reader* under the ambitious category of literary Vergangenheitsbewältigung. The need to camouflage or de-emphasize the concern for the second generation's pain furthermore helps to explain Berg's obsessive confessions of guilt that we identified in Chapter 3. Apart from serving as a badge of undeserved suffering, his guilt discourse constitutes a kind of "code" for expressing the second generation's sense of victimization without seeming to intrude on Jewish suffering. Germans may express *guilt* all they like—that works like a charm. Schlink's achievement consists in having Berg broadcast the victim message in, and through, the relentless confession of guilt. It may well be, as Bill Niven argues in his study *Germans as Victims*, that we now find ourselves in a quite different dispensation—an era in which Germans are much freer to see and depict themselves as victims of World War II.[42] But there is no symmetry of suffering here: portraying oneself as a victim of Allied fire bombing, of Soviet rape and plunder campaigns, or of other postwar privations is simply of a different order, as we can see in the many works that document this suffering but are careful to code it as a *consequence of* Germany's war of aggression and the genocide against the Jews.[43] Indeed, in contemporary German society, there apparently remains a powerful taboo against acknowledging second-generation suffering in any commensurate way unless it comes wrapped with the acceptable label of "Holocaust literature," accompanied by copious, even obsequious, expressions of German guilt.

But what if Berg were not (or not only) an icon of second-generation *German* suffering but an emblem of the burden *any* member of a subsequent generation must feel in coping with atrocities of this magnitude that he or she had nothing to do with in the first place? What may seem to require careful narrative choreography in the German context may strike American readers as much less fraught. As an innocent who has the Holocaust thrust upon him and who does his best to deal with all its complex (and seemingly contradictory) requirements, Berg presents a very respectable and attractive figure with whom to identify. Well into the arduous trial, after having learned of horrendous crimes and listened to difficult testimony, he confesses that he has had enough. And in this, he anticipates the (American) reader's sense of exhaustion with and "entrapment" by the Holocaust: "I had had enough too. But I couldn't put it behind me. For me, the proceedings were not ending, but just beginning. I had been a spectator, and then suddenly a participant, a player, and member of the jury [Mitentscheider]. *I had neither sought nor chosen this new role, but it was mine whether I wanted it or not, whether I did anything or just remained completely passive.*"[44]

By the late 1990s, when *The Reader* first hit U.S. bookstores, "official" U.S. Holocaust commemoration had been in force for almost twenty years. It is not far-fetched to imagine that a number of those visitors who flocked to the USHMM in unexpectedly high numbers emerged from that experience, or from some other venue of Holocaust education, with a sense of injury or frustration. Of course exposure to the unvarnished representation of atrocity is itself extremely draining; this we can intuitively affirm from our own experience. Even patient, open-minded, and genuinely curious citizens may legitimately have wondered what on earth was to be done with this horrible knowledge, especially in light of the Rwandan and Bosnian genocides that occurred concurrently with unprecedented levels of Holocaust education and commemoration in the United States.[45]

In his account of the founding of USHMM, Linenthal reports, "By the time the President's Commission was created in 1978, a canonical reading of the Holocaust had already been established in American culture, thanks largely to . . . Elie Wiesel."[46] His statement is worth quoting in full because of its resonance with Berg's language in *The Reader*. Indeed, this "American" reading of the Holocaust sounds strikingly similar to Berg's and that of his generational cohort:

> The Holocaust could never be understood but, for the sake of humankind, had to be remembered. It was an event that transcended history, almost incapable of being represented except through survivor testimony. When one was speaking of the Holocaust, it was unwritten etiquette to begin by saying that no one could understand the Holocaust, but it needed to be spoken of so "it" would not happen again, or be forgotten. The Holocaust was not only a transcendent event, it was unique, not to be compared to any other genocidal situation, and its victims were Jews. Any comparison of event or linkage to any other victim group could be, and often was perceived as, if not the murder of memory, at least its dilution.[47]

Linenthal cites this "canonical reading" only to introduce the impossibility of enshrining it as such in the USHMM. But for Berg—and the generation he stands for—this becomes an expression of the exacting and ultimately impossible demands made by official Holocaust commemoration. Notice how the aporias of Wiesel's mode of Holocaust commemoration become a series of unreasonable and mutually exclusive mandates for Berg:

> At the same time I ask myself, as I had already begun to ask myself back then: What should our second generation have done, what should it do with the knowledge of the horrors of the extermination of the Jews? We should not believe we can comprehend the incomprehensible, we may not compare the incomparable, we may not inquire because to inquire is to make the horrors an object of discussion, even if the horrors themselves are not questioned, instead of accepting them as something in the face of which we can only fall silent in revulsion, shame, and guilt. Should we only fall silent in revulsion, shame, and guilt? To what purpose? . . . that some few would be convicted and punished while we of the second generation were silenced by revulsion, shame, and guilt—was that all there was to it now?[48]

By juxtaposing these two passages, it is easy to see how Berg transforms Wiesel's paradoxical agenda into a set of impossible-to-fulfill requirements, a kind of permanent scourge upon second-generation Germans. If one cannot comprehend, compare, and analyze, how can one apply the "lessons of the Holocaust" to contemporary politics? How then can one possibly ensure that something of this kind never happens again—this being, after all, the avowed purpose of so much Holocaust commemoration?

This impossible dilemma—which falls so onerously upon the second (and subsequent) generations, reemerges in slightly different form when Berg visits the Struthof concentration camp, which he does twice in the novel.[49] There he is confronted with the same problem that many American visitors to the USHMM will have experienced: exactly what or how is one supposed to feel? What is the appropriate reaction? What if one cannot quite muster it, whatever that "it" ultimately may be? Using the camp's realia, Berg tries to imagine the horrors: "I really tried; I looked at a barracks, closed my eyes, and imagined row upon row of barracks. I measured a barracks, calculated its number of occupants from the informational booklet, and imagined how crowded it had been . . . But it was all in vain, and I had a feeling of the most deplorable, shameful failure."[50] Although, by one set of criteria, Berg claims to have "failed," at the same time, he does not really know what is being asked of visitors.[51] And later, after having completed the tour, he lies in his hotel room bed wondering if, and how, he can ever lead a normal life after this harrowing experience.[52] He thus registers the full—and contradictory—set of expectations of Holocaust pedagogy in his personal life. And likewise, when the film takes Berg through the Natzweiler-Struthof camp, the emphasis is also on his tortured response, as we will see in the following chapter. Moreover, the Strutthof camp exhibit—particularly with its mound of expropriated shoes—is starkly reminiscent of one of the most commented upon exhibits at the USHMM, thus merging Berg with the "American" viewer even further.[53]

This hermeneutic dilemma plays out quite differently, depending on whether one is a German or an American. In Germany, the decade just prior to the appearance of *The Reader* was marked by a stormy debate about the proper context for Holocaust commemoration and historiography. The conservative historian Ernst Nolte launched a furious debate by suggesting that the Nazi genocide against the Jews should be understood as a kind of response to the Soviet purges and mass murder of the 1930s; from this perspective, German mass murder was neither unique nor "original" within the European context. Nolte's critics, led by Jürgen Habermas, vehemently argued that such comparisons were illegitimate because their real aim was to "unburden" German history. Of course, Habermas never denied the fact of Soviet mass murder nor its historical primacy. The disagreement rather focused on the putative purpose of such a comparison—namely, as was alleged, to make the Holocaust look slightly less abhorrent by comparison. But this was hardly the effect the debate—known in German as the *Historikerstreit* (historians' debate)—had on German intellectual and popular culture. Instead, it saturated the media and gave Germany bad press abroad, setting back the official Vergangenheitsbewältigung agenda by perhaps a decade.

It may be of value to review these facts, even briefly, since adult readers of German would have known them as part of their basic cultural competence in the mid-1990s. And it adds considerable heft to Berg's lamentations: not only were Germans "forbidden" to draw comparisons, in the general sense that Wiesel—already in 1974—believed applied to *all* observers of the Holocaust. Now, in the wake of the *Historikerstreit*, the injunction against any kind of relativizing historical comparisons took on a more punitive tone, where those perceived to be proscribing any and all comparisons were not only politically liberal Germans like Habermas but also American Jews, who, once again, were "dictating" how the Holocaust was to be remembered in Germany.[54]

Although the *Historikerstreit* made headlines in the United States, it never penetrated the popular culture to the extent it had in Germany.

And though there were (and still are) many who believe the Holocaust's singularity—they would say uniqueness—is seriously degraded whenever it is invoked as part of a comparison with other genocides, this view was challenged early on. In fact, as Linenthal shows, the very founding of the USHMM testifies to the plurality of views that necessarily replaced the erstwhile "canonical reading." Simply in order to lay out the permanent exhibit, scholars had to conclude that the Holocaust is in fact comprehensible—though perhaps not fully. As an object of historical analysis, it simply could not remain a transcendent event. And as the museum's series of temporary exhibits demonstrates, it would indeed serve as a touchstone for coming to terms with other atrocities and genocides—though here, too, not without arousing considerable debate from time to time. As Raul Hilberg has argued, the USHMM could sensibly uphold both terms of the debate—the Holocaust's singularity as well as its comparability—because there are valid arguments for maintaining both views. They are formally, but not actually, mutually exclusive positions, he has argued.[55] So while there was an official consensus against comparison in Germany (because it was held to represent the first step toward relativizing the Holocaust), the American approach—to the extent that one may speak so broadly—was more pragmatic and heterogeneous.

But if it permitted both views (the Wiesel view of the Holocaust as uniquely transcendent and the Holocaust as an object of historical study) to coexist more or less peacefully side by side, the American approach did not necessarily seek to resolve, or even make conscious, their differences, let alone take account of the cognitive and emotional dissonance this might create within observers. For example, to explicitly suggest that studying the Holocaust provides valuable lessons for ethnically mixed societies—as the USHMM and numerous state Holocaust curricula do—and then to "fail" to apply these lessons meaningfully to contemporary atrocities, can lead some observers to the very same conclusion articulated so eloquently by Berg. Such people may wonder, as Berg does, what the point of this painful pedagogy is, sometimes feeling overwhelmed by the flood of information about atrocities and unsure about what to "do" with it. In some way, they may feel "victimized" by the unrealistic promises (if not demands) of Holocaust commemoration itself. And, over time, this feeling of frustration—perhaps even resentment—may increase.[56] Thus, American observers, despite all the obvious differences enumerated here, may have a substantial commonality with second- (and subsequent) generation Germans. Since "we" are now all innocent of the Holocaust, chronologically, we cannot have had anything to do with it. But there it is, refusing to go away, making us feel uncomfortable—perhaps even "guilty"—as we wonder what to do with this terrible knowledge.

Despite all of his anguished protestations to the contrary, Berg's trip to New York indeed offers a kind of closure fully in keeping with genre expectations. Though all manner of ethical ambiguity has ostensibly been aired in the pages of *The Reader*, what we get in the end is one more confirmation of the standard view that underprivileged people are more likely than others to be involved in criminality, but that, in spite of it all, rehabilitation is possible. Hanna's eleventh-hour "enlightenment" after learning how to read is, in this sense, little more than a gloss on the (overused) Anne Frank quote to the effect that "in spite of everything, I believe that people are really good at heart."[57]

Above all, *The Reader* offers the implicit assurance, by way of Berg's own biography, that if we cannot be spared from confronting such atrocity, and are unable to avoid some damage to ourselves, we can ultimately move beyond it. Does this conclusion offer a troubling refuge to those unwilling to face the historical truth? Or does it represent a defensible mode of reception, precisely for those who have done this important work elsewhere? The answers are very likely mixed. Yet regardless of how we may individually respond to these questions, we might be able to agree that this celebration of the secondary "victims," this articulation of the plight of the post-Holocaust generation(s) in coming to terms with the genocide, is itself fundamentally appealing. In this way, the novel becomes essentially about *us*—which may explain why not just Germans but Americans as well—and readers around the world, for that matter—find it so compelling. If this is the case, Hoffman's admonition must haunt the global appeal of this book: "The statute of limitations on the Holocaust is running out, as it must. Living memory fades, the fierceness of feeling subsides . . . We must reflect on the past, but we cannot dwell in it forever. But how we turn away from the Holocaust matters . . . It matters enormously that we do not use the Holocaust for our own self-serving purposes."[58]

Chapter 6

Going Global

The Hollywood *Reader*

> Walter Benjamin asked me once in Paris during his emigration . . . whether there were really enough torturers back there to carry out the orders of the Nazis . . . Benjamin sensed that the people who *do* it, as opposed to the bureaucratic desktop murderers and ideologues, operate contrary to their own immediate interests, *are murderers of themselves* while they murder others . . . I fear that the measures of even an elaborate education will hardly hinder the renewed growth of desktop murderers. But that there are *people who do it down below, indeed as servants, through which they perpetuate their own servitude and degrade themselves, that there are more Bogers and Kaduks: against this, however, education and enlightenment can still manage a little something.*
>
> —Theodor W. Adorno, "Education after Auschwitz"

IT CAN BE A DREARY AND DEEPLY unimaginative process to tot up all the things a film gets "wrong" about a novel. And it may, in any event, be simply unfair to ask a primarily *visual* medium to remain faithful to its textual predecessor. Would we even want that? Yet as we know from *Harry Potter* aficionados the world over, there is no stopping viewers from doing just this. Whenever a book has achieved such widespread advance circulation as *The Reader*—translated now, as Ari Shapiro notes, into almost forty languages[1]—and serves as the explicit inspiration for "its" film, people are simply bound to ask about how the two line up. How do Schlink's novel and Stephen Daldry's film compare? And how do we explain the inevitable alterations? Film scholars may understandably cry foul, insisting that we not subordinate one medium to another. This is a valid point for many reasons, not the least of which is the fact that many people who view the film may never have read the book. But the novel—and the various debates it has engendered—was, as we have noted, already a mass-market phenomenon, and it shows no signs of abating. It would be naïve, I think, to exclude from consideration the myriad ways in which the film revises and expands upon—even "corrects"—the novel. This genetic approach does not compel us to neglect the film's distinctive contributions either.

Indeed, Daldry has given us striking scenes that appear nowhere in the novel, and, in so doing, he has significantly altered the trajectory of Schlink's narrative. By placing a tearful Hanna in a gorgeous, baroque country church, and by lingering over the lower- and working-class faces of visitors in a prison waiting room—to name just two examples I will treat in this chapter—he has poignantly streamlined the story. The Hollywood version of *The Reader*, I argue, makes a far more credible case for sympathetically viewing the disadvantaged perpetrators within a context that both includes and transcends the Holocaust. Yet the potential for this approach to spill over to other historical events featuring similarly underprivileged perpetrators—one thinks, for example, of the torture carried out by certain U.S. soldiers at the Abu Ghraib prison—represents a direction the film clearly does not want to take. It hesitates to walk through the door it has opened, and thus the film's "analysis" of such perpetrators—its greatest achievement, in my view—remains muted. The larger, more forceful, countervailing movement is its rage for closure. This, too, can be epitomized by two compelling visuals that will be explored here: one of the narrator, Michael Berg, as he is melodramatically restored by the very act of storytelling, and the other of the lone surviving Jew after the atrocity referenced in the story, who, for her part, is depicted as wholly removed from the Holocaust due to her extreme affluence.

All feature films that are based on novels must make huge cuts or leave vast tracts of the novel untreated. In the German tradition, there is probably no better example than Grass's *Tin Drum (Die Blechtrommel)*. Schlöndorff's remarkable film of 1979 takes up only the first quarter of that far-flung novel—to the chagrin of some students who make this discovery only as a result of encountering an exam question focused on one of the many passages that Schlöndorff left out. It is simply impossible to make a standard feature film—even one that exceeds the customary ninety-minute formula by a third, as does *The Reader*—and still do justice to every twist and turn of the "parent" novel. Yet I contend that screenwriter David Hare's emendations go well beyond such basic considerations of time. It is almost as if, prior to rewriting the novel into a film script, he first reviewed the major charges made against the novel. This supposition is not hard to imagine, given the availability of the criticism in widely accessible media venues such as *The New Republic*, *Commentary*, and *The*

Times Literary Supplement. We may not know precisely what governed Hare's "corrections," but it is clear that he has given us a substantially different *Reader* by pruning away problematic—and in some cases even embarrassing—portions of the original plot. To speak of "subtraction" as the dominant editorial principle vis-à-vis the novel is accurate enough as a rule of thumb. But it simultaneously fails to capture the sundry additions and substitutions that together make Daldry's film not only a cleaner, more streamlined version of the original story but also a work of considerable beauty in its own right.

RECASTING HANNA: CORRECTION VIA SUBTRACTION

One of the earliest and most vociferous objections to the novel had to do with its suspect deployment of illiteracy as an implicit defense. We have seen throughout this study—particularly in the considerable play given illiteracy in numerous teachers' editions—how large this disability looms in readers' assessment of Hanna's culpability. Daldry takes it off the table, so to speak, by having the lone Jewish survivor lecture Berg rather sternly about using illiteracy as an alibi.[2] This exchange comes near the end of the film—a privileged scene in any event, and one I will discuss in some detail in this chapter—but it is made to frame the entire film insofar as this interview prominently leads the trailer advertisement. In unmistakable terms, and with the special authority of the survivor, Ilana (as she is called in the film) names, and then eliminates, the illiteracy excuse, which gives the film much-needed deniability on a particularly sensitive issue.

But if we are honest, illiteracy plays somewhat less of a role in the film than in the novel—as counterintuitive as this may sound. Of course it remains a lynchpin of the plot, and it motivates the most endearing part of the love affair between Hanna and Berg. Indeed, it gives David Kross, who plays the young Berg, the opportunity to display his charming acting skills. Instead of just moping around, staring in teary disbelief or showing how aloof he can be (which he does for much of the second part of the film), here he gets the chance to ham it up. By allowing him to read not only the classics of eighteenth- and nineteenth-century German and Russian literature but also raucous comic books and the American classic *The Adventures of Huckleberry Finn* as well, Daldry has given the character greater, and far more imaginative, leeway than did Schlink. Kross's enthusiastic rendering of the slave Jim—an audio equivalent of "black face"—may prove discomfiting to contemporary American audiences, but I think it fits 1958 postwar Germany rather well. Recording literature for Hanna in prison also gives the middle-aged Berg (played by

Ralph Fiennes) a welcome break from those melancholy blank stares that he does so well.

In the film, illiteracy without a doubt remains the hallmark of Hanna's disability. But it is somehow less of a secret—and not only, I think, because so many of us will have read the book in advance. The film depends less on its discovery as a plot device and instead extensively "telegraphs" her problem almost from the outset. Even if we have not quite figured out that she cannot read or write, we see the unmistakably distraught expression on Kate Winslet's face when she is offered the promotion that would take her from being a streetcar ticket-taker to working in the office. Office work—something about that prospect makes her very nervous, anxious enough to pack her bags and move on without even saying good-bye to young Berg.

Later, through a less-than-subtle series of flashbacks highlighting all the times she refused to read (pushing a proffered book back toward Berg for him to read; nervously asking him to order when given a menu; and rejecting the guidebook he offers in order to show her the route for their planned vacation), we directly learn of Berg's "discovery" of her illiteracy. But its function instead metamorphoses into a vehicle for depicting his "betrayal" of her. Recall that in the novel we were asked to entertain the possibility that young Berg betrays Hanna by refusing to recognize her when she unexpectedly appears at the local swimming pool. All this has been—wisely, I think—excised from the film. Berg's "disloyalty" in the film becomes his failure to get up the nerve to speak to her about her hyperbolic confession of guilt in court. He sets up an appointment but flees at the last moment. He thinks better of it, returns, but is too late. This is ultimately not much of a failure, however, because it can never really have been his responsibility to confront her in this way.

In the film, therefore, illiteracy does not mitigate responsibility for Holocaust crimes *per se* but instead motivates the injustice done in the present by the court. *This* effect of illiteracy—one that victimizes Hanna before our very eyes—the stern Jewish survivor never places in doubt. Yet these two time levels cannot, in the end, be separated so cleanly. When the chief judge seeks to know if Hanna joined the SS of her own free will, we learn that her "decision" to do so came in the wake of the threat of another promotion. Yet this is not so much free choice as anxious flight, just as when she so abruptly abandons Berg after being offered a promotion in the local mass transit company. This particular deployment of illiteracy casts an exonerative glow over the conditions of Hanna's Nazi-era employment—how she came to "serve" in the SS— rather than upon her actual collaboration in deportations and death marches, resulting in the effective bifurcation of illiteracy into an illegitimate alibi (which Ilana forcefully challenges) and a legitimate source of sympathy, which the film encourages.

Illiteracy can take a backseat, so to speak, because two other pertinent factors—Hanna's gender and her lower-class provenance—are deployed to soften her criminality; and they are portrayed in such a manner that may indeed generalize the film's message to a broader, international audience. But before discussing these larger terms, it may be valuable to enumerate a series of further "subtractions" from the novel as well as one significant *addition*, which together serve to importantly upgrade the figure of Hanna Schmitz. First is the decision to cast Kate Winslet in this role. In one fell swoop, Daldry (or perhaps Anthony Minghella before him) altered the characterization of Hanna Schmitz by making her more feminine, more petite, and far less intimidating. Given the actress's delicate frame—she visibly struggles with the coal bucket as she lugs it up the stairway—it becomes clear from the moment of her appearance on screen that she could never inspire the nickname "Pferd" (horse) that Berg gives his lover in the novel.[3] She lacks the "broad back and powerful arms" of Schlink's Hanna,[4] whose rippling musculature of the upper back and neck feature so prominently throughout the novel and at the trial in particular.[5] The physical threat implicit in this strength—which gave so many teachers' commentaries reason to compare Hanna with the real-life convicted murderer, the notorious "Mare of Maidanek" ("Stute von Majdanek")[6]—utterly vanishes.

And there are other key changes. Gone is the scene of Hanna's most serious actual brutality toward Berg, when she flies into a rage at his having "abandoned" her during their country vacation and splits his lip with the buckle of her belt. Absent, too, is the one-sided obsequiousness that reduced Berg, in the novel, to the role of subordinate petitioner.[7] In the film, he complains that it is always he who has to apologize, but the script belies this claim. When they have their first fight—about who is to blame for the failed meeting in the streetcar—it seems like a genuine misunderstanding: Winslet's facial expression leaves little doubt as to her surprise at seeing him in this unexpected place. He remains in the adjoining car, and so she felt rejected, she says, and proceeds to pay him back with cruel words about how little he matters to her, which sends him running from her apartment. But when he returns and tearfully tries to talk it out, she relents. Indeed, she admits that she did not mean what she said and that she loves him,[8] confirming the existence of a reciprocal relationship of a kind the narrator of the novel never enjoys.[9] In other words, in the film, it is much more of a conventional lovers' quarrel. Granted, they are not

fully equals—Berg is articulate, while Hanna seems trapped in speechless-
ness—but neither is it the master-slave relationship of the novel.

Later, when Berg complains about being the one who has to subordinate himself, the film establishes *him* as the unambiguous aggressor.
It is his birthday, and he feels torn between the attractions of friends his
own age and Hanna's charms. He acts impatiently toward Hanna, who
has just gotten word that she is to be promoted to "office work," and
she is visibly anguished. In the midst of their battle, Berg grabs her and
kisses her—forcefully, even violently. She responds by slapping him across
the face, offering Hollywood's conventional female response to unwanted
male advances. This is Hanna at her most aggressive. I recount this much
plot because it represents a starkly different picture from the woman we
encounter in the novel. In the film, her anger is motivated by plausible
and immediate circumstances, and her response is fairly measured. She
never appears out of control or as if she is trying to suppress some kind
of violent rage that may have characterized her in an earlier phase of her
life; nor is she particularly authoritarian in her dealings with Berg. There
is no obvious trace, in other words, of the Auschwitz guard in this postwar
lover. On the contrary, the Hanna as portrayed by Winslet is vulnerable,
sensitive, and sometimes quite willing to submit herself (and not just
because of her illiteracy) to her young lover—as we see when she scrubs
every inch of his naked body prior to their final lovemaking scene.

There are further deletions that directly affect our view of Hanna but
none perhaps more important than the excision of all of Berg's mental
pleadings and bizarre fantasies of the concentration camp Hanna. Recall
that, in the book, the trial is intercut with Berg's running commentary:
when, for example, the inexperienced lawyer fails to vigorously defend
Hanna, Berg rushes (employing the literary device that Dorrit Cohn has
labeled "narrated monologue") to provide a proper defense. But in a film,
especially an aesthetically traditional one, this kind of intrusion would
be awkward. Instead, we watch the trial *with* Berg or, better, we often
watch the impression the trial is having *on* him. His face—registering,
by turns, astonishment, grief, and revulsion—commands our attention
and constitutes the film's central focus.[10] But if the filmic Hanna does not
profit from Berg's *sotto voce* defense, neither does she suffer from association with Berg's erotic fantasies, which picture her as a dominatrix clad
in black leather and wielding the requisite whip: "Die harte, herrische,
grausame Hanna [die mich] sexuell erregte."[11] (A hard, imperious, cruel
Hanna [who] aroused me sexually.)[12]

This pared-down filmic version of Hanna may at first glance appear to
be a cruder, less nuanced depiction—the classic compromise demanded

by the so-called dominant cinema, with its commercial drive to please large audiences. If we simply go by the math, this would be a convincing conclusion, for in addition to all the foregoing, the film dispenses with a key alibi. In the novel, as we saw in some detail in Chapter 3, Hanna denies ever possessing the key to the locked church and names others who quite plausibly would have been expected to take charge during the night of the awful fire, such as the armed male guards who were her superiors. They fled the scene, ostensibly to accompany some wounded to the hospital; but they were supposed to return. Why didn't they? Why didn't at least some of them come back? Why didn't they send the female guards with the wounded? Why didn't the villagers intervene, once they saw that the church was burning, to save the lives of those trapped inside? Where were these other actors when the Allied bombs hit? And where were they somewhat later, when it became clear that the church was burning? The book raises all these questions—it even suggests that the prisoners could have saved themselves[13] had they acted differently—so that, in the end, we have no definitive answer to the question of who had the last clear chance to save the lives of these Jewish women?[14] The book allows—even encourages—us to believe that not only were there serious mitigating circumstances but also alternate perpetrators, and that while Hanna was by no means a hero, she may not have been guilty of anything more than neglect or—as trite and hollow as this must sound when baldly stated—of following the orders of those immediately in charge. As Oprah memorably concluded, the Hanna of the novel can easily seem a "guilty bystander."

But not so in the film, and I would argue that this is one of the film's chief "corrections" as against the novel. At least at the level of dialogue—later we will return to the level of image, which tells an intriguingly different story—these other potential perpetrators have been cut from the script. Granted, Daldry's Hanna reminds us of the general confusion and chaos of that night, but she does not accuse anyone else. In the film, one of Berg's fellow law students summarizes it quite pithily: "Six women locked three hundred Jews in a church, and let them burn. What is there to understand?"[15] On the plane of explicit courtroom testimony, then, we could view this reduction as a simplification of a far more complex situation, as it is conceived of in the novel (and therefore as the kind of aesthetic impoverishment we might well expect from popular cinema). But it might equally well represent a rectification of the novel's "error" of obfuscating Hanna's criminality. In this way, the film makes Hanna a lot less ambiguously guilty—she is one of six who could have, and clearly should have, released the prisoners. And to the extent that the film does not equivocate about her guilt in the same "sophisticated" (or sophistic?) way the novel does, we can say that it does better in living up to Schlink's original agenda—that of portraying the plight of one who loved an actual criminal, for Daldry's Hanna, frankly, is guiltier than Schlink's.

She is so not only because film viewers lack the benefit of Berg's eloquent interior monologue defenses on her behalf. This less-debatably guilty Hanna is also a result of the film's deployment of the Holocaust survivor's testimony—particularly that of the daughter Ilana. As discussed in this chapter, the novel positions this young survivor quite differently, namely, *in response* to the ugly allegations of Hanna's codefendants, who suggest that Hanna's "special selections" may also have involved some kind of sexual abuse. Recall that in the novel, the Jewish surviving daughter is not even on the witness stand; she is sitting in the audience, listening to the testimony, when she suddenly remembers the true nature of these special selections. Her intervention, as I argued in Chapter 3, functions as a corrective to the darker interpretation offered by the codefendants, whom we know to be offering other false testimony about Hanna in order to shield themselves. The survivor solves the mystery of this "special treatment" by relating what she learned from a few of the inmates who were under Hanna's direct command. Reversing the malignant innuendo offered by the codefendants, she reveals that they were in fact treated well by Hanna—received better rations and lighter working conditions—and that they were only required to read aloud to her. Since even those who received this special treatment were, in the end, deported back to Auschwitz, the daughter does wonder aloud (and this is included in the film) whether Hanna's special treatment was ultimately any better for them. In the novel, Hanna emerges from this colloquy as a relatively humane guard. Yes, she, like all the guards, cooperated in the "selections,"[16] the guiding principle of which was that the weakest would be deported. But her wards had it relatively easier for a time—she afforded them a reprieve, though not a rescue.

Daldry stages this quite differently. The codefendants have virtually nothing to say until the matter of the contested SS report on the church fire is raised. In the film, all the damning information about Hanna comes from the surviving daughter, and not in a manner that qualifies or answers the graver charges of others. She grants that Hanna may have treated her charges better for a short time, but her final question—whether this "kindness" made any difference—is delivered more as an accusation than as an open question. The result is to render Hanna the only guard about whom we hear anything of substance. Her past thus becomes more immediate to us, more palpable, and, in this sense, "more real," while the participation of the others remains relatively more abstract. So with regard to the two main charges—the guards' responsibility on the night of the church fire and their role in the selections—the film is unambiguous in implicating Hanna. It offers no alternate perpetrators, nor does it (on this point at least) show her to be much better than her fellow guards.

The importance of this "correction" vis-à-vis the novel should not be underestimated. It is surely not merely a concession to literary critics—even to those far better known, such as Jeremy Adler (whose father, Hans Adler, was the well-known refugee from Hitler's Germany)—who complained about the way in which the novel effectively obfuscates Hanna's criminality. However, the filmmaker may well have wanted to avoid any controversy that could arise if a short clip were taken out of context, perhaps one in which Berg defends his lover to the hilt or one in which Hanna fumblingly suggests that she was waiting for guidance from her male superiors in the SS. Why risk such potentially exculpatory material, especially when it presents a danger of shifting the film's focus to the Holocaust and away from the second generation, not to mention the possibility of being quoted out of context in support of deniers?

As a binary proposition—up or down, yes or no—the film leaves the *fact* of Hanna's guilt uncontested. And I would argue that this is a distinct improvement rather than an awkward simplification, as it removes a potentially distracting debate about her actual culpability and paves the way for us to pity her. The Hanna of the film, despite her one big cover-up lie, comes across, paradoxically, as more "truthful" than her literary counterpart. She not only offers a capacious confession (as in the novel) but also resists the temptation to point to others as an alibi—a strategy that, in the novel, as we saw, had the effect of undoing the substance of the confession. Hanna's codefendants receive four years and three months each for "aiding and abetting murder in three hundred cases," and the implication is clearly that she—though more humane than they, and plainly more forthcoming during the trial—is no guiltier than they are. Hanna repeatedly says—naively turning toward her codefendants for an affirmation that, of course, never materializes—"but we all did it." Nevertheless, she alone is given a life sentence.[17]

Class Critique and the Rage for Closure

Visually, however, the film sends a more complex and far more interesting message. It provides a nonverbal, multivalent perspective on this class of perpetrators. Specifically, by depicting Hanna as a vulnerable, underprivileged woman—one of many—the film offers not a simple alibi or excuse but a kind of visual investigation of the social provenance of the lower-level collaborators with the Nazi regime. The most poignant scene in this respect is the visitors' waiting area in the prison where Hanna is being held during the trial. The camera drinks in the spare setting, and though we are ostensibly here to witness Berg's anguish as he tries to decide whether he can actually speak to Hanna about her cover-up, we enter another world. The camera becomes, in a sense, promiscuous or, perhaps, forgetful of its mission, for instead of focusing on its character of alleged interest—the beleaguered young Berg—and moving the plot along expeditiously, it lingers over the hardened faces of the down-and-out visitors waiting along with him to visit their loved ones. Berg stands out—even in his disheveled state—as distinctly bourgeois. We see the faces of the postwar, modestly dressed working class.

And they are all working-class, which is a circumstance that Daldry clearly wants us to ponder, for he positions his camera in a manner that contravenes dominant cinematic expectations. It does not record exclusively from the perspective of Berg, who is clearly so wrapped up in his inner anguish that it is doubtful whether he is registering any of this carefully rendered social reality. On the contrary, the camera briefly takes on a documentary perspective, framing its lower-class subjects in the manner, say, of Ansel Adams or Paul Graham.[18] This filmic intermezzo presents at least three portraits—the disoriented elderly couple; the middle-aged man with his ill-matched, worn tweed outfit; and a close-up of a woman's disoriented, quizzical face. There is unmistakable beauty in this sketch. The filmmaker captures, fleetingly, the grief and confusion in the faces of people who do not seem to know how to proceed or what kind of consolation to offer. They are being directed, instructed, herded—as we can imagine they have been, as members of the working class, all their lives. Each is apparently there to visit someone on the inside. Yet given the manner in which the camera captures them—huddled in confined quarters, mutely waiting for further guidance, prodded to move on at the behest of a gruff guard, responding unquestioningly to authority—they do not seem all that different from the prisoners they are there to visit.

Where have we seen this before? One does not have to think long before answering this question. The film opens in Hanna's working-class neighborhood, and though it is in many respects faithful to Schlink's description in the novel, the film medium is simply superior at rendering the vast differences in social privilege that separate Hanna from Berg. His romantic escapade is no dangerous liaison with an insatiable housewife from his own social class. When he goes to visit Hanna in the *Bahnhof-strasse*, he is clearly "slumming it." The visual evocation of the West German working class of the late 1950s is deliberate—down to the chipped

Figure 6.1   A fleeting portrait of working class visitors at the prison where Hanna is being held. (Still from *The Reader*.)

enamel of the doorbell plaque and the peeling linoleum on the floors. Her apartment is the rough equivalent of a cold-water flat: a simple, two-room efficiency. She lives in what Germans will recognize as a workers' tenement, a *Mietskaserne*—literally, a "renters' barracks."

Intermittently we hear the buzz of a ripsaw, marking the site as one of small industry as well. The lumber yard that occupies the "Hof" portion of Hanna's building may be a homage to Alfred Döblin, who begins his iconic novel of working-class criminality, *Berlin Alexanderplatz* (1929), with just such a scene: Franz Biberkopf, recently released from prison, returns to a tenement cum lumberyard very reminiscent of this setting. And for those who may miss the literary allusion, Rainer Werner Fassbinder's 1980 film adaptation, complete with ripsaw audio track, may still reverberate in cultural memory. In this milieu, work never really ends; it is the antithesis of the bourgeois bedroom community, or *Villenviertel*, of Berg's upbringing. As the young Berg hesitantly approaches Hanna's apartment for the second and third times, he pointedly makes way for the gritty, overall-clad workmen carrying bundles of lumber who cross in front of him. They are not masses used for decoration—as Siegfried Kracauer argues in *From Caligari to Hitler* (with respect to Weimar-era film)—but, rather, are individual members of the working class metonymically deployed to indicate masses of workers like themselves. For a few moments, they emerge from the film's background in order to characterize Hanna and Berg. Though Berg temporarily defers to their activity, briefly yielding center stage to them, his erotic trysts with Hanna are themselves emblems of his class privilege. In becoming Hanna's lover, he, in a sense, poaches "their" woman: the rich boy who does not need to work has the leisure to pursue a woman who "should" be one of theirs. At any rate, Berg is fascinated with—maybe even frightened by—this milieu, even before he discovers Hanna as erotic object. Later on, he will tear up the stairs (and the camera with him), but at first, both sets of eyes—the camera's and his—dwell upon the details and trappings of working-class living arrangements.

Though the film has vastly reduced the plot-time spent in Berg's middle-class house, it takes us there frequently enough for us to appreciate the difference. The film never reveals that Berg's father is a professor of philosophy or that he was a minor resister during the war (having dared to lecture on Spinoza, even after the Nuremburg laws had been enacted). All of this falls away, but not the economic privilege. In the novel, it was Hanna who was dumbstruck by the sheer excess of the father's library; in the film, this task—not this precise observation, of course, for there is no library in Daldry's story—falls to us. When the thirty-something Berg returns home to tell his mother about his impending divorce, the visual register—with its focus on the substantial dining room set and Biedermeier sideboard—seems anxious to pursue this other story—the class divide that has been depicted for much of the early part of the film.

With Berg's rushing to and fro from after-school beach parties to Hanna's tenement, we are regularly reminded of the economic gap he bridges with each trip. His classmates—all seemingly members of the solid middle class—dangle their feet in the water, read by the waterside, splash each other playfully, gossip idly, giggle impulsively, ogle their peers, and plan parties and sexual conquests. In the novel, this segment was intended to

Figure 6.2   Berg's affluent upbringing on display. (Still from *The Reader*.)

show how Berg is drawn both to a beautiful young girl his own age (the pretty, Teutonic-looking Sophie) and to Hanna. It was meant to supply further evidence of how his experience with Hanna distorted his normal development (which is not really left to our imagination, insofar as the Sophie of the novel returns to accuse Berg of being maladjusted). Daldry retains Sophie—the other potential love interest—but uses her principally in order to oppose her to the working-class Hanna.[19] In Berg's pendulum between these two worlds, it is Hanna, the anti-Sophie, who stands out starkly as one who clearly never enjoyed such a childhood. She does not have the luxury of whiling away afternoons at a gorgeous lake resort and obviously never did. Unlike Sophie, she will not study at the university, nor will she ever really have much of a career.

All this we understand well before the "discovery" of her illiteracy, which really only confirms and caps a view of her underprivileged life that we have been given from the beginning. By making her, in addition, an "ethnic German" (a *Volksdeutsche*), Schlink places her clearly on the margins of German culture.[20] The novel gives her place of birth as Hermannstadt,[21] Romania, suggesting that she is, in a sense, twice orphaned. Not only is she deprived of a family, she is also without a proper "German" cultural milieu of origin as well. Her Volksdeutsche heritage not only signals outsider status in a general sense; in addition, certain readers may be invited to see her as the victim of anti-German persecution conducted against ethnic Germans during the Hitler period, which was not only the subject of lurid Nazi propaganda (patterned, as it turns out, precisely on the kind of persecution then being perpetrated upon Jews) but highlighted as well by the Adenauer government in the postwar era.[22] Indeed, the Federal Republic of Germany issued commemorative stamps enshrining the plight of the ethnic Germans up until the late 1950s, giving them prominent status as a victim group.[23] This Volksdeutsche heritage may powerfully communicate to certain German readers,[24] but it does not transfer well to the film—or to the English version of the novel, for that matter, and neither is it necessary, given all the other visual markers of Hanna's social and cultural deprivation we have been given. Reduced to casting Hanna in starker relief, the filmic Sophie functions as the classic foil. Unlike this pretty young schoolgirl, the darling of Berg's Gymnasium class, Hanna lives a life of drudgery, routine, and duty. She gets up early, puts on a uniform, and performs simple, repetitive tasks all day long. When she comes home from work, she is exhausted, sweaty, and dirty—and yet her work is never done. We see her hauling a pail of coal up the stairs, ironing, and doing laundry. Her whole life—except for the respite offered by

Berg—is a chore. Even her promotion comes from above, as something unanticipated, unasked for, imposed, and ultimately unwanted.

These two sites—Hanna's working-class apartment and the prison waiting room—conduct a visual dialogue between the singular and the plural; she is the particular case of a more general phenomenon, the film seems to suggest. Those downtrodden people in the prison waiting room may not all be waiting to see prisoners being held for war crimes or crimes against humanity; in fact, this is unlikely. But neither is the point of these images merely to underscore the sociological fact that involvement in crime—the particular kinds of crime that tend to be prosecuted vigorously—is inversely related to class privilege. In the context of *The Reader*, whose theme is the Holocaust—whether or not Schlink would like to admit it—this studied attention to the working-class provenance of the film's chief perpetrator is not meant to excuse or expunge her guilt but rather to reflect upon how she became an SS guard in the first place. More successfully than the book, the film explores the intriguing question of criminal causality.[25]

When, during a charged exchange with the presiding judge, Hanna responds that she cooperated in the selections because "new women were arriving all the time, so of course we had to move some of the old ones on. We couldn't keep everyone. There wasn't room,"[26] she is exhibiting the classic behavior of the subordinate worker who takes for granted the boss' right to make the rules. She may not have liked them, but she felt she had no business questioning them. In effect, she is expressing a very familiar defense, though somewhat indirectly. It differs not only in its inarticulateness—she never actually says that she was "just following orders," though this is clearly implied in her earnestly affirmed words "we had to." What makes this "defense" different from the one so familiar to us from other tribunals such as the Nuremberg and Frankfurt Auschwitz trials is that it is "spoken" from a clearly demarcated lower-class perspective. Or, better, it is spoken on her behalf by the film.

What Hanna does not need to say is that her whole underprivileged life—and not just the particular fact of her illiteracy—prepared her for just this kind of "service." To the film's credit, it offers this contextualization without simplistically imposing it as grounds for exculpation. This interpolated working-class tableau does not say that it is acceptable, or inevitable, that the Hannas of this world cooperate in genocide. But it does suggest reasons why it may have been relatively easy to recruit guards from the ranks of those depicted waiting in the anteroom of the prison: these are the people who desperately need to work, who are not educated, who do not have many options, and whose economic status has kept them in a subordinate position all their lives, such that the "Kantian autonomy" the novel makes so much of is surely foreign to their everyday experience.[27] It is a controversial message because it implies that this class of collaborator was not in the first instance induced to cooperate because of specifically Nazi convictions or sympathies. Hanna mentions nothing of the sort as a factor in her "decision" to join the SS. Unlike her literary "cousin," the privileged and highly educated Gerhard Selb (see Chapter 1), she never was a "convinced Nazi."

Seen from this perspective, the portrayal of Hanna as a collaborator with a criminal regime becomes relevant to an international audience in a manner that Schlink has surely not anticipated. In the popular U.S. film *A Few Good Men* (dir. Rob Reiner, 1992), two U.S. Marines from very modest backgrounds—one is black; the other, a slow-witted white youth—are charged with the murderous hazing of a fellow soldier, Private Santiago. There is no doubt that they did it: they carried out a "code red" assault that resulted in the death of their comrade. They were the proximate perpetrators. The only question is whether they acted on their own or whether the action was ordered by higher authorities. Most viewers will recall the brilliant dialogue between the JAG defense lawyer Daniel Kaffee (played by Tom Cruise) and Colonel Nathan Jessep (played by Jack Nicholson), in which the young and inexperienced lawyer ultimately gets the better of the older colonel, forcing him into admitting that he ordered the deadly hazing.[28] We experience a sense of euphoria and relief at Kaffee's having nailed the bastard behind the crime. It is especially satisfying because Jessep is a highly placed, highly educated, and highly privileged figure. The satisfaction of the sense of justice we feel has as much to do with vindicating the two socially disadvantaged Marines who are being court-martialed, it seems, in place of the truly responsible party. In its focus on rival perpetrators (the real one versus the duped, lower-level, and, in some sense, unwitting collaborators), the film virtually forgets the dead Marine himself.

Yet following the cathartic release of emotion connected to Jessep's dramatic admission, the two Marines are convicted after all, albeit on far lesser charges. As one manfully advises the other, they should have known better than to harass their buddy, even if the commander ordered it. The white defendant, Private First Class Downey, who does not seem intellectually on a par with high school graduates, accepts this verdict with tears in his eyes.[29] As in *The Reader*, *A Few Good Men* not only withholds exoneration, it explicitly punishes these two low-level perpetrators. But simultaneously, by furnishing us the sad images of these two handsome but hapless youths, who frankly do not seem to have had many other

career options, the film supplies a powerful, if only implicit, "explanation" of their criminal actions. And we are left thinking that this calami-
tous turn of events, while perhaps not quite their foreordained fate, is
hardly surprising given their socioeconomic background.

The portrayal of Hanna and these two young Marines contains, at its
core, a potentially provocative proto-Marxist critique. Why are the poor
and economically underprivileged, as a group, predisposed to obedience
and submission? The answer is not difficult to divine: such has been their
lot the whole of their lives. This is not the case for those middle- and
upper-class defendants we know from the Nuremberg and Frankfurt Auschwitz trials. Recall, for example, the case of SS Corporal Stark, featured
unforgettably in Peter Weiss's documentary play *The Investigation*: he is
studying for his *Abitur* (the leaving exam of the exclusive college preparatory school) between acts of murderous brutality at Auschwitz. One
hardly need review the high level of education and cultural sophistication
of leading Nazi perpetrators; indeed, the cultivated Nazi, listening to a
Mozart sonata while resting from the "work" of genocide, has become
almost a cliché of Nazi iconography.[30] When such defendants offer the
defense that they were only following orders, they can at best call upon
an authoritarian, militaristic ethos and culture that encouraged such
behavior. But they cannot invoke a life of backbreaking labor in low-
level employment or the systematic deprivation of education and other
cultural resources that might well have made such obedience seem if not
natural, then somewhat less than surprising, at any rate.

As poignant as Daldry's working-class scenes are, however, they really
only whisper their backstory. Later in the novel—once again, this passage
is notably dropped from the film—Berg tells us that in finally learning
to read during those final years in prison, Hanna put her "self-imposed
immaturity" (*selbstverschuldete Unmündigkeit*) behind her.[31] The film
clearly distances her from this robust reference to the Kantian autonomy
of the self-legislating subject. While making her unambiguously corespon-
sible for some crimes, through these images, it simultaneously communicates that her predisposition to do so was anything but "self-imposed."
But this is all it wants to achieve, so the implicit Marxist critique remains
latent and muffled. Otherwise it might spill over and cling to unwanted,
uncomfortable realities in the present, for if there is any truth to this
account, then it should apply just as much today, within a modern capi-
talist society that produces—perhaps demands—an extensive supply
of uneducated drones to carry out low-level, routinized, and physically
exhausting labor the world over. One might well begin to ask, for example, why in the U.S. armed forces such a high percentage of troops are

recruited from the lower classes, and why it includes, most recently, even those with a criminal record.[32] Can it really be a coincidence that such a disproportionate number of relatively uneducated, economically underprivileged, and sometimes criminal young people "volunteer" for military duty? The American Lynndie England, a lower-class, unemployed, and uneducated woman convicted of carrying out torture at the Abu Ghraib prison, is just one example of this larger phenomenon.[33]

When Schlink opined that *The Reader* is not, in the end, really about the Holocaust but instead is concerned with more general phenomena that apply equally well internationally,[34] this proto-Marxist critique can hardly have been on his mind. Nor, if we are honest, is this in any sense part of the film's overt ideology. If "class analysis" plays any role in Daldry's film, it does so in the sense that Lukács argued it functions in the great bourgeois novels of "critical realism"—those "loose and baggy" novels (to use J. P. Stern's phrase for the "excess" of literary realism) that, in a sense, inadvertently betray their class.[35] Simply by telling such a comprehensive story—by presenting a social "totality"—they unintentionally reveal the cracks and strains in bourgeois ideology, as Lukács famously argued. In this way, even a fairly conservative artist like Thomas Mann (and *mutatis mutandis*, Daldry) can be seen as offering an incisive social critique. If we are tempted to overlook this radical narrative strand, it may be due to the fact that these works sometimes retract, soften, or distort the very critique they purvey. The fate of the two Marines becomes, as we saw, an anticlimactic footnote to the identification of the real villain, the commander. The intense emotional focus on his indictment necessarily drains energy away from the subplot. Moreover, one could argue that the penultimate punishment of these two minor perpetrators points only fleetingly to the social milieu that "produced" them, while more powerfully affirming the supremacy of the principle of *personal* responsibility. On this reading, their visually quite poignant salute of their defense lawyer at the conclusion of the trial signals their manful acceptance of individual responsibility *despite* the social determinants that predisposed them to the uncritical carrying out of orders, let alone military service in the first place.[36] A similar dynamic may be at work, as we will see here, in Daldry's *The Reader*.

Obviously, there is no menacing, macho commander in *The Reader* to draw culpability off from Hanna. But male privilege is at issue from the very outset. Indeed, to understand the way in which gender issues will cushion Hanna's blameworthiness as a camp guard, we need to return to the exposition, to the love story itself. As pedagogues do not tire of mentioning, lurking behind this romantic liaison is an unequal relationship between an adult woman and a boy of 15.[37] Technically, Hanna is a sexual predator. The classic method of flushing out the implications of this relationship of radically unequal power is to switch the genders: if this were a 36-year-old man seducing a 15-year-old girl, few would hesitate to indict the predatory older male. The novel goes to some lengths—as it does in so many other respects—to have it both ways: it wants to establish this sexual relationship—Berg's first—both as an empowering rite of passage and as a deeply traumatizing event that derails his subsequent maturation. But the film clearly emphasizes the former.

Now there is no dispute that Daldry faithfully depicts the wreck of Berg's adult life. There is no missing this. When Ralph Fiennes, as the older Berg, tearfully confesses to his adult daughter that he was indeed "distant" as a father and "not really open with anybody," we are to clearly understand this to be a result of his aborted relationship with Hanna.[38] However, the wound issues not from child abuse but from a more universal story of failed love. We see the young Berg lying alone on the bed of Hanna's now abandoned apartment and recognize the pain of a forsaken lover. This was not the case in the narratively more confused novel, where the scene in which Hanna splits his lip with the buckle of her belt could give rise to charges of physical abuse, and where her repeated, insistent demand that he submit to her make an easy case for emotional abuse. But these, as we have already seen, are notably lacking in the film.

The film shows us a newly confident Berg: the scene in the school gymnasium where he displays a newly acquired athletic prowess by scoring goal after goal (to the surprise of his classmates) depicts an alpha male who has come into his own. Sitting peacefully in the bathtub, Hanna compliments him on his academic gifts and he realizes—for the first time, he says—that he actually is good at something. Like a good lover (not just one who exploits the other's body for self-gratification), she takes the time to see things in him that he had not even grasped himself. And like any lover, she possesses the power to hurt him deeply. But when she does so, as I have said, the film presents this as a lovers' quarrel among coevals and one that, in any case, ends with her gestural affirmation of love and forgiveness. It is an exchange in which Berg—with his ability to tenderly articulate their misunderstanding—is positioned as a partner capable of offering a gift in return. The lovemaking scenes are gentle and (for Berg) didactic: "Like this?" he asks; "No," she says, "slower." It is true that he does not have time for his friends who are his age, but as we noted in the first part of this chapter, the Sophie plot is radically reduced in the film, and, at any rate, Berg seems a good deal more upset to be away from Hanna than from these friends.

The film, in other words, portrays their relationship much more as a love affair—one that abruptly ends with Hanna's departure but that somehow never ends with regard to their mutual emotional investment. In the novel, we are invited to believe that Hanna's suicide follows, in substantial part, from her reading of the classics of Holocaust literature. She seems, through her newfound literacy, to have finally grasped her guilt—as George Steiner famously argued in his review of the novel—and thus carries out this measure of justice as a sentence she pronounces on herself, the one she said no one else (except for the dead) had a right to render. (This improbable bit of plot was also deleted from the film.)[39] But Daldry gives us a woman who kills herself because she sees that there is no future with Berg, despite his having continued the relationship for over twenty years by personally recording books on tape for her. The film streamlines the plot by locating the "abuse" in the Holocaust *per se* but not by making it intrinsic to the unequal age or gender relationship. And this is sensible, because if Berg had instead met her while in college (which would have removed the specter of sexual abuse of a minor from their relationship) and then only later discovered her Holocaust past, he obviously would have been confronted with the same problem: having loved a criminal.

As counterintuitive as this may sound, the film exploits the age-gender difference not to indict Hanna as the senior, and therefore responsible, party, but instead to awaken sympathy for her as a woman within a deeply patriarchal society.[40] Again, as in the working class scenes discussed in this chapter, the point is not some crude exoneration but a relatively subtle contextualization of her plight. What the love affair between Hanna and Berg reveals is not (or certainly not only) her domination of him but his privilege as a young male. Even when they are mistaken as a mother and son pair by the waitress at the outdoor country café, Berg is not moved to flee or conceal the relationship. Instead, he flaunts it: following a series of three emphasized glances back to the waitress—he wants to be sure that she witnesses his visual correction of her assumption about their relationship—he confidently strides up to Hanna and plants an unmistakably romantic kiss on her lips. She is somewhat taken aback; her furtive glances signal that she is unsure of whether this is acceptable in public, reminding us of her confusion in the tram when Berg appears but does not step forward to greet her. Berg, in contrast, is the proud, young buck who displays his erotic conquest without regard for possible societal sanctions or disapproval.[41] Not only does Daldry demur from depicting Hanna as sexual predator, he also deploys the affair to underscore her gender inequality and relative vulnerability. For example, as we have already noted, she seems genuinely flummoxed when Berg attempts to meet up with her while she is on duty in the streetcar. Her face registers indecision, confusion, and anguish before she simply returns to her duties. In stark contrast to the novel, when this rejection scene seemed more like a unilateral act of cruelty on her part (in the novel, she has no work to return to, since there are no other passengers in the street car), here the scene becomes a commentary on Berg's greater freedom as the young male "suitor." He has the time and leisure to pursue his lover at work and even contemplates (to her chagrin) the prospect of kissing her in this public place.[42]

This same message is underscored in other powerful visuals. Whereas the novel tells us that Hanna was initially the sexual aggressor—straddling him in the dominant position and "riding me until she came"[43]— the film sends a more egalitarian message.[44] When she is "on top," we do not get the sense that she is taking sexual gratification in a way that is indifferent to, or exploitive of, her neophyte lover. For one, the camera focuses in these scenes on Berg's pleasurable response; and secondly, her "dominance" is so tightly framed and briefly held that it simply does not gain much traction. The longer and more memorable erotic scenes position Berg in the traditionally male role—the so-called missionary position. With her left leg placed deliberately over his right shoulder, and offering commentary on his technique during coitus, she is clearly the more experienced partner. And he is a happy and grateful apprentice who seems to profit in ancillary ways from these lessons in manhood.

Finally, there is the fact of his adult male body. We do not encounter a boy halfway through puberty. Visually, the young Berg remains a physical constant—youthful yet virile—from the first lovemaking scenes through his university years. When he makes love to his girlfriend in law school, his naked body does not appear any more or less mature than it did in the earlier scenes with Hanna. This is of course no accident: though the director first cast Kross when he was just 15 years old, he deliberately waited 3 years until the young actor reached the age of majority (18) before proceeding with the love scenes. We can well imagine the extrafilmic reasons for this arrangement; Daldry will have wanted to avoid the controversy he knew the novel had already ignited in some quarters (Oprah, for example). For the film, however, this decision effectively takes the charge of rape of a minor off the table. As Mark Jenkins writes in his review, "When his teenage self is in bed with Hanna, in scenes that are alluringly lighted and frankly erotic, the lovers appear quite happy. The legal age of consent aside, Michael does not look like he's being manipulated or molested."[45]

The film is replete with additional images of the explicit male privilege that characterized the Adenauer period of postwar "Restauration." Father Berg is the undisputed authority at the family dinner table—all eyes (including the camera's) go to him whenever a decision is to be made; the mother really has no say until after her husband has died;[46] and the sister's role is reduced to that of a pesky irritant, whose views are regularly dismissed whenever they appear to cast aspersions on her brother. The fact that young Berg regularly lies about his whereabouts at the family table—and nevertheless retains his parents' trust—only underscores his privilege.

All of this prepares us for the court scene in which the presiding judge and the lawyers are, of course, all men. (The second tier of justices does indeed include women. But I suspect this reflects a rogue bit of gender-blind casting. Like those recent Broadway revivals of musicals pointedly set in the 1930s that nevertheless now cast interracial couples—in flagrant, and anachronistic, defiance of the miscegenation laws then in effect throughout most of the United States—this retrospective infusion of women in the court may be a bit of ahistorical fantasy, perhaps a trace of the film's desire to have it both ways.) Thus, while the prior love affair sets up Berg's great shock and dismay at discovering Hanna among the defendants, it simultaneously has prepared us for this specifically gendered contextualization of Hanna's guilt. The images of patriarchy and male privilege discussed above make it unnecessary for Hanna to explicitly mention the male guards as alternate, and perhaps as the logically more responsible, perpetrators.[47] These visuals have already powerfully sensitized us to the fact of male dominance in society, so that when Hanna is questioned about the church fire and the selections, we must wonder—consciously or not—where were the men? The oft-rehearsed images of female subordination—of Hanna's own deference precisely within a relationship in which she is the alleged dominant party—create a hermeneutic context of considerable sympathy. Under the pressure of interrogation from the presiding judge to justify her participation in the selections, Hanna once again defers to her male superior—this time, to the judge himself. Her very subaltern behavior in court, in a sense, makes the case for explaining her prior behavior during the war: this disingenuous witness would also have turned to the men then in charge when it came to making the key decisions. Much more so than in the novel, which features a feisty and assertive defendant, the Hanna of the silver screen is badgered, inarticulate, and helpless.[48] In the novel, her most memorable line, "What would you have done?" represents a kind of victory for her, because she manages to stump the judge. In the film, this scene underscores not the judge's but Hanna's helplessness.

Moreover, when she says that she and the other female guards had no choice because more and more women prisoners were being brought to the satellite camp that had limited capacity,[49] we may of course wish

Figure 6.3   Hanna as victim in (and of) the male-dominated courtroom—"What would you have done?" (Still from *The Reader*.)

that she had more independence of mind or simply had the courage to say no. Yet while her testimony provokes moral indignation, it simultaneously serves to remind us of the gendered hierarchy that placed men in all the key positions of power within the military and the specialized Nazi organizations. It was the men—who do not really need to be accused directly—who set up the rules for this genocide, a fact that has led one critic to charge that Schlink "misrepresents the historical role of women in SS posts" by casting "Hanna simply as a member of the SS" without acknowledging the subordinate and minority status of women in that organization.[50] Furthermore, Hanna's *perception* that she had no choice—as long as we accept it as an honest self-assessment—automatically reduces her crimes to a lesser level of severity. As we noted above, she clearly invokes, if obliquely, the excuse of having simply "followed orders." Those men who gave the orders and devised the system of deportation and extermination remain offscreen, but are "present" nonetheless, indirectly evoked not only via the film's images of male privilege but also—and very powerfully—by way of classic Holocaust intertexts.[51]

In the novel, Berg complains about these iconic images of the genocide that have flooded popular culture and have become shopworn over the years, tending to obscure any more nuanced accounts of the genocide: "Today there are so many books and films that the world of the camps is part of our collective imagination and completes our ordinary everyday one. Our imagination knows its way around in it, and . . . actually moves in it, not just registering, but supplementing and embellishing it."[52] Yet the film (as much as the novel) also fully exploits this storehouse of Holocaust iconography, such that as soon as we hear the word "selections," we envision a grim scene in which women with young children, and the elderly, are commanded to step to the right, while those able to work are directed to the left. The person wielding such power will inevitably be a jack-booted, leather-clad man. Whether we turn to classic literary treatments of the Holocaust (e.g., Wiesel, Klüger, Hochhuth, or Weiss) or restrict ourselves to memorable filmic moments (*Sophie's Choice* or *Schindler's List*), those in culpable positions of authority are principally, if not exclusively, men. Our collective cultural memory will, in any case, populate all the leading roles in the prosecution of the Holocaust with men, a fact that makes Hanna's subordination and deference—both from a class and gender point of view—utterly plausible. And as we know, Hollywood films typically do not abstain from stating the obvious. In this case, it is none other than the surviving Jewish daughter, Ilana, who refers to the female guards on trial as "the girls," reminding us (because we all know that "girls" did not mastermind the Holocaust) once more of the defendants' subsidiary role in war crimes. This is how the film, by virtue of the images it directly proffers, as well as those it triggers by way of intertextual allusion, renders Hanna "guilty, but not as guilty as it seemed" (Berg).

There are two other techniques the film engages to effectively upgrade the Hanna of the novel. The first is pure innovation; the second elaborates a motif from the book. During the halcyon days of their bicycle tour (not marred in the film by an outburst of violence on Hanna's part, as in the novel), at one point, Hanna wanders off without notifying Berg. She is attracted (as are we) by the stunning voices of an *a cappella* children's choir practicing in a nearby church. She strolls in, sits down, and listens to them sing a classical composition of the "Gloria in Excelsis Deo" (Glory to God in the Highest) with tears running down her cheeks. Her eyes (and those of the camera) explore the painted ceiling of the apse while she listens to the great doxology of the Christian church. Berg walks in and finds her; the camera assumes his perspective, framing her for us within his visual field.

We can be certain that this is no accident of editing, for Daldry returns us to this very church at the end of his film; the actual choir is of course no longer present, but their singing fills our ears via voiceover technique. It is an obvious and heavy-handed reprise, but it is also a turning point for Berg. Repeating an earlier segment with his daughter as a young girl, he now takes his adult daughter to this very churchyard to show her Hanna's grave—but without telling her in advance, ostensibly because of the daughter's lifelong love of surprises. He melodramatically wipes away the brush from her gravestone, revealing Hanna's name and dates, and in this

gesture finds the inspiration to tell the story of *his* painful youth. Echoing the opening lines of Homer's *Odyssey* (a text he has been reading and
rereading to Hanna at various points in the film), he will now sing *his*
song, for he has found his muse. And we can fully expect that it will be a
story of ultimate mastery.

Let us consider the two images consecutively, despite their obvious
interdependence. What are we to make of that initial image of Hanna
sitting in the church pew? On the one hand, it presents a modicum of
interpretive multivalence. Is she reminded, sitting here, of the fire that
destroyed the church she guarded some 15 years earlier? Is this repentance
after the fact? A sign of nonverbal remorse despite herself (recall that she
will later deny ever having thought of these events in the postwar years
before her trial)? May we see her tears as a sign of spiritual melding with
the *Gloria*—an alliance with this age-old Christian plea for mercy and
forgiveness? Is she in a sense *praying* along with these words?

> O Lord, the only begotten Son Jesu Christ;
> O Lord God, Lamb of God, Son of the Father,
>> that takest away the sins of the world,
>>> have mercy upon us.
>> Thou that takest away the sins of the world,
>>> have mercy upon us.
>> Thou that takest away the sins of the world,
>>> receive our prayer.
> Thou that sittest at the right hand of God the Father,
>> have mercy upon us.[53]

The woman before us is, at any rate, a very good, culturally sensitive Hanna—surely not the "launisch und herrisch" (moody and domi-
neering)[54] and even brutal one that we are sometimes invited to imagine
in the novel. We might even wonder if this image, which shows her to
be in intensive emotional contact with Christian hymnody, in a sense
retracts what turned out to be the highly suspect illiteracy alibi. Does her
immediate response to the power of sacral music—one that transcends
any dependency on the written word—not establish her as an ethically
worthy subject? Given the provenance of this baroque country church,
are we perhaps not precisely invited to recall a time (i.e., the Catholic
Church prior to the Reformation) when the bulk of the populace was still
illiterate, and when the church depended upon music, painting, and the
spoken word to communicate its message?

The beauty of this scene may also have something to do with its central paradox. For the very hymn that establishes her inclusion within

Figure 6.4   Hanna experiences a moment of transcendence as she tearfully takes in the strains of the *Gloria* in the country church where she will later be buried. (Still from *The Reader*.)

Figure 6.5   Hanna rests in peace in the same country churchyard. The gravestone serves as a prompt for Berg's retrospective story that marks reconciliation with his daughter. (Still from *The Reader*.)

European Christendom also marks her distance from high culture. She is listening to Latin, after all, and we cannot help but be reminded of the Latin and Greek lines Berg recites to her uncomprehending ears.[55] As Berg perhaps tactlessly points out, she does not understand the content of the quoted lines from Horace and Homer, so how can she deem them beautiful? Perhaps it is their "musicality," and an intuition of their broad meaning, that justifies her response. At any rate, the youths in the choir, as well as Berg himself, are all thus marked as children of privilege insofar as they have the luxury of time and training to learn classical languages and enlarge their cultural horizons. Sitting alone in the pews, spatially set off from the others, she is therefore also contemplating an upbringing she never had. And thus those tears might be for herself as well, for the childhood of innocence and comfort that was denied her by her lower-class provenance, her heritage as a "Volksdeutsche," the economic crises of the Weimar period, and then the war itself. Let us not forget that she is just 17—not much older than Berg at the time of their meeting—when Hitler invades Poland in 1939.

While this central image of Hanna can invite different readings, it is also an iteration of a widespread trope about the "civilizing" power of music.[56] There are many examples of this motif in Western culture, but the most notable within the German tradition is probably that given to us by Mozart in *Die Zauberflöte*: when the evil sycophant Monostatos, along with his nasty crew, is about to abduct and rape Pamina, Papageno saves her the only way he can, by recourse to his magic carillon. The music instantly disarms and transforms these would-be thugs into merry model citizens who dance in tune with the magic carillon's rhythm but implicitly also with its Enlightenment values. Though amusing, the message is also serious: no one, according to this optimistic Enlightenment credo, is beyond redemption—not the "savage" Monostatos (still played in black-face in Germany to this very day) and certainly not the "Naturmensch" Papageno. As an extension of this trope, Hanna's responsiveness to music that speaks, as it were, directly to the heart is also meant to communicate a redemptive moment. And it is no accident that she is framed in this way well before we discover her SS past.

This is how the film, without speaking a word, announces that Hanna is not beyond the pale—not a brute or a monster but one of us. Unlike those infamous Nazi elites who listened to classical music as a respite from their murderous "work," she is deeply touched by sacred music that carries a humanizing mission. The children's choir itself suggests a new beginning, one the film envisions by rehabilitating the perpetrator. None of this occurs at the level of dialogue or even plot, but it is strongly suggested by the subsequent inclusion of Hanna's grave within the churchyard. She is, at least in death, welcomed back into the community. Her crimes while with the SS—conditioned but not foreordained by her lower class and "lesser" gender—are not sufficient to posthumously exile her from the community. When Berg brings his daughter to this hallowed spot—a plot sequence wholly invented for the film—he is recruiting the third generation along with the film's viewers to this conciliatory point of view. It is a reversal of Bitburg.[57]

Thus Hanna's act of suicide—unlike the most famous suicide in German literature—does not require her banishment from sacred soil. Apart from this larger symbolic meaning—connoting reconciliation and closure—the cemetery scene has a narrower and more commonplace function within the film: it repeats and cements our image of Hanna, quietly sobbing, as she takes in the sublime "Gloria." It guarantees that this will be our final and perhaps dominant view of her. In this sense, her burial marks not a process of dispersal or displacement but a revivification of a particular and very positive image that is obviously important to the filmmaker. In this sense, it represents a powerful visual framing device that establishes not only *ex post facto* but also *preemptive* reintegration—telegraphing to the audience that the confession she will later offer in court (the confession that Peter Brooks tells us is so crucial to the social reintegration of the criminal) will suffice.[58] At this semiotic level, the first church scene effectively relegates the entire trial to a kind of flashback, because she already achieves here what only the trial (according to Brooks) can grant.

RESTORING BERG, RETIRING THE HOLOCAUST

Drawing upon a key passage in the novel, Daldry had already sounded the dominant conciliatory note during Berg's interview with the now middle-aged surviving daughter. This may well appear rather counterintuitive, because the daughter does not exactly offer him a warm reception. Indeed, one critic notes, "The older Michael gets a sharp lecture from a Holocaust survivor."[59] It is, at any rate, quite true, as we noted at the outset, that the daughter immediately and forcefully debunks illiteracy as being in any way exonerative. She furthermore tells Berg that she cannot accept the money—Hanna's life savings—because that would imply absolution, something she is "neither willing nor in a position to grant."[60] She is cool, clear, and commanding.

But in this instance, too, the verbal and visual registers appear to be somewhat at odds with each other, for while she is in one sense putting him in his place, she is also offering him a very special place. She demands to know about Berg's relationship with Hanna: "Why don't you start by being honest with me? At least start that way. What was the nature of your friendship?"[61] Yet this colloquy that begins as stern chiding ends by paying rich dividends for Berg, because once he reveals the affair, Ilana asks compassionately, "And did Hanna Schmitz acknowledge the effect she'd had on your life?"[62] In the novel as well as in the film, this amounts to a conferral of victim status from an unimpeachable source. But Daldry seems to know about the controversy that this problematic "equivalence" instigated in the reception of the novel, beginning with Ernestine Schlant's thoughtful analysis of this scene in *The Language of Silence* (1999). He therefore has Berg respond with humility, "She'd done much worse to other people."[63] This appropriately qualifies—and thus rescues—his victim status. By dutifully subordinating himself, he maintains this valuable affiliation.

But it is at the level of image that this message is perhaps most effectively communicated. He is placed visually on par with the survivor—for he, too, is a survivor. Sitting on a couch opposite her guest and prompting him to speak of his pain, she functions almost as his therapist. She mandates (rather than coaxes) a response, and he obligingly reveals, for the first time, his love affair—"I've never told anyone,"[64] which constitutes a dry run for the subsequent breakthrough scene with his daughter, when the whole story will come to light and thus make possible the very film we are watching. Ilana's austere tone may camouflage the pastoral role she assumes vis-à-vis this damaged "survivor" of Hanna. Her no-nonsense reception of Berg at once authenticates and intensifies the film's characterization of him: "Long divorced and distant from his grown-up daughter, the morose lawyer is supposedly scarred by his underage fling with a woman twice his age . . . Michael is apparently meant to be the last of Hanna's victims, the postwar equivalent of the doomed children who read to her while behind barbed wire."[65] Precisely because she is so cool, and not mawkish or sentimental, we accept her view of him as Hanna's casualty.

Most revealing, however, is Ilana's "response" to Michael's story. Using diction familiar from Ruth Klüger's Holocaust memoir (*weiter leben*), she begins a disquisition on what the camp experience meant to her; specifically, she disputes the thesis that the camps offered some kind of edifying experience: "The camps weren't therapy. What do you think these places were? Universities? . . . Nothing comes out of the camps. Nothing."[66] But who within this narrative ever contended that the camps built character? At first blush, we might well wonder about the impetus for this speech, for on the surface it is a clear *non sequitur*: no one had asked her about her experience, least of all Berg, who has already read her book and attended every session of the trial—as he has just reminded her.[67] Has she mistaken this interview with one of the many speaking engagements to which she, as a middle-aged Holocaust survivor, would certainly have been invited during the mid-1990s when Holocaust education and awareness were all the rage in the United States? Is this the speech she gives at schools and synagogues? Maybe; but in the context of the interview with Berg, it does indeed comprise part of a *dialogue on victimhood*, a rejoinder she offers to his revelations about Hanna as lover.

Looking into his brimming eyes, and considering the abuse he suffered, she is prompted to tell *her* story. She does so in such strong and compelling terms that one could easily focus on the content of her story to the exclusion of the dialogic structure that frames their conversation. At the level of discourse, we notice that it is she who sponsors the juxtaposition, suggesting the interrelatedness of their respective stories, if not their full "equivalence." Simply by occupying the same stage with him, and by freely placing her story of suffering side by side with his, she lends credence to his claim of victimhood. With this supreme affirmation of his woundedness, Berg can proceed to the next stage in his *Bildungsroman*, namely to the mastery that will come in narrating his story.[68]

But the function of this lone survivor of the Holocaust is not just to certify Berg's victimhood. She is also there in order to step aside—for in order tell the story of the second generation, the Holocaust must itself be made to recede into the background. It is one thing to have the Holocaust unexpectedly "intrude" within a plot apparently unrelated to it,[69] but how does one both insert a war crimes trial and a visit to a concentration camp into the central action of the film, and then somehow push them into the background so that the woes of second-generation Germans can be foregrounded?[70] There are surely other strategies that bear examination, but here I want to focus on the depiction of the surviving daughter during this climactic interview. Here she is no longer the tearful young woman testifying in a German courtroom. When Berg enters her lavish Fifth Avenue apartment, he is greeted by a black maid, clad in traditional servant's uniform, complete with apron and cap. Only after the maid has taken his coat and he has had a chance to drink in the majestic views of Manhattan through the floor-to-ceiling windows and glance around the elegantly appointed living room replete with original works of art, does the lady of the house sweep into the room and offer him a seat. The Master of Metropolis never had it this good. Her clothes, manners, jewelry, and apartment do not evoke even a hint of victimhood or oppression. All that belongs to the past. This is an image of a victor, a ruler, a master. She is a rich New York Jew.

While there is some danger here of reviving an anti-Semitic stereotype, this cannot have been Daldry's purpose. When Ilana gnomically speaks to Berg about "*the* camp experience," she is, however, speaking in general terms, and thus for an entire group. As a representative of this group, the picture she presents is of someone who has mastered this horrible past as much as is humanly possible. Her wealth and comfort, symbolized by

Figure 6.6   Ilana's well-appointed Fifth Avenue apartment: a rich New York Jew confronts a repentant second-generation German. (Still from *The Reader*.)

this fabulous piece of New York real estate as well as by all the gorgeous accoutrements it displays, signify, more than anything else in the film, the "pastness" of the Holocaust. Visibly and palpably, it puts distance between the genocide of the 1940s and the present—and it does so without in any way denying the truth of the event.

Ilana's last act in this scene is silent. After Berg leaves, she takes Hanna's tea tin and gives it a place of honor on her dressing table, arranging it carefully next to an old family picture. She (and along with her, we viewers) gaze into this dog-eared black-and-white photograph of a family gathering. The men are in suits, the women in skirts, and they are all lounging on a lawn, perhaps out for a picnic or a Sunday stroll. These are her relatives who, we are given to understand, were murdered in the Holocaust. It is next to this precious family relic that Hanna's tin now stands. The final composition is rich in signifiers: of Hanna, the film's chief perpetrator; of Ilana's murdered Jewish relatives; and of her considerable fortune.

Ilana accounts for the apparent contradiction of rejecting Hanna's money but accepting the tea tin because the latter item reminds her of a tin she had as a child, one that held prized childhood treasures and was stolen in the camps. Accepting the tin thus amounts to a kind of restitution, whether or not the survivor wants to view it this way. She may value it because of its incidental likeness to the one she lost. But we know—and, of course, so does she—that this one came from a female guard who participated in death marches and selections, and then failed to intervene during the horrible fire. When one considers the fact that Holocaust survivors often cannot even relax in the presence of Germans "of a certain generation"; how, in the postwar period, Jews would often boycott German cars and other export items; and how even the sound of the German language would set some survivors' teeth on edge, it seems incredible indeed to imagine that this survivor would accept Hanna's "gift," even if she interprets it on her own terms. But there it is: this woman who could have afforded any tea tin in the world chooses this one. She cannot erase its provenance, nor does the film want us to. Her prior unforgiving words notwithstanding, this emotional embrace of the tea tin functions as a sign of conciliation pure and simple, and it too serves to put the Holocaust to rest. More powerfully even than having her buried within the churchyard, this placement of Hanna's tin next to the cherished image of a murdered Jewish family represents a rapprochement, or truce, with the Holocaust.

True to Hollywood formula, the melodramatic turning point will come in the final scene with the visit to the cemetery, when Berg begins to tell his story. But this scene with the survivor constitutes the film's more fundamental turning point, and not only because it is actually at this point that Berg first starts to tell his story, for in this stunning Fifth Avenue apartment—the visual antithesis of "l'univers concentration-naire" (the concentration camp world)[71]—we are given powerful images of Holocaust closure. It is this sense of finality, qualified and contested by the dialogue and even some of the images themselves, that removes the Holocaust as a rival narrative. The well-to-do Jewish survivor gives Berg the "permission" he needs to sing his own song—which may be ours as well.

Figure 6.7   Ilana accepts the gift of Hanna's tea tin—a kind of restitution after all. (Still from *The Reader*.)

Figure 6.8   The aggrieved adolescent Berg—scarred for life? (Still from *The Reader*.)

Figure 6.9   The adult Berg—a successful judge, father, and story-teller confronts his past. (Still from *The Reader*.)

It would be flippant simply to mock the desire to move on. Few of us could live in the "Holocaust present," and few really want to engage the pain of the Holocaust in the unremitting manner prescribed by Lawrence Langer. But, as Hoffman has cautioned, we should at least be cognizant of what we are doing when we redraw the boundaries of "Holocaust" litera-ture and film. I have argued that Daldry's film is less schizophrenic about Hanna's guilt because it refrains from introducing alternate perpetrators.

It also eliminates—wisely, I think—what I have elsewhere called the "numbness doctrine," which is Berg's excuse for shutting down during the trial (and later during his visit to one of the camps) in the face of "atrocity overload." Though he feels bad about this in the book, we are to understand that his *Betäubung* radically reduces his ability to process Holocaust events in any sustained manner—and thus to relate them to us. Perhaps the director sensed that this is an unworthy attempt to garner the equivalent of the "illiteracy alibi" for Berg.

"Correction through subtraction" does not, in the end, capture the full extent of Daldry's substantial filmic translation of *The Reader*, for he not only excised a series of questionable and problematic themes, motifs, and passages, but also poignantly amplified the key factors of class and gender. In this respect, the visual evocation of Hanna's lower-class neighborhood and her simple "workers'" apartment; the much more delicate and vulnerable casting of Winslet as Hanna; and the supplementary images of the humbly clad working-class visitors to the prison all contribute to a potentially more differentiated view of the perpetrators. But in the end, the film's rage for order and closure gains the upper hand.[72]

In an interview with National Public Radio (NPR), Schlink expressed this hope: "I wanted it to be an international movie because even though it's a very German topic, I think it's not just a German topic" (NPR Weekend Edition, Jan 3, 2009). This "international" message, however, was never meant to query the sensitive topic of how a number of governments (not just Germany during the "Third Reich") continue to recruit lower-level collaborators to become, in some cases, "willing executioners"—one thinks, for example, of the burgeoning international catastrophe of child soldiers. The message Schlink thought would appeal across national boundaries is not this explosive one but rather one of self-pity—one that is, frankly, much less difficult to air because it makes us, all of us, the victims: "The problem of what does it mean to us, how do we cope with the fact that someone whom we love, admire, respect has—turns out to have committed an awful crime, I think is not just a German problem."[73] In this respect, Daldry turns out to be a very faithful disciple of Schlink after all.

And we are perhaps now, finally, in a better position to understand why the filmmaker found it necessary to link an upgraded image of Hanna with Berg's own recovery and ultimate mastery, for a film that seeks to retire the Holocaust cannot risk reopening the wounds by asking uncomfortable questions about actual crimes and those who committed them. If Daldry were to take seriously his own imagistic discourse about class and gender disadvantage, we might be moved not only to ask about contemporary instances of this truly international phenomenon but also to refine our understanding of the full range of Holocaust perpetrators. Since those scenes that contextualize Hanna within larger trends of gender and class oppression fail to open onto the larger phenomenon of the recruitment of guards, torturers, and executioners—both within and beyond the Holocaust—they are left with the much narrower task of rendering a single character more sympathetic.

From this perspective, Hanna's posthumous icons—the grave marker and the tea tin—represent what Marxist critics of an earlier era would have called a premature, or "false," reconciliation, because we are given images of her reintegration without full consideration of the (social) conditions of her criminality. This commitment to the twinned redemption of Hanna and Berg ironically undercuts the very premise of the film. By pursuing a strategy of containment vis-à-vis the Holocaust, we are less able to appreciate the pain it caused to the second generation. Relegating its horrors to the past risks underplaying the second generation's fundamental trauma. Similarly, by glibly indicating Berg's mastery of these wounds in the final scene, the film jeopardizes its stated concern with this ostensibly *ongoing* distress. One of the standard critiques of Hollywood cinema is that it too neatly resolves all the conflicts it depicts. Daldry's film is no exception—it abounds with closure with respect to both generations. Perhaps this is its real appeal—proffering the consoling notion of Hollywood optimism that all conflicts are surmountable, at least in our filmic dreams.

NOTES

PREFACE

1. The editors of the highly esteemed *Die Zeit* characterized the state of Jews and Jewish studies in Germany thus: "Besonders sensibel und wichtig für die deutsch-amerikanischen Beziehungen." Editor's introduction to Donahue and Cohn, "Ein Besuch, der manche Fragen offenließ."

2. An English language version of the article ("Ein Besuch") was published in the *Harvard Divinity Bulletin* 26, no. 1(1996): 13. A longer reflection on the Fulbright seminar appeared as "Cultural Reparations? Jews and Jewish Studies in Germany Today," *German Politics & Society* 15, no. 1 (Spring 1997): 94–116.

3. Mahnke writes in his letter to the author regarding the "prejudice" of American Jews: "Mir [war] doch schon bei unserem Treffen in Bonn aufgefallen, daß viele in Ihrer Gruppe Deutschland mit Voreingenommenheit und wenig Wohlwollen entgegentraten, auch mit wenig Offenheit gegenüber dem, was wir tun und in den vergangenen fünfzig Jahren getan haben." Letter to Robert L. Cohn and William C. Donahue, August 13, 1996.

4. Manhke formulates his accusation that virtually no German could satisfy the requirements of American Jews thus: "Einige Bekannte, die den Artikel ebenfalls gelesen haben, haben mich gefragt, ob es wohl sein könnte, daß jeder Deutsche, der Ihnen nicht gesenkten Hauptes und 'mia culpa' [sic] murmelnd entgegentritt, Ihnen 'barsch' oder gar 'drohend' vorkommt." Letter to Robert L. Cohn and William C. Donahue, August 13, 1996.

5. Mahnke defends his diction by putting it in the mouth of an American Jew: "Das hat der amerikanische—jüdische—Student aus Stanford, den ich zitierte, gemeint, als er von 'overkill' sprach, und ich gebe zu, daß es ein schlechtes Wort ist, aber es trifft die Sache." Letter to Robert L. Cohn and William C. Donahue, August 13, 1996.

6. Mahnke warns about overburdening and exhausting young people in the following: "Aber man kann junge Menschen, für die das Vergangenheit ist, überlasten und ermüden—und genau das will ich nicht!" Letter to Robert L. Cohn and William C. Donahue, August 13, 1996.

7. Smelser, "The Holocaust in Popular Culture."

8. For a recent affirmation of this chronology, see Jarausch, *After Hitler*, 270.

INTRODUCTION

1. See Fatima Naqvi-Peters, "Laugher in the Darkness."
2. Zelizer, *Remembering to Forget.*
3. See Niven, *Facing the Nazi Past*; Cooke, *German Culture, Politics, and Literature*; and Taberner, *Contemporary German Fiction.*
4. See Niven, *Facing the Nazi Past*, 105ff.
5. Gavriel D. Rosenfeld, "Alternate Holocausts," 241, 243–44, 247, 248. The leftist critique of "normalization" crystallized to a significant extent in response to Martin Walser's controversial 1998 Nobel Peace Prize speech at the Frankfurt book fair. For a more capacious treatment of the term, one that accounts for its changing meaning over time, see Konrad Jarausch, "Searching for Normalcy," in *After Hitler*, 214–38.
6. These commemorative sites have, of course, also aroused controversy. A recent critical view of the Berlin Museum's permanent exhibit (not the Libeskind building) can be found in Rothstein, "In Berlin, Teaching Germany's Jewish History"; an account of the debates attending the Berlin "Holocaust Memorial" (as it is widely known, despite its official title) can be found in Young, "Teaching German Memory and Countermemory," 274–85. A positive discussion of German normalization can be found in McGlothlin, *Second Generation Holocaust Literature*, 201–2.
7. Ash, "The Stasi on Our Minds," 6, 8. Ash writes, "The enterprise in which the Germans truly are *Weltmeister* is the cultural reproduction of their country's versions of terror. No nation has been more brilliant, more persistent, and more innovative in the investigation, communication, and representation—the representation, and re-representation—of its own past evils." See also Jarausch, *After Hitler*, 279–80.
8. Duke Jewish Studies Seminar, "Friedländer's Debate with Broszat Reconsidered," November 10, 2008, Freeman Center, Duke University. Friedländer proposes, on the contrary, that while younger historians will inevitably write about the Holocaust with fewer constraints than his own generation did, attention to and interest in these events has only become more intense over time. Summarizing his position succinctly, Friedländer maintains, "Yes, it can be historicized. [But] time does not put an end to it. The *Schlußstrich* idea is simply not workable"; see also "A Controversy about the Historicization of National Socialism" in *Reworking the Past: Hitler, the Holocaust, and the Historians' Debate*, 102–34.
9. From a publicity flyer during Schlink's guest professorship at Princeton University School of Law, 1999.
10. Mittelberg, *Bernhard Schlink, Der Vorleser*, 3. A mark of distinction in this regard is the 2005 Reclam publication meant to facilitate school and university teaching; see Heigenmoser, *Der Vorleser.*
11. Lamberty, *Literatur-Kartei "Der Vorleser,"* 4. For an example of the use of *Der Vorleser* in U.S. collegiate programs in German Studies, see Schaumann, "Erzählraum im virtuellen Raum." For this Mellon Foundation project, Schaumann tracked the widespread use of Schlink's novel in U.S. postsecondary education.

12. Taberner and Berger, *Germans as Victims*, 7; Taberner and Berger, *Germans as Victims*, 5.

13. Schaumann, *Memory Matters*, 25.

14. Taberner and Berger, *Germans as Victims*, 6.

15. Taberner, Berger, and their collaborators are, of course, keenly aware of the existence of earlier texts that feature German victimhood. See, for example, chapter three, "Expulsion Novels of the 1950s," in *Germans as Victims*, 42–55. The key determinant in the "changed memory discourse," they rightly note, has to do with the "contextualization of [German] suffering within the overarching reality of German perpetration" (6; on the need for proper contextualization, see also 4). But what qualifies as evidence of this contextualization? Precisely this crucial point requires careful interpretation and, I would argue, adjudication on a case-by-case basis, using the tools (also) of reception analysis. Does a passing reference to the Holocaust suffice? Do "off stage" summaries of the genocide provide the necessary context? Schlink's detective novels provide both, but the quality of this contextualization leaves, I would argue, a great deal to be desired.

16. See Donahue, "Of Pretty Boys and Nasty Girls," for an illustration of this point.

17. Turow, *One L*.

18. Bernhard Schlink, email message to author, November 22, 2005. In an email to me, Schlink seems rather resigned about this: "Lieber Herr Donahue, haben Sie besten Dank fuer Ihre Sendung. Mit Interesse habe ich Ihre Aufsätze gelesen. Mit Interesse habe ich dabei gelernt, dass es eine beträchtliche germanistische Beschäftigung mit meinen Büchern gibt. Die wissenschaftlichen Diskurse der Germanisten und der Juristen berühren sich so wenig, daß es mir bisher entgangen war. Ich sehe, wie Sie und nicht nur Sie meine Bücher lesen. Ich sehe, daß man sie also auch so lesen kann. Ich mag mich dazu nicht erklärend, ergänzend, berichtigend äußern." (Dear Mr. Donahue, many thanks for sending your materials. I have read your essays with interest. With interest I have in the process learned that my books have generated considerable interest among Germanists. The academic discourses of Germanists and jurists intersect so rarely that until now I didn't know of this. I see how you [and not only you] read my books. I see also that they can be read in this manner. I'd rather not take a position meant to explain, complete or correct.) On the other hand, Schlink has repeatedly suggested that any criticism of his book results from ideological prejudice or "misunderstandings" of his work. See Doerry and Hage, "Ich lebe in Geschichten"; Schlink, "Als Deutscher im Ausland"; and Geisel, "Der Botschafter des deutschen Buches." In another case, Schlink insists that the novel's political incorrectness accounts for criticism (Sauer, "Man mag es traurig").

19. For example, Baron, "Schlink Als Neuestes Opfer Des Deutschen Feuilletons."

20. See for example Clee, "Matter of Interpretation"; Krause, "Gegen die Verlorenheit an sich selbst"; and especially Geisel, "Der Botschafter des deutschen Buches."

21. Schlink, "Auf dem Eis" and "Rede zur Verleihung des Fallada-Preises der Stadt Neumünster."

22. Lamberty, *Literatur-Kartei "Der Vorleser,"* 49. Lamberty quotes extensive portions of Schlink's "Auf dem Eis" essay and then gives students the discussion question, "Diskutieren Sie, ob für die heutigen Jugendlichen überhaupt noch eine Notwendigkeit der Vergangenheitsbewältigung besteht." (Please discuss whether for the youth of today there exists any obligation at all to confront the Nazi past.)

23. Möckel, *Bernhard Schlink*, 15. "Hier deckt sich die Einstellung des Protagonisten und Erzählers mit der des Autors." (In this respect the view of the protagonist and narrator overlaps with that of the author.)

24. See for example Ostermann, who writes "In seinem Aufsatz 'Die Bewältigung der Vergangenheit durch Recht' führt Bernhard Schlink in den rechtstheoretischen Kontext ein, der schon seinem Roman *Der Vorleser* zugrunde liegt" (45). (In his essay "Mastering the Past through Law," Schlink introduces the juridical-theoretical context that also forms the basis of his novel.) This is a hermeneutical strategy many teachers' manuals use, as we will see in this study. See also Ostermann's Chapter 3.1 "Schlinks Schuldbegriff" (Schlink's Concept of Guilt), 56ff.

25. Bernhard Schlink, email message to author, November 22, 2005. I have translated the German to provide an abbreviated sense rather than the literal equivalent. The original is as follows: "Mit Interesse habe ich Ihre Aufsätze gelesen . . . Sie interpretieren aus meinen Büchern auch theoretische Positionen zum Umgang mit der Vergangenheit. Lassen Sie mich darauf hinweisen, dass ich, was ich theoretisch zum Umgang mit der Vergangenheit zu sagen habe, in mehreren Aufsätzen gesagt habe."

26. See, for example, Schlink's "Sommer 1970"; *Vergangenheitsschuld und gegenwärtiges Recht*; and *Vergewisserungen: Über Politik, Recht, Schreiben und Glauben.*

27. Lamberty, *Literatur-Kartei "Der Vorleser,"* 4.

28. Urban, *Bernhard Schlink*, 7. "Der Roman eignet sich als Textgrundlage für den Deutsch-, Literatur-, Pädagogik-, Geschichts- und nicht zuletzt für den Ethik- bzw. Philosophieunterricht. Aufgrund der Komplexität des Romans und des nötigen Hintergrundwissens eignet er sich in erster Linie für die gymnasiale Oberstufe. Zudem ist er für Juristen und Jurastudenten relevant." (The novel is suitable as a textbook for courses in German, Literature, Pedagogy, History, and not least, Ethics and Philosophy. Because of its complexity and the background knowledge it presumes, it is most suitable for upper level students. In addition, it is relevant to jurists and law students.)

29. Lamberty, *Literatur-Kartei "Der Vorleser."* Lamberty recommends using the novel in class in part because Michael Berg represents an easy identification figure for young readers (4). Mittelberg argues that "die 'menschliche' Gestaltung Hannas in der 'Liebesgeschichte' so viel Identifikation mit dieser Romanfigur aufgebaut hat, dass ihre Vergangenheit auch heutigen Schülerinnen und Schülern als bedrängend erscheint" (5). (The "human" portrayal of Hanna in the "love story" has built up so much identification with her that her past seems in the eyes of today's students to harass [besiege] her.)

30. Möckel, *Bernhard Schlink*, 5–6. The following is the original text in German: "Meiner Erfahrung nach hat er sich als ein Text bewährt, der für Leser/innen der verschiedenen Altersstufen faszinierend ist. Er hat eine packende Geschichte, enthält überraschende Wendungen der Ereignisse, fesselt den Leser durch die Erzählweise bis zum Schluss." Mittelberg concurs, assuring pedagogues that though Michael's verbose reflections on the Nazi past might appear langatmig (long-winded), this can be diffused with proper pedagogical technique. "Erfahrungsgemäß wird der Roman bei den Schülerinnen und Schülern überwiegend auf Zustimmung stoßen" (5). (Experience tells us that the novel generates a preponderance of resonance [agreement] among students.)

31. McGlothlin, *Second Generation Holocaust Literature*, 208.

32. Ibid.

33. Ibid., 214.

34. Ibid., 208.

35. Ibid., 206. Later in her analysis, McGlothlin wavers in her ascription of this position to the novel, suggesting that it may in fact be due to the errant narrator, as in the following: "Such a reading reveals a false understanding of the inner workings of the text, yet it is the text (or more precisely, Michael's overt claims to generational representation) that promotes this misreading" (208). This is an important distinction, as I will argue below.

36. Though academic studies often treat journalistic reviews as "popular," this overlooks the elite status of many of these publication venues. For a rigorous definition of elite and popular cultural arenas, see Andrei S. Markovits, "Germany and Germans."

37. See Donahue, *The End of Modernism*, 174–205.

38. I am aware that I have, for my purposes here, truncated a much richer tradition of Aphrodite representation within the visual arts. For that longer view, see, for example, Seifert, *Aphrodite*.

39. Schaumann, *Memory Matters*, 14–17.

40. For an insightful discussion of the terms "second generation" and "second-generation literature," see McGlothlin, *Second-Generation Holocaust Literature*, 13–18. There is a larger literature on this problem as well. See, for example, my reflections on this matter when applied to the so-called '68ers: "Elusive '68," 118–119. Yet historians have, with good reason, persisted in the use of these generational groupings. Though he at times prefers the term "birth cohorts," historian Richard Bessel employs generational analysis in his excellent new study *Germany 1945: From War to Peace* (New York: Harper Collins, 2009); see, for example, page 8. See also Hughes, "Reason, Emotion, Force, Violence," who introduces the neologism "'45ers" to refer to members of the first generation.

41. Rogowski, "Born Later," chap. 7, *113–26*. In his contribution to this volume, Rogowski identifies himself as a representative of second generation stigma that attaches to Germans teaching in the United States.

42. See the expanded, German version of this book, Bernhard et al., "Die Nachwirkungen des Holocaust in der deutschen Gegenwartsliteratur: ausgewählte

Fallstudien [The Afterlife of the Holocaust in Contemporary German Literature: Select Case Studies]," *Holocaust Lite: Bernhard Schlinks "NS-Romane" und ihre Verfilmungen*, chap. 5.

43. There are numerous and profitable studies of German literature of Vergangenheitsbewältigung, ranging from Judith Ryan's award-winning *The Uncompleted Past* (1983) to Katja Garloff's insightful recent study of trauma in second-generation literature, *Words from Abroad: Trauma and Displacement in Postwar German Jewish Writers* (2005). My contribution to this otherwise well-plowed field lies, I would hope, in my effort to delineate epiphonemenal Holocaust literature that offers this critical vantage point from that which favors evasion and "mental comfort" (Langer, note 42). I argue that attention to textual detail, while crucial, cannot fully answer this question. For this reason I seek to include the political and cultural context, changeable though that is, in my analyses.

44. Langer, *Admitting the Holocaust*, 5ff. The term is most closely associated with Langer, who deploys it (and related phrases like "discourse of consolation" and "culture of consolation") throughout his work as the measuring rod for (un)acceptable Holocaust literature. He borrows the term "mental comfort" from the Russian poet Joseph Brodsky.

45. Rosenfeld, Alvin, "Problematics of Holocaust Literature," 25, 27 respectively; see also Lang, "Image and Fact."

46. In a recent exchange with Christopher Browning, Saul Friedländer softened his objections to Holocaust representation (articulated in the often-cited and highly regarded book *The Limits of Representation*). Now he admits of no restrictions other than that the narrative must somehow convey a "sense of disbelief." Precisely this, he avers, is found again and again in the diaries of Jews as well as those of German and other perpetrator soldiers. Though he is principally thinking of historical writing, I think his insistence that "extreme events must retain a moment of disbelief" could apply equally well to Holocaust fiction. From the November 10, 2008, lecture at Duke University's Freeman Center for Jewish Life.

47. Huyssen, Andreas, "The Politics of Identification." For a more critical view of the television series, though without attention to the specific arena of West German public culture, see Langer, *Admitting the Holocaust*, 9.

48. See Hanno Loewy, "Tales of Mass Destruction and Survival," 7.

49. See Cohn, "Optics and Power in the Novel," chap. 10, 163–80.

50. Downing, *Double Exposures*.

51. See Holub, "Review: Double Exposures," and also my review in *The European Legacy*. A classical assumption regarding what is often referred to as the ideological reading of literary realism is that it aids and abets the formation of "reified consciousness," which Adorno defines in "Education after Auschwitz," chap. 2, 28, as "a consciousness blinded to all historical past, all insight into one's own conditionedness, and posits as absolute what exists contingently." Holub's own *Reflections of Realism* provides a locus classicus of Frankfurt School apprehensions about realism. See also Russel Berman's "The Dialectics of Liberalism: Gustav Freytag," chap. 7, 79–104.

52. Nevertheless, their arguments could easily have given comfort to those seeking absolution for popular realism, particularly in the "posttheory" era of cultural studies. After all, any number of the canonical or even high (poetic) realists authors they treat were, in their day, exceedingly popular, accessible, and, in some senses, quite conventional—for example, Dickens, Fontane, and Storm.

53. "Der Roman beweist . . . dass die Skepsis gegenüber unterhaltsamer und fesselnder Literatur unbegründet ist, dass eine verständliche und klare Sprache nicht notwendigerweise den Verzicht auf ästhetisches und intellektuelles Vergnügen bedeuten muss" (Möckel, *Bernhard Schlink*, 6). (The novel proves . . . that the skepticism regarding entertaining and gripping literature is unfounded, [and] that comprehensible and clear language must not necessarily mean the renunciation of aesthetic and intellectual pleasure.) The suggestion that Schlink is a neorealist who makes no concessions to popular entertainment (Möckel 12) was first propounded by the critic Tilman Krause.

CHAPTER 1

1. A thoughtful reassessment can be found in Sansom, "Doubts About The Reader." A Holocaust historian takes issue with the novel in Neander and Körner, "Auschwitz im Roman als Schullektüre?" See also Adler, "Bernhard Schlink and 'The Reader'"; Bartov, "Germany as Victim"; Norfolk, "Die Sehnsucht nach einer ungeschehenen Geschichte"; Ozick, "The Rights of History"; Schlant, *The Language of Silence*; Hoffman, "The Uses of Illiteracy"; and Donahue, "Illusions of Subtlety."

2. See Huyssen, "The Politics of Identification." One of the chief critics of the television series was Elie Wiesel, who doubted the wisdom of "selling soap" with such a broadcast. Elie Wiesel, "Trivializing the Holocaust" and "Art and the Holocaust: Trivializing Memory."

3. "Gleichzeitigkeit des Ungleichzeitigen." See Durst, "Ernst Bloch's Theory of Nonsimultaneity" and Bloch, *Heritage of Our Times*, especially page 116, where Bloch characterizes modernity as a "collection of unresolved contradictions."

4. See Heineman, "The History of Morals." Heineman points out that Beate Uhse's Nazi past was largely overlooked in the postwar fascination with her life and career as entrepreneur of the erotic. The "real work" of Vergangenheitsbewältigung appears to have been reserved for other, more "serious," establishment figures. No one appears to have demanded that she confront her Nazi past (a past about which she offered various versions). Even the rather highbrow, left-leaning *Der Spiegel* covered her, but not critically, Heineman reports. The story of Beate Uhse demonstrates that public efforts to come to terms with the Nazi past, while significant, were by no means monolithic or applied evenly across classes and persons.

5. Wilson, "Why Do People Read," 595.

6. Brecht, "Let's Get Back," 30–32 (doc. 7), 263–70 (doc. 59); Bloch, "A Philosophical View" 209–227; on Benjamin's view of the detective novel see Bloch,

"A Philosophical View" 216–17. For an overview of theory of detective fiction, including the central theoretical documents, see Vogt, *Der Kriminalroman.*

7. Wilson, "Who Cares," 392. But this is not the worst; in the same piece he refers to detective fiction as "rubbish" (397), and "degrading to the intelligence" (396).

8. As the poet W. H. Auden famously observed, "the most curious fact about the detective story is that it makes its greatest appeal precisely to those classes of people who are most immune to other forms of daydream literature. The typical detective story addict is a doctor or clergyman or scientist or artist, i.e., a fairly successful professional man with intellectual interests and well-read in his own field, who could never stomach the *Saturday Evening Post* or *True Confessions* or movie magazines or comics." Auden, "The Guilty Vicarage," 269. While this appears to be a widely held view, one may well wonder where Auden and Wilson get their certainty.

9. Tannert and Kratz, Early German and Austrian Detective Fiction, 7. Tannert and Kratz argue that detective fiction inevitably proves a valuable source of social commentary: "The act of solving serious crimes," they propose, "especially murder (and there is nearly always a murder in a detective story), involves not merely ratiocination applied to the physical evidence, but—even if unconsciously—also the whole of a society's values with regard to justice and punishment."

10. Loewy, "Tales of Mass Destruction," 3.

11. "Eine besondere Qualität fast aller Texte Schlinks liegt darin, dass sie brisante Themen der deutschen Zeitgeschichte auf eine brillante Weise verhandeln und gekonnt spannende Unterhaltung mit Tiefgang verbinden. Auch in den Kriminalromanen werden thematische Felder wie die deutsche Vergangenheit, das Verhältnis von Ost und West oder das Verhältnis von Deutschen und Juden auf eine Art und Weise angesprochen, die ihrer Komplexität gerecht wird." Mall-Grob, "Grossartiger Abgang einer literarischen Figur."

12. Doerry and Hage, "Spiegel-Gespräch." Here Schlink remarks, "Beim Schreiben mache ich in gewisser Weise keine Unterschiede, ob ich nun einen Krimi, einen anderen Roman, Erzählungen oder einen Beitrag für eine wissenschaftliche Zeitschrift verfasse. Ich bin gleichermaßen dabei . . . Im Übrigen ist das alles ein fortlaufender Prozess: Ich hätte den 'Vorleser' nicht ohne die Erfahrung mit den Büchern davor schreiben können." The Nazi thematic continuity in Schlink's novel writing was emphasized by Christoh Stölzel in his "Laudatio" for the author: "Wie ihn die NS-Zeit beschäftigt, wird auch aus den früheren Krimis ersichtlich, die Schlink geschrieben hat" ("'Ich hab's in einer Nacht ausgelesen.' Laudatio auf Bernhard Schlink," *Die Welt*, November 13, 1999). On the minimal cultural knowledge presupposed by popular culture, see Sagan, *I Want to Go on Living.*

13. Schlink has authored a fourth novel in this genre, namely *Die gordische Schleife* (Zurich: Diogenes, 1988), which is unrelated to the Selb trilogy and therefore not treated here.

14. 1"Ein Mann mit gebrochenem Lebenslauf, aber einer, der daraus gelernt hat." Mall-Grob, "Grossartiger Abgang."

15. See, for example, "Das Tschernobyl Der Wasserwirtschaft," *Der Spiegel*, November 10, 1986, 161–66a; "Was Da Fließt, Weiß Nur Der Liebe Gott," *Der Spiegel*, December 29, 1986, 22–25; "Unterschiedliche Konsequenzen aus der Rheinverseuchung gezogen. Regierungserklärung und Debatte über die Basler Brandkatastrophe und ihre Folgen in der 246. Sitzung des 10. Deutschen Bundesages am 13.11.1986-Reden von: Walter Wallmann, Klaus Matthiesen, Hannegret Hönes, Harald Schäfer, Bernd Schmidbauer." Bonn, Germany: *Das Parlament* 48 (1986), 4–5. My thanks to Aaron Lee for his assistance with this note.

16. "Eine Klarheit über mich selbst." Schlink and Popp, *Selbs Justiz*, 186. Subsequent page references to the original German edition are preceded by the abbreviation "SJ." Longer quotations appearing in the body of this chapter will be given in English and are from the English language edition, which is abbreviated as "SP." German original quotes (of lengthier or linguistically ambiguous passages) are given in the notes. In cases where I have revised the translation, I will use the abbreviation "trans. rev."

17. SP, 104. "Ich war überzeugter Nationalsozialist gewesen, aktives Parteimitglied und ein harter Staatsanwalt, der auch Todesstrafen gefordert und gekriegt hat. Es waren spektakuläre Prozesse dabei. Ich glaubte an die Sache und verstand mich als Soldat an der Rechtsfront, an der anderen Front konnte ich nach meiner Verwundung gleich zu Beginn des Krieges nicht mehr eingesetzt werden" (SJ, 146–47).

18. SP, 104.

19. SP, 104.

20. SP, 104. "Mein Glaube war verlorengegangen. Sie können sich wahrscheinlich nicht vorstellen, wie man überhaupt an den Nationalsozialismus glauben konnte. Aber Sie sind mit dem Wissen aufgewachsen, das wir 1945 erst Stück um Stück bekamen . . . Um die Zeit der Währungsreform begann man, belastete Kollegen wieder einzustellen. Da hätte ich wohl auch wieder zur Justiz gekonnt. Aber ich sah, was die Bemühung um die Wiedereinstellung und die Wiedereinstellung selbst aus den Kollegen machte. Anstelle von Schuld hatten sie nur noch das Gefühl, man habe ihnen mit der Entlassung Unrecht getan" (SJ, 147).

21. While not entirely complete or historically accurate, the *Braunbuch* represents one of the acknowledged methods the GDR employed to fuel the discontent of the West German student movement. For more on the *Braunbuch*, see below. As this book goes to press, it has come to light that Benno Ohnesorg's murder—widely viewed as the catalyst that turned student protest into a mass movement—was carried out by a member of the SED and an unofficial employee of the *Stasi*. See "Neue Recherchen: Ohnesorgs Todesschütze soll Stasi-Spion gewesen sein," *Spiegel*, May 21, 2009; see also Kulish, "Spy Fired Shot."

22. SP, 104, trans rev. "Schlimm war's mit meiner Frau, die eine schöne blonde Nazisse war und auch blieb, bis sie zur vollschlanken Wirtschaftswunder-deutschen wurde" (SJ, 147).

23. SJ, 242.

24. SP, 182, trans rev. "Natürlich hatte ich mich als Staatsanwalt mißbrauchen las-sen, das hatte ich nach dem Zusammenbruch gelernt . . . Dennoch war es für mich auf Anhieb nicht das gleiche ob ich im Dienst einer vermeintlich großen, schlechten Sache schuldig geworden war oder ob man mich als dum-men Bauern, meinethalben auch Offizier, benutzt hatte auf dem Schachbrett einer kleinen, schäbigen Intrige, die ich noch nicht verstand" (SJ, 256). This corny, self-consciously trite imagery is a staple of the genre and perhaps even a homage to that master of detective fiction, Raymond Chandler. Chandler's Detective Marlowe, for example in *The Long Good-Bye*, is forever spouting the most shop-worn vernacular and yet somehow capable of nuanced descriptive prose, not to mention insightful detective work. I thank Alfredo Franco for introducing me to the pleasures of Chandler.

25. SJ, 299, 325.

26. SP, 180, trans rev. "Sie haben ihm dafür nicht einmal das Leben versprochen, sondern nur, daß er noch ein bißchen überleben kann" (SJ, 253).

27. SP, 179. "Mein Mann war nicht sehr lebenstüchtig und auch nicht sehr tapfer" (SJ, 252).

28. SP, 179; SJ, 252.

29. SP, 227–28, trans rev; "Das Komplott, für das ich den nützlichen Idioten abgegeben hatte. Eingefädelt und durchgeführt von meinem Freund und Schwager. Den nicht in den Prozeß ziehen zu müssen, ich auch noch froh gewe-sen war. Er hatte sich meiner überlegen bedient" (SJ, 321).

30. "Schuldete ich irgend jemand irgendwas? . . . Sollte ich an die Presse gehen? Was machte ich mit meiner Schuld?" (SJ, 325).

31. SP, 161–62, 165, 171–72; SJ, 228; cf. 232.

32. See Hilberg, *The Destruction*, esp. ch. 7, "The Nature of the Process."

33. SP, 162.

34. SP, 246, trans rev; "Tyberg hatte verstanden. Es tat mir gut, einen heimlichen Mitwisser zu haben, der mich nicht um Rechenschaft fragen würde" (SJ, 344).

35. "Das Unheil, das ich als Staatsanwalt damals angerichtet hatte." Schlink, *Selbs Mord*, 107. Subsequent page references to this novel are preceded by the abbreviation "SM" and provided parenthetically within the text. The German "Unheil" can range from meanings like "calamity" all the way to mere "mis-chief"; and the verb "anrichten" is frequently associated with things like "dam-age," "harm," "mischief," "mess," and so on.

36. *Self's Deception* (henceforth abbreviated "SD"), trans. rev., 39. "Ich erinnerte mich an den Vermerk des Generalstaatsanwalts, der 1943 oder 1944 über mei-nen Schreibtisch bei der Staatsanwaltschaft Heidelberg gegangen war und ver-fügt hatte, daß wer von den russischen und polnischen Arbeitern lässig arbeitet, Zwangsarbeit im Konzentrationslager bekommt. Wie viele hatte ich dorthin geschickt? Ich starrte in den Regen." Schlink, *Selbs Betrug*, 36–37. Subsequent page references to the German original are preceded by the abbreviation "SB."

37. For another example of an apparent admission of guilt, which, however, lacks any real substance, see SB, 227–28.

38. These include conversations with himself (monologues), with Frau Buchendorf (*Selbs Justiz*), and Leo Salgar (*Selbs Betrug*).

39. SD, 152–53; "1945 hatte man mich als Nazi-Staatsanwalt nicht mehr gewollt, und als man die alten Nazis wieder wollte, wollte ich nicht mehr. Weil ich kein alter Nazi mehr war? Weil mich das Schwamm-drüber-Denken derer störte, die in der Justiz meine alten Kollegen gewesen waren und meine neuen geworden wären? Weil ich mir die Frage, was Recht und was Unrecht ist, von niemandem anderes mehr beantworten lassen wollte? . . . Ich kann's nicht genau sagen, Leo. Staatsanwalt—das war für mich 1945 einfach vorbei" (SB, 136).

40. "Ich konnte nun einmal nicht mehr Staatsanwalt sein, zuerst, weil man mich wegen meiner Vergangenheit nicht mehr haben wollte, und dann, weil sich in mir alles dagegen sträubte, mit den anderen zu tun, als hätten wir keine Vergangenheiten, auch wenn man uns dazu aufforderte" (SM, 170–71).

41. I mention this in part because Schlink is better known for chiding the '68ers, in particular their undifferentiated accusations of "the fathers." See c. four below.

42. SB, 92; SM, 56, 72.

43. SM, 89

44. This is not to suggest that German suffering is somehow a less legitimate topic. Uwe Timm, in his novella *Die Entdeckung der Currywurst* (1993), and more recently Günter Grass, with his novel *Im Krebsgang* (2002), but, above all, Walter Kempowski in his masterpiece *Alles umsonst*, have shown how this topic can be handled with varying degrees of poignancy.

45. SM, 90–93.

46. SM, 107–8.

47. Author's translation; "Ich war nicht ernsthaft zu Schaden gekommen . . . Aber weh tat etwas anderes. Ich hatte die Gelegenheit gehabt, richtig zu machen, was ich seinerzeit falsch gemacht hatte. Wann hat man das schon! Aber ich habe es wieder falsch gemacht" (SM, 93).

48. "Ich habe es nie bereut. Manchmal habe ich gedacht, ich müßte es bereuen, weil es weder rechtlich noch moralisch in Ordnung war. Aber das Gefühl der Reue hat sich nicht eingestellt. Vielleicht gilt die andere, ältere, härtere Moral, die vor der heutigen galt, in unseren Herzen doch noch fort" (SM, 223).

49. SB, 274, 280.

50. SB, 124.

51. For example, "Wie damals bei Baader und Meinhof," SB, 117–21.

52. SD, 159; "Ich bin viel zu oft bei meinem Leisten geblieben. Als Soldat, als Staatsanwalt, als Privatdetektiv—ich habe gemacht, was man mir gesagt hat, daß es mein Handwerk ist, und habe den anderen nicht in ihres gepfuscht. Wir sind ein Volk von Schustern, die bei ihrem Leisten bleiben, und schauen Sie sich an, wohin uns das gebracht hat" (SB, 142).

53. SD, 158; "Sie meinen das Dritte Reich?" (SB, 142).

54. SM, 212–13.

55. Author's translation; "Ja, so waren sie. Drittes Reich, Krieg, Niederlage, Aufbau und Wirtschaftswunder—für sie waren es nur verschiedene Umstände, unter denen sie das gleiche betrieben: Sie mehrten, was ihnen gehörte oder was sie

verwalteten . . . Was zählten Regierungen, Systeme, Ideen, die Schmerzen und Freuden der Menschen, wenn die Wirtschaft nicht florierte? . . . Korten war so gewesen . . . Wie den anderen [Weller und Welker] waren auch ihm Macht und Erfolg des Unternehmens und der eigenen Person eins geworden" (SM, 222).

56. SP, 5.

57. SM, 17.

58. Author's translation; "im Fernsehen haben wir verfolgt, wie Bill Clinton wiedergewählt und vereidigt wurde" (SM, 18).

59. For just a few of the many, many instances that mention Selb's age sympathetically, see SP, 14, 22, 54, 175, 179.

60. Selb reports that he joined the public prosectuor's office in 1942 and served there through 1945; SP, 4.

61. This data was culled from the *Braunbuch* entries by Mr. John T. Grimaldi, to whom I owe a debt of gratitude. See also Donahue, "The Popular Culture Alibi."

62. Kaes argues that German Weimar-era film in large part responds to the trauma of WWI. This dialogical relationship is often a layered and indirect phenomenon, as he demonstrates. See, for example, his *M* (a concise and valuable guide to the famous Fritz Lang film of this title) and especially *Shell Shock Cinema*.

63. On this see Mann, xvii. For the purposes of this discussion, I focus on the way in which *Judgment at Nuremberg* seeks to establish the responsibility of a wider sphere of educated and socially privileged adults, rather than focus on the notorious perpetrators who actually conducted the genocide first hand. This discussion is necessarily selective and unfortunately overlooks the relatively bold social criticism aimed at the United States and certain American institutions. Herr Rolfe (played by Maximilian Schell) is, for example, a compellingly mixed figure; his dramatic question about the American nuclear bombing of Hiroshima and Nagasaki—"Is that their superior morality?"—raises serious ethical questions. Similarly, when the Nazi T4 project is referenced, the presiding U.S. judge, Dan (played by Spencer Tracy), quotes none other than Oliver Wendell Holmes approving the practice of sterilization of the mentally handicapped in the state of Virginia. After the films from the camps are shown, the camera intentionally focuses on the only African American MP in the courtroom, raising the thorny question of civil rights (or the lack thereof) in 1961 America. A further object of critique is the American public's indifference to the trials and fickleness when it comes to foreign affairs. Indeed, Dan's final speech from the bench appears to be aimed more to cold-war America than to postwar Germany.

64. *Judgment at Nuremberg*, directed by Stanley Kramer, (MGM, 2004), DVD. The DVD provides background information on the film's Berlin premier, including coverage of the postscreening press conference in which mayor Brandt is clearly tongue-tied. As the background material provided on the DVD attests, the film did not, in any case, do very well in Germany, despite its star-studded cast. This is true at least for first-run theater screenings. Later, the film was shown on German television.

65. Mann, 91.

66. Ibid., ix.

67. As chief prosecutor Colonel Lawson (Colonel Parker in the play) contends—using language that virtually quotes Taylor—"Their minds were not warped at an early age. They had attained maturity long before Hitler's rise to power. They embraced the ideologies of the Third Reich as educated adults. They, most of all, should have valued justice" (Mann 17).

68. The principal reason for rejecting the Nuremberg Trials as the "victors' justice" was the Allies' refusal to consider the bombing of Dresden and Soviet crimes, such as the 1940 mass shooting of Polish officers at Katyn. But the long-term cultural impact of the Nuremberg Trials should not be underestimated, as Konrad Jarausch observes, for "roughly half of the German population considered the punishment of the perpetrators to be just," and "all told, the Nuremberg trials bolstered the impression of the leading Nazis' guilt. At the same time, this unprecedented experiment in international justice also contributed to a feeling of exculpation among the population since many Germans could now claim that they had either known nothing of the crimes in the first place or had only followed orders handed down from above" (Jarausch, *After Hitler*, 8).

69. The play debuted in Germany in 2001 in Nuremberg. Press, photos, the cast list, and an interview with Mann can be found at http://www.staatstheater-nuernberg.de/02_03/Schauspiel/Produktionen/Urteil/urteil_pres.html.

70. In the novel *Selbs Justiz*, it is the Jew Vera Mueller who invites Selb in for pizza and a drink, and, most importantly, forgives him of his Nazi past (SP, 186); whereas "Frau Weinstein" (Sarah Hirsch) dismisses Selb in anger (SP, 178–80).

71. The novel justifies her baldness by explaining that she was a victim of medical experiments having to do with the scalp. However, the image of a bald survivor, which refers back to famous images of camp inmates at the time of their liberation, seems to be the point of this physical characteristic.

72. It is also much more effective than inserting a third party, such as the novel does in the person of Vera Mueller. Indeed, this figure appears to me to serve as a buffer in another sense: unlike Hofmann, Schlink hesitated to link German and Jew so directly, worrying, perhaps, as he said about *The Reader*, that it might come across as "a kind of white-washing novel" (see below).

73. Bloch, "A Philosophical View," 219; emphasis in original.

74. Bloch, "A Philosophical View," 219.

75. "The problem of the omitted beginning affects the entire detective genre, gives it its form: the form of a picture puzzle, the hidden part of which predates the picture and only gradually enters into it." Bloch, "A Philosophical View," 227.

76. "It is sometimes said that detective stories are read by respectable law-abiding citizens in order to gratify in fantasy the violent or murderous wishes they dare not, or are ashamed to, translate into action. This may be true for readers of thrillers . . . but it is quite false for the reader of detective stories" (Auden, "The Guilty Vicarage," 270).

77. Ibid.

78. "Morden heißt, nicht verzeihen müssen" (SJ, 342)

79. Adorno and Horkheimer develop their critique of affirmative culture in "The Culture Industry: Enlightenment as Mass Deception," in *Dialectic of Enlightenment*. See also Marcuse, "The Affirmative Character."

80. SP, 181.

81. "Alle sind wir verstrickt" (SJ, 331).

82. Konrad Jarausch argues that the process of denazification, though intrinsically problematic and widely discredited, was in fact a qualified success: "The actual paradox of the great purge is thus the contradiction between the fact that it undoubtedly petered out in the short term but nonetheless achieved most of its aims in the long run" (*After Hitler*, 55).

83. Author's translation; "Ich bin immer wieder zu langsam, nicht erst seit ich älter werde" (SM, 187).

84. SM, 142, 160, 182, 255–56.

85. Metz, "'Truth is a Woman.'"

86. This is, to my mind, the most persuasive of this kind of argument. See Swales, "Sex, Shame and Guilt."

87. Beissner, *Der Erzähler Franz Kafka*. Walter H. Sokel translates this as "unimental perspective"; see his *The Myth of Power and the Self*, 14–15.

88. Donahue, "Illusions of Subtlety," 73–75.

89. Huyssen, "Politics of Identification," 94–114.

90. Many readers—including participants in Oprah Winfrey's Book Club and the more elite press venues—advocate The Reader as an important contribution to the literature of Vergangenheitsbewältigung, but they do so on the basis of a consonant reading of Berg. See Donahue, "Illusions of Subtlety," esp. 63–72.

91. If the ironic reading is to prevail in some fashion, it must either (1) exclude the consonant (or einsinnig) reading as mistaken, or (2) in a mood of postmodern inclusivity, concede that the consonant reading is at least as plausible, which then undermines the case for viewing the novel as a serious intervention in Vergangenheitsbewältigung. If one is just as welcome to read with Berg as to critique him, where is the impulse to confront the past critically? I have argued this point at greater length in "Revising '68," esp. 307–9.

92. SJ, 332–33

93. My translation; "der Täter will Richter spielen, was? Fühlst du dich unschuldig mißbraucht?" (SJ, 334).

94. Jarausch, *After Hitler*, 6, 8, 49.

95. John M. Reilly, "Detective Novel," 117.

96. Talburt, "Religion," *The Oxford Companion*, 383. See also Auden, "The Guilty Vicarage."

97. While it is generally assumed that Nazis were far more rigorously pursued in the Soviet Zone, a correction in this understanding may now be called for, as Jarausch cautions, because "in some areas—for example, medicine, technology, and the military—high percentages of Nazis were tolerated there as well" (*After Hitler*, 47).

98. Nadya Aisenberg, "Resolution and Irresolution," 384–85.

99. See Giordano, *Die zweite Schuld*.

100. In a 1955 speech marking West Germany's entry into NATO, Adenauer asserted that Germans had "paid hard for the misdeeds that were committed in their name by corrupt and blind leaders" (in Niven, *Facing the Nazi Past*, 103). Regarding Helmut Kohl, Niven observes, "Throughout his chancellorship, his commemorative speeches displayed a typical tendency to pin sole responsibility for the war on Hitler or the Nazi party, while implicitly exonerating the broad mass of Germans. 1995 was no exception in this regard" (Niven, *Facing the Nazi Past*, 113). Niven furthermore rightly depicts the Kohl-sponsored "House of History" (Haus der Geschichte) in Bonn as "Holocaust-marginalizing" (Niven, *Facing the Nazi Past*, 213; cf. 58–59; 200–2). See also Donahue and Cohn, "Cultural Reparations."

101. Judith Ryan, *The Uncompleted Past*.

CHAPTER 2

1. Schlink, *Der Vorleser*, 103. Further references appear in the text.

2. Ibid., 107; see also 123.

3. Schlink, *Der Vorleser*, 107–8.

4. The English translations of *Der Vorleser* throughout this book represent my revisions of Carol Brown Janeway's translation, *The Reader*, here 112. Henceforth noted only as Janeway, *The Reader*. J/TR 112.

5. Quoted in the *Oprah Winfrey Show* transcript, March 31, 1999, 8. Further references appear in the notes as "Oprah."

6. Ozick, "The Rights of History," 27.

7. Hoffman, "The Uses of Illiteracy," 35.

8. Bartov, "Germany as Victim," 29–40; see also Adler, "Die Kunst, Mitleid mit den Mördern zu erzwingen."

9. *The Economist*, June 13, 1998, R16–17.

10. Schlink, *Der Vorleser*, 196.

11. Löhndorf, "Die Banalität des Bösen."

12. See Ruta, "Secrets and Lies"; Scherer, "Spitzfindigkeiten."

13. On the genre of Holocaust courtroom drama, see Loewy, "Tales of Mass Destruction."

14. Ruta, "Secrets and Lies," 9.

15. Ernestine Schlant argues that in asserting this defense for his own sudden inability to narrate, Berg commits the same kind of error that became infamous during the *Historikerstreit* of the 1980s, namely the confusion of Germany and the Germans with the immediate and principal victims of the Holocaust, the Jews of Europe, in *The Language of Silence*, 214.

16. Schlink, *Der Vorleser*, 98–99.

17. Janeway, *The Reader*, 103.[0]

18. Hilberg, "Seminar," June 7. According to Hilberg, Himmler, in reaction to von dem Bach's query regarding the effect of mass murder on German men, went so far as to recommend a kind of talk therapy for the murderers: they would meet together at the end of the day over a meal, find support in the fact that they

were all executioners, and then proceed to listen to music or a lecture together. See also Hilberg's discussion of the psychological effects of killing and various bureaucratic strategies for dealing with it (ideological indoctrination, strict rules about not killing or pillaging without authorization, "humane" methods like the gas van, which make killers feel better, etc.) in *The Destruction of the European Jews*, 136ff, 274ff.

19. Bauman, *Modernity and the Holocaust*.

20. See Hoffman, chapter 4, 114.

21. For an authoritative introduction to posttraumatic stress disorder as well as a helpful bibliography of current findings, see http://www.nimh.nih.gov/health/topics/post-traumatic-stress-disorder-ptsd/index.shtml. In addition, LaCapra's *Writing History* provides an overview of trends in trauma theory across the humanities.

22. Schlink, *Der Vorleser*, 142–43.

23. For a significant exception to this rule, see Feuchert and Hofmann, discussed at length in Chapter 4.

24. The blanket application of Berg's Betäubung thesis to camp inmates is further contested in the more nuanced account of Des Pres, *The Survivor*.

25. See Naumann, *Auschwitz*. See also Wittmann, *Beyond Justice*. Wittmann analyzes the actual voice recordings from these trials and confirms the defendants' combativeness and wiliness; their behavior in court was not characterized by "numbness."

26. Schlink, *Der Vorleser*, 99.

27. Carole Angier's review reflects the manner in which the renunciation of repugnant ideas fails to cancel their effect: "But 'can one see them all as linked in this way?' No, he answers; the person who endures suffering and the person who imposes it are incommensurable. But the question has been raised." Indeed it has. See Angier, "Finding Room for Understanding."

28. "Dort in jener moralischen Betäubung, über die Berg später grübeln muß, ihren grausigen Dienst versah." And elsewhere, too, it is clear that Berg has harvested approval on precisely this point. Though Berg has formally withdrawn—or qualified—his views on "numbness," they clearly live on: *The Guardian* found his thoughts on numbness "most striking" ("The Digested Read," 16) and *Publishers Weekly* (1999) considered them "philosophical."

29. Lamberty, Literatur-Kartei "Der Vorleser," 64. "Weshalb ist diese 'Betäubung' eine notwendige Reaktion?" See Möckel, Bernhard Schlink, Der Vorleser, who draws attention to the "Betäubung/Erstarrung/Kälte" motifs in her teaching guide as well (75).

30. Schlink, *Der Vorleser*, 114–15.

31. Janeway, *The Reader*, 118–19.

32. Berg reprises the Betäubung narrative to various ends in the following places: 152 (his reaction to Struthof), 155 (his feelings after failing to raise the issue Hanna's illiteracy with the judge), 159–60 (his overall response to the trial). Page references here are to Schlink, *Der Vorleser*.

33. Schlink, *Der Vorleser*, 117–18.

34. Oprah, [0]13, 18.
35. Malcomson, "Lost Love."
36. Bernstein, "Once Loving."
37. Oprah, 14, cf. 8.
38. Similar views can be found in Demmer, "Die Liebe zu einer KZ-Aufseherin" and Michalzik, "Das Monster als Mensch."
39. See Mejias, "Schlink ist okay!"; Saur, "Man mag es traurig"; wink, "Fräulein Lehrer."
40. Annan, "Thoughts about Hanna," 22. Others who champion the novel's moral finesse are Enright, "Modern Love"; Hage, "Der Schatten der Tat"; Maristed, "The Secret"; Moritz, "Die Liebe zur Aufseherin"; Ploetz, "Vom Verlust der Unschuld"; Stölleis, "Die Schaffnerin," "and Walter, "Secrets and Lies"
41. The following explicitly cite Steiner: Clee, "Matter of Interpretation"; Krause, "Wunder und Zeichen" 9; McCrum, "Book of the Week"; and the unsigned review ("The Digested Read") in The *Guardian*. It is a common reviewing practice, it should be noted, to consult earlier reviews; so even when Steiner is not explicitly acknowledged, his influence may still be in effect. Reviews too numerous to list routinely refer to prior critical praise. And, of course, the Vintage paperback edition features Steiner's enthusiastic endorsement on the back cover. Neither is Steiner alone in this; Paul Bailey cites the authority of "Jorge Semprun, the great Spanish writer who is a survivor of Buchenwald" (4) in his praise of the novel as well in "The Heartbreaking Consequences of a Liaison."
42. This and subsequent quotations of Steiner from "He Was Only a Boy but He Was Good in Bed," reprinted with the telling title "Reading's Seductive Power" in the *Manchester Guardian Weekly*.
43. See, for example, *Lamberty, Literatur-Kartei "Der Vorleser,"* 66f.; Mittelberg, *Bernhard Schlink, Der Vorleser*, 30–33; Möckel, *Bernhard Schlink, Der Vorleser*, 83–85; Urban, *Bernhard Schlink, Der Vorleser*, 42–46; Greese and Peren-Eckert, *Unterrichtsmodell Bernhard Schlink*, 49–53; Köster, *Bernhard Schlink*, Der Vorleser, 49–54; Reisner, *Lektürehilfen Bernhard Schlink*, 75–83.
44. Carl Macdougall, "Guilt Edged Ideas."
45. Schlink, *Der Vorleser*, 142–43.
46. Hanks in *The Independent*.
47. Bernstein, "Once Loving, Once Cruel."
48. Ibid.
49. Natasha Walter, "Secret Love and the Holocaust."
50. Hanks in *The Independent*.
51. "If the Nazis had been monsters," Schlink says, "we would not have a problem. We would be here, and they would be out there. It is precisely because they were not monsters that what happened is so challenging for us, and so frightening" (quoted in Clee, "Matter of Interpretation").
52. Peter Schneider, "German Postwar Stategies of Coming to Terms with the Past," 283.

53. On this, see Gail Hart's excellent discussion of Schiller's *Verbrecher aus ver-lorener Ehre* in *Friedrich Schiller: Crime, Aesthetic and the Poetics of Punishment* (Newark, DE: University of Delaware Press, 2005).

54. On the question of moral obfuscation via apparent nuance, see MacKinnon's excellent "Law and Tenderness." Here MacKinnon grants the novel "a certain moral poise," but concludes that this is "overwhelmed by Schlink's studied effort throughout the novel to erode moral distinctions, to establish personal circumstances and debilities as mitigating even the most horrible crimes, and to attribute criminal conduct not so much to individuals as to the desperate shortcomings of human nature" (195).

55. Petropoulos and Roth, *Gray Zones*, xix. Here also the authors formulate pithily their central point: "Levi argued that nothing revealed the gray zone more grimly than the *Sonderkommando*'s plight."

56. Levi, *The Drowned and the Saved*, 59.

57. Petropoulos and Roth, *Gray Zones*, 94.

58. Levi, *The Voice of Memory*, 180.

59. Petropoulos and Roth, *Gray Zones*, 294.

60. Ibid.; emphasis added.

61. Ibid., 3.

62. Ibid.

63. This view of moral sophistication arising out of the inability to attribute guilt and innocence is also evident in a number of teaching guides, particularly in their extensive treatments of guilt. See, for example, Möckel, who argues, "Gerade weil keine eindeutigen Rollenzuweisungen zu Nur-Schuldigen oder Nur-Unschuldigen entstehen, die Umstände, die zur Schuld führten verstehbar und erklärbar gemacht warden, aber deutlich darauf hingewiesen wird, dass gleichzeitiges Verstehen und Verurteilen nicht geht, *bekommt der Roman eine universelle Bedeutung mit fast philosophischen Bezügen.*" Bernhard Schlink, *Der Vorleser*, 93; my emphasis.

64. "Levi minced no words about German murderers and their accomplices, the experts at planning and implementing the 'useless violence' that was rife in the Holocaust. They were the ones who initiated, built, and maintained the system. Apart from them—from Hitler and Himmler to Muhsfeld and Pannwitz—it had no reality, but with them the degradation and killing went on and on." Petropoulos and Roth, *Gray Zones*, 295.

65. Langer, *Versions of Survival*.

66. For an explanation of this phenomenon in Africa in recent years, see Chelala, "Child Soldiers: Skipping Childhood."

67. Schieber, *Soundless Roar*.

68. Oprah, 14.

69. Sympathy for Hanna as victim of forces beyond her control abounds. Robert Hanks, in *The Independent*, offers one particularly revealing example of how the overturning of moral conventions is linked to viewing Hanna as victim. The novel presents "the possibility—no more than that—that Hanna is a sort of victim, and that Michael's generation, babies during the war, are at least as

guilty." If Michael is really "at least as guilty" as Hanna, then Hanna cannot be very guilty after all.

70. Levi, *The Drowned and the Saved*, 48.
71. Battersby, "Reading in the Dark."
72. Clark in the *Sunday Times*.
73. Wyss, "Fragen auf Antworten."
74. Krause, "Keine Elternaustreibung," *Der Tagesspiegel*, September 3, 1995.
75. Schlink, *Der Vorleser*, 187.
76. Hösle, *Objective Idealism*, 16.

CHAPTER 3

1. "Man muß auch vergeben können. Man weiß ja nicht, wie man selbst in dieser Situation gehandelt hätte." Quoted in Lamberty, *Literatur-Kartei "Der Vorleser,"* 36.
2. For a balanced and insightful discussion of the portrayal of Hanna within a broader philosophical context see MacKinnon, "Crime, Compassion, and The Reader."
3. Schlink, *Der Vorleser*, 107–8.
4. For translations from the German original I have consistently consulted and used (with some minor revisions in each case) Carol Brown Janeway's *The Reader*. Noted below as Janeway, *The Reader*, here 112.
5. Roche, *Why Literature Matters*, 23–30.
6. Donahue, "Illusions of Subtlety," 78.
7. For a contrasting point of view, see Micha Ostermann, "Täter–Opfer–Zuschauer," in *Aporien des Erinnerns*, chap. 3, 56–103. Ostermann reads Hanna as unambiguously guilty of the specific counts against her, and takes her "conversion" in prison quite seriously.
8. Janeway, *The Reader*, 97.
9. Schlink, *Der Vorleser*, 92.
10. Loewy, "Tales of Mass Destruction and Survival."
11. Schlink, *Der Vorleser*, 105.
12. Janeway, *The Reader*, 110.
13. Speer, *Inside the Third Reich*. Speer set himself apart from his codefendants precisely by taking at least a modicum of responsibility for some wrongdoing. Whereas the other defendants claimed not to know of the genocide, or only to have followed orders, he alone took responsibility and thus gained a tremendous amount of prestige in the postwar period. See esp. chap. 34 ("Nuremberg") and 35 ("Conclusions"), where Speer distinguishes himself from the other Nuremberg inmates as uniquely willing to confess his guilt and responsibility. See also Pabsch, "Albert Speer."
14. Schlink, *Der Vorleser*, 104–5.
15. Janeway, *The Reader*, 109.
16. Jarausch, *After Hitler*, 49. Jarausch documents the widespread denial by Nazi elites of responsibility for war crimes: "At first, most could barely grasp the

reality of Germany's collapse, and, clinging bitterly to their national pride, claimed to have no knowledge whatsoever of Nazi crimes: 'Ultimately, it turned out that they all together rejected any "blame" for themselves.'" This focus on the prosecution of Nazi elites, albeit in many respects unsuccessful, "contributed to a feeling of exculpation among the population since many Germans could now claim that they had either known nothing of the crimes in the first place or had only followed orders handed down from above" (8; see also 6).

17. *Die bleierne Zeit* was distributed in the United States both under the title *The German Sisters*, and (the better known) *Marianne and Juliane*.

18. "'Ich bin nicht schuldig,' sagt der Kapo. 'Ich bin nicht schuldig,' sagt der Offizier. 'Ich bin nicht schuldig.' Wer also ist schuld?"

19. "If one tries to give a historical account of the various stages of German efforts to master the past—efforts at Vergangenheitsbewältigung—key political and cultural events that have provoked brief periods of intense confrontation with this past come to mind when one speaks of such confrontations, [however,] one is speaking of a relatively small segment of the population for whom the imperative to work through the past is a given." Santner, *Stranded Objects*, xi–xii.

20. See Jauß, "Literary History As a Challenge" [1967], reprinted in *Toward an Aesthetic of Reception*, trans. T. Bahti (Minneapolis: University of Minnesota Press, 1982).

21. Janeway, *The Reader*, 97.

22. Wittmann, *Beyond Justice*.

23. Jarausch, *After Hitler*, 9.

24. Schlink, *Der Vorleser*, 111.

25. Janeway, *The Reader*, 115.

26. Ibid.

27. Schlink, *Der Vorleser*, 111.

28. Novik, *The Holocaust in American Life*.

29. Janeway, *The Reader*, 116.

30. Ibid.

31. Ibid.; emphasis added.

32. Ibid., 116–17.

33. Ibid., 117.

34. Ibid.

35. Ibid., 133–34.

36. This technique of retracting what has been said can of course cut both ways, as we will see in the case of the novel's "numbness" doctrine. In that case, a weak series of retractions is actually meant to leave the initial charges in place. Here we see the opposite: Berg names the charges in order to undermine and defang them.

37. See also the apostrophe to Hanna and her court-appointed attorney (V 113) and the imagined conversation with the presiding judge (V 132).

38. Janeway, *The Reader*, 4.

39. Schlink, *Der Vorleser*, 122. The idea that SS guards were routinely shot for objecting to carry out executions and other genocidal actions is not true, though it is still widely entrenched in popular culture (see Hilburg, *The Destruction of the European Jews*). On the other hand, German soldiers who deserted their units, as well as members of the SS who surrendered to the Allies without an explicit order (which rarely came), were indeed treated harshly by roving summary courts well into 1945 (see Bessel, Germany 1945).

40. Janeway, *The Reader*, 125.

41. "Wir haben uns zusammen überlegt, was wir schreiben sollen. Wir wollten denen, die sich davongemacht hatten, nichts anhängen. Aber daß wir was falsch gemacht hätten, wollten wir uns auch nicht anziehen" (V 123).

42. Janeway, *The Reader*, 127.

43. Schlink, *Der Vorleser*, 156.

44. Janeway, *The Reader*, 135.

45. Ibid., 162–63.

46. Ibid., 163.

47. Mittelberg, *Berhard Schlink*, 29. "Ungeachtet der fragwürdigen Beschuldigungen der Mitangeklagten wird . . . die Schwere von Hannas Schuld unterstrichen."

48. Mittelberg, *Berhard Schlink*, 29.

49. Ibid.

50. Janeway, *The Reader*, 48.

51. Ibid., 49.

52. Schlink, *Der Vorleser*, 50. Referring to his practice of submitting to Hanna in person, even when he thought he was not at fault, Berg says, "Ich konnte mit ihr nicht darüber reden. Das Reden über unser Streiten führte nur zu weiterem Streit. Ein- oder zweimal habe ich ihr lange Briefe geschrieben. Aber sie reagierte nicht, und als ich nachfragte, fragte sie zurück: 'Fängst du schon wieder an?'"

53. Janeway, *The Reader*, 79.

54. Schlink, *Der Vorleser*, 77.

55. Ibid., 72.

56. Ibid., 78.

57. Janeway, *The Reader*, 80.

58. Ibid., 83.

59. Schlink, *Der Vorleser*, 129.

60. Janeway, *The Reader*, 134.

61. The meaning of her illiteracy, as we noted in Chapter 2, has been hotly debated in the secondary literature. True to his "sowohl-als-auch" strategy that permeates the novel (the "Aphrodite" structure, as I have dubbed it in the Introduction), Schlink has managed also in his commentary to occupy both sides of the argument. On the one hand, he dismisses the notion that this disability is exonerative (Schlink, "Matter of Interpretation"). On the other, he offers this extended reflection on the limitations imposed by this disability: "Es gibt eine Theorie zum Analphabetismus, die besagt, dass die eigene Lebensgeschichte

von Analphabeten viel schwieriger erinnert und begriffen wird als von Menschen, die lesen und schreiben können. Wer das Vergangene nicht im Umgang mit Texten präsent halten kann, wird zu einer geschichtslosen Existenz." (Schlink, "Lesen muss man tranieren."). There is a theory of illiteracy according to which illiterates find it much more difficult to recall and understand their own life story compared with those who can read and write. Those who can not, with the aid of texts, access (or grasp) the past become people without history."

62. Schlink, *Der Vorleser*, 129.

63. Janeway, *The Reader*, 134.

64. Schlink, *Der Vorleser*, 162–3; Janeway, *The Reader*, 171.

65. Schlink, *Der Vorleser*, 163.

66. Janeway, *The Reader*, 171.

67. Schlink, *Der Vorleser*, 163. For a concise overview of *Väterliteratur*, see Schaumann, *Memory Matters*, introduction and chap. 1.

68. Janeway, *The Reader* 171.

69. Ibid.,169.

70. "Solidarität mit dem Täter verstrickt in dessen Verbrechen und Schuld—dies ist der rationale Kern der Vorstellung einer Kollektivschuld . . . Schuld wird nicht von den kranken, schuldigen Teilen der Gemeinschaft auf die gesunden übertragen wie ein Bazillus und nicht von der einen Generation auf die nächste vererbt wie ein Gen. Die Vorstellung einer Kollektivschuld kann sinnvoll nur meinen, daß eine Gemeinschaft dadurch, daß sie mit den Tätern eines Verbrechens Solidarität übt, auch an deren Schuld teilhat und gegenüber den Opfern des Verbrechens Verantwortung übernimmt." Schlink, *Vergangenheitsschuld*, 97.

71. Schlink, *Vergangenheitsschuld*, 13.

72. Ibid., 97–98; German original: "Daß die Täter des Dritten Reichs nicht ausgestoßen, nicht verfolgt und verurteilt, sondern toleriert, respektiert, in ihren Positionen belassen und bei ihren Karrieren gefördert, als Eltern und Lehrer akzeptiert wurden, hat die Generation der Täter und die ihrer Kinder in die Verbrechen und Schuld des Dritten Reichs verstrickt." Schlink takes up this matter again in the final chapter, entitled "Die Gegenwart der Vergangenheit," 145–56; see also Schlink, "Kollektivschuld?"

73. See Schlink, "Recht—Schuld—Zukunft," in *Vergangenheitsschuld*, 10–37, esp. 20–26.

74. "Kinder sind nicht frei, ihre Eltern, die zweite Generation ist nicht frei, die erste auszugrenzen." Schlink, *Vergangenheitsschuld*, 98.

75. "Eine hinreichende konsequente Ausgrenzung hätte es aber nicht geben können, so daß die Verstrickung ein Moment des Unvermeidlichen und, wenn man so will, Tragischen hat." Schlink, *Vergangenheitsschuld*, 98.

76. Though in his legal writings Schlink includes the second generation within this soft indictment, the novel, with its very young protagonist, seems calculated to exonerate this group. Schlink proclaims the third generation unreservedly free of this "Verstrickung"; see *Vergangenheitsschuld*, 98; see also 147, 153–54.

77. Jarausch, *After Hitler*, 59.

78. Ibid. 63; cf. 66, 70.
79. "Occupation, captivity, hunger, and cold formed a new kind of collective experience whose inescapable common denominator was membership in the German nation. In wide sections of the populace, feelings of self-pity for their newfound role as victims helped transform the formerly aggressive nationalism into a defensive resentment toward 'the awful things that have been done to the German people.'" Jarausch, *After Hitler*, 60.
80. Schlink, *Der Vorleser*, 163.
81. Brooks, *Troubling Confessions*, 9.
82. Ibid., 21.
83. Ibid., 23, see also 24, 46.
84. Schlink, *Vergangenheitsschuld*, 151.
85. See Rogowski, "Born Later."
86. Niven, *Facing the Nazi Past*.

CHAPTER 4

1. For another comparative analysis of these two works, albeit from a different perspective, see Paver, "Generation and Nation: Peter Schneider's *Vati* and Bernhard Schlink's *Der Vorleser*," chap. 2, 29–51.
2. *Die Klage unter dem Kreuz* ("Lamentation under the Cross," also known simply as Crucifixion of Christ, 1503) by Lucas Cranach, the Elder (1472–553). Part of the permanent collection of the Alte Pinakothek, Munich. Inventory number 1416. One distinctive feature of this composition is Cranach's placement of the three crosses in a circle, allowing the viewer to notice the contrastive depiction Christ and the "good theif."
3. An der Heiden, *Die alte Pinakothek*, 140–45.
4. An der Heiden remarks, "Wie der noch im Tod athletisch schöne Leib am Kreuz hängt" (ibid., 144). However, he attributes the billowing loincloth exclusively to natural causes (i.e., the rising storm), which strikes me as less convincing, since the garments of the disciple John appear undisturbed by the supposed strong wind.
5. On the larger culture of victimhood, with special attention to theoretical reflections, see Naqvi's *The Literary and Cultural Rhetoric of Victimhood*.
6. Jensen, "Peter Schneider's *Vati*," 90; cf. Riordan, "The Sins of the Children," 176.
7. Morgan, "The Sins of the Fathers," 109–12, 125.
8. Riordan notes this in the case of Schneider's *Vati*, 176.
9. See also Franklin, "Immorality Play."
10. "Im Kern," he observes, "geht es in Schlinks Roman um die simple Tatsache, dass man einen Menschen, den man in seiner Jugend geliebt hat, nicht einfach fallen lassen kann, wenn sich herausstellt, dass er ein Verbrecher ist. In einer solchen Situation findet tatsächlich eine Perspektivenverschiebung zu Gunsten der Täter statt."

11. In the worst of all cases, she stood by while women prisoners burned to death in a church. Not coincidentally, it is on this point that Schlink rushes in to supply a plethora of mitigating circumstances: the presence of other guards who obviously were literate; higher-ranking male guards who might have intervened but instead fled; villagers who also could have stopped the catastrophe; a door key that may have been too hot to touch (and one Hanna testifies, in any case, not to have had); general confusion and panic engendered by an enemy (i.e., Allied) bomb attack as well as a raging and quickly spreading inferno; and, finally, Hanna's own submissive mind-set about following orders, nourished by years of servitude in low-end employment.

12. Janeway, *The Reader*, 142. R 142. "Wir reden nicht über Glück sondern über Würde und Freiheit" (Schlink, *Der Vorleser*, 136).

13. "The sole end for which mankind are warranted, individually or collectively, in interfering with the liberty of action of any of their number, is self-protection. That the only purpose for which power can be rightfully exercised over any member of a civilised community, against his will, is to prevent harm to others." Mill, *On Liberty*, 13.

14. Janeway, *The Reader*, 188; Schlink, *Der Vorleser*, V 178.

15. Schlink, *Der Vorleser*, 178.

16. Janeway, *The Reader*, 188. "Indem Hanna den Mut gehabt hatte, lesen und schreiben zu lernen, hatte sie den Schritt aus der Unmündigkeit zur Mündigkeit getan, einen aufklärerischen Schritt" (Schlink, *Der Vorleser*, 178).

17. "*Der Vorleser* scheint als einer der wenigen Romane der Gegenwartsliteratur den Weg in den Kanon der Oberstufenliteratur zu finden." Greese and Peren-Eckert, *Unterrichtsmodell Bernhard Schlink*, 15.

18. Ibid., "Die Relevanz des Romans in historischer Hinsicht liegt darin, dass er sich mit zentralen Fragen der Nachgeborenen an die Zeit des Nationalsozialismus beschäftigt. Die Fragen nach Schuld, Verantwortung und Vergangenheitsbewältigung sowie 'schuldlos-schuldigem' Verstricktsein in verbrecherische Zusammenhänge werden für die Schüler konkreter fassbar."

19. Ibid., 68.

20. Ibid. "Hierdurch wird deutlich, dass der Tätertypus, in der Figur Hannas vorgeführt, Analogien in der realen Welt findet—ja sogar stellvertretend für viele Lebensläufe steht, auch wenn es für die Figur Hannas kein direktes Vorbild gibt."

21. "Aus egoistischem Interesse eilfertig zum befohlenen Mord beigetragen, sich durch eigenen Beitrag die Tat zu eigen gemacht." "Die Stute von Majdanek," 126.

22. "Er habe recherchiert, das Wenige gelesen, was es über Frauen als Wärterinnen im KZ gebe." Geisel, "Der Botschafter Des Deutschen Buches," 33.

23. See especially "Rechtstaat und revolutionäre Gerechtigkeit," "Die Bewältigung von Vergangenheit durch Recht," and "Recht—Schuld—Zukunft," all in *Vergangenheitsschuld und gegenwärtiges Recht*.

24. "Zum Schluss dreht sie den Spieß herum—und klagt das Gericht an: 'Was wissen Sie, meine Herren, was wissen die Menschen, die hier Zuhörer waren, von uns?'" Greese and Peren-Eckert, *Unterrichtsmodell Bernhard Schlink*, 126.

25. Ibid.

26. Ibid., "Ich trage Schuld, aber ich bin keine Mörderin."

27. Janeway, *The Reader*, 137. "Ich konnte zum Vorsitzenden Richter gehen und ihm sagen . . . daß sie schuldig, aber nicht so schuldig war, wie es den Anschein hatte." (Schlink, *Der Vorleser*,132).

28. Schlink, *Der Vorleser*, 68. Later Berg wonders whether Hanna is identifiable in the lone survivor's book about the camps: "Manchmal glaubte ich, sie in einer Aufseherin zu erkennen, die jung, schön und in der Erfüllung ihrer Aufgaben von gewissenloser Gewissenhaftigkeit geschildert wurde, aber ich war nicht sicher . . . Aber es hatte weitere Aufseherinnen gegeben. In einem Lager hatte die Tochter eine Aufseherin erlebt, die 'Stute' genannt wurde, ebenfalls jung, schön und tüchtig, aber grausam und unbeherrscht. An die erinnerte sie die Aufseherin im Lager. Hatten auch andere den Vergleich gezogen? Wußte Hanna davon, erinnerte sie sich daran und war sie darum betroffen, als ich sie mit einem Pferd verglich? (Schlink, *Der Vorleser*, 115).

29. "Hierbei sollte deutlich werden, dass der Prozessbericht konkrete Details der Verbrechen Hermine Braunsteiners verhandelt (sie habe Kinder mit Schöpfkellen totgeschlagen), auf die der Roman verzichtet. Der Perspektive des Romans ist es geschuldet, dass ein Großteil der Lagervergangenheit Hannas im Dunkeln bleibt. Hanna wird vorgeworfen an Selektionen beteiligt gewesen zu sein; was genau dies bedeutet, kommt nicht zur Sprache." Greese and Peren-Eckert, *Unterrichtsmodell Bernhard Schlink*, 68. A biographical summary of Hermine Braunsteiner's life, crimes, and prosecutions is at http://www.variationsphase.de/seminar/index.php?site=orte/stute&language=de.

30. "Folglich sind sowohl ihre Einsicht als auch ihr Vermächtnis dem utopischen Potenzial von Literatur zuzuschreiben." Greese and Peren-Eckert, *Unterrichtsmodell Bernhard Schlink*, 68.

31. "Monster. Ich hatte allergrößte Schwierigkeiten, sie als normale Menschen zu betrachten" "Die Stute," 127.

32. *Dead Man Walking*, directed by Tim Robbins (1995; MGM, 2000). DVD.

33. Another example from the many inspired by the desire to explore the simultaneous humanity of the "inhuman" murderer is the *Showtime* series "Dexter," in which the protagonist is a vigilante serial killer by night and a devoted, very human husband, brother, and police department lab technician by day.

34. "Vielleicht wird Ihr Buch [in den deutschen Schulen] auch besonders lange durchgekaut, weil es sich als Einstieg in einen ganzen Themenkomplex eignet, den Holocaust" ("Lesen muss man trainieren").

35. See, for example, Möckel, *Bernhard Schlink, Der Vorleser*, 13.

36. Köster, *Bernhard Schlink, Der Vorleser*, 11ff.; Möckel, *Bernhard Schlink, Der Vorleser*, 106; Schäfer, *Bernhard Schlink, Der Vorleser*, 39; Lamberty, *Literatur-Kartei "Der Vorleser*," 35; Mittelberg, *Bernhard Schlink, Der Vorleser*, 12–13. The other relevant teaching guides are Urban, *Bernhard Schlink, Der Vorleser*;

Moers, *Bernhard Schlink, Der Vorleser*; Taberner, *Der Vorleser, Bernhard Schlink*; Reisner, *Lektürehilfen Bernhard Schlink*, and the unattributed *Lektürehilfen (Stuttgart: Klett, 2001)*. To this list we should add the two Reclam books: Heigenmoser (*Der Vorleser: Erläuterungen und Dokumente*) and Feuchert and Hofmann (*Bernhard Schlink: Der Vorleser. Lektüreschlüssel.*). While I am emphasizing commonalities here, one also notes interesting and substantive disparities among these pedagogical works. Indeed, we are now in need of a more detailed study of *The Reader* in the schools and universities both in Germany and globally.

37. Köster, *Bernhard Schlink, Der Vorleser*, 8.

38. Ibid., 7.

39. This is a fundamental problem endemic to all teaching guides. In attempting to provide historical background, they inevitably suggest rather strong interpretive perspectives. For example, Lamberty provides admirable information on the infamous "death marches" in an effort to illuminate Hanna. But Schlink studiously avoids this aspect of her characterization. So when Lamberty asks his students to imagine "welchen Handlungsspielraum es für Hanna gab" (What kind of freedom of action was there for Hanna?), he is already asking a leading question, and one students are not really in a position to answer. Lamberty, *Literatur-Kartei "Der Vorleser,"* 59.

40. Peter Schneider, "German Postwar Strategies"; see also the 2002 interview "Peter Schneider über die Studentenbewegung."

41. Davis "Handmaid of the Future," 13–14; see also Davis, "New Leftists and West Germany."

42. Ibid., 14.

43. Ibid., 14ff.

44. Donahue, "Elusive '68."

45. Quoted in Davis, "Handmaid of the Future," 15.

46. Davis, "Handmaid of the Future," 5.

47. Ibid., 19.

48. The German press in particular was eager to embrace this apparently self-deprecatory gesture as a marked advance over the moralizing crudity of the '68ers' muckraking élan. See Krause, "Keine Elternaustreibung"; Mosler, "Ein Generationen-Vorfall"; Ziegler, *Die Woche*. But they are not alone; writing for the *Times Literary Supplement*, Bryan Cheyette, in "The past as palimpsest," applauds this disavowal of youthful moralism as progress "beyond the usual clichés" and "such banal certainties."

49. Helmut Moers, *Bernhard Schlink, Der Vorleser* (Freising: Stark, 1999), 30.

50. Janeway, *The Reader*, 169. This point is worth bearing in mind in light of the claim, repeated on numerous occasions by the book's most prominent and avid promoter, Tilman Krause, that the novel's chief attraction lies in its apolitical renunciation of *literature engagée*. No journalist has written more extensively on this novel than Krause, whose newspaper, *Die Welt*, has featured Schlink in several favorable interviews and feature stories and awarded him its first literature prize. Krause's enthusiasm for Schlink's accessible, apolitical, and

inoffensive text is, as Gregor Dotzauer notes, a quite political attempt to set him apart from and above the literary tradition of Böll, Grass, and Walser. See Krause, "Keine Elternaustreibung," and "Die Freiheit des Arrivierten; "Wunder und Zeichen," *Die Welt*, April 3, 1999; as well as "'In Berlin fehlt es an Bürgersinn,'" *Die Welt*, October 14, 1999.

51. "Manchmal denke ich, daß die Auseinandersetzung mit der nationalsozialistischen Vergangenheit nicht der Grund, sondern nur der Ausdruck des Generationenkonflikts war, der als treibende Kraft der Studentenbewegung zu spüren war. Die Erwartungen der Eltern, von denen sich jede Generation befreien muß, waren damit, daß diese Eltern im Dritten Reich oder spätestens nach dessen Ende versagt hatten, einfach erledigt." Schlink, *Der Vorleser*, 161.

52. Janeway, *The Reader*, 170. "Der Fingerzeig auf die Schuldigen befreite nicht von der Scham . . . Und die Auseinandersetzung mit schuldigen Eltern war besonders energiegeladen." Schlink, *Der Vorleser*, 161–62. On the topic of shame, see Swales, "Sex, Shame and Guilt" and Bill Niven, "Bernhard Schlink's *Der Vorleser* and the Problem of Shame."

53. Janeway, *The Reader*, 171. "War die Absetzung von den Eltern nur Rhetorik, Geräusch, Lärm, die übertönen sollten, daß mit der Liebe zu den Eltern die Verstrickung in deren Schuld unwiderruflich eingetreten war?" Schlink, *Der Vorleser*, 163.

54. Taberner, *Der Vorleser, Bernhard Schlink*, 27.

55. Schlink, *Der Vorleser*, 87–89.

56. Ibid., 160–63.

57. Janeway, *The Reader*, 170. "Das aber, was andere aus meinem sozialen Umfeld getan hatten und womit sie schuldig geworden waren, war allemal weniger schlimm, als was Hanna getan hatte." Schlink, *Der Vorleser*, 162.

58. Janeway, *The Reader*, 171.

59. Ibid., 171. "In gewisser Weise das Schicksal meiner Generation, das deutsche Schicksal" (Schlink, *Der Vorleser*, 163).

60. The tension and outright anger that sometimes surfaces between the narrator and this unspecified friend boils over when the former accuses the latter of hypocrisy. This well-known passage culminates with Rolf (the narrator) saying, "Als du mir dann noch erklärt hast, dein 'Alter' sei für dich 'gestorben' und jede Verbindung zu ihm abgebrochen, habe ich nur gedacht: bis auf den Monatsscheck, den nimmt er!" (When you then made clear to me that your "old man" was as far as you're concerned "dead" and that you broke off all contact with him, I could only think: ya, sure, but he doesn't refuse his father's money—that he takes!) (Schneider, *Vati*, 23). If the "friend" is indeed one incarnation of an implied reader, then it is no wonder that we are, almost from the outset, enmeshed in a distinctly discordant relationship with this narrator.

61. Greese and Peren-Eckert, *Unterrichtsmodell Bernhard Schlink*, 86. And they are not alone. Reisner (*Lektürehilfen Bernhard Schlink*, 41) can stand for numerous others who see the writing of the fictional memoir itself as a sign of Berg's ultimate mastery. Feuchert and Hofmann provide a dissenting view,

which I treat in some detail in part two of this chapter, "Berg as Schlink's Alter Ego."

62. "Mit dem gleichen Abwehrmechanismus hält sich der Zuschauer die Exekutoren des Holocaust vom Leib: Es waren ein paar abartige Monster, die das getan haben, wir haben nichts mit ihnen zu tun!" Schneider, *Vom richtigen Umgang mit dem Bösen*, 92.

63. "Das Monsterbild, das sie von ihm entwarfen, machte ihn beinahe unsichtbar." Schneider, *Vati*, 11.

64. Schneider was first drawn to the topic because Rolf Mengele, as he was quoted in *Bunte Illustrierte*, referred to the infamous war criminal Josef Mengele as "Vati." It is this intimate form of address that dissolves the distance we seek to establish between criminals and ourselves. From Schneider's Harvard seminar on contemporary literature, Department of German, Spring 1991.

65. Riordan, "The Sins of the Children," 175. See also Riodan's introduction to his 1993 edition of *Vati*. This point about the novella's essential historicity seems to have evaded (or failed to convince) Gordon Burgess, who argues that the novella's fictionality is a weakness vis-à-vis other forms of *Väterliteratur* ("'Was da ist, das ist (nicht) mein': The Case of Peter Schneider,"in Williams, Parkes, and Smith, eds., 107–22).

66. Peter Schneider, *Vati*, 19.

67. Ibid. "Die ganze Welt war hinter meinem Vater her, Millionen kleiner Täter suchten den einzigen, allmächtigen Täter, um selber unschuldig zu sein" (Schneider, *Vati*, 19).

68. Ibid., 49–52.

69. Lamberty, *Literatur-Kartei "Der Vorleser,"* 41.

70. "Zuerst irritierte mich der Ton, mit dem die Lehrer mich aufriefen—dieses Zögern, dieses Senken der Stimme vor den drei Silben, ganz so, als sei der gut schwäbische Familienname ganz unaussprechlich" (Schneider, *Vati*,13).

71. Ibid., 99–100; 103.

72. Ibid., 102–3.

73. For compelling analyses of the scandal surrounding the publication of *Vati* (as well as other issues not touched on here) see Jensen, "Peter Schneider's Vati"; Morgan, "The Sins of the Fathers"; Riordan, "The Sins of the Children"; and Elizabeth Snyder Hook, "The Sins of the Fathers," chap. 4 of *Family Secrets*, 69–102.

74. "Die Erzählung *Vati* fußt auf einer authentischen Begebenheit. Es handelt sich um die erste und einzige Begegnung zwischen dem KZ-Arzt Josef Mengele und seinem Sohn Rolf." Schneider, *Vati*, 64.

75. "Macht die Geschichte bedrängender oder auch nur aufklärender, daß ein Mengele den Fall für den Mythos abgibt? Aber welche Bedeutung hätte eine solche Erzählung ohne das verbürgt Grausige dieses wahren Hintergrunds? Ein erfundener Auschwitzmörder ließe nur den echten einmal davonkommen."

76. Schneider, "Vom richtigen Umgang mit dem Bösen," 86, 120, for example. Schneider argues that reviewers were eager to condemn Rolf's obvious shortcomings to the exclusion of identifying with him as a "son" and therefore a

member of their own generation: "Sie lesen die Erzählung eben nicht als poten-
tielle Söhne und Töchter des Dr. Mengele. Sie urteilen darüber so, wie sie sich
vorstellen, daß die Opfer von Mengele urteilen würden" (120).

77. "Ich wollte ihn stellen, ihn mit dem Recht meines schuldlos schuldbeladenen
Lebens zu Fall bringen" (Schneider, *Vati*, 25).

78. "Ja, statt meinen Vater habe ich in diesem Augenblick die Opfer gehaßt, die
sich, nur von einem Dutzend SS-Schergen bewacht, zu Tausenden in die
Todeskammern führen ließen und mich, ausgerechnet mich, zu ihrem Rächer
ernannten" (Ibid., 33).

79. "Das aber, was andere aus meinem sozialen Umfeld getan hatten und womit sie
schuldig geworden waren, war allemal weniger schlimm, als was Hanna getan
hatte" (Schlink, *Der Vorleser*,162).

80. Dorrit Cohn, *Transparent Minds*, 153ff. The reminiscence about Schneider's
public readings of early drafts of *Vati* are from his 1991 Harvard seminar on
contemporary literature.

81. "Ich kann und werde das Verbrechen, das sie bezeugen, niemals leugnen"
(Schneider, *Vati*, 19).

82. "Wenn ich auch zugeben muß, daß ich bis heute nicht fähig bin, sie in allen
Einzelheiten zu erfassen, da mich, wo immer ich ihnen begegne, ein blind
machender Schwindel erfaßt—eine Schwäche meiner Konstitution, ein
Schutz—oder Fluchtreflex, mag sein, ich kann das nicht ändern" (Ibid.).

83. See Niven, *Facing the Nazi Past*, 53–56.

84. "Eine überwältigende, jeden Impuls vernichtende Gleichgültigkeit legte sich
auf mich" (Schneider, *Vati*, 53).

85. "Es war nicht zu erkennen, ob sie als Angeklagte oder als Beschwerdeführer
hierhergekommen waren. Dieser Unterschied schien bei der Hitze auch völlig
belanglos" (Ibid., 56).

86. Ibid.

87. "Was ich in Belem wollte, habe ich dir erklärt. Ich wollte ihn zur Rede stellen,
ihn dazu bewegen, sich vor einem deutschen Gericht zu verantworten. Heute
weiß ich, daß diese Erklärung eher dazu taugt, mein Vorhaben zu verschleiern.
*Ich wollte ihn stellen, ihn mit dem Recht meines schuldlos schuldbeladenen Lebens
zu Fall bringen. Nein, ich will es mit einfacheren, ebenso falschen Worten sagen: ich
wollte durch ihn erlöst werden* (Ibid., 25; my emphasis).

88. In *Second Generation Holocaust Literature*, Erin McGlothlin provides an incisive
reading of *Vati*, which she chiefly credits with breaking out of the generic shack-
les that seek to limit *Väterliteratur* to "self-evidently autobiographical prose narratives" (148). In her plaidoyer to include Schneider's fictional *Vati* within this
genre she is quite convincing (see also 151, 156, 172). Less persuasive, I think,
is her diagnosis of the son's "guilt," which she sees as virtually replicating that
of the father. She writes, for example, "The father's legacy, which the son had
carefully attempted to rewrite, suppress, and keep apart from himself, breaks
down and becomes indistinguishable from his own" (170; see also 156, 169,
171–72). The son's "guilt" has little to do with direct parallels with the father
(from whom he was, after all, separated for most of his life) and more to do with

the way in which he "uses" the Holocaust to pursue his own misunderstood "redemption."

89. See Schlink, *Der Vorleser*, 114.

90. Donahue, "Illusions of Subtlety," 72.

91. Adler, "Bernhard Schlink and *The Reader*."

92. For example, Klein, "Schlink Evokes Certain Realities"; Möckel, *Bernhard Schlink, Der Vorleser*, 15; Moers, *Bernhard Schlink, Der Vorleser*, 30.

93. "Wer allerdings leichtsinnig Michael Bergs Argumente mit Bernhard Schlinks Meinungen gleichsetzt, verletzt elementare Grundsätze einer literaturwissenschaftlichen Analyse fiktionaler Texte" (Feuchert & Hofmann, 51).

94. "Hier hat der Leser den Eindruck," "der Autor und Jurist Bernhard Schlink äußert sich durch seine Romanfigur" (Urban, *Bernhard Schlink, Der Vorleser*, 40).

95. See also Urban 39, 41. Mittelberg asserts, to further illustrate, "Bernhard Schlinks Skepsis gegenüber der Art, wie sich die so genannte zweite Generation, die auch seine eigene ist, mit der nationalsozialistischen Vergangenheit auseinander setzte, artikuliert Michael" (17). Less direct affirmations of identity or near-identity (at least on certain key issues) can be found in Möckel, *Bernhard Schlink, Der Vorleser*, 15; and Stölzel, "'Ich hab's in einer Nacht ausgelesen.'"

96. "B. Schlink ist Sohn eines Theologieprofessors, auch der Vater der Romanfigur Michael ist Professor . . . B. Schlink wächst mit drei Geschwistern auf, ebenso Michael" (Mittelberg, 43).

97. See Cohn, *Transparent Minds*, 153ff.

98. Some academic critics who argue that Schlink sets up Berg for critique in the general manner that Feuchert and Hofmann outline are Metz, "'Truth Is a Woman'"; Niven, "Bernhard Schlink's Der Vorleser"; Schmitz, "Malen nach Zahlen?"; Swales, "Arthur Schnitzler"; and Taberner, *Bernhard Schlink, Der Vorleser*, 37.

99. "Wichtig bei der Analyse des *Vorlesers* ist die klare Unterscheidung zwischen der Ebene des Romans, dessen Autor Bernhard Schlink ist, und der der Erzählung des fiktiven Ich-Erzählers Michael Berg. Die Kontroverse um den Roman . . . wurzelt nicht selten in der allzu leichtfertigen Gleichsetzung beider Ebenen" (Feuchert and Hoffmann, 6).

100. Ibid., 66–67.

101. "Genau in dieser Hinsicht muss die Rückblende verstanden werden: Erneut dient ihm eine Erinnerung dazu, Täter allgemein und Hanna im Besonderen zu entlasten: Betäubung, Gleichgültigkeit, 'Es' –alle diese Stichworte laufen im Endeffekt auf eine Entschuldigung Hannas hinaus. Berg nimmt dabei billigend in Kauf, dass seine Argumente für alle Täter gelten können und damit letzlich kaum ein Verantwortlicher für den Holocaust übrig bleibt" (Ibid., 47).

102. For a blistering and entertainingly polemical critique of the novel in general and of the numbness strategy in particular, see Justus Wertmüller's "Deutsche Soap zum Massenmord," which largely concurs (though for sometimes different reasons) with my "Illusions of Subtlety." In *Bahamas* 39 (2002): 14–19.

Available at http://riotelectricdisco.blogsport.de/images/39DeutscheSoapzum Massenmord.pdf.

103. Even the highly critical second wave of criticism is not willing to touch Berg, and may blame Schlink in part because of the literary cues that essentially "protect" the narrator. In other words, the impetus to deflect criticism from the narrator to the author may emanate from the novel's own coding.

104. They deem this technique tantamount to "ein komplexes Spiel" that culminates in "die Entlastung des Ich-Erzählers von seiner eigenen Schuld, eine SS-Täterin geliebt zu haben." Feuchert and Hofmann, *Bernhard Schlink: Der* Vorleser, 6. We have already seen (in Chapter 3), that this manner of "guilt" (if it is guilt at all) tends to exonerate and function as a code for having been vicitimized.

105. This is not an idiosyncratic error on the part of Feuchert and Hofmann. In failing to note how the middle-aged Berg frames the entire narrative, and intervenes from this more mature perspective at key junctures, they typify other similar approaches that would "save" the novel by having us see the narrator as fundamentally flawed. Of course, rescuing the novel in this way also means freeing the author from the very criticisms they now seek to lay at the feet of the narrator alone. Furthermore, their division of criticism into overwhelmingly positive reception (during the first seven or so years) and a negative wave (commencing, they incorrectly say, in 2002) is rather misleading. For example, Lamberty (who can be taken as just one of numerous other commentators in this vein) continues to advocate Berg as an identification figure to this day (*Literatur-Kartei "Der Vorleser,"* 4).

106. See, especially, the interview "Ich lebe in Geschichten."

107. Feuchert and Hofmann, *Bernhard Schlink, Der Vorleser*, 30.

108. "Michael Berg steht *pars pro toto* auch für die erste deutsche Nachkriegsgeneration, die vom Umgang mit der Vergangenheit überfordert wird." Ibid., 19.

109. "Es gibt keinen Weg, diese Analyse Michaels zu entschärfen: Sie dient letzlich eindeutig auch der Legitimierung der Täter und ihres Handelns." Ibid., 44–45.

110. "Deshalb muss ein wacher Leser sie selbstverständlich zurückweisen." Ibid., 45.

111. Ibid., 51.

112. Ibid., 30.

113. For a brief but valuable discussion of shame grounded in the wider political culture of the FRG, see Reiss, "Selbstkritik," especially 179–80.

114. Reiss concurs that the portrayal Berg's extensive self criticism is actually meant to stifle vigorous debate about the Nazi past. See Reiss, "Selbstkritik," 183–89.

115. Erlanger, "Postwar German Writer."

116. Janeway, *The Reader*, 213. "Was ist diese Frau brutal gewesen. Haben Sie's verkraftet, daß sie Sie mit fünfzehn. . . . Hatten Sie . . . jemals das Gefühl, daß sie wußte, was sie Ihnen angetan hat?" (Schlink, *Der Vorleser*, 202).

117. Schlant, *The Language of Silence*, 214ff.

118. The analogy of camp inmate to Berg receives further elaboration in Berg's fantasies of Hanna as a Nazi dominatrix clad in leather and equipped with a whip. Of course, he is quick to dismiss these erotic fantasies as unfounded—just as he was quick to see the error of his ways in promulgating the all-encompassing

"numbness doctrine." But just as with the Betäubing matter, this comparison of himself to camp inmates does not disappear when it is recanted. It can be said to live a narrative afterlife "under erasure"—to speak with Roland Barthes—that is, nominally withdrawn, but still semantically in force.

119. See Tatar, "'We Meet Again, Fräulein.'"

120. Hoffman, *After Such Knowledge*, 174–77. While not concerned specifically with popular literary realism, Hoffman gives voice to the overexpansion of the Holocaust as metaphor for evil itself, for example, "the Shoah is in danger not so much of vanishing into forgetfulness as expanding into an increasingly empty referent, a *symbol* of historical horror, an allegory of the Real, the familiar catastrophe and a stand in for authenticity and for history" (177).

CHAPTER 5

1. On the difference between elite and mass venues, see Markovits, "Germany and Germans."

2. See Oprah, 5.

3. See Oprah, 12.

4. On the use of this problematic locution, see Markovits, "Germany and Germans," *Germany in the American Mind*, 143–64; and Donahue and McIsaac, "Introduction," ibid. pp. 1–5.

5. Some critics (above all, Tilman Krause) and pedagogues (e.g., Möckel, *Bernhard Schlink, Der Vorleser*, 12) have highlighted Schlink's allegedly "American" style of very accessible, neorealist prose. There may be some truth to this but it cannot sufficiently explain Schlink's particular success in the United States. See Krause, "Schwierigkeiten beim Dachausbau."

6. Ash, "The Stasi on Our Minds."

7. See "The Holocaust in Popular Culture" (273) in which Smelser shows, for example, how widespread the *Wehrmacht* myth is in American popular culture. Smelser also documents the popularity in the United States of a spate of memoirs by former German soldiers who highlight German victimhood on the Eastern Front (see 277–79). "This 'glorification' (not too strong a word) of the German military," he cautions, "continues in the popular literature, in war gaming, on the Internet, resonating with hundreds of thousands if not millions of Americans who read these books, play these games, and surf the Web" (279).

8. Tatar, "'We meet again, Fräulein.'"

9. See Schaumann, *Memory Matters*, 143.

10. Smelser, "The Holocaust in Popular Culture," 277.

11. Smelser entertains a more complex view of (popular) culture and reception praxis, namely one that allows for the possibility that individuals consume various kinds of literature, film, and so on. Regarding the counternarrative he has been documenting (i.e., the story of German soldiers as victims without reference to the Holocaust), he says, "No one suggests that this narrative is anywhere close to challenging the master-narrative at this point in time. It remains on the margins but is by no means negligible. Nor are the people who are captured

by this mythology Holocaust deniers. They share in the same mass culture that watches *Schindler's List* and reads *The Diary of Anne Frank*." Smelser, "The Holocaust in Popular Culture," 280.

12. Gavriel Rosenfeld, "Alternate Holocausts," 247.

13. Gavriel Rosenfeld calls this exhaustion with memory "conservative" (ibid., 245), which I consider a premature judgment. He appears at times to equate the desire for "normalcy" with repression of Holocaust memory per se, and to oppose these as the only available options. However, problematizing the official memory rituals of German and Austrian public culture can constitute a legitimate brand of Holocaust literature and one that need not be read in simple opposition to the canon but as complementary to it. See my "Nachwirkungen des Holocaust in der deutschen Gegenwartsliteratur," chap. 5, *Holocaust Lite*.

14. "Aber laßt euch doch mindestens reizen, verschanzt euch nicht, sagt nicht von vornherein, das gehe euch nichts an oder es gehe euch nur innerhalb eines festgelegten, von euch im voraus mit Zirkel und Lineal säuberlich abgegrenzten Rahmens an, ihr hättet ja schon die Photographien mit den Leichenhaufen ausgestanden und euer Pensum an Mitschuld und Mitleid absolviert. Werdet streitsüchtig, sucht die Auseinandersetzung." Klüger, *Weiter leben*, 141; quoted as English translation in Schaumann, *Memory Matters*, 121, 141.

15. Hofmann, *After Such Knowledge*, 23. In the context of recent evocations of German suffering, Hofmann notes a similar phenomenon of atrocity overload: "More horrors to add to the catalogue, more images one doesn't want to image. And more moral problems to confront, of the kind that have no answer" (132).

16. See Linenthal, *Preserving Memory*, 1–2, 91, 193. Ironically, it was also Eisenhower who rehabilitated the German *Wehrmacht* for the American reading public. Ronald Smelser writes, "Dwight Eisenhower, as NATO commander, in a sense set in motion this mythologizing of the German military by famously giving it a clean bill of health in 1951. His son continues that tradition." Smelser, "The Holocaust in Popular Culture," 273.

17. Linenthal, *Preserving Memory*, 167. See also Rabinbach, "From Explosion to Erosion."

18. Linenthal, *Preserving Memory*, 194; photo reproduced on 197.

19. A. Rosenfeld, "The Americanization of the Holocaust," 14.

20. Quoted in A. Rosenfeld, "The Americanization of the Holocaust," 15.

21. A. Rosenfeld, "The Americanization of the Holocaust," 15.

22. This is true for a number of reasons, not the least of which is the fact that some camp exhibits and memorials do indeed provide comfort, if not quite pride.

23. In *The Holocaust in American Life*, Novik reminds us that "close to 100 million Americans watched all or most of the four-part, 9½ hour program. As was often observed at the time, more information about the Holocaust was imparted to more Americans over those four nights than over all the preceding thirty years" (209).

24. Novik explains, "The airing of the series, in January 1979, became the turning point in Germany's long-delayed confrontation with the Holocaust, which, albeit not without bumps in the road, has continued ever since. It enabled

Germans to connect with the Jewish victims, and the crime, as never before. It was widely credited with a decisive role in the Bundestag's decision, later that year, to abolish the statute of limitations on war crimes . . . It was the German reception of that American 'soap opera' which, as a practical if not theoretical matter, ended debate in America on the ability of the popular media to present the Holocaust effectively." Novik, *The Holocaust in American Life*, 213.See also 234.

25. "Indeed, at a time when moral categories, at a certain level of intellectual discourse, are generally seen as suspect or outmoded . . . the arena of collective violence—especially the violence of genocide—is the one place where our ethical instincts cannot be denied, and the moral response cannot be gainsaid" (Hoffman, *After Such Knowledge*, 104; see also 157–58, 175–77).

26. Novik, *The Holocaust in American Life*, 233. For a strongly worded rebuke of Novik, see Lang, "Lachrymose without Tears."

27. This constitutes Alvin Rosenfeld's chief criticism of *Schindler's List*: while hailed as a quintessential Holocaust story, it could not possibly be less representative, given the historical paucity of rescuers and the relative minority of survivors. Yet he fears that viewers see it in this representative, and thus idealized, manner.

28. Novik, *The Holocaust in American Life*, 231.

29. A. Rosenfeld, "The Americanization of the Holocaust," 22–23. Regarding this tendency in Germany, see Tönnes, "Die Klagemeute," and Donahue "Der Holocaust als Anlass zur Selbstbemitleidung."

30. Ibid., 23.

31. Ibid.

32. Novik, *The Holocaust in American Life*, 231.

33. This is a point Holocaust historian Omer Bartov made in his commentary on the occasion of the novel's English-language publication over a decade ago. For Bartov, this constitutes an egregious lacuna, insofar as it entails a kind of implicit fraud, posing as something it is not.

34. Janeway, *The Reader*, 158.

35. This contrasting kind of victimhood—one kind repellent, the other idealized—is fundamentally similar to the one I have drawn in Chapter 4 in the context of my discussion of Peter Schneider's novella *Vati*.

36. See Kristeva, *Powers of Horror*, 2, 128–29, and 185, for example.

37. Brooks, *Troubling Confessions*, see especially chap. 2 and 4.

38. Quoted in Novik, *The Holocaust in American Life*, 236.

39. I think this also reveals an error in the conception of the novel. What could Hanna have learned in all those books about the Holocaust that she could not have gleaned—perhaps far more immediately—from the protracted trial itself? Recall that during the trial she is extremely engaged, going toe to toe with the prosecutor (see Schlink, *Der Vorleser*, 105, 131). The film, on the other hand, gives us a much more passive, defeated defendant who objects only briefly, as we shall see in the subsequent chapter. Why did her ultimate "illumination" require literacy? This plot inconsistency—like many in detective fiction—may

not be evident upon the first, quick reading; but neither does it withstand close scrutiny.

40. See Weinthal's article about Broder, "The Raging Bronx Bull of German Journalism," in the *Jewish Daily Forward*, June 8, 2007.

41. Tönnies, "Die Klagemeute."

42. Niven, ed., *Germans as Victims*.

43. For a thoughtful reflection on the representation of German suffering within the context of the Holocaust and World War II, see Hoffman, *After Such Knowledge*, 127–34.

44. Janeway, *The Reader*, 137. "Auch ich hatte genug. Aber ich konnte die Sache nicht hinter mir lassen. Für mich ging die Verhandlung nicht zu Ende, sondern begann. Ich war Zuschauer gewesen und plötzlich Teilnehmer geworden, Mitspieler und Mitentscheider. *Ich hatte diese neue Rolle nicht gesucht und gewählt, aber ich hatte sie, ob ich wollte oder nicht, ob ich etwas tat oder mich völlig passiv verhielt*" (Schlink, *Der Vorleser*, 131, my emphasis).

45. Donahue, "Holocaust as History Lesson?"

46. Linenthal, *Preserving Memory*, 4.

47. Ibid.

48. Janeway, *The Reader*, 104.

49. Janeway, *The Reader*, 154; Schlink, *Der Vorleser*, 144–52.

50. "Ich versuchte es wirklich, schaute auf eine Baracke, schloß die Augen und reihte Baracke an Baracke. Ich durchmaß eine Baracke, errechnete aus dem Prospekt die Belegung und stellte mir die Enge vor . . . Aber es war alles vergeblich, und ich hatte das Gefühl kläglichen, beschämenden Versagens" (Schlink, *Der Vorleser*, 149).

51. Ibid., 150.

52. Ibid., 151.

53. I thank Molly Donahue for bringing Daldry's "citation" of the USHMM shoe exhibit to my attention.

54. See Donahue and Cohn, "Cultural Reparations?"

55. Raul Hilberg, Seminar for University-level Holocaust educators, USHMM, June 1999. Lectures recorded by, and available from, the USHMM.

56. The phenomenon of "Holocaust exhaustion," while difficult to quantify, has been widely noted and variously diagnosed in Germany. Schlink, for example, blames the second generation for overdoing Holocaust pedagogy: "Der Überdruß gegenüber der Vergangenheit von Drittem Reich und Holocaust, den die nächste Generation oft zeigt, hat seinen Grund in der banalisierenden Häufigkeit, mit der sie der Vergangenheit in Schule und Medien begegnet." Schlink, "Die Gegenwart der Vergangenheit" in *Vergangenheitsschuld*, 147. The difficulty of gaining the interest of contemporary German schoolchildren for this topic emerges also from the extensive pedagogical materials surrounding the (state subsidized) play *Ab heute heißt du Sara*, the dramatization of Inge Deutschkron's autobiography *Ich trug den gelben Stern*. Materials available from the Museum Blindenwerkstatt Otto Weidt (now a part of the Gedenkstätte Deutscher Widerstand), Rosenthaler Straße 39, 10178 Berlin. Deutschkron

observes that the play, which emphasizes German heroes who hid Jews during the Nazi period, has a better chance of appealing to young Germans than traditional efforts at *Vergangenheitsbewältigung*. An effort to overcome this disinterest, and to succeed where the schools have not, is documented in *Jugendliche interviewen Zeitzeugen für Jugendliche*, 5–6. See also online material at http://www.museum-blindenwerkstatt.de/de/projekte/jugendliche-interviewen.

57. See Sagan, "An Optimistic Icon."
58. Hoffman, *After Such Knowledge*, 266.

CHAPTER 6

1. Shapiro, "For *The Reader*."
2. Hare, "The Reader. Based on the novel by Bernhard Schlink," online film script, 77. Henceforth abbreviated as Hare, filmscript (plus page number). A note of caution in using this version of the script: without warning, it diverges from the actual film dialogue at a number of points. The quotations in this chapter are from this online source. The book version, with an interesting introduction by Hare, is now available; see Hare, *The Reader: A Screenplay*.
3. Schlink, *Der Vorleser*, 68–69.
4. Ibid., 91.
5. Berg "reads" Hanna's reactions to the court proceedings by watching her muscular body: "Wenn sie sich ungerecht behandelt, verleumdet, angegriffen fühlte und um eine Erwiderung rang, rollte sie die Schultern nach vorne, und der Nacken schwoll, ließ die Muskelstränge starker heraus- und hervortreten" (Schlink, *Der Vorleser*, 95–96).
6. The surviving daughter, it should be noted, finds Hanna similar in appearance to the barbarous "Stute"; but importantly she distinguishes the two. Berg remarks that others, too, may have noticed the physical resemblance (ibid., 115). Nevertheless, pedagogues frequently suggest that Hanna is precisely meant to evoke the cruelest of female guards ever tried for war crimes, namely Hermine Braunsteiner, the so-called Stute von Majdanek (see Chapter 4).
7. For example, "Wenn sie drohte, habe ich sofort bedingungslos kapituliert" (Schlink, *Der Vorleser*, 50).
8. Hare, filmscript, 18.
9. Indeed, the Berg of the novel bitterly complains, "über ihre Liebe zu mir weiß ich nichts" (Schlink, *Der Vorleser*, 67). The film resolves this uncertainty and thus shifts the entire narrative trajectory.
10. This interest in the effect of the revelation of Holocaust truths on the second generation has a specific genealogy. It was first premiered in Margarethe von Trotta's *Die bleierne Zeit* (The German Sisters, 1981), in which we watch, sympathetically, as the young Marianne and Juliane are compelled to screen Alain Resnais' *Night and Fog* (*Nuit et brouillard*, 1955) in a school auditorium (see Chapter 3). Because von Trotta's film has multiple agendas, it is often forgotten that it includes the first widely distributed portrayal (to my knowledge) of female guards as aggressive and active (rather than merely passive) agents.

11. Schlink, *Der Vorleser*, 142.

12. Janeway, *The Reader*, 147.

13. Schlink, *Der Vorleser*, 117.

14. The novel suggests additional or alternate perpetrators in at least five places; see Schlink, *Der Vorleser*, 102, and especially 109–10; 121–22; 123; 130–31. Repeatedly, Berg inquires as to the whereabouts of the missing camp commandant. One can speak here of an evidentiary campaign that calculatedly creates a plausible case for mitigating circumstances.

15. Hare, filmscript, 50

16. I put "selections" in quotation marks to acknowledge that the word itself is a euphemism for murder or aiding and abetting in the same.

17. Hare, filmscript, 60.

18. A selection of Graham's photos was recently exhibited at the Museum of Modern Art (New York) under the title "shimmer of possibility" (http://www.moma.org/visit/calendar/exhibitions/321). See also http://www.paulgrahamarchive.com/index.html.

19. Even Hare's script makes more of the Sophie subplot (see 26–28), but this did not survive Daldry's final cut.

20. Schlink, *Der Vorleser*, 40.

21. Ibid., 91.

22. Walter Kempowski unforgettably captures this sentiment in his novel *Alles umsonst*, where, for example, the Nazi violin player (a woman who entertains wounded troops) passes on reports about Poles having massacred "Volksdeutsche" as if they were uncontested truth (42).

23. For this fascinating story, see Bergen, "The Volksdeutsche of Eastern Europe." Here, Bergen is primarily concerned with the last year of the war, a time that witnessed a great spectrum in Volksdeutsche behavior and commitments, ranging from Nazi collaboration to partisan resistance. Though some Volksdeutsche suffered persecution during the Nazi period (despite their favored racial categorization), it was primarily during the postwar period, particularly the 1950s of the Federal Republic, that the Volksdeutsche story became one of paramount victimhood (see especially 118–19). I am grateful to Matthias Pabsch, who urged me to be skeptical of this "Volksdeutsche" alibi. Hanna's heritage as an ethnic German from Hermannstadt (Siebebürgen) does not in itself "explain" her illiteracy, because this community in particular retained its German language traditions and to this day boasts very accomplished German-language authors.

24. German pedagogues have certainly gotten the message: Reisner, who makes a great deal of Hanna's illiteracy, imagines that her Volksdeutsche heritage—having grown up "bei Hermannstadt"—explains her handicap (*Lektürehilfen Bernhard Schlink*, 76–77); Urban links the two as well, though less firmly (*Bernhard Schlink, Der Vorleser*, 33–34). Möckel goes so far as to suggest (albeit obliquely) that Hanna's illiteracy is a response to an education system infused with Nazi ideology; her illiteracy, we are left to surmise, was perhaps intentional and maybe even a kind of resistance (*Bernhard Schlink, Der Vorleser*, 86). This is

not only wildly speculative but illogical insofar as Hanna would have learned to read and write at an age long before the rise of Nazism. See also, Schlink, "Lesen muss man tranieren."

25. While I argue that the evocation of class difference is communicated more powerfully in the film, the novel, in its own way, certainly emphasizes Hanna's lack of economic and cultural privilege. For example, Berg remarks that the avoidance of violence (within the family) is a factor of his upbringing (Schlink, *Der Vorleser*, 55) in contrast to hers. Further, when he gives us the four critical pictures of Hanna he carries around in his mind (all positive, by the way), he first expounds upon the image of Hanna standing—confused, disconcerted, yet also fascinated—in his father's library (ibid., 62). In her lack of discrimination with regard to cinema and her total inexperience with theater, Hanna exhibits her cultural limitations (ibid., 69, 76). At the trial, too, we are of course reminded of her relative poverty insofar as she receives a "Pflichtverteidiger," or court-appointed lawyer (ibid., 106), whose incompetence in the novel is meant to explain (at least in part) the unfair verdict and sentence she receives.

26. Hare, filmscript, 45.

27. Schlink, *Der Vorleser*, 178.

28. *Col. Jessep*: You want answers?
Kaffee: I think I'm entitled.
Col. Jessep: You want answers?
Kaffee: I want the truth!
Col. Jessep: You can't handle the truth!
[pause]
Col. Jessep: Son, we live in a world that has walls, and those walls have to be guarded by men with guns. Whose gonna do it? You? You, Lt. Weinburg? I have a greater responsibility than you could possibly fathom. You weep for Santiago, and you curse the marines. You have that luxury. You have the luxury of not knowing what I know. That Santiago's death, while tragic, probably saved lives.
Kaffee: Did you order the Code Red?
Col. Jessep: I did the job I . . .
Kaffee: Did you order the Code Red?

29. The following dialogue excerpt from the trial gives an example of how utterly lost Downey is without someone telling him what to do. "Hal" is his codefendant and friend, Lance Corporal Harold Dawson:

Capt. Ross: Why did you go into Santiago's barracks room that night?
Galloway: The witness has rights!
Capt. Ross: The witness has been read his rights, Commander!
Judge Randolph: The question will be repeated.
Capt. Ross: Why did you go into Santiago's barracks room that night?
Downey: Hal?
Capt. Ross: Did Lance Corporal Dawson tell you to give him a code red?
Downey: Hal?
Capt. Ross: Don't look at him!
Downey: Hal?

Dawson: Private, answer the captain's question!

Downey: Yes, captain, I was given an order by my squad leader Lance Corporal Harold W. Dawson, United States Marine Corps and I followed it!

James Marshall, who plays Downey superbly, communicates poignantly the Private's modest mental capacities. Dialogue source: http://www.imdb.com/title/tt0104257/quotes.

30. Timothy Garton Ash argues that the cliché cuts both ways. Classical music is deployed both to reveal its civilizing, humanizing potential (as it is in Daldry's film), as well a marker of alleged cultivation that stands in stark contrast to Nazi brutality: "Surely we think of Roman Polanski's *The Pianist*, with the German officer deeply affected by the Polish Jewish pianist's playing of Chopin, and therefore sparing his life—as Wiesler now spares Dreyman. Surely we think, too, of the educated Nazi killers who in the evening listened to the music of Mendelssohn, then went out the next morning to murder more Mendelssohns. Did they not *really* hear the music? Does high culture humanize?" Ash, "The Stasi on Our Minds," 8.

31. Schlink, *Der Vorleser*, 178.

32. See "More Army Recruits Have Criminal Record."

33. See, for example, Emma Brockes, "Interview: She's Home from Jail."

34. Interview with Ari Shapiro, National Public Radio.

35. The concept of "critical realism," which of course ran afoul of orthodox Marxist aesthetics, is introduced and elaborated in the seminal works by Lukács: *Studies in European Realism, The Historical Novel, Essays on Realism*, and *Realism in our Time: Literature and the Class Struggle*. For lucid commentary, see Tavor, "Art and Alienation."

36. The intradiegetic cue that Jessep's conviction might fully account for any guilt in this matter is provided by the defendants themselves, who, to their surprise, are found guilty—though not of murder or conspiracy to commit murder but rather of "conduct unbecoming of a Marine." They are sentenced to time served and given a dishonorable discharge from the Marines. Pfc Downey—the dim-witted youth—is particularly confused and slow to accept responsibility of any kind, as the following dialogue demonstrates:

Downey: I don't understand. Colonel Jessep said he ordered the Code Red. . . . Colonel Jessep said he ordered the Code Red, what did we do wrong?

Jo [one of the defense lawyers]: It's not as simple as—

Downey: What did we do wrong?

Dawson: We did nothing wrong.

The film diverges from the published script (as is often the case), placing Dawson in the role of eleventh-hour mentor to Downey regarding their (residual) guilt.

37. Lamberty, *Literatur-Kartei "Der Vorleser,"* 18, and Möckel, *Bernhard Schlink, Der Vorleser*, 93, make the point that Hanna is in violation of paragraph 182 of the German federal penal code, which prohibits having sex with minors. Some

pedagogues play up this point in order to underscore the way in which Berg was victimized by Hanna.

38. Even this Daldry chooses to play down, however, as can be seen from the scene with Gertrud (Berg's soon to be ex-wife) that he excised from the script (Hare, filmscript, 62–64).

39. This deletion may constitute not only a "correction" vis-à-vis the novel in the sense argued for above but in an additional sense as well, for this may be one of the novel's technical errors. What can Hanna have possibly learned from these classical works of Holocaust literature that she would not, in one form or another, have already heard from eye-witnesses during her own lengthy trial? The notion that she can only come to a proper realization of her guilt—indeed of the scope of the Holocaust—years later is one we encounter also in Schlink's detective novels, where the loveable Gerhard Selb repeatedly proffers the notion that the second generation is "privileged" with regard to Holocaust education, privy to information that the perpetrators lacked. Berg offers the notion of "numbness" (extensively discussed in chaps. 3 and 4) to explain why the perpetrators, judges, jurors, and trial attendees (such as himself) shut down in the face of testimony about atrocities. The only way that Hanna's eleventh-hour insight (via the classics of Holocaust literature she is said to have read) can be rendered plausible even in a *prima facie* manner is that we readers have—along with her—been spared these gory "details" in Berg's account of the trial. If the novel had included thorough and detailed accounts of brutality in the manner we encounter them in *Die Ermittlung* (e.g., the description of the Boger swing), this claim to *ex post facto* illumination would seem, I propose, patently absurd.

40. To see this should not blind us to the undercurrent of Hanna's alluring sexuality, which, particularly in the novel, positions Berg as kind of victim. What heterosexual young man could say no to her naked advances? It is undeniably *her* sexuality that inaugurates the relationship and thus Berg's lifelong distress. Except for the innuendo about Hanna's "special selections" (discussed in Chapter 3), and Berg's erotic fantasies about a Nazi dominatrix, however, I see no connection between Hanna's "predatory" sexuality and Holocaust crimes. For a different view, see Metz "Truth is a Woman," and Schipplacke, "Enlightenment, Reading, and the Female Body." For a broader discussion of the representation of sex, gender, and the Holocaust, see Horowitz, "The Gender of Good and Evil."

41. This particular display of macho pride is of course anachronistic for 1950s West Germany; neither is it part of the script referenced above. On the sexual mores of the time, see Lamberty, *Literatur-Kartei "Der Vorleser,"* 13.

42. Says Berg, "I sat in the second carriage because I thought you might kiss me." Hanna responds, "Kid, you thought we could make love in a tram" (Hare, filmscript, 17).

43. Schlink, *Der Vorleser,* 33.

44. The novel is unambiguous on this point: "Auch wenn wir uns liebten, nahm sie selbstverständlich von mir Besitz. Ihr Mund nahm meinen, ihre Zunge spielte mit meiner, sie sagte mir, wo und wie ich sie anfassen sollte, und wenn sie

mich ritt, bis es ihr kam, *war ich für sie nur da, weil sie sich mit mir, an mir Lust machte* . . . Ich war jung, und es kam mir schnell, und wenn ich danach langsam wieder lebendig wurde, ließ ich sie gerne von mir Besitz nehmen. Ich sah sie an, wenn sie über mir war" (Schlink, *Der Vorleser*, 33–34; my emphasis). "When we made love, too, she took possession of me as a matter of course. Her mouth took mine, her tongue played with my tongue, she told me where to touch her and how, and when she rode me until she came, *I was there only because she took pleasure in me and on me* . . . I was young, and I came quickly, and when I slowly came back alive again afterwards, I liked to have her take possession of me. I would look at her when she was on top of me . . ." (Janeway, *The Reader*, 33; emphasis added).

45. Jenkins, "'The Reader': A Holocaust Story Lost in Translation."

46. Hare, filmscript, 62.

47. In addition to the absent camp commandant and other (male) members of the command, about whom we are insistently reminded in the novel, Hanna draws our attention during a key point in the testimony to the marginal status of the female support staff: "Einige von uns waren tot, und die anderen haben sich davongemacht. . . . Wir wären auch mitgefahren, aber sie haben gesagt, die Verwundeten brauchen den Platz, und sie haben sowieso nichts . . . waren sowieso nicht scharf darauf, so viele Frauen mit dabei zu haben. . . . Wir haben nicht gewußt, was wir machen sollen. Es ging alles so schnell, und das Pfarrhaus hat gebrannt und der Kirchturm, und die Männer und Autos waren eben noch da, und dann waren sie weg, und auf einmal waren wir allein mit den Frauen in der Kirche. Irgendwas an Waffen haben sie zurückgelassen, aber wir haben nicht damit umgehen können, und wenn wir's gekonnt hätten—was hätte uns das geholfen, uns paar Frauen?" (Schlink, *Der Vorleser*, 121–22). "Some of us were dead, and others slipped away . . . We would have gone with them, but they said they needed the room for the wounded, and had no room in any case . . . We didn't know what to do. It all happened so fast, with the priest's house burning and the church spire, and the men and the cart were there one minute and gone the next, and suddenly we were alone with the women in the church. They left behind some kind of weapons, but we didn't know what to do with them, and even if we had, what could we have done, we few women?" (Janeway, *The Reader*, 126–27). None of this is spoken in the film, but the same message, as I argue later in this chapter, is taken up by the visual register and other elements of the plot.

48. "Sie fragte nicht laut," Berg observes, "nicht rechthaberisch, aber beharrlich . . . Sie widersprach baharrlich und gab bereitwillig zu . . . Aber sie merkte nicht, daß ihre Beharrlichkeit den Vorsitzenden Richter ärgerte" (Schlink, *Der Vorleser*, 105). "She didn't ask loudly or arrogantly, but with determination . . . But she did not notice that her insistence annoyed the presiding judge" (Janeway, *The Reader*, 109–10). And, again later, we are reminded of a tenacity that never appears on screen: "Hanna kämpfte weiter . . . Sie wurde nicht laut. Aber schon die Intensität, mit der sie redete, befremdete das Gericht" (Schlink, *Der Vorleser*, 131).

"Hana continued to fight . . . She didn't raise her voice, but the very intensity with which she spoke alienated the court" (Janeway, *The Reader*, 136).

49. Hare, filmscript, 45.

50. McGlothlin, *Second-Generation Holocaust Literature*, 207, 9n. To bolster her critique, McGlothlin cites Patricia Herberer of the Center for Advanced Holocaust Studies at the USHMM, who observes that "women could not be members of the SS proper" and "were technically termed 'weibliche SS-Gefolge' . . . an auxiliary group of the SS" (ibid.). To make Hanna a kind of perpetrator type, as I argue in Chapter 1, only magnifies the historical misrepresentation. On this point, I concur with Mahlendorf, "Trauma Narrated," 459–69.

51. In his teaching guide to the novel, Lamberty provides assistance on how to assess Hanna by informing his readers of the historical unlikelihood of female perpetrators (*Literatur-Kartei "Der Vorleser,"* 54). He furthermore provides historical material on the recruitment of unemployed women into positions such as Hanna's; underscores the dominance of the male hierarchy in the chain of command; and quotes Ruth Klüger to the effect that, in general, the men were in fact much worse (55). He later makes essentially the same point by placing Hanna in the context of brutal, elite perpetrators, all of whom are men (72).

52. Janeway, *The Reader*, 148. The full German text reads: "Heute sind so viele Bücher und Filme vorhanden, daß die Welt der Lager ein Teil der gemeinsamen vorgestellten Welt ist, die die gemeinsame wirkliche vervollständigt. Die Phantasie kennt sich in ihr aus, und seit der Fernsehserie Holocaust und Spielfilmen wie *Sophies Wahl* und besonders *Schindlers Liste* bewegt sie sich auch in ihr, nimmt nicht nur wahr, sondern ergänzt und schmückt aus"[0] (Schlink, *Der Vorleser*, 142–43).

53. I have given the English language version from the *Book of Common Prayer* (1662). The Latin sung in the church (and in the film) is as follows: Dómine Fili Unigénite, Jesu Christe, / Dómine Deus, Agnus Dei, Fílius Patris, / qui tollis peccáta mundi, miserére nobis; /qui tollis peccáta mundi, súscipe deprecatiónem nostram. / Qui sedes ad déxteram Patris, miserére nobis.

54. Schlink, *Der Vorleser*, 76.

55. Hare, filmscript, 13–14.

56. See Ash, "The Stasi on Our Minds," 15n.

57. President Reagan's 1985 visit to Kolmeshohe, the German military cemetery outside of Bitburg, had ignited a controversy because among the 2,000 graves of regular infantrymen were 49 of the Waffen SS. For an account and critical assessment, see Hartman, ed., *Bitburg in Moral and Political Perspective*.

58. See Chapter 3.

59. Jenkins, "'The Reader.'"

60. Hare, filmscript, 79.

61. Ibid.

62. Ibid., 78.

63. Ibid.

64. Ibid.

65. Ibid; see also Jenkins, "'The Reader.'"

66. I am grateful to Karina von Tippelskirch for pointing this out to me at the Duke German Jewish Workshop, February 2009.

67. Ilana: "You attended the trial?" Michael: "Yes. Almost twenty years ago. I was a law student. I remember you, I remember your mother very clearly" (Hare, filmscript, 76).

68. The fact of Berg's restoration via this fictional memoir is stressed in many of the pedagogical manuals. See, for example, Möckel, *Bernhard Schlink, Der Vorleser*, 17, 45, 90–91; Reisner, *Lektürehilfen Bernhard Schlink*, 31, 40–41; Urban's assessment of the positive trajectory of the novel can be seen in the term she applies to it, "Entwicklungsroman" (novel of development); *Bernhard Schlink, Der Vorleser*, 29).

69. In the expanded German version of this book, I include a chapter on "epiphenomenal" Holocaust literature, in which I argue that indirection and "secondary" Holocaust allusions can comprise a very compelling strategy. It is not an oblique reference to the Holocaust itself, therefore, that makes *The Reader* problematic. See my "Die Nachwirkungen des Holocaust."

70. Of course this technique of citation and diversion would not have been possible had the filmmaker decided to actually film the church fire, the selections, or the death march itself. These are narrated (as in the novel) in a succinct and summary fashion—one that allows the film to be both truthful about these events yet not "distract" us with emotionally charged images of death and suffering that would surely alter our sympathies and interests. In this sense, *The Reader* is a Holocaust film without the Holocaust.

71. Rousset, *L'univers Concentrationnaire.*

72. Advancing the sociological view of criminality—which the film poignantly does—is, after all, itself a kind of consolation, a form of "mental comfort" against which Lawrence Langer has so tirelessly inveighed. It reprises one of the most widely embraced views of criminality and simultaneously marginalizes the confounding questions about the Nazi leadership as well as Hanna's own sphere of volition and agency. Even the austere and hardly sentimental Adorno, who felt that Holocaust education may in the end constitute nothing more than a consoling illusion, conceded that it might just work with lower tier perpetrators like Hanna. See especially, Adorno's "Education After Auschwitz," 22.

73. Schlink, Interview. NPR Weekend Edition, Jan 3, 2009.

BIBLIOGRAPHY

Adler, Jeremy. "Bernhard Schlink and 'The Reader.'" *Times Literary Supplement* no. 22. March 3, 2002: 17.

———. "Die Kunst, Mitleid mit den Mördern zu erzwingen. Einspruch gegen ein Erfolgsbuch: Bernhard Schlinks 'Der Vorleser' betreibt sentimentale Geschichtsfälschung." *Süddeutsche Zeitung*, April 20, 2002.

Adorno, Theodor. "Education after Auschwitz." In *Can One Live after Auschwitz? A Philosophical Reader*, edited by Rolf Tiedemann. Translated by Rodney Livingstone, 19–33. Stanford, CA: Stanford University Press, 2003.

Adorno, Theodor, and Max Horkheimer. *Dialectic of Enlightenment: Philosophical Fragments*. Edited by Grunzelin Schmid Noerr. Translated by Edmund Jephcott. Stanford, CA: Stanford University Press, 2007.

Aisenberg, Nadya. "Resolution and Irresolution." In *The Oxford Companion to Crime & Mystery Writing*, edited by Rosemary Herbert, 384–85. Oxford: Oxford University Press, 1999.

Angier, Carole. "Finding Room for Understanding." *The Spectator*, October 25, 1997, 54–55.

Annan, Gabriele. "Thoughts About Hanna." *London Review of Books*, October 30, 1997, 22–23.

Ash, Timothy Garton. "The Stasi on Our Minds." *New York Review of Books*, May 31, 2007, 6, 8.

Auden, W. H. "The Guilty Vicarage: Notes on the Detective Story, by an Addict." In *The Complete Works of W.H. Auden: Prose: Volume II. 1939–1948*, edited by Edward Mendelson, 261–69. Princeton, NJ: Princeton University Press, 2002.

Bauman, Zygmunt. *Modernity and the Holocaust*. Cambridge: Polity Press, 1989.

Bailey, Paul. "The Heartbreaking Consequences of a Liason." *The Daily Telegraph*, November 1, 1997, 4.

Baron, Ulrich. "Schlink als neuestes Opfer des deutschen Feuilletons." *Der Tages-Anzeiger am Samstag*, May 11, 2002.

Bartov, Omer. "Germany as Victim." *New German Critique* 80 (2000): 29–40.

Battersby, Eileen. "Reading in the Dark." *The Irish Times*, January 3, 1998, 67.

Beissner, Friedrich. *Der Erzähler Franz Kafka*. Ein Vortrag Stuttgart: Kohlhammer, 1952.

Bergen, Doris. "The Volksdeutsche of Eastern Europe and the Collapse of the Nazi Empire, 1944–45." In *The Impact of Nazism: New Perspectives on the Third Reich and Its Legacy*, edited by Alan E. Steinweis and Daniel E. Rogers, 101–25. Lincoln: University of Nebraska Press.

Berman, Russell A. *The Rise of the German Novel: Crisis and Charisma*. Cambridge: Harvard University Press, 1986.

Bernstein, Richard. "Once Loving, Once Cruel, What's Her Secret?" *The New York Times*, August 20, 1997, C-16.

Bessel, Richard. *Germany 1945: From War to Peace*. New York: Harper Collins, 2009.

Bloch, Ernst. *Heritage of Our Times*. Cambridge: Polity Press, 1991.

———. "A Philosophical View of the Detective Novel." *Bloch: Literary Essays*. Translated by Jack Zipes and Frank Mecklenburg. Stanford: Stanford University Press, 1998.

Brecht, Bertolt. "Let's Get Back to Detective Novels." In *Brecht on Art and Politics*, edited by Tom Kuhn, 30–32, 263–70. London: Methuen, 2004.

Brockes, Emma. "Interview: She's Home from Jail, but Lynndie England Can't Escape Abu Ghraib." *The Guardian*, January 3, 2009.

Brooks, Peter. *Troubling Confessions: Speaking Guilt in Law and Literature*. Chicago, IL: University of Chicago Press, 2000.

Burgess, Gordon. "'Was da ist. das ist (nicht) mein': The Case of Peter Schneider." In *Literature on the Threshhold: The German Novel in the 1980s*, edited by Arthur Williams, Stuart Parkes, and Roland Smith, New York: Berg, 1990, 107–22.

Chelala, Cesar. "Child Soldiers: Skipping Childhood." *The New York Times*, July 17, 2003.

Cheyette, Bryan. "The Past as Palimpsest." *Times Literary Supplement*, November 28, 1997, 23.

Clark, Alex. "Review of *The Reader*." *Sunday Times*, July 12, 1998.

Clee, Nicholas. "Matter of Interpretation." *The Times*, June 27, 1998.

Clendinnen, Inga. *Reading the Holocaust*. Cambridge: Cambridge University Press, 1999.

Cohn, Dorrit. *The Distinction of Fiction*. Baltimore: Johns Hopkins University Press, 1999.

———. *Transparent Minds: Narrative Modes for Presenting Consciousness in Fiction*. Princeton, NJ: Princeton University Press, 1978.

Cooke, Paul. *German Culture, Politics, and Literature into the Twenty-First Century: Beyond Normalization*. Rochester, NY: Camden House, 2006.

"Das Tschernobyl der Wasserwirtschaft." *Der Spiegel*, November 10, 1986, 161–66.

Davis, Belinda. "Handmaid of the Future or Specter of the Past? Violence and Leftist Activism in West Germany 1967–1977," Lecture, Rutgers Center for Historical Analysis, New Brunswick, NJ, February 13, 2001.

———. "New Leftists andWest Germany: Fascism, Violence, and the Public Sphere." In *CopingWith the Nazi Past: West German Debates on Nazism and Generational Conflict, 1955–1975*, edited by Philipp Gassert and Alan Steinweis. New York: Berghahn, 2006, 210–37.

Demmer, Erich. "Die Liebe zu einer KZ-Aufseherin: mehrmals lesen. Bernhard Schlinks Roman 'Der Vorleser.'" Die Presse, November 11, 1995.

Dead Man Walking. DVD. Directed by Tim Robbins. MGM, 2000.

Des Pres, Terrence. *The Survivor: An Anatomy of Life in the Death Camps*. New York: Oxford University Press, 1976.

"Die Stute von Majdanek." *Süddeutsche Zeitung Magazin*, December 13, 1996. Reprinted in Greese and Peren-Eckert, 122–29.

"The Digested Read." *The Guardian*, August 29, 1998, 16.

Doerry, Martin and Volker Hage. "Spiegel-Gesprach: 'Ich lebe in Geschichten.'" *Der Spiegel.* January 24, 2000.

Donahue, William Collins. "Elusive '68: The Challenge to Pedagogy." *Die Unterrichtspraxis/Teaching German* 41, no. 2 (Fall 2008): 113–23.

———. *The End of Modernism: Elias Canetti's Auto-Da-Fe*. Chapel Hill: University of North Carolina Press, 2001.

———. "Der Holocaust als Anlass zur Selbstbemitleidung: Geschichtsschüchternheit in Bernhard Schlinks Der Vorleser." In *Rechenschaften. Juristischer und literarischer Diskurs in der Auseinandersetzung mit den NS-Massenverbrechen*, edited by Stephan Braese. Göttingen: Wallstein, 2004, 177–97

———. "Holocaust as History Lesson? Contestatory Voices." *Österreich in Amerikanischer Sicht: Das Österreichbild im Amerikanischen Schulunterricht* 9 (1999): 28–40.

———. *Holocaust Lite: Bernhard Schlinks "NS" Romane und ihre Verfilmungen.* Bielefeld: Aisthesis, 2010.

———. "Illusions of Subtlety: Bernhard Schlink's Der Vorleser and the Moral Limits of Holocaust Fiction." *German Life and Letters* 54, no. 1 (2001): 60–81.

———. "Die Nachwirkungen des Holocaust in der deutschen Gegewartsliteratur: ausgewählte Fallstudien (Bernhard, Brüssig, Walser, Timm, Kempowski)." *Holocaust Lite.* Bielefeld: Aisthesis, 2010.

———. "Of Pretty Boys and Nasty Girls: The Holocaust in Two German Films of the 90s." *New England Review* 21, no. 4 (2000): 108–24.

———. "The Popular Culture Alibi: Bernhard Schlink's Detective Novels and the Culture of Politically Correct Holocaust Literature." *German Quarterly* 77, no. 4 (Fall 2004): 462–81.

———. "Review: Double Exposures by Eric Downing." *The European Legacy: Journal of the International Society for the Study of European Ideas* 8, no. 5 (October 2003): 662–63.

———. "Revising '68: Bernhard Schlink's Der Vorleser, Peter Schneider's Vati, and the Question of History." *Seminar: A Journal of Germanic Studies* 40, no. 3 (September 2004): 293–311.

Donahue, William Collins and Robert L Cohn, "Cultural Reparations? Jews and Jewish Studies in Germany Today." *German Politics & Society* 15, no. 1 (Spring 1997): 94–116.

———. "Ein Besuch, der manche Fragen offenließ: Amerikanische Wissenschalftler auf den Spuren jüdischen Lebens in Deutschland," *Die Zeit* 31 (July 26, 1996): 8.

Downing, Eric. *Double Exposures: Repetition and Realism in Nineteenth-Century German Fiction.* Stanford, CA: Stanford University Press, 2000.

Durst, David C. "Ernst Bloch's Theory of Nonsimultaneity." *Germanic Review* 77, no. 3 (2002).

The Economist. June 13, 1998, R16–17.

Enright, D. J. "Modern Love." *New York Review of Books*, March 26, 1998, 4–5.

Erlanger, Steven. "Postwar German Writer a Bard of a Generation." *The New York Times*, January 19, 2002, A4.

Feuchert, Sascha, and Lars Hofmann. *Berhnard Schlink: Der Vorleser. Lektüreschlüssel.* Ditzingen: Reclam, 2005.

Franklin, Ruth. "Immorality Play." *The New Republic*, January 15, 2001, 54–60.

Friedlander, Saul. "The Controversy about the Historicization of the Holocaust Reconsidered," Lecture, Freeman Center, Duke University, Durham, NC, November 10, 2008.

Garloff, Katja. *Words from Abroad: Trauma and Displacement in Postwar German Jewish Writers.* Detroit: Wayne State University Press, 2005.

Geisel, Sieglinde. "Der Botschafter des deutschen Buches." *Neue Züricher Zeitung*, March 27, 2000. 33.

Giordano, Ralph. *Die zweite Schuld oder von der Last Deutscher zu sein.* Munich: Knaur, 1990.

Greese, Bettina, and Almut Peren-Eckert. *Unterrichtsmodell Bernhard Schlink, "Der Vorleser."* Paderborn: Verlag Schöningh, 2000.

Hage, Volker. "Der Schatten der Tat." *Der Spiegel* 47, 1995, 258–63.

Hanks, Robert. *The Independent*, July 5, 1998, 32.

Hare, David. *The Reader: A Screenplay.* New York: Weinstein Books, 2009.

———. "The Reader. Based on the Novel by Bernhard Schlink." Screenplay. The Weinstein Company. Accessed: January, 2009. http://www.weinsteincohighlights.com/screenings/the-reader/screenplay.

Hartman, Geoffrey. Bitburg in Moral and Political Perspective. Bloomington: Indiana University Press, 1986.

an der Heiden, Rüdiger. *Die Alte Pinakothek. Sammlungsgeschichte, Bau und Bilder.* Munich: Himmer Verlag, 1998.

Heigenmoser, Manfred, ed. *Der Vorleser. Erläuterungen und Dokumente.* Ditzingen: Reclam, 2005.

Heineman, Elizabeth. "The History of Morals in the Federal Republic: Advertising, PR, and the Beate Uhse Myth." In *Selling Modernity: Advertising in Twentieth-Century Germany*, edited by S. Jonathan Wiesen, Pamela E. Swett, and Jonathan R. Zatlin, 202–29. Durham, NC: Duke University Press, 2007.

Hilberg, Raul. The Destruction of the European Jews. 3rd ed. New Haven, CT: Yale University Press, 2003.

———. "Seminar for University-Level Holocaust Educators." Lecture, United States Holocaust Memorial Museum, June 1999.

Hoffman, Eva. *After Such Knowledge: Memory, History, and the Legacy of the Holocaust.* New York: Public Affairs, 2004.

———. "The Uses of Illiteracy." *The New Republic*, March 23, 1998, 33–36.

Hollinger, David A. "The Knower and the Artificer, with Postscript 1993." In *Modernist Impulses in the Human Sciences 1870–1930*, edited by Dorothy Ross, 26–53. Baltimore: John Hopkins University Press, 1994.

Holub, Robert C. "Review: Double Exposures by Eric Downing." *The German Quarterly* 75, no. 3 (Summer 2002): 312–13.

Horowitz, Sara R. "The Gender of Good and Evil: Women and Holocaust Memory." In *Gray Zones: Ambiguity and Compromise in the Holocaust and Its Aftermath*, edited by Jonathan Petropoulos and John K. Roth, 165–78. New York: Berghahn, 2005.

Hösle, Vittorio. *Objective Idealism, Ethics, and Politics.* Notre Dame, IN: University of Notre Dame Press, 1998.

Hughes, Michael L. "Reason, Emotion, Force, Violence: Modes of Demonstration as Modes of Political Citizenship in 1960s West Germany." Lecture, *North Carolina German Studies Seminar and Workshop*, University of North Carolina at Chapel Hill, February 22, 2009.

Huyssen, Andreas. "The Politics of Identification: 'Holocaust' and West German Drama." In *After the Great Divide: Modernism, Mass Culture, Postmodernism*, chapter 6. Bloomington: Indiana University Press, 1986.

"Internet Movie Database: A Few Good Men." IMDb. Accessed: January, 2009. http://www.imdb.com/title/tt0104257/quotes.

Jarausch, Konrad. *After Hitler: Recivilizing Germans.* Oxford: Oxford University Press, 2006.

Jauß, Hans-Robert. "Literary History as a Challenge to Literary Theory,"chapter 1, *Toward an Aesthetic of Reception.* Translated by Timothy Bahti. Minneapolis: University of Minnesota Press, 1982.

Jenkins, Mark. "'The Reader': A Holocaust Story Lost in Translation." Movie review: NPR, December 10, 2008. http://www.npr.org/templates/story/story.php?storyId=98883419.

Jensen, Birgit A. "Peter Schneider's Vati: Contesting a German Taboo." *Critique: Studies in Contemporary Fiction* 43, no. 1 (Fall 2001): 84–92.

Judgment at Nuremberg. Special Edition DVD. Directed by Stanley Kramer. Screenplay by Abby Mann. MGM, 2004.

Jugendliche interviewen Zeitzeugen für Jugendliche. Berlin: Museum Otto Weidt, 2007. Online materials from this project available at: http://www.museum-blindenwerkstatt.de/de/projekte/jugendliche-interviewen/.

Kaes, Anton. *M.* London: British Film Institute, 2008.

———. *Shell Shock Cinema: Weimar Culture and the Wounds of War.* Princeton: Princeton University Press, 2009.

Kempowski, Walter. *Alles umsonst.* Munich: btb, 2008.

Klein, Julia M. "Schlink Evokes Certain Realities but Eludes Moral Certanties." *Chronicle of Higher Education*, December 7, 2001, B18.

Klüger, Ruth. *Still Alive: A Holocaust Girlhood Remembered.* New York: The Feminist Press at the City University of New York, 2001.

———. *Von hoher und niedriger Literatur.* Göttingen: Wallstein, 1996.

———. *weiter leben. Eine Jugend.* Göttingen: Wallstein, 1994.

Köster, Juliana. *Bernhard Schlink, Der Vorleser.* Munich: Oldenburg, 2000.

Kracauer, Siegfried. *From Caligari to Hitler: A Psychological History of the German Film.* 1947. Translated by Leonardo Quaresima. Princeton, NJ: Princeton University Press, 2004.

Kratz, Henry, and Mary W. Tannert, eds. *Early German and Austrian Detective Fiction: An Anthology.* Jefferson, NC: McFarland, 1999.

Krause, Tilman. "Die Freiheit des Arrivierten. Bernhard Schlink, Schriftsteller und Juraprofessor." Die Welt, April 28, 1996.

———. "'In Berlin fehlt es an Bürgersinn': Welt-Literaturpreisträger Bernhard Schlink über seinen Beruf, seine Vorbilder und die deutsche Geschichte." Interview with Tilman Krause. *Die Welt*, October 14, 1999.

———. "Keine Elternaustreibung: ein Höhepunkt im deutschen Bücherherbst. Bernhard Schlinks Roman über 68er und die deutsche Schuld." *Der Tagesspiegel*, September 3, 1995.

———. "Schwierigkeiten beim Dachausbau." *Die Welt*, January 29, 2000.

———. "Wunder und Zeichen." *Die Welt*, April 3, 1999.

Kristeva, Julia. *Powers of Horror: An Essay in Abjection*. Translated by Leon S. Roudiez. New York, Columbia University Press, 1982.

Kulish, Nicholas. "Spy Fired Shot That Changed West Germany." *The New York Times*, May 26, 2009.

LaCapra, Dominick. *Writing History, Writing Trauma*. Baltimore: Johns Hopkins University Press, 2001.

Lamberty, Michael. *Literatur-Kartei "Der Vorleser": Schülerarbeitsmaterial für die Sekundärstufen*. Mühlheim an der Ruhr: Verlag an der Ruhr, 2001.

Lang, Berel. "Image and Fact: The Problem of Holocaust Representation," part 1, chapters 1–5, *Holocaust Representation: Art within the Limits of History and Ethics*. Baltimore: Johns Hopkins University Press, 2000.

———. "Lachrymose without Tears: Misreading the Holocaust in American Life," chapter 10, *Post-Holocaust: Interpretation, Misinterpretation, and the Claims of History*. Bloomington: Indiana University Press, 2005.

Langer, Lawrence. *Admitting the Holocaust: Collected Essays*. New York: Oxford University Press, 1995.

———. *Versions of Survival: The Holocaust and the Human Spirit*. Albany: SUNY Press, 1982.

Levi, Primo. *The Drowned and the Saved*. Trans. Raymond Rosenthal. New York: Summit Books, 1988.

———. In *The Voice of Memory: Interviews, 1961–1987*, edited by Marco Belpoliti and Robert Gordon. Trans. Robert Gordon. New York: The New Press, 2001.

Linenthal, Edward. *Preserving Memory: The Struggle to Create America's Holocaust Museum*. New York: Viking, 1995.

Lektürehilfen: Bernhard Schlink, Der Vorleser. Stuttgart: Klett, 2001.

Loewy, Hanno. "Tales of Mass Destruction and Survival: Holocaust, Genre and Fiction in the Movies and on TV." *Rutgers German Studies Occasional Papers* 4. New Brunswick, NJ: Rutgers Department of German, Russian, and East European Languages & Literatures. 2005.

Löhndorf, Marion. "Die Banalität des Bösen: Bernhard Schlinks Roman 'Der Vorleser.'" *Neue Züricher Zeitung* 28/29 (October 1995): 251.

Lukács, György. *Essays on Realism*. 1948. Translated by David Fernbach. Cambridge, MA: MIT Press, 1980.

———. *The Historical Novel*. 1937. Translated by Hannah Mitchell and Stanley Mitchell. Boston: Beacon Press, 1964.

———. *Realism in Our Time: Literature and the Class Struggle*. 1958. Trans. John Mander and Necke Mander. New York: Harper & Row, 1964.

———. *Studies in European Realism*. 1930. Translated by Edith Bone. New York: Grosset & Dunlap, 1964.

Macdougall, Carl. "Guilt Edged Ideas." *The Herald*, January 1, 1998, 12.

MacKinnon, John E. "Crime, Compassion, and *The Reader*." *Philosophy and Literature* 27 (2003): 1–20.

———. "Law and Tenderness in Bernhard Schlink's *The Reader*." *Law and Literature* 16 no. 2 (2004): 179–201.

Mahlendorf, Ursula R. "Trauma Narrated, Read and (Mis)Understood: Bernhard Schlink's The Reader." *Monatshefte* 95, no. 3 (2003): 458–81.

Malcomson, Scott L. "Lost Love: A Postwar German's Romance with the Past." *The New Yorker*, August 18, 1997: 72–73.

Mall-Grob, Beatrice. "Grossartiger Abgang einer literarischen Figur: Bernhard Schlinks neuer Roman Selbs Mord." *Der kleine Bund*, October 11, 2001, Z6.

Mann, Abby. *Judgment at Nuremberg*. [Play]. New York: New Directions, 2002.

Marcuse, Herbert. "The Affirmative Character of Culture," chapter 3, *Negations: Essays in Critical Theory*. Translated by Jeremy J. Shapiro. Boston: Beacon Press, 1968.

Maristed, Kai. "The Secret." *Los Angeles Times Book Review*, August 31, 1997.

Markovits, Andrei. "Germany and Germans: A View from the United States." In *Germany in the American Mind: The American Postwar Reception of German Culture*, edited by William Collins Donahue and Peter M. McIsaac. Special Issue of *German Politics & Society* 13, no. 3 (Fall 1995): 142–64.

McCrum, Robert. "Book of the Week." *The Observer*, November 9, 1997, 80.

McGlothlin, Erin. *Second-Generation Holocaust Literature: Legacies of Survival and Perpetration*. Rochester, NY: Camden House, 2006.

McIsaac, Peter, and William Collins Donahue. "Introduction." *German Politics & Society* 13, no. 3 (Fall 1995): 1–5.

Mejias, Jordan. "Schlink ist okay! Oprah bleut's den Amerikanern ein: *Der Vorleser* sei super." *Frankfurter Allgemeine Zeitung*, April 3, 1999.

Metz, Joseph. "'Truth is a Woman': Post-Holocaust Narrative, Postmodernism, and the Gender of Fascism in Bernhard Schlink's *Der Vorleser*." *German Quarterly* 77.3 (Summer 2004): 300–23.

Michalzik, Peter. "Das Monster als Mensch." *die tageszeitung* December 9, 1995, 8.

Mill, John Stuart. *On Liberty*. 1859. Cambridge: Cambridge University Press, 1989.

Mittelberg, Ekkehart. *Bernhard Schlink. Der Vorleser. Unterrichtsmodelle Mit Kopiervorlagen. Litera Nova*. Edited by Helmut Flad. Berlin: Cornelsen, 2004.

Möckel, Magret. *Bernhard Schlink, Der Vorleser*. Hollfeld: C. Bange Verlag, 2001.

Moers, Helmut. *Bernhard Schlink, Der Vorleser*. Freising: Stark, 1999.

"More Army Recruits Have Criminal Record." *Associated Press*, October 10, 2007.

Morgan, Peter. "The Sins of the Fathers: A Reappraisal of the Controversy About Peter Schneider's Vati." *German Life and Letters* 47, no. 1 (January 1994): 104–33.

Moritz, Rainer. "Die Liebe zur Aufseherin: Bernhard Schlinks Roman 'Der Vorleser'—ganz einfach ein Glücksfall." *Weltwoche*, November 23, 1995.

Mosler, Peter. "Ein Generationen-Vorfall: ein Buch über den heißen Sommer von '68—aus der Feder des Krimiautors und Rechtprofessors Bernhard Schlink." *Frankfurter Rundschau*, January 6, 1996.

Naqvi, Fatima. *The Literary and Cultural Rhetoric of Victimhood: Western Europe, 1970–2005*. New York: Palgrave Macmillan, 2007.

Naqvi-Peters, Fatima. "Laughter in the Darkness: La Vita E Bella [Life Is Beautiful]. Reflections on Benigni's Holocaust Film." *World Order* 31, no. 1 (2000): 46–48.

Naumann, Bernd. *Auschwitz. A Report on the Proceedings against Robert Karl Ludwig Mulka and Others before the Court at Frankfurt*. New York: Praeger, 1966.

Neander, Joachim and Kristof Körner, "Auschwitz Im Roman Als Schullektuere? Eine Kontroverse." Sozialwissenschaftliche Informationen 2 (2001): 151–61.

"Neue Recherchen: Ohnesorgs Todesschütze soll Stasi-Spion gewesen sein." *Der Spiegel*, May 21, 2009.

Niven, Bill. "Bernhard Schlink's Der Vorleser and the Problem of Shame." *Modern Language Review* 98, no. 2 (April 2003): 381–96.

———. *Facing the Nazi Past: United Germany and the Legacy of the Third Reich*. London: Routledge, 2002.

Niven, Bill, ed. *Germans as Victims: Remembering the Past in Contemporary Germany*. New York: Palgrave Macmillan, 2006.

Norfolk, Lawrence. "Die Sehnsucht nach einer ungeschehenen Geschichte: warum Bernhard Schlinks Roman 'Der Vorleser' ein so schlechtes Buch ist und allein sein Erfolg einen tieferen Sinn hat." *Süddeutsche Zeitung*, April 27, 2002.

Novik, Peter. *The Holocaust in American Life*. Boston: Houghton Mifflin, 1999.

"Oprah's Book Club," *Oprah Winfrey Show*, March 31, 1999. Harpo Productions. Livingston, NJ: Burrelle's Information Services.

Ostermann, Micha. *Aporien des Erinnerns: Bernhard Schlinks Roman Der Vorleser*. Bochum: Verlag Dolega, 2004.

Ozick, Cynthia. "The Rights of History and the Rights of Imagination." *Commentary* (March 1999): 22–27.

Pabsch, Matthias. "Albert Speer: Des Teufels Architekt," chapter 10, *Berlin und seine Künstler*. Darmstadt: Wissenschaftliche Buchgesellschaft, 2006.

———. "Luftschlösser: The Reconstruction of the Berlin City Palace." Lecture, Duke University, Durham, NC, April 2, 2009.

Paver, Chloe. *The Third Reich in German and Austrian Fiction and Film*. Oxford: Oxford University Press, 2007

Petropoulos, Jonathan, and John K. Roth, ed. *Gray Zones: Ambiguity and Compromise in the Holocaust and Its Aftermath*. New York: Berghahn, 2005.

Ploetz, Dagmar. "Vom Verlust der Unschuld: 'Der Vorleser'—ein deutscher Roman." *Freitag*, November 17, 1995.

"Post-Traumatic Stress Disorder (PTSD)." National Institute of Mental Health website. http://www.nimh.nih.gov/health/topics/post-traumatic-stress-disorder-ptsd/index.shtml.

Rabinbach, Anson. "From Explosion to Erosion: Holocaust Memorialization in America since Bitburg." History and Memory 9, no. 1–2 (Spring-Winter 1997): 226–55.

Reilly, John M. "Detective Novel." In *The Oxford Companion to Crime & Mystery Writing*, edited by Rosemary Herbert, 117. Oxford: Oxford University Press, 1999.

Reiner, Rob, dir. *A Few Good Men*. Perf. Tom Cruise Jack Nicholson, Demi Moore. DVD. 2001. 1992.

Reisner, Hans-Peter. *Lektürehilfen Bernhard Schlink, Der Vorleser*. Stuttgart: Ernst Klett Verlag, 2005.

Resnais, Alain, dir. *Nuit et brouillard* (Night and Fog). 1955.

"Review of the Reader." *Publishers Weekly*, June 2, 1997, 51.

"Review of the Reader." *Publishers Weekly*, March 1, 1999, 20.

Baldwin, Peter, ed. *Reworking the Past: Hitler, the Holocaust, and the Historians' Debate*. Boston: Beacon Press, 1990.

Riordan, Colin. "The Sins of the Children: Peter Schneider, Allan Massie and the Legacy of Auschwitz." *Journal of European Studies* 27 (1997): 161–80.

Robbins, Tim, dir. *Dead Man Walking*. Perf. Susan Sarandon and Sean Penn. Gramercy Pictures. 1995.

Roche, Mark W. *Tragedy and Comedy: A Systematic Study and a Critique of Hegel*. Albany: SUNY Press, 1998.

———. *Why Literature Matters in the Twenty-First Century*. New Haven, CT: Yale University Press, 2004.

Rogowski, Christian. "Born Later: On Being a German Germanist in America." In *A User's Guide to German Cultural Studies*, edited by Irene Kacandes, Scott Denham, and John Petropoulos, 113–26. Ann Arbor: University of Michigan Press, 1997.

Rosenfeld, Alvin. "The Americanization of the Holocaust," chapter 6, *Thinking about the Holocaust after Half a Century*. Bloomington: Indiana University Press, 1997.

———. "The Problematics of Holocaust Literature," chapter 1 in *A Double Dying: Reflections on Holocaust Literature*. Bloomington: Indiana University Press, 1980.

Rosenfeld, Gavriel D. "Alternate Holocausts and the Mistrust of Memory." chapter 16. In *Gray Zones: Ambiguity and Compromise in the Holocaust and Its Aftermath*, edited by John Petropoulous and John K. Roth, 241–48. New York: Berghahn, 2005.

Rothstein, Edward. "In Berlin, Teaching Germany's Jewish History." *The New York Times*, May 1, 2009.

Rousset, David. *L'univers Concentrationnaire*. Paris: Editions du Pavois, 1946.

Ruta, Suzanne. "Secrets and Lies." *New York Times Book Review*, July 27, 1997: 8–9.

Ryan, Judith. *The Uncompleted Past: Postwar German Novels and the Third Reich*. Detroit: Wayne State University Press, 1983.

Sagan, Alex. *"I Want to Go on Living Even after My Death": The Popularization of Anne Frank and the Limits of Historical Consciousness*. Ph.D. diss., Harvard University, 1998.

———. "An Optimistic Icon: Anne Frank's Canonization in Postwar Culture." *German Politics & Society* 13, no. 3 (Fall 1995): 95–107.

Sansom, Ian. "Doubts About the Reader." *Salmagundi* 124/125 (1999–2000): 3–16.

Santner, Eric. *Stranded Objects: Mourning, Memory and Film in Postwar Germany*. Ithaca: Cornell University Press, 1990.

Saur, Michael. "Man mag es traurig." *Das Sontagsblatt*, April 9, 1999.

Schäfer, Dietmar. *Bernhard Schlink, Der Vorleser*. Munich: Mentor, 2000.

Schaumann, Caroline. "*Erzählraum im virtuellen Raum*: Rewriting Bernhard Schlink's *Der Vorleser* on the Web." *Die Unterrichtspraxis* 34.2 (Fall 2001): 150–57.

———. *Memory Matters: Generational Responses to Germany's Nazi Past in Recent Women's Literature*. New York: W. De Gruyter, 2008.

Scherer, Benedikt. "Spitzfindigkeiten: Bernhard Schlinks Roman 'Der Vorleser.'" Tages *Anzeiger*, October 9, 1995.

Schieber, Ava Kadishson. *Soundless Roar: Stories, Poems, and Drawings*. Chicago: Northwestern University Press, 2002.

Schipplacke, Heidi M. "Enlightenment, Reading, and the Female Body: Bernhard Schlink's Der Vorleser." *Gegenwartsliteratur* 1 (2002): 310–28.

Schlant, Ernestine. *The Language of Silence: West German Literature and the Holocaust*. New York: Routledge, 1999.

Schlink, Bernhard. "Als Deutscher im Ausland wird man gestellt." Interview with Gunhild Kübler. *Die Weltwoche*. January 27, 2000.

———. "Auf Dem Eis." Interview. *Der Spiegel* 19. May 7, 2001, 82–86.

———. *Der Vorleser*. Zurich: Diogenes Taschenbuch, 1997.

———. *Die Gordische Schleife*. Zurich: Diogenes, 1988.

———. "Kollektivschuld?" Chapter 1, *Vergangenheitsschuld:Beiträge zu einem deutschen Thema*. Zurich: Diogenes, 2007.

———. "Lesen muss man tranieren." Interview. *Der Spiegel* 39. January 7, 2002.

———. *The Reader*. 1997. Trans. Carol Brown Janeway. New York: Vintage Press, 1997.

———. "Recht–Schuld–Zukunft," chapter 1, *Vergangenheitsschuld und gegenwärtiges Recht*. Frankfurt am Main: Suhrkamp, 2002.

———. "Rede Zur Verleihung Des Fallada-Preises Der Stadt Neumunster." *Salatgarten Heft* 1 (1998): 44.

———. *Selbs Betrug*. Zurich: Diogenes, 1992; Diogenes Taschenbuch, 1994.

———. *Selbs Mord*. Zurich: Diogenes, 2001.

———. *Self's Deception*. 1992. Trans. Peter Constantine. New York: Vintage Books, 2007.

———. *Self's Murder*. 2001. Trans. Peter Constantine. New York: Vintage Books, 2009.

———. "Sommer 1970. Kleine Bewältigung einer kleinen Vergangenheit." *Merkur: Deutsche Zeitschrift für europäisches Denken* 57, no. 12 (2003): 1120–34.

———. *Vergangenheitsschuld und gegenwärtiges Recht*. Frankfurt am Main: Suhrkamp, 2002.

———. *Vergewisserungen: Über Politik, Recht, Schreiben und Glauben*. Zurich: Diogenes, 2005.

Schlink, Bernhard and Walther Popp. *Selbs Justiz*. Zurich: Diogenes, 1987.

———. 1987. *Self's Punishment*. Trans. Rebecca Morrison. New York: Vintage Books, 2005.

Schmitz, Helmut. "Malen nach Zahlen? Bernhard Schlinks Der Vorleser und die Unfähigkeit zu trauern." *German Life and Letters* 55, no. 3 (2002): 296–311.

Schneider, Peter. "German Postwar Strategies of Coming to Terms with the Past." In *Legacies and Ambiguities: Postwar Fiction and Culture in West Germany and Japan,* edited by Ernestine Schlant and J. Thomas Rimer, 279–88. Washington: Woodrow Wilson Center Press, 1991.

———. "Peter Schneider über die Studentenbewegung, die USA und Deutschland, Literatur und Politik. Gespräch mit Siegfried Mews." *German Quarterly* 75, no. 1 (2002): 9–19.

———. Seminar on Contemporary German Literature. Harvard University, Department of Germanic Languages and Literatures. January-May, 1991.

———. *Vati. Erzählung*. Reinbek: Rowohlt Taschenbuch, 1996.

———. "Vom richtigen Umgang mit dem Bösen," chapter 7, *Deutsche Ängste. Sieben Essays*, Darmstadt: Luchterhand, 1988.

Seifert, Martina, ed. *Aphrodite: Herrin Des Krieges, Göttin Der Liebe*. Mainz: Verlag Philipp von Zabern, 2009.

Shapiro, Ari. "For The Reader, Guilt Travels from Page to Screen." Radio commentary: NPR, January 3, 2008. http://www.npr.org/templates/story/story .php?storyId=98883419.

Smelser, Ronald. "The Holocaust in Popular Culture: Master-Narrative and Counter-Narratives in the Gray Zone." In *Gray Zones: Ambiguity and Compromise in the Holocaust and Its Aftermath*, edited by Jonathan Petropoulos and John K. Roth, 270–85. New York: Berghahn, 2005.

Smith, Dinitia. "'The Reader' Digs into German's Guilt." *The New York Times*. March 30, 1999. E-1.

Snyder Hook, Elizabeth. *Family Secrets and the Contemporary German Novel*. Rochester, NY: Camden House, 2001.

Sokel, Walter H. The Myth of Power and the Self: Essays on Franz Kafka. Detroit: Wayne State University Press, 2002.

Speer, Albert. *Inside the Third Reich: Memoirs*. Translated by Richard Winstons and Clara Winston. Introduction by Eugene Davidson. New York: Simon & Shuster, 1970.

Steiner, George. "He Was Only a Boy but He Was Good in Bed." *The Observer*, November w, 1997, 15.

———. "Reading's Seductive Power." *Manchester Guardian Weekly*, November 23, 1997, 35.

Stölleis, Michael. "Die Schaffnerin." *Frankfurter Allgemeine Zeitung*, September 9, 1995.

Stölzel, Christoph. "'Ich hab's in einer Nacht ausgelesen.' Laudatio auf Bernhard Schlink." *Die Welt*, November 13, 1999.

Swales, Martin. "Arthur Schnitzler." In *Handbuch der deutschen Erzählung*, edited by Karl Konrad Pohlheim, 421–32, 603–5. Dusseldorf: Bagel, 1981.

———. "Sex, Shame and Guilt: Reflections on Bernhard Schlink's Der Vorleser (the Reader) and J. M. Coetzee's Disgrace." Journal of European Studies 33, no. 1: 7–22.

Taberner, Stuart. *Contemporary German Fiction: Writing in the Berlin Republic*. Cambridge: Cambridge University Press, 2007.

Taberner, Stuart, ed. *Der Vorleser, Bernhard Schlink*. London: Bristol Classical Press, 2002.

Taberner, Stuart, and Karina Berger, eds. *Germans as Victims in the Literary Fiction of the Berlin Republic*. Rochester, NY: Camden House, 2009.

Talburt, Nancy Ellen. "Religion." In *The Oxford Companion to Crime & Mystery Writing*, edited by Rosemary Herbert, 383. Oxford: Oxford University Press, 1999.

Tatar, Maria. "'We Meet Again, Fräulein': Hollywood's Fascination with Fascism." *German Politics & Society* 13, no. 3 (Fall 1995): 190–98.

Tavor, Eva. "Art and Alienation: Lukács' Late Aesthetic." *Orbis Litterarum* 37 (1982): 109–21.

Tönnies, Sibylle. "Die Klagemeute: warum sich Deutsche den Opfern aufdrängen." *Frankfurter Allgemeine Zeitung*, April 23, 1996.

von Trotta, Margarethe, dir. *Die bleierne Zeit.* 1981.

Turow, Scott. *One L.* New York: Putnam, 1977.

Tyson, Ann Scott. "Youths in Rural U.S. Are Drawn to Military: Recruits' Job Worries Outweigh War Fears." *The Washington Post*, November 4, 2005, A01.

"Unterschiedliche Konsequenzen aus der Rheinverseuchung gezogen. Regierungserklärung und Debatte über die Basler Brandkatastrophe und ihre Folgen in der 246. Sitzung des 10. Deutschen Bundesages am 13.11.1986-Reden von: Walter Wallmann, Klaus Matthiesen, Hannegret Hönes, Harald Schäfer, Bernd Schmidbauer." *Das Parlament* 48 (1986): 4–5.

Urban, Cerstin. *Bernhard Schlink, Der Vorleser.* Hollfeld: Joachim Beyer, 2000.

Vogt, Jochen, ed. *Der Kriminalroman. Poetik-Theorie-Geschichte.* Stuttgart: UTB, 1998.

Walter, Natasha. "Secret Love and the Holocaust." *The Evening Standard*, December 22, 1997, 39.

"Was da fließt, weiß nur der liebe Gott." *Der Spiegel*, December 29, 1986, 22–25.

Weinthal, Ben. "The Raging Bronx Bull of German Journalism." *Jewish Daily Forward*, June 8, 2007.

Wiesel, Elie. "Art and the Holocaust: Trivializing Memory." *The New York Times*, June 11, 1989, 2:1.

———. "Trivializing the Holocaust." *The New York Times*, April 16, 1978, 2:1.

Wilson, Edmund. "Who Cares Who Killed Roger Ackroyd?" In *The Art of the Mystery Story: A Collection of Critical Essays*, edited by Howard Haycraft, 390–97. New York: Simon & Schuster, 1946.

———. "Why Do People Read Detective Stories?" In *The Edmund Wilson Reader*, edited by Lewis M. Dabney, 595–98. New York: De Capo Press, 1997.

wink. "Fräulein Lehrer." *Stuttgarter Zeitung* 24/25, April 1999.

Wittmann, Rebecca. *Beyond Justice: The Auschwitz Trial.* Cambridge, MA: Harvard University Press, 2005.

Wyss, Martin. "Fragen Auf Antworten." *Tages Anzeiger*, June 15–21, 1996.

Young, James E. "Teaching German Memory and Countermemory: The End of the Holocaust Museum in Germany." In *Teaching the Representation of the Holocaust*, edited by Marianne Hirsch and Irene Kacandes, 274–85. New York: Modern Language Association of America, 2004.

Zelizer, Barbie. *Remembering to Forget: Holocaust Memory through the Camera's Eye.* Thousand Oaks, CA: Sage, 2004.

Ziegler, Helmut. *Die Woche*, October 6, 1995.

Index

Page numbers in *italics* indicate photos.